ANNA BARRIE was born in 1946 and lives with her husband in a village  published in 1986; he the Rain and Briar Ros currently working on h

Also by Anna Barrie

Shadows in the Rain
Briar Rose

The Butterfly

A Novel by
ANNA BARRIE

———

PIATKUS

First published in Great Britain in 1996 by
Judy Piatkus (Publishers) Ltd of
5 Windmill Street, London W1

First published in paperback in 1997

**The moral right of the author
has been asserted**

*A catalogue record for this book is available
from the British Library*

ISBN 0-7499-3010-1

Set in 11/12pt Times by
Creative Print and Design, Harmondsworth
Printed and bound in Great Britain by
Mackays of Chatham Plc, Chatham, Kent

For Alex Edwards
with all my love

Part One

Chapter One

The place was packed, and in spite of the open door and open windows, it reeked of cigarette smoke, stewed tea and fish-paste sandwiches. A typical village beano in a typical village hall, whose walls were still plastered with war-time propaganda – 'Dig for Victory', 'Careless Talk Costs Lives' – although the war was over, at least in Europe. For Leo, of course, it was completely over: he'd been liberated from a prisoner-of-war camp and demobbed, awarded his new suit, paid his gratuity and told to go home and enjoy himself, as if nothing had happened, as if it was as easy as that.

Actually, he'd thought it *would* be that easy. He'd thought a good night's sleep in his own bed would bring the soul back to his body much as the tooth-fairy had brought the silver threepenny-bit when he was a child, leaving it under his pillow with a magic touch, so that when he woke up in the morning he was rich. But it hadn't worked. His soul was still out there, somewhere, flying around in a panic, looking for the way home.

He leaned out of the window as far as its high sill allowed, watching black specks of swallows swooping through the blue and gold of a glorious June evening. He wanted to be out there, not jammed in here like a blasted sardine with hordes of people he didn't know. His sister, who had promised not to leave his side, was now trapped on the far side of the hall, her face (like everyone else's) lobster-red and glistening, with a smile of fake enthusiasm stretching it beyond its natural limits.

The party had been arranged to give the retiring vicar 'a good send-off', and someone was making a speech in his honour – usual jokes, usual sentiments, everyone shouting, 'Hear, hear!' – but Leo felt more like shouting, 'Oh, sod the bloody vicar!' and getting out of it, fast.

This visit of his to Prue and her husband had been a mistake from the first, but his tactful attempts to wriggle out of it had been too tactful by half. He'd forgotten that Prue (like their mother) could be as deaf as a post when she was in danger of hearing something she didn't like, and as for Gerald . . . Leo had met his brother-in-law only once before this week and was already wishing he'd never have to meet him again. Damn silly fool of a man. He'd spent the entire war sitting safely at a desk and thought he knew it all.

A smattering of applause signalled the end of the eulogy and Leo heaved a sigh of relief, only to swallow it again as, to cries of 'Speech! Speech!' from the floor, the vicar clambered on to the platform, modestly flapping his hands for silence.

'My dear friends, I scarcely know how to thank you –'

Inwardly groaning, Leo thought it a pretty poor show if a blasted clergyman didn't know how to say thank you. Two words. Just two words and it would be over. But no. It would be embroidered in every shade of sky-blue, pink and purple. It would go on for hours. They'd all suffocate before he'd finished.

Aware that he was beginning to panic, Leo shut his eyes, clenched his jaw and hoped that Prue might look at him and see that she had to get him out of here before he went crazy.

'I shall miss you all –'

I shan't, Leo thought bitterly. Be glad to see the back of you.

'– and shall always remember you with gratitude –'

'Oh, put a sock in it,' Leo whispered. He opened his eyes and met the cold, glittering gaze of a young woman across the hall who, judging from the expression on her face, could lip-read abusive whispers at a range of thirty paces. Dark girl, taller than most of the others, with a haughty tilt to her chin and a contemptuous stare that seemed to sum Leo up and discard him as of no account. Nasty piece of work. Needed taking down a peg or two. Leo thought he might do it for her, just to pass the time . . .

He was tall, too, and as fair as she was dark, with triangular blue eyes and a jaw which, since he'd lost so much weight, looked as if it had been shaped with three clean blows from a hatchet. His mother had said he looked like a Viking warrior (an elegant euphemism for 'You look a wreck') and, taking courage from that, he fixed his gaze on Lady Muck across the room and thought piratical thoughts about rapine and pillage, willing her to blush, willing her to lower her eyes and admit she'd met her match.

Nothing happened. Her gaze didn't flicker, and the disdainful cast of her mouth seemed to be set in stone. Leo, on the other hand, could feel a new heat scorching his neck, scalding his eyes. Furious with himself, hating himself, he lowered his gaze, acknowledging (not for

4

the first time) that he was not the man he used to be. But it wasn't his fault! Who the hell was she to look at him as if he was dirt under her foot?

He might have wept had not the vicar at last said 'Thank you', and stepped down into the crowd. Applause. *For he's a jolly good fellow*. Prue's hand on his arm.

'Sorry about that, Leo. You all right?'

'Fine.' He wiped the sweat from his face and added faintly, 'I'll go now, Prue. Bit much. Too many people. Too hot.'

'Cup of tea before you go?'

'No. No. I've got to get out of here . . .'

'So this is your brother, Prue.' (It was the vicar again.) 'How are you, my dear boy?'

He seemed a sweet old chap, with a depth of suffering in his eyes that Leo instantly recognised and respected. He couldn't just growl at him and walk off. He had to shake his hand, wish him well, answer his questions . . .

Yes, it was hard to come home after years away to find everything so changed, so strange. His sister married, his father dead, his home a near-ruin . . .

'Beautiful old place,' the vicar said. 'I used to drive over that way before the war and we'd sit – my wife and I –'

Leo had never met him before, yet knew from the way he'd said 'my wife' that she was dead, and that he had loved her.

'– and gaze at it for an hour or more, weaving our little dreams. It had – I'm sure it still has – a warmth, a beauty, that has nothing at all to do with its fabric or design. Its history glows in its walls. And it's been in your family . . .?'

'Since the Restoration.'

'A long time, Captain Chantry. And now you can live there in peace for a good while longer, I hope.'

Six months at the outside, Leo thought grimly. He was broke. So was Molliston's roof and most of its windows. There were mushrooms growing in the drawing room and frogs breeding in the cellar. It would take a fortune to save it.

Gerald had told him to knock it down and build prefabs in its place. Although he'd laughed, he hadn't been joking and was lucky Leo hadn't strangled him for meaning every word of it.

Leo's mother (typically) had told him he should marry money. She hadn't been joking, either – 'perfectly respectable, darling. At one time, you know, it was the only way of keeping a place like Molliston going from one generation to the next' – although she'd known how funny it was, in the circumstances. A man who marries for money

5

needs to know a woman who has some, and he knew no one, rich or poor. And a man who marries for money needs to offer something in return: his charm (huh), his good looks (gone), or his protection (couldn't swat a fly). Still, it was a nice idea . . .

Prue had wandered off again and now came back with two cups of tea and a small boy called Reggie who was dying to meet someone who'd met *a real German* (or fifty).

'What were they like, sir? Were they –?'

'Just like me,' Leo said, 'tired, bored and longing to go home.'

Not the answer Reggie wanted, but it was the only one he was going to get. It was impossible to talk about it to anyone who hadn't been there, who hadn't shared it, who didn't know at first-hand the feeling that one's soul had been hung up on a hook and left to rot. After four years of that, you didn't much care if you hurt some kid's feelings, disappointed his hopes. Nevertheless, there was no honour in a man who deprived another of his own, so he smiled and added respectfully, 'And what kind of a war have you had, Reggie? Pretty tough, I suppose?'

With his cup of tea in one hand and a dried-up sandwich in the other, he kept edging his way towards the door, but never quite got there. Reggie introduced him to his mother; she introduced him to a snooty old dragon in a black frock who introduced him to his own sister – 'Mrs Gerald Whiteway, Captain Leo Chantry' – and strolled regally away, her social duty done.

'Who the devil –?' Leo whispered.

'Mrs Westley from Priory Farm,' Prue chuckled. '*Not* one to argue with. Her granddaughter's here somewhere.' She stood on her toes and twirled around, but failed to locate her. 'Lovely girl. Very tragic. She's just inherited a packet from her godfather and there's nothing to spend it on. Can you think of anything worse than being rich when everything you want's on ration?'

She laughed up at her brother. 'You're looking a bit better, Leo. Any chance of you hanging on for an hour? I promised I'd help with the washing up, but if you'd rather go home . . .?'

'No, no. I'm all right.'

He was fine, his blue Viking eyes pillaging the company for the girl of his dreams. A packet? How much was that? He needed five thousand pounds just to keep the weather out, another five to repair the damage the weather had already done, another five . . .

He found her. She was the only one in the place wearing a decent frock, the only one wearing stockings. She had a wonderful figure, too: small, but nicely rounded in all the right places.

'Is that the one?' he asked, *sotto voce*.

Prue tossed her head in disgust. 'Oh, *Leo* . . .'

'What?'

Prue sighed, despairing of his ignorance of the world she knew so well. 'A woman doesn't dress like that unless she does things she shouldn't, and Josie Moore does them *all*.'

'Oh.' He shrugged and turned away, his heart constricting with a feeling very like fear. The England he'd returned to, after so many years away, was nothing like the England he'd left behind, and although he was learning the rules, a bit at a time, most of them were still a mystery to him. He was like an innocent abroad. Abroad in his own land . . . He looked at Josie Moore again, his brow creasing with bewilderment. She looked exactly as a respectable girl had looked before the war: clean, smart and well-fed. But now it wasn't respectable for a girl to look like that. The respectable ones wore neatly patched rags and ankle socks. They were thin and drab, worn to the bone on patriotic war-work and Dig for Victory . . . And he hated it. He *hated* it.

Someone was playing 'The White Cliffs of Dover' on an out-of-tune piano, people were settling in for a sing-song, and Leo, abandoned again by his sister, edged once more towards the door, fresh air and freedom.

'Ah, Captain Chantry.' An aged, bony hand tapped his sleeve. It was the old dragon again, the black-clad Mrs Whatsit from Priory Farm. 'I've learned,' she said graciously, 'that I made the quite ridiculous error of introducing you to your own sister just now. I do apologise. Would you allow me to make amends and introduce you to my granddaughter? Miss Lydia – Lydia? Ah, here she is . . .'

Leo turned his head and met the cold, contemptuous stare of the girl he'd hoped never to see again. Just his luck. If there was only one woman in the world he might marry for money, it would have to be the one he couldn't stand the sight of.

'My granddaughter, Miss Lydia Westley, may I introduce Captain Leo Chantry? Mrs Whiteway's brother, you know.'

Miss Lydia Westley smiled stiffly. 'I'm delighted to meet you, Captain Chantry. Your sister's told me so much about you.'

Leo was not fooled by the pleasantry, but he was shocked by her voice, which didn't seem to belong to her. He'd expected a thin, languorous sneer, and heard instead an almost boyish medley of husky low notes and squeaky highs, all the more curious for being off-set by near-perfect diction and a formality of address which precisely echoed her grandmother's. Close up, she was really quite pretty, but even her prettiness was strange. Her eyes were as black as jet and a little smaller than perfection dictated. Her brows were thin, high arches of an almost furry texture; her skin (which would be bone-white in winter) was the pale gold of clotted cream, without a touch of pink to enliven it, although a faint sprinkling of freckles on her cheekbones did the job well enough. Her hand, as he shook it, was ice cold, dry to the touch and as narrow as a ribbon.

'I hope you're enjoying our little party, Captain Chantry. You've had some tea? Something to eat?' She pursed her mouth – a thin, disapproving mouth – which seemed to indicate that eating was something she considered beneath her status.

With some difficulty, Leo smiled, crinkling his eyes as he'd learned to do as a boy. It had proved, then, to be the perfect way of 'charming the socks off 'em', although he doubted it would work with this little madam. 'Best party I've been to in years,' he said, quite truthfully.

'Oh, dear.' She looked away. 'I know where you've been for the past few years and I don't suppose there were many parties there.'

'We did our best. The high spot was a performance of *Carmen*, in which I danced the flamenco, in a frock.'

She took a sharp, hissing breath and said crisply, 'I think it best if I try not to imagine that. Did you also sing, Captain Chantry?'

'Yes, I did. After my fashion.'

She sucked her cheek. 'And did you assume a woman's voice to – er – match the frock?'

'In times of war, a man must do many things he wouldn't otherwise do. But that wasn't one of them. The point of the exercise was to make the men laugh –' the point of *this* exercise was to make Lydia Westley laugh, but she still looked like the chief mourner at Prince Albert's funeral '– and the flamenco had achieved the purpose quite adequately. If they'd laughed any more, they might have injured themselves.'

She closed her eyes briefly. 'Yes,' she said. 'I can quite see that.'

'And you, Miss Westley?' he enquired through his teeth. 'Did the war make *you* smile at all?'

She sighed. 'We've had *ITMA* and *Worker's Playtime* on the wireless, although I imagine you think them rather tame, after *Carmen*. Men –' She paused, turning her gaze to the wall.

'Men?' he prompted.

'Laugh best when they're laughing at women, don't they?'

'On the contrary. Both men and women laugh best when they laugh at themselves.' He stared up into the rafters of the hall. 'As I think I'm about to do,' he added under his breath.

God, this was deadly! He didn't care how rich she was. She could have half a million for all he cared. It was quite clear that she despised him as much now as at first sight, and perhaps she had reason to despise him. After all, he didn't amount to much now. He was as thin as a rake and his suit only fitted where it touched. He was confused and afraid, and was sure it must show – in his voice, in his stance, even in the slick of sweat on his forehead which was about to run into his eyes. Oh, he hated her. He hated all of this. He wanted to go home!

'I *can* still laugh at myself,' he said, 'but I find it rather tiring, so if you'll excuse me, I think I'll . . .' He smiled and sketched her a bow. 'It's been a great pleasure to meet you, Miss Westley. Goodnight.'

He had gone almost before Lydia realised he was going, slipping through the open door so fast, she could almost have convinced herself she'd imagined the whole thing. But why had he gone? Was it something she'd said? She couldn't actually remember what she'd said – she'd been feeling sick all night, fighting it off with every ounce of concentration she could muster – the whole thing was a blur. But she remembered what *he'd* said – 'I danced the flamenco, in a frock' – although if she'd laughed as he'd intended she'd have thrown up all over his shoes. Oh, God, what an awful night. What an awful *life*, and the worst thing about hers was that it was all her fault, which meant that she couldn't even complain about it. Just take it on the chin, like a soldier.

She wandered to the door and leaned against the jamb, trying to get some air into her lungs. The sun had set some time ago but the sky was still light and a soft breeze stirred the air, cooling her face. She imagined how it might feel for Leo Chantry, that breeze. A breath of freedom and renewed hope? She doubted it. Prue had said he'd been very depressed since he'd come home, and in spite of his claim, 'I *can* still laugh,' she thought he was probably laughing more in desperation than in hope. There'd been something awfully grim about him, anyway, as if he was tensed to his limits, the muscles in his gaunt cheeks working like pistons, the sparkle in his eyes more like the spark of a flint on stone than of happiness. But at least he had the comfort of knowing that his unhappiness *wasn't* his fault. He couldn't help having been taken prisoner so early in the war. He'd fought bravely, kept his honour, his dignity and decency, his sense of humour . . .

'Men and women laugh best when they laugh at themselves.' Probably true. But, oh, God, this wasn't *funny*!

She darted out from the doorway and hid herself behind a patch of brambles to be sick. It didn't take long – she'd eaten almost nothing all day – and although she didn't expect to feel better afterwards, in fact she did. The nausea seemed to have gone. Now she just had heartburn – and an overwhelming desire to go home and sleep. No one would notice if she crept away. The vicar was singing his party-piece, 'Did You Not See My Lady . . .?', which also happened to be Gran's favourite, so she'd be happy for a while, and Prue or one of the others would walk home with her when the party was over. She'd be furious, probably, but Lydia was past caring about that sort of thing, the little things. It would be better to go home.

She walked along the path at the rear of the hall, turned the corner and halted, startled to see Captain Chantry still there, leaning thoughtfully on the gate, admiring the view. The village stood at the edge of a high plateau, with a view of the City of Bath, far below. A year ago it would have been just a shadow, hiding itself under the cover of blackout like a beetle under a stone. Now it was twinkling with lights, calling attention to itself: its beauty, its strength, the proud history that stretched in an unbroken line all the way back to the Romans.

Captain Chantry had taken off his jacket and the ill-cut trousers of his demob suit cruelly emphasised his skinny hips, his long, bony shanks, the wicked waste of a young man in his prime. He'd been liberated on his thirtieth birthday, Prue had said, and everyone knew how lucky he was to have survived that far. The last six months must have been hell. The Germans, who had run out of food and fuel for themselves, could have had nothing to spare for their prisoners. And, oh, they had such cold, hard winters in Germany . . .

If he could survive that, surely Lydia could survive this? But she wasn't as brave as he was. She couldn't laugh at herself. Only hate herself and wish she was dead.

He moved very suddenly, slinging his jacket over his shoulder as he opened the gate to walk away and, on an impulse she didn't quite understand, Lydia stepped briskly forward and called, 'If you're walking back to the village, Captain Chantry –?'

He wasn't pleased. She saw it in the sudden droop of his shoulders and the absence of any reply, save that he held the gate open for her, as a gentleman should. He'd been thinking, poor man; trying to put his life in order, no doubt, and since Lydia had been doing very much the same thing during the past few weeks, she knew just how annoying it was to be interrupted in the middle of it. She wanted company now, but he clearly didn't. It would be kinder to let him go.

'I just want to stroll,' she said. 'So if you'd rather go on?'

'No,' he said, his tone very flat, expressing more courtesy than enthusiasm. 'Strolling will be fine.'

The village was a rather strung-out affair, over a mile long, with the church at one end and the village hall at the other. Remembering Sinden St Michael, which was the Chantrys' home village – ten miles distant on the Trowbridge side – Lydia said with forced brightness, 'This must seem huge to you, compared with Sinden.'

'Hmm.'

'Prue's been so looking forward to your visit, Captain Chantry. You must have a lot to talk about, a great deal to catch up on.'

'Hmm.'

'But perhaps you find it difficult to talk?'

'Yes, I'm afraid I do. Everything's changed, you see. I can't quite get a grip on it.'

'Your father . . .?'

'No. My mother wrote to me about that. I've had time to come to terms with it. But – you can't – put –'

As he hesitated she looked at him and caught him looking at her, his face pale in the dusk, his eyes glittering with a strange, bewildered hostility. 'You can't explain a social revolution on an official letter-form. There isn't room. And anyway, people who live through such things experience them gradually, scarcely noticing they've happened until . . . Until someone who's been away comes back.'

'A social revolution? What do you mean?'

He laughed shortly. 'There. You've lived through the middle of it and don't even know it's happened. *Everything's* changed, don't you see? Food, clothing, manners, customs, morality.'

Lydia darted him a sideways look, wondering if he'd guessed her secret, but he'd turned his head away from her and appeared to be talking to himself.

'Even the landscape! Sinden's been in sheep and wool since the days of the Black Death. Now it's all grain and dairying and it looks completely different.' He stopped suddenly and pointed into old Mr Snook's front garden. 'Look at that! Beans and cabbages where there used to be roses! I know *why* Miss Westley. I understand the *principles* of it all. I just can't –' He sighed.

'Take it all in?' she suggested nervously.

'Quite.' He said it with a snap and a sudden quickening of pace which seemed to Lydia to indicate that she was one of the things he couldn't 'take in'. An insult, an irritation, a denial of everything he knew and believed in. Yes, she was all of those things . . .

He'd marched a few yards up the road before he noticed he'd left her behind. Then, his shoulders sagging again, he turned and held out his arm to shepherd her forward. 'Forgive me,' he said wearily. 'I'm afraid my manners aren't all they should be, just lately. Where do

11

you live?'

'Next door to Prue. At Priory Farm.'

He clicked his teeth with annoyance. 'Drat it, I *knew* that.'

'I imagine you can only concentrate on the important things at the moment and where I live is hardly important – except to me, of course. Once you've settled down –'

'Hmm.'

'I'm saying all the wrong things, aren't I?'

'No, no. I think I'm probably hearing all the wrong things, which is quite a different matter, Miss Westley. I'm like a child hearing a cathedral organ for the first time. There's no music in it. Only noise.'

A real gentleman. It was the way he'd been brought up. No matter what, he'd always turn the blame on himself, always volunteer to take responsibility for someone else's mistakes . . .

Lydia's eyes widened. Her heart thumped as the idea struck her. A gentleman always gives way to a lady . . . She peered at him covertly through the gathering gloom. Too thin to be handsome. Too sad to have any of Nigel's glamour, his style, his charismatic charm. But Nigel had been no gentleman and Leo Chantry was worth ten of him . . . in more ways than one. Fine old family, beautiful old house, everything just as Gran would want it . . .

They'd reached the gate of Priory Farm and Captain Chantry had said goodnight and walked on before Lydia dared to speak. She bit her lip, watching him – a mere shadow now – as he stooped to find the latch of Prue's garden gate.

'Captain Chantry?'

'Yes?'

'Prue's told me you're a good horseman and I was wondering . . . If you have time, would you like to ride with me tomorrow? I usually go out at about eight.'

He was silent for a moment. 'You're very kind,' he said at last. 'But I'm afraid I haven't ridden since . . . And I'm not –'

She waited, swallowing hope.

'Yes,' he said at last. 'I'd like that very much, Miss Westley. Thank you.'

She closed her eyes on a prayer of gratitude. 'Oh,' she called out brightly, 'and would you please call me Lydia? I'm only twenty-two, you see, and "Miss Westley" makes me feel rather ancient.'

He laughed and opened the gate, calling, 'Leo, then,' over his shoulder. 'Goodnight . . . Lydia.'

He'd been locked away for four years, and unless he'd visited a brothel on his way home (she shuddered at the thought), he was ripe for a quiet ride out to the Red Barn. When you weren't accustomed to it, riding could be a quite stimulating exercise and when Lydia wasn't feeling as sick as a dog, so could she.

Morning sickness! If ever there was a misnomer, that one was. She had it every hour of the day and night, although it wouldn't make her sick enough to miss a chance like this. Poor Leo Chantry. Lost and bewildered in a world he no longer knew . . . But so was Lydia, in her way. As Leo had hinted, the morals of the nation had gone down the drain during the war years – and Lydia's had gone with them. In wartime, there's no tomorrow. In wartime, anything goes – a solid, Christian upbringing, a good education, the love and respect of one's family . . .

Lydia's mother had died when she was very young and her life had been guided since then by her grandmother, whose rigid, Victorian ideas of right and wrong would never – never in a million years – accommodate an illegitimate child in the family. Or, for that matter, its mother. Its *adulterous* mother. And it was no good saying she'd been deceived, that she hadn't known he was married. If she'd conducted herself as she ought, she'd never have put herself in a position to be deceived. And *what* a position, too! The tiny back seat of an Austin Seven was no place for a girl to lose her virtue, let alone sell her soul!

God, oh *God*! As soon as the news came out – and you couldn't hide this kind of news indefinitely – Lydia would be turned out of house and home and the door shut against her. She had money of her own; she wouldn't be destitute. She could go where no one knew her and call herself a war widow. But that wasn't the point! She loved her grandmother. She adored her father. They deserved so much more from her than shame, pain and broken hearts.

They deserved . . . Leo Chantry.

Chapter Two

Gerald had stayed at home to catch up on some work, but he couldn't have worked very long before going to bed, for the house was dark save for a small electric lamp on the hall table, and silent, save for the heavy tick of the clock in the drawing room. Leo was disappointed. He'd hoped to be offered a drink of some kind – even if it was only Prue's elderberry wine – to melt the tension from his nerves, to help him sleep. He knew where the bottle was kept but couldn't possibly help himself. A man's pantry was like his purse nowadays; every crumb in it hard-won and anxiously counted. Leo had come very close to starvation during the past year and the British rationing system still seemed to him a cornucopia of plenty, but still . . . He would have liked a drink, if only to keep Lydia Westley from tramping through his brain all night.

Strange girl. Very strange. She'd spoken to him exactly as she'd looked at him – as if he was something unpleasant she'd stepped in – and then asked him to *ride* with her! What was he meant to make of *that*, for heaven's sake? He'd been confused enough (and angry enough) to turn her down flat, but just as he reached the point of declining, he'd remembered her money and decided he could stand being insulted a little while longer.

Now that he'd committed himself, of course, he wasn't sure he *could* stand it. He'd never met anyone so abrasive and insensitive, so certain of her own superiority. 'Lordly', that was the word for it. Certainly not ladylike, which implied a degree of tenderness, and 'tender' wasn't a word to describe Lydia Westley. 'Ruthless' was nearer the mark.

It was odd, though. He'd revealed more of his feelings to her than he had to his own mother, and all because she'd annoyed him so much. Just the way she'd told him he 'couldn't take things in' had been contemptuous and patronising. She was right, of course; he

14

couldn't take any damn thing in, but how clever would *she* be, he wondered, if she'd had *his* kind of war? Still, maybe she couldn't help sounding patronising with that ridiculous voice of hers. She seemed unable to control it as most people did and he couldn't imagine her putting on a girlish 'poor little me' voice: 'Oh, Leo, you're so big and strong, you make me feel quite helpless!'

The very thought of it was enough to make him laugh. Enough to make him weep, too, for no woman was likely to feel very helpless with him now. He wasn't so much big and strong as tall and spindly, hollow-cheeked, hollow-chested, and probably too feeble even to keep his seat on a horse . . . Hell, what had he let himself in for?

As he'd anticipated he slept very badly. In his long, waking hours he worried about Molliston: the holes in its roof and floorboards, the cracks in its plasterwork, the many varieties of insect and fungus that were eating its heart out. And eating his. Molliston was all he had left of his life, the only thing he loved, the only thing, if the truth were told, that had kept him sane while he was away from it. When his house had endured for five hundred years, a man can convince himself that a year wasted from his life – even two or three – don't count for very much. He can tell himself that he can wait just so long as his home waits for him.

But Molliston hadn't waited. It had been dying even before the war, although Leo hadn't known it. A man of twenty-two, twenty-three, what does he know about woodworm and dry rot? What does he care? True, he'd seen the occasional carpenter or plumber at work, replacing a floorboard, repairing the leads, but it hadn't crossed his mind that such things cost money. A great deal of money. Enough to bleed his father dry and leave Leo with scarcely a penny to his name. The only funds coming in now were the rents from a couple of farms; a poor enough income even to keep body and soul together, let alone a place like Molliston.

He woke, finally, soon after six and dressed in his only spare set of clothes, a pair of second-hand cavalry twills which his mother had acquired for him by means too subtle to mention. He had a feeling, sometimes, that she was capable of having pinched them from someone else's washing line; her ideas of honour had always been a little different from the norm and one could guarantee that she'd taken the 'make do and mend' philosophy an inch or two further than the government had intended. Just the way she'd suggested he marry for money was an example of that. Never mind that by modern standards it would be thought totally immoral. The fact that it had once been 'perfectly respectable' was quite enough for her!

As he knotted his tie Leo scowled at himself in the glass, raising a despairing eyebrow as he recalled that it had been quite enough for him, too, until he'd met Lydia Westley. But at least he'd found something good to say about her now: she was a moral force, a living example of the 'wages of sin'. He'd rather die a pauper than marry her! Not that he'd get the chance. Miss Westley was saving herself for a viscount, at least. A duke, if she could get him. She'd make a terrific duchess, anyway. Born for it!

He arrived in the stable yard at Priory Farm just before eight. The horses were already saddled and Lydia, with her back to him, was adjusting the girth of a spirited grey gelding and talking to him in that peculiar voice of hers as if he was the junior partner in a law firm. 'I've had quite enough of this nonsense, young man. Stand still. Where are your manners?' That apart, he could find nothing to criticise in the way she handled the gelding. He was the type to take fright at sudden movements, but Lydia had him where she wanted him, soothing and smoothing, her hands and head moving as softly as the breeze.

She looked very different this morning. She had long hair, for one thing, and he certainly hadn't noticed *that* last night; she must have been wearing it 'up'. A marvellous figure, too; straight and slim, with nicely shaped hips very nicely set off by her riding breeches and narrow-waisted shirt. She didn't quite answer the fantasies he'd entertained during the past four years (Josie Moore had come nearer the mark), but oh, Lord . . . what was a fantasy compared with the real thing? Whatever else she might be, Lydia Westley was most certainly a *woman*.

Leo coughed, partly to announce himself and partly to pull his wandering thoughts into order, and she turned at once, lifting her chin and peering at him disdainfully down the length of her nose as if . . . Well, as if she hated the sight of him.

'You did say eight, didn't you?' he asked, astonished.

'Oh, hello, Leo.' She glanced at her wristwatch. 'Yes, you're dead on time. How are you this morning? Did you sleep well?'

Very strange woman . . . She was smiling now; smiling as if, on second thoughts, she really wanted to know how he was and how well he'd slept, although he didn't suppose she'd appreciate a truthful reply. He smiled, nodded and approached the grey, murmuring soothing nothings by way of introduction. The touch of the gelding's velvet nose, the smell of oats and grass and leather, had an immediate effect on his nerves, relaxing him so completely that, for a moment, he forgot Lydia Westley until she said briskly, 'Shall we go?'

They'd ridden some distance before either of them spoke again and then both spoke at once: Leo in praise of his mount, a gentle chestnut hunter, and Lydia to ask, 'You've no horses at Molliston, now?'

They apologised as people do in such circumstances, as embarrassed by the clash as if they'd bumped into each other in a doorway, each giving way only to find themselves in the same predicament as before.

'No,' Leo said firmly at last. 'My mother couldn't manage them after my father died.'

'You must have missed them.'

'Not in particular. Just . . . it's hard to know what things you miss when the thing you really miss is the sum of several parts.'

'A way of life.'

'Yes.' He sighed and changed the subject. 'Lovely view. Is that another farm down there, or –?'

'No, it's one of our barns. We call it the Red Barn . . . Probably because it's orange.'

In its syntax, at least, it sounded suspiciously like a joke, but there was nothing in her voice to confirm the suspicion. She sounded, as ever, as solemn as a hanging judge. Leo sent her a sideways glance and discovered that although she wasn't exactly smiling, she looked curiously exultant and pleased with herself. Yes, it seemed she'd made a joke.

'You're a strange girl,' he said softly. 'I can't make you out.'

'You aren't the first to say so, but I don't think anyone realises how lonely it makes me feel.'

He looked at her again, blinking with surprise. It was her voice. She'd made a deeply emotional statement and made it sound as if she was ordering a pound of onions! So, take the statement for its own sake and ignore its mode of expression . . . Lonely? Yes, she must be. She was riding with *him*, wasn't she?

'Let's try and make each other out, then,' he said. 'Tell me a little about yourself. I suppose you've done your share of war-work?'

'Oh, Lord, let's not talk about that. War-work is something you do because you have to, not because . . . Well, I'm sure you know exactly what I mean. I suppose one day we might feel enriched by the experience, but it's hard to believe just now.'

'Enriched?' he murmured dryly. 'Yes, that's certainly hard to believe. But surely you've snatched a few pearls out of the mud? Something to laugh at, something to admire, something to absorb your mind so that time passes painlessly, if only for an hour. Books, music, radishes . . .'

She laughed at last: a deep, husky chuckle which brought a faint flush of pink to her cheeks and a jetty sparkle to her eyes. '*Radishes*?'

'We had little vegetable gardens. Hardly anything grew, but we managed a few rows of radishes. It's quite a thrill when you see that thin line of green coming through. Makes you feel a little less powerless.'

Their ride so far had taken them along the hedgerows of newly mown hay-fields and then down a long, earthen lane, overarched with elder blossom and edged with drifts of cow parsley and wild campion. But suddenly the sky opened as they came to the gateway of another field, where the hay had already been gathered and stacked into two neat ricks, like a pair of thatched, windowless cottages. At the far side of the field, hidden – save for its rusty galvanised roof – by a rise in the land, stood the Red Barn. Even from this angle it looked extraordinarily beautiful, as if the scene had been painted by an Impressionist master. The pale gold of the grass set against lush green hedgerows; green against the rusty barn; rust against bright, cobalt sky.

'Now there's a tasty-looking radish,' Leo murmured.

Their eyes met. Lydia straightened her spine. 'Race you to it,' she said. 'On your marks . . .'

Although it lasted scarcely a minute, that gallop gave Leo his first moments of pure happiness since his return home. It made him feel like a man again: strong and free, in full control of everything that was happening to him. The sun on his face, the rush of wind through his hair, the feeling of perfect harmony between horse and man . . . It was almost a sexual experience: an answering of both one's physical nature and one's spiritual needs, a complete negation of grief in a soaring sweep of pleasure.

Lydia won the race. She'd taken advantage of him, in fact, spurring the grey just before she'd said 'Go!' and she was already dismounting as Leo arrived at the barn. She looked marvellous: skin flushed, dark hair glinting with auburn lights, her eyes aglow with the excitement of the gallop.

'You cheated,' he teased, narrow-eyed. He expected her to laugh, deny it and accuse him of being a slow-coach – all the things girls usually did in such circumstances. Instead, to his amazement, she blushed and turned away to extract something from her saddle-bag. 'Yes, I did, didn't I?' she admitted coolly. 'I've brought a flask of coffee. Will you have some?'

'Coffee? *Real* coffee?'

'I've an uncle in America. He's the black sheep of the family,

18

trying to worm his way back into our affections with a regular supply of food-parcels.'

'Is he having any luck?'

'Good Lord, no.' Her chin went up in that disdainful way he so disliked. 'We can't possibly forgive him until rationing eases up. How would we eat?'

Another joke. It *was* another joke, yet unaccompanied by even the ghost of a smile! God, she was strange! In fact she was becoming rather fascinating, although Leo still couldn't say he liked her. She set his teeth and his nerves on edge just because she met none of his expectations. She was by no means a typical girl, but neither, according to his original judgement of her character, was she a typical Lydia Westley! Every time he thought he'd got her measure, she surprised him with another twist. He'd thought her totally devoid of humour and she wasn't. He'd thought her crass and insensitive and she wasn't. But it was no good to say what she *wasn't*. What the hell *was* she?

She was terrified. She was also a little drunk. Having raided her grandmother's secret hoard of 'medicinal' brandy with the intention of spiking Leo's coffee, she'd taken one or two gulps just to calm her nerves. She'd spiked the coffee, too, of course – not as heavily as she would have liked (the secret hoard had its limits) – but it was worth giving Leo a weaker cocktail just to have given herself a spot of Dutch courage. She needed it.

He wasn't acting at all as she'd imagined a sex-starved P.O.W. would. No lavish personal compliments, no steamy, lingering glances. The nicest things he'd said so far he'd addressed to her father's hunter, and it was going to be hard – very hard – to seduce a chap who preferred the blasted horse!

But even if he'd shown more interest in her, she wasn't at all sure she could go through with it. In spite of his confessed confusion of mind, he struck Lydia as being remarkably self-contained, as if he existed in a world of his own and wasn't at all keen to enter anyone else's. It was a terribly noble world he lived in, too: the pre-war model, all honesty and heroism, chaperones and virgins. He'd given her such a filthy look when he'd accused her of cheating, as if her idea of a silly game was his idea of collaborating with the enemy – and if he disapproved of *that* kind of cheating ... No, she didn't stand a chance. But she had to try.

The flask, a precious survivor from pre-war days, had only one cup and Lydia's plan had been to give Leo the coffee and pretend not to like it. Now, wanting more Dutch courage, she asked, 'You don't mind sharing?' and took a long, warming gulp before he had a chance to reply, 'No, of course . . .'

'Your turn.'

'You haven't had enough.'

'There's more in the flask.' She took a deep, calming breath and strolled into the shadow of the barn where a deep drift of wasted hay made a soft couch along the wall. 'Shall we sit down?'

He didn't reply. He made no move to join her. He took the little metal cup to his lips and then closed his eyes as the reek of brandy hit his nostrils.

Lydia held her breath.

'Oh, Lord,' he said, 'Manna from heaven. I'd forgotten what good coffee smells like.'

Yes, he certainly had . . .

Smiling, Lydia patted the hay, encouraging him to join her. 'How's the taste?'

'Wonderful. Have some more?'

'No, no. We've plenty at home. This is for you.'

He smiled and sat beside her with his legs crossed: an armoured posture, the equivalent of a curled-up hedgehog, with all the spines pointing outwards. 'You're very kind,' he said formally.

'It isn't kind to enjoy someone else's pleasure. Kindness is when you sacrifice your own enjoyment for someone else's, and I never do that.'

'Don't you?' He sounded politely unconvinced. 'You sound as if you've thought it through rather thoroughly.'

'Yes, I have. People who make sacrifices usually end up regretting them,' (she was thinking about Nigel's Austin Seven) 'and no good comes of that. Here –' She reached for the flask and took the cup from his hand, brushing his fingers as if by accident. 'Have some more.'

He could be no more accustomed to strong drink than she was, and if she could only get another cupful into him . . . Or less. He was already looking more relaxed. He'd stretched out his legs, leaned his back against the barn wall, and the flinty sparks in his eyes were misting over very nicely . . .

'It'll be all right,' she said softly.

'What will?'

'Everything. Things fall into place, don't they? And the best man always wins, in the end.'

'Yes, so they say. My difficulty is that I'm by no means the best man.'

'Nonsense,' she said huskily.

He smiled. 'No, not nonsense. I've met many better men. Enough, anyway, to have made comparisons and found myself wanting.'

'Except in humility, perhaps. I've met many men who *thought* themselves the best. But they were usually the worst, deceiving themselves in an attempt to deceive everyone else.'

Leo gave her a long look from the corner of his eye. 'You've met *many* men?'

'Mmm. Most of the Royal Navy, in fact. I worked at the Admiralty, you see. It's just down the road. Very brave men, of course, but . . .'

'But?'

She let out a wild little giggle. 'Too fond of the grog.'

'Ah . . .' He sighed rather wistfully. 'Never touch it, myself.'

'No. That's what I thought.' She reached out to pat his hand. He caught her hand and stroked it. He looked dreamily into her eyes.

'Isn't there anyone? One of these – many?'

'No.'

He was breathing like a cornered fox. His eyes were glazed, drooping with brandy-induced languor. Lydia touched his cheek with the tips of her fingers and he turned his mouth into her palm, sighing with pleasure.

As his lips met hers, she was already composing the letter she'd be posting to Molliston a few weeks from now.

Dear Leo,
Dreadful news. I've missed my monthly and can only suppose the Red Barn is to blame . . .

Some time passed before Leo entertained his next conscious thought, and it was a curious thought, culled from the story of the Prodigal Son: 'He was lost and is found . . .'

His soul had come back to him. He was alive again and only now realised how close to death he'd been before. He was aware of every inch of his skin, every hair, bone and fibre of his body. In the purely physical sense, he was exhausted, and had Lydia suggested going home now, he couldn't have done it, but in the spiritual sense he was strong enough to leap the moon.

An illusion, of course. It would wear off. He'd always been inclined to be sentimental in such circumstances, even with girls of the 'wrong sort', whose attractions were purely physical. Lydia hadn't attracted him at all at first, and even now he wasn't quite certain how – or why – his feelings had changed towards her. That joke about her uncle, perhaps, had had a softening influence on his nerves. Or perhaps it had just been the luxury of drinking real coffee, the generous way she'd said, 'This is for you,' and then denied she was being in the least generous.

He blinked with sudden disbelief at the extent of her generosity. She couldn't possibly be accustomed to such goings-on, for she'd blushed crimson when he'd peeled off her clothes. He hoped 'peeled' was the word and not 'torn', although he could scarcely remember how any of it had happened and now felt an urgent desire to find out, to be sure he hadn't frightened her.

He plucked a strand of dark, silky hair from her face and stroked it over her brow until she opened her eyes and, to his astonishment, blushed again.

'All right?' he smiled.

'Yes . . .'

'I didn't hurt you?'

'No.' She sounded sad, and that distant look had returned to her eyes as if she'd withdrawn from him and was wishing none of it had happened. Had she been a virgin? He didn't know. It was a question a man should ask before the event, not after it, and he despised himself for not asking, for not being aware enough of her feelings to even notice how she'd responded to him.

'I don't suppose . . .' she murmured, and then stopped, averting her eyes.

'What?'

'I don't suppose it really meant anything to you?'

'Oh, Lydia.' He gathered her against him, rocking her in his arms, trying to think of the right thing to say. In the sense that she meant it, she was right, of course; it had meant very little. A man with a need had found a woman to supply it – and that was all. Within certain limits, she could have been anyone. In fact, she still could be anyone, for he knew too little about her to claim otherwise and even his guesses about her had fallen far wide of the mark. Who'd have guessed – who in the world, who'd observed their meeting last night, would have guessed – that they'd spend the morning like *this*? But he was beginning to wish they hadn't spent it like this. He scarcely knew her, barely liked her, had used her, in fact, as no decent woman should ever be used: casually, carelessly . . .

'It meant everything to me,' he whispered, and thought he was lying until the next comforting insincerity passed his lips. 'You were the only girl I saw last night, the only one I wanted.'

It was true, at least from the point when Prue had mentioned Lydia's money, and perhaps that was what had brought them to this, for such things could influence one's behaviour beyond conscious knowledge or intention. But there was another side to that coin. Try as he might, he couldn't honestly find a point at which he'd pursued Lydia without her cooperation. He'd walked away from her at the party and she'd followed. He'd said goodnight to her and she'd invited him to ride. He'd certainly had no thoughts, as they rode, of a *possible* seduction, if only because the *impossibility* of such a development had excluded such thoughts from his mind.

But unless he was dreaming, it had happened, and Lydia must have played a part in it somehow. A man could act beyond his knowledge only so far. If she had kicked him or slapped him, if she'd screamed, he'd have *noticed*. He hoped.

'But how do *you* feel?' he whispered. 'You aren't sorry?'

'Not sorry, exactly. Just a bit scared, that's all.'

'Of *me*?' He was appalled.

'No.' She smiled weakly. 'I know you've been away an awfully long time, but . . . unless nature has altered in the meantime, and I don't think it has, because the hens are still laying, the cows still calving, the lettuce still bolting to seed . . .'

'Oh, dear,' Leo said.

Lydia had covered herself (rather ineptly – she'd done up her shirt on the wrong buttons), but now an image of her naked body came back to his mind – her firm, rose-tipped breasts and flat, creamy belly. But if nature was already at work behind the scenes . . . Oh, damn it, he couldn't bear that!

'My grandmother,' Lydia whispered, 'would never forgive me.'

He did not need the solemnity of her tone to make him realise the solemn nature of her fears. It was a story as old as the world – the God-fearing world, at least – and one he'd heard before, many times. It was a risk you took. He knew that for a woman the risk was greater than for a man: there seemed to be two moral codes in such matters and the woman usually caught the worst of it – but although he'd taken the risk on several occasions before the war, he'd never made a baby then, so why should he make one now? Because it would be just his bloody rotten luck . . .

He was about to say the usual, reassuring things when a new – and horribly devious – though crossed his mind. If she *was* pregnant . . . if she *was* pregnant he'd have to marry her! No choice! All cut and dried! For her, because it would be the only alternative to utter disgrace. For him, because a gentleman does not leave a lady to face such disgrace all alone. Even by today's fast declining moral standards, an unmarried mother was an outcast in the world and her child scarcely better. No matter how much money she had (Lord, he wished he knew how much!), it couldn't save her from that. Only a husband could save her from that . . .

'I'm sure it won't come to that,' he sighed, feeling pretty certain that it would not, for nothing in life is so easy. But never mind . . . Even if he couldn't get his hands on Lydia's money, she'd given him something else, which was probably more valuable in the long run. A renewal of his power. A reminder of his manhood. And he was a bright enough chap. He'd rescue Molliston, somehow or other.

'Come on,' he said. 'They'll be wondering where we've got to, and we don't want the search-party to find us like this, do we? You've buttoned your blouse all askew.'

'Oh, Lord, have I?'

Rather touchingly, he thought, she turned away from him to adjust the fastenings, her hay-tousled hair parting at the back to reveal the fragile nape of her neck. She was only twenty-two. He'd found it hard to believe last night, but he believed it now. She looked so vulnerable and unsure of herself, arousing feelings of tenderness in him that took him completely off his guard.

'We'd better get that hay out of your hair, too,' he said. 'I don't suppose you've brought a comb?'

She shook her head and stood quietly while he ran his fingers through the dark, silky mane, pausing occasionally to pick out a loose hay seed, a burr, a petal.

He realised suddenly that she was crying, although she didn't even cry as other women did, sniffing and bawling, making a meal of it. She just stroked her eyes with her fingertips, scooping up tears as if she were panning for gold.

'Don't cry,' he said. 'I won't let you down.'

'Easy to say –'

'Yes, except that I say it with the full knowledge of its difficulty, which should make it easier for you to believe.'

'Mm.'

He laughed. 'You aren't convinced, I take it?'

'Oh . . . Oh, I am. I knew as soon as I saw you that you were a gentleman. It's just . . .'

Leo blinked and drove his tongue into his cheek, remembering how she'd looked at him the first time she saw him. A *gentleman*? She'd thought he'd crawled out from under a stone!

'Love at first sight,' he murmured cynically.

'Yes, I suppose it must have been.' The dryness of her tone matched his, but there was never any knowing what Lydia's tone implied, for she went on hoarsely, 'How else could this have happened?'

Love at first sight? She *meant* it? She couldn't. But she *had*

24

followed him home; she *had* asked him to ride. And she most certainly *hadn't* kicked him . . .

Strike while the iron's hot, then? Even if she had only a thousand, it would patch the roof until he could think of something more permanent.

'Oh, Lydia,' he breathed. 'You can't mean that, surely?' He turned her into his arms and would have done all the things a romantic lover should in such circumstances – had Lydia let him. But she tore herself free and turned to face the barn, wrapping her arms around her stomach as though to suppress a rising tide of nausea.

'Do you imagine –?' she cried out angrily. 'Do you think I do this sort of thing every day, for God's sake? Oh, I *know*! I know how it must *seem*! But I'm not that kind of girl, Leo! I'm –' Her voice fell to a husky whisper as she concluded helplessly, 'I'm not.'

Leo had heard such protests before and they usually made him think of the ham-fisted excuse, 'It just slipped out of my hand!' But he felt certain Lydia was telling the truth, that she wasn't at all 'that kind of girl' and that something – something in him, perhaps, as well as the sensual influences of sunshine and warm hay – had broken down her natural defences. He was probably deceiving himself; he certainly *needed* to feel that he still had the ability to attract a woman, to melt her reserve, to think him worthy of the sacrifice of her virtue. But since Lydia *had* made the sacrifice, she deserved all the reassurance he could give her.

'I know,' he said.

She turned to him then, her dark eyes as wide and as anxious as a chastened child's. Strange, strange girl . . .

'How do you know?' she whispered.

'You blushed,' he said gently. 'It was the first time for you, wasn't it?'

Her face reddened again and she lowered her eyes. Leo laughed. He took her in his arms and did all the things a romantic lover should, but at least half his mind was at Molliston, fixing the roof. Home and dry, his thoughts ran. Home and dry . . .

Chapter Three

Given the use of her father's car (which she hadn't been; he hadn't enough petrol) Lydia could have arrived at Molliston in half an hour, but the bus took twice the time, and that hour was one of the longest she'd ever known. She felt rotten. Rotten right through: mind, body and soul. She could have borne it if only the wretched bus had kept going, let some air in, given her any hope of ever getting anywhere. But the dratted thing kept stopping. And every time it stopped someone else got on: someone red in the face and reeking of sweat, someone gasping, 'Phew, ennit a *scorcher*?' as if no one else had noticed it was the hottest day of the year.

'Enjoy yourself,' Gran had said crisply. 'A change of scene will do you the world of good. I haven't liked the look of you just lately, Lydia. You've lost your glow.'

She had been expecting something like this and had already worked out which face-saving lies would cover it, at least for a little while. 'Mm,' she'd murmured. 'I think I'm in love, Gran.'

'In love?' It was more typical of Gran to have said this with a disapproving snap rather than in the anxiously sympathetic tone she'd used instead. 'Not – Captain Chantry?'

'Mm.' She'd affected a dreamy air to hide her panic. 'I'm not optimistic, though. I know he's invited me to visit Molliston, but I think it was only good manners. To thank me, I suppose, because he'd enjoyed . . . the ride.'

'Nonsense. He could have just said "thank you" and been just as well-mannered. Not –' Gran had added darkly '– that I think you should hope for too much. He told your father he scarcely knew if he was on his head or his heels, and who can blame him after all he's been through, poor man? You have to bear that in mind, Lydia.'

'Yes, I suppose I do . . .'

'And there's something else you should bear in mind. The

26

Chantrys are gentry and we are not. Oh, I know you think all that kind of thing is old-fashioned, but there's nothing so old-fashioned as old blood, Lydia, nor so keen on self-preservation. I hope I've brought you up to behave like a lady, but the fact remains that you are an ordinary farmer's daughter. Captain Chantry might – indeed he'd be foolish if he did not – think very highly of you as a friend, but when it comes to marriage . . .' She'd raised her eyebrows. 'Be careful, Lydia. Don't wear your heart on your sleeve, my dear.'

She wasn't wearing it on her sleeve. She was carrying it in her mouth, and finding that it didn't function half so well there as when – before Nigel – she'd kept it in its proper place. It had been a quiet little thing then, getting on with its business without drawing much attention to itself. Now it acted like a raw wound and fluttered like a frightened bird. And no matter how hard she tried to ease it – with a half-baked plan, a still-born hope – it swelled up like a barrage balloon and threatened to choke her.

Until Gran had mentioned it, it had never crossed her mind that in Leo's eyes (or anyone else's, for that matter) she might be seen as 'an ordinary farmer's daughter'. She hadn't been brought up to think of herself in such a way but, now that she'd begun to think of it, it was all so humiliatingly obvious she could scarcely bear it. He wouldn't marry her. He'd rather die. It would be like marrying the parlour maid!

All this agony was for nothing, then. She'd have done better to have thrown herself *under* the bus than to get on it. She'd even blown the last of her clothing coupons on a new dress. It was one size too big, for although she wasn't yet 'showing', she soon would be, which would make most of her old clothes unwearable. In a month or so, this one would be unwearable, too, and what would she do then, for crying out loud? What the devil would she do then?

Aware that she was likely to faint if she continued to think like this, Lydia took a deep breath and tried to relax. The bus – at last – had broken free of its chain of villages and was jouncing merrily through the lanes at a breathtaking speed of about twenty miles an hour. All the windows were open and a dusty breeze, scented with hay and cow parsley, freshened the heat-stifled air. The hedges were a riot of fresh green leaf and wild roses, the sky a pure, radiant blue, without even a smudge of cloud to mar it. She couldn't see much beyond the hedges – a green blur merely – but the things she could see near at hand were enough to inform her of everything that lay beyond. Peace and beauty . . . Everything she'd longed for . . . And she'd ruined it all. It meant nothing. All the fear, the anxiety and misery of the war was nothing compared with this.

Although she'd been to Sinden St Michael at least once before the war, Lydia could barely remember it, and was surprised, as the bus trundled through it, to find it so different from the villages nearer home, which – in their essential character – were so reminiscent of Bath's elegant Georgian buildings and pale yellow stone. Sinden was an older place, built largely on much older money – the great wealth of the wool trade which had flourished here during the Middle Ages. Many of the houses and cottages were timber-framed, and although few of them had been painted during the war years, most were still coloured with a variety of lime-wash hues – dark gold, pale green and mildewed pink – which looked rather lovely under their wreaths of rambling roses and soot-darkened thatch. There was also a 'wool church' – St Michael's, of course – which, although it served such a tiny parish, was as lavishly ornamented as a cathedral, with a tall spire scratching the sky above towering churchyard elms.

The bus slowed. Frantic to escape, Lydia stood up. 'No, no, this ent your stop.' The conductress held out a hand as if to press her back into her seat. 'Manor's dewn t'other end.'

Lydia smiled weakly. 'I need the walk,' she said, and then wished she hadn't as the bus shuddered to a halt and the temperature shot up another ten degrees. This side of the village street was in full sun which, reflected from the high stone wall which seemed to run its full length, made the heat well-nigh unbearable. As soon as the bus had puttered away, belching blue smoke and a whiff of burning rubber, Lydia hurried to the shaded side of the street where Sinden's population of cats had draped themselves over walls, windowsills and doorsteps to sleep off the heat of the day. All the windows were open to the street and she heard little snatches of people's lives filtering out to her as she walked by. A child practising piano scales, a baby screaming, a woman crying out, 'In *this* heat? Are you mad?' and another saying firmly, 'I tell you, it's upside down, Arnold.'

She walked the full length of the village without catching sight of anything that could be Molliston and then, wishing she'd brought her glasses (pure vanity, of course: she hated them) and fearing that the manor might be a part of the 'green blur', which was all she could see without them, she walked back again, deciding that her best bet was to ask at the shop.

A tall man in a pale summer suit, his face shaded by an elegantly tilted Panama hat, stood opposite the shop, looking up and down the street as if he'd lost a pound and found a penny. Lydia peered into the shop window, but the blinds had been pulled down to shield it from the sun and instead of the interior she saw a reflection of the man crossing the street towards her.

'Lydia?'

'Leo!' She blushed and laughed with embarrassment. 'I didn't recognise you.'

'I met the bus,' he said. 'Thought you'd missed it.'

He looked almost as uncomfortable as she felt.

'I couldn't find it,' she said. 'Molliston, I mean.'

He pointed to the high wall on the far side of the street. 'There it is,' he said. 'That's our boundary wall. If you stand on your toes, you can just see the chimneys.'

He gave her his arm (the sleeve of his suit was peppered with moth holes, which marked it out, like its wearer, as a pre-war model) and they crossed the road in silence. Lydia felt she'd been hit by something large and very heavy. Her brain seemed to have slipped sideways. She was numb with shock. She'd walked half a mile, at least, from the bus stop by the church, and Leo's garden wall had run the entire distance! She hadn't expected this! He'd told her that Molliston was one of the finest *small* Elizabethan manor houses in England, and although she hadn't seen many of the Elizabethan variety, she'd certainly seen 'small' and knew what it looked like! Oh, God, oh, God, she didn't stand a chance! Ordinary farmer's daughter . . . Ordinary farmer's daughter . . .

'How was your journey?' he asked.

'What? Oh . . . hot.'

'It'll be cooler indoors.'

They turned between two stone gateposts she hadn't noticed before, into a weed-infested gravelled drive lined with elm trees. The house stood on a small rise. As they drew closer to it, she saw that it was built of honey-gold stone, with pointed gables and three courses of stone-mullioned windows. Compared with Buckingham Palace it was tiny. Compared with most of the houses Lydia had ever seen, it was huge.

'It's beautiful,' she said flatly.

'Not at its best, I'm afraid. The war . . .'

She felt sick. Worse than sick. If she hadn't been holding his arm, she'd have fallen to her knees and quietly died.

Leo was talking about the house, the many repairs he'd need to do as soon as the men came back from the war, but she could barely hear him and anyway didn't care. It didn't matter any more.

Leo was angry. He'd specifically told her not to get off at the church, and although he hadn't said he'd meet her at the next stop, it was something he'd *thought* she could take for granted! And then, when he'd finally found her, she'd coolly and quite brazenly snubbed him:

looked straight into his eyes and turned away to look in the shop window, as if . . . *Yes, I thought you'd wait for me,* she'd seemed to say, *but now you can wait a little longer, until I'm ready for you.* Love at first sight, indeed! What kind of fool did she think he was?

He didn't like her, that was the long and short of it; and he'd liked her less (much less) in the instant she'd seen Molliston and said, 'It's beautiful,' as if her next words should have been, 'For a pig-sty.' Superior little madam!

She made him feel like a worm. She made him feel small and defensive and . . . and frightened, for there was nothing he could say or do to make her feel the same. She was in control. All he could do was suffer it. But not for long. Once today was over and the exchange of hospitality complete, he'd say goodbye and that would be the end of it. Whatever she was worth – one thousand or ten – she wasn't worth all this.

'The biggest problem is the roof,' he said with exaggerated calm. 'The slates seem to be all right, but most of the leads are broken and we can't find anyone to do the repairs. The water pours in when it rains.'

She didn't reply.

'It's caused a fair bit of damage inside, of course,' he said desperately. 'But if we can fix it this side of winter . . .'

Lydia stopped walking. 'I think –' she said abruptly, '– that I'm going to faint.'

He couldn't see her face. She was wearing a rather jaunty straw hat which obscured his view and at first he thought she was making some kind of sarcastic comment about Molliston's roof. But as her hand gripped his arm with uncharacteristic urgency, he stepped ahead of her and caught her in his arms just as her knees buckled.

They sat in the long grass under the trees, Leo fanning her face with his hat. 'Travel sickness,' she muttered feebly. 'The heat . . .'

She hadn't quite fainted, but was still as near to collapse as made no difference, her face chalk-white, her mouth drooping with nausea. 'I'm so sorry,' she whispered. 'What on earth must you think of me?'

He stared at her in bewilderment, scarcely knowing what to think, except that she'd foxed him yet again. Poor kid, no wonder she'd got off the bus at the church! 'I think,' he said, 'you'll feel better if we can get you indoors. It's like an ice-box in there.'

'Oh.' She almost smiled at the thought before her face fell again. 'What will your mother think?'

'My mother? *Think*? Never.' He grinned and stroked her cheek with his finger. 'Gives her headaches.'

She smiled. 'What a dreadful thing to say.'

30

'No, it's true.'

'But the truth usually is dreadful, isn't it? You've got grass stains on your knees. Your lovely suit . . .'

She looked as if she might cry about his lovely suit (which he'd found in a chest in the gallery, covered with mildew and full of moth), but there was a trace of colour in her cheeks now, and he pulled her gently to her feet, holding her against him until he was certain she could stand unaided.

'A cool drink from a wet glass,' he teased gently. 'Come on.'

'I'm all right now.' She spoke almost harshly, turning her face from him, but when he offered his arm, he felt her trembling and knew she hadn't recovered. Funny little soul . . . maddening. He felt quite protective of her now, yet at the same time was afraid of showing it in case he rubbed her up the wrong way. It was like having an unexploded bomb in his hands. If he so much as cleared his throat, he'd be a gonner.

In the week since he'd seen her last, he'd worked a few miracles in the house, mostly miracles of obliteration – a harvesting of mushrooms, a scrubbing of stains and mildew, a removal to the gallery of torn rugs, soggy armchairs, and the few dozen tin baths and galvanised buckets which had been dotted here and there to catch the drips. Every door and window had been left open to kill the reek of mould, and now, as he led Lydia through to the lofty 'great hall', he saw it as she might see it: a pure, if rather stark, representation of Elizabethan architecture at its finest. There was only the old refectory table here, with its great carver chair and plain oaken benches, a brass jug filled with roses, the enormous, carved stone fireplace.

Her face should have lit up with pleasure. It didn't. She looked appalled, as if she'd expected something far better than any of his feverish spring-cleaning could have produced.

'Sit down,' he said wearily. 'I'll fetch you a drink. What would you like? No real coffee, I'm afraid, but the tea's genuine enough.'

'Just water, I think.' He was halfway to the kitchen before she added, 'Please.'

His mother, done up in her best (which wasn't much different from her worst) summer frock, was putting the finishing touches to the lunch. 'Where is she?' she asked excitedly.

'In the hall. Travel sick.'

'Oh. You might sound more sympathetic, darling.'

'Might I?' He sighed as he filled a glass with water. 'Yes, I suppose . . . Come and meet her, will you? I'm all nerves; can't think of a damn thing to say.'

Peggy Chantry laughed. 'Not a problem I'd know much about, of course. With nerves or without, I can *always* think of something to say!'

She was a tall woman, but not nearly so tall as Leo and he could see over her head as she preceded him back to the hall. Lydia was sitting where he'd left her, but she'd straightened her spine against the carver-back, lifted her chin, and as his mother made the usual welcoming sounds, Lydia narrowed her eyes in an icy, contemptuous stare. Leo's jaw dropped. He could have slapped her. Instead, grinding his teeth in rage, he said, 'My mother, Peggy Chantry.'

Lydia jumped to her feet and smiled. She held out her hand.

'May I introduce –' Leo murmured, amazed.

'Oh, never mind all that,' his mother laughed. 'If I don't know her name by now, I never shall. He's told me all about you, Lydia, and the wonderful ride you gave him.'

Lydia blushed. Leo smiled and turned away.

'But what a lovely dress!' his mother went on. 'Where on earth did you find it?'

Leo slid the glass of water across the table and perched on the windowseat to watch and listen as they exchanged the usual stories of queues and clothing coupons and making do. Now that he came to notice the new frock, he didn't think highly of it. The print was all right, but the colours, a combination of red, blue and beige, were too harsh for Lydia's colouring, making her face look too pale and her dark eyes unfathomable. It was also too big. Did nothing at all for her figure . . .

As if she'd guessed what he was thinking, she said, 'They didn't have my size, but I decided too big was better than too small. It leaves more scope for alterations, doesn't it?'

Friendly enough. And she was smiling now. So what had that look meant?

And, after all, what did it matter? When he put her back on the bus this evening, he'd never see her again.

Leo smiled and closed his eyes. Oh, what a blissful thought!

Peggy Chantry was not at all the kind of woman Lydia had expected Leo's mother to be. She'd expected someone more like Gran: someone aloof, dignified and very 'proper'. Mrs Chantry was none of those things. Although she couldn't be more than a decade younger than Gran, and had the grey hair and wrinkles to prove it, she talked and acted like a girl of twenty, laughing at the least provocation, chattering about nothing in particular, seeming to have nothing more serious on her mind than to make Lydia feel welcome, comfortable and at ease. In fact, although Lydia appreciated the 'welcome' part of it, she felt quite the opposite of 'comfortable and at ease'. She felt confused and on the defensive, afraid to relax in case she said or did something she shouldn't.

She was horribly aware that Leo was watching her, listening to every word she said as if to catch her out in some awful lapse of taste or good manners. And she was terrified of eating lunch with them! Gentry or not, they were as much at the mercy of rationing as everyone else, and could not be depended on to serve something that didn't turn her stomach inside out. It would be just as much a disaster to refuse it as to eat it and throw up, although it wouldn't, probably, get that far. She might have fooled Leo with the excuse of 'travel sickness', but she had an idea that Mrs Chantry would be much harder to convince.

'If you're feeling better, Lydia?' Leo said.

'Yes, yes, I feel –'

'I'll show you around, then. What time's lunch, Mother?'

'Whenever you like, darling. Floral's just picking the lettuce, so shall we say half an hour?'

'Flora?' Lydia asked tentatively.

'Flora*l*,' Leo corrected crisply, 'is our evacuee. She's been here since the Bristol blitz and is planning to stay until Armageddon.'

'She's a darling,' Mrs Chantry chuckled. 'Couldn't manage without her, could we, Leo?'

'Hmm,' he said. 'What would you like to see first, Lydia? The hole in the drawing-room ceiling, or the hole in the library floor?'

He seemed almost as abrasive now as on the night of the vicar's party, and while it was clear that he didn't think very highly of Floral, whoever she was, Lydia had a suspicion that *she* was the real fly in the ointment, although she had no idea of what she was doing wrong. Except, perhaps, to be an ordinary farmer's daughter . . . Oh, if only Gran hadn't *said* that! She hadn't had much faith in herself to start with, but those few words had destroyed her every shred of confidence, making her feel beaten before she'd even begun.

Leo showed her into another hallway, with a fine dog-leg staircase of carved oak, and then through to a long, spacious room with tall windows and panelled walls. The hole in the ceiling was not very big, not anywhere big enough, in Lydia's opinion, to merit all the attention Leo gave it, if only because everything else was so beautiful. The windows were the originals, she guessed, with square lattices, bubbly blown glass, and here and there a tiny coloured pane: red or green or dark, golden yellow. There were no curtains and hardly any furniture, but a sofa of worn blue brocade, a couple of leather wing chairs, a table and an enormous Persian rug made a cosy setting in front of the fireplace.

Lydia didn't know what to say. She felt a great deal, but couldn't find words to express it. It was a feeling of peace, of belonging, as if the history of the room was her own history and that nothing bad could happen to her while she stayed here.

'Well?' Leo said, and there was a look in his eyes that made her heart thud. He cared about this house more than he cared for anything else in the world, and if that was the way to catch him . . .

Lydia turned away to gaze out of the window. 'It's perfect,' she said. 'I love it.'

'Really? Why?'

'I don't know. It feels . . . It makes me want to stay.'

He laughed shortly. 'It's the sunshine. You wouldn't feel the same if it was raining, I can promise you. Come on. There are twenty more rooms still to go.'

As she turned to join him, Lydia saw a movement from the corner of her eye and turned again to see a thin, wizened little woman marching across the terrace with a basket on her arm. As she came closer, Lydia saw her more clearly: her hair a frizz of mousy brown, her face as tanned and wrinkled as a walnut. Lydia's first thought was that she looked like a leprechaun, a creature of nature and as happy as the day.

'Is that Floral?'

'Mm,' Leo said.

'She looks rather sweet.'

'Mm,' he said again.

'You don't like her, I take it?'

'I don't really know.' He opened the door and bowed her through, looking at his feet. 'She seems to have claimed squatter's right to the place. She thinks Molliston belongs to her. I've dropped hints so heavy, anyone else would have been crushed under the weight.'

'But your mother said –'

'My mother doesn't *think*. If it's all right now, she supposes it'll be all right for ever, but . . . Oh, well, never mind. It doesn't really matter.'

Lydia took the distinct impression that she'd been told to mind her own business.

Having decided that he would *never* marry Lydia – even if she paid him – Leo spent most of the day pointing out Molliston's worst points and not caring much what she thought of them. It wasn't until he took her around the garden – the little that was left of it – that he realised she'd fallen in love with the place and wouldn't have noticed its faults if he'd cast them in bronze and dropped them on her head.

'This used to be the rose walk,' he said, pointing out a lush growth of nettles between two collapsing yew hedges. 'There's meant to be a topiary arch at the end, with a view down to the woods at the bottom of the park. The park's gone, of course. Ploughed up for grain.'

'Oh, it's wonderful,' Lydia breathed. 'I can just see it . . . As it used to be, I mean. Will you restore it?'

She'd been the same about everything, asking him what he would do to set things right, and how he'd go about it. She'd had some pretty good ideas, in fact, and he hadn't been able to bring himself to say that none of it would happen. That none of it *could* happen. That it would cost a fortune even to reclaim the confounded rose walk.

'But the woods are still there, aren't they? Would it matter if one saw wheat fields through the arch instead of parkland?'

He smiled wearily. 'I suppose not. But the arch has collapsed.'

'You can grow it back again. It'll take time, obviously, but all it really needs is work, and when a place is as lovely as this, what's a little work?'

'Hmm,' Leo said again.

He was aware that his depressed frame of mind was beginning to tire her, even to worry her a little, because she kept darting him frantic little glances under her eyelashes, as if wondering what next she could say to raise his spirits. But he didn't really care. He didn't understand her. She'd kept his mother at arm's length all day, talking to her in that annoyingly formal tone of hers that made it sound as if she was organising a funeral. His mother either hadn't noticed or didn't care, but it was driving Leo to distraction. He wanted to shake her. Or, rather, to put her back on the bus and see the last of her.

'Yew hedges,' she said, 'can regenerate from old wood.'

'What?'

'You can cut them back as hard as they need, and they'll grow again as strong as before.'

He smiled wanly. 'I'll remember that,' he said. 'If only because it sounds like a proverb. The kitchen garden's through here. Floral's kept it going, within her capabilities.'

He showed her through a broken doorway in a collapsing stone wall and let her wander around on her own while he stood waiting, idly inspecting Floral's cabbage patch. Lydia's enthusiasm for Molliston had had the opposite effect from the one she'd intended. He hadn't told her he was broke – there'd been no point, it was none of her business – but without that information, none of her helpful

35

suggestions had had any meaning except to make him realise, once and for all, that the case was hopeless and doomed to fail. He'd have to sell up.

The cabbages were alive with caterpillars, ugly little creatures whose unpleasant, contorted form of locomotion indicated that life was as much a torment for them as it was for him. They were at the mercy not only of their own needs, but of Floral's for cabbage and the birds' for caterpillars. For all their efforts, their endless, voracious munching, scarcely one in a hundred would live to become a butterfly.

He whispered a curse and turned away. 'We'd better go back to the house,' he called harshly. 'Your bus leaves in an hour.'

Lunch had been easy: a few slices of cold meat with new potatoes and salad, all of which Lydia's stomach had found quite acceptable. Tea was even easier and much more welcome, but it was over too soon, leaving her in a state very like grief and close to tears. She couldn't say she'd enjoyed her day – it had been a failure from the first, and she was sure Leo had hated every minute of it – but when it was over, her last hope of salvation would be over too and the horrors of tomorrow would be upon her. *I'm pregnant, Gran . . .*

Her heart lurching with terror, she jumped to her feet. 'I'd better powder my nose before I go, Mrs Chantry. And find my things.'

She'd left her hat in Mrs Chantry's bedroom and, as they went to fetch it, Lydia noticed a painting on the landing she hadn't seen earlier. It was a landscape – a little too modern for a house like this – and it looked strangely familiar . . .

'Who painted this, Mrs Chantry? It reminds me –'

Mrs Chantry laughed. 'Oh, it's there mostly for sentimental reasons, my dear. An old friend of mine painted it – an old beau, in fact, from my long-ago girlhood – for a wedding present. Terribly gracious of him, I thought. I'd sent him off with a flea in his ear, which he by no means deserved. But by that time I'd fallen for Lionel – Leo's father, you know – and couldn't be bothered to be tactful.'

'Was his name Avery? Avery Moreton?'

'Why, yes! How did you know? He hasn't signed it, surely? I've had it all these years and never noticed . . .'

'No, I just recognise his style. He was my godfather. His wife was a friend of my mother's. He died, I'm afraid, only a few months ago.'

Mrs Chantry stared at her. 'Yes,' she said. 'I saw the obituary in *The Times*. So sad . . . But how very curious! And you say he was your godfather? Goodness, isn't it a small world!'

They'd had tea on the terrace. When the ladies went off to 'powder their noses', Leo sat and gazed around him as if trying to commit Molliston and its surroundings to memory. The long boundary wall existed only on the village side of the house and the rest of the grounds lay open to a gentle, rolling landscape of woodland and pasture, half-hidden farmsteads, the nearest and oldest of which nestled in a snug fold of land barely half a mile distant. Had his father not let it out so successfully, Leo might – when he sold up – have moved there and worked it for himself. Now he had no idea where he'd end up or how he'd earn his living. He knew he'd have to make himself think of such things before long, but somehow . . .

'Leo! Leo!' His mother sped around the corner of the house, clutching one of her many scrapbooks to her chest. 'Leo, you'll never guess,' she whispered excitedly. 'I don't know why I didn't realise it before! Her name's here, as plain as day, but I just didn't make the connection! She's Avery's god-daughter!'

'Avery? Avery who?'

'Avery Moreton! Chap who did the painting on the landing! You know, darling, the one your father hated because . . . Oh, never mind that! Quick, quick, before Lydia comes down! I cut out his obituary from the paper and . . . oh, *read* it! Quick!'

Avery Moreton, architect and landscape painter, had died in February after a short illness, aged seventy-two. His marriage had been without issue and the bulk of his fortune had been left to his three nephews, with a 'small' legacy – *of thirty thousand pounds* – to his god-daughter, Miss Lydia Charlotte Westley, of Duncombe, near Bath.

Leo's heart began to thud. He'd spent the entire day being a misery with Lydia, the entire day longing for her to go, when he should have been wooing her half to death, charming the socks off her, kissing her breathless . . . Thirty thousand pounds! Oh, damn it all to hell! He'd missed his chance!

They walked to the bus stop in an embarrassed silence which they both broke at once, Leo saying stiffly, 'I hope it hasn't been too boring for you?' and Lydia breaking in, 'I've had such a lovely day, Leo.'

'Have you?' he asked, astonished. 'But I've been so –'

'So *worried*,' she interrupted breathlessly. 'And I can quite see why, but I do think you're being too pessimistic. Of course it'll be hard to put everything right again, but you'll do it, I know you will. You *must*. It's the sort of place that deserves everything you can give it. If it was mine . . . it isn't, of course, and I shouldn't . . .'

'No, go on. Please,' he prompted faintly.

'If it was mine, I'd get it right if it killed me. If it took every penny I possessed, I'd get it *right*.'

Leo threw back his head and laughed. He swung her off her feet and kissed her. 'You're wonderful,' he said. 'You're adorable. When can I see you again?'

Chapter Four

Leo walked home the long way round, feeling a little shaken by Lydia's emotional leave-taking, which – rather like his own – had had so little in common with the mood of the rest of the day. He'd kissed her in the full knowledge that he'd fallen in love with her bank-balance, but why the devil had Lydia kissed *him*? Why had she clung to him like that, as if . . .? Well, as if she really cared! *Did* she care? Or was she just hedging her bets in case their little lapse at the Red Barn went against her? Yes, it must be that. It must be. A few weeks from now, when she realised she was safe, it would be *Goodbye, Leo, I didn't like you anyway*.

And yet, if all she'd wanted was to hedge her bets, wouldn't she have behaved differently *during* her visit, as well as after it? If she'd wanted to keep him sweet, wouldn't she have tried a little harder, laughed a little more, attempted to charm his mother at least, instead of fending her off with the proverbial bargepole? She'd been so *solemn*, so frigidly polite, so ridiculously *proper*!

He shrugged and turned into the narrow lane which led to the rear gate of Molliston. Without actually entering the grounds or walking on farmland, this was the only spot where one could view the house entire, and it looked wonderful from here, bathed in the golden light of evening, its tall, ornate chimneys set against the lucid green of the elms.

This was where Prue's retiring vicar must have come with his wife, before the war, to gaze at it and dream . . . But what had they dreamed of? On a day like today, they might have seen a few flashes of white and heard the echo of laughter as Leo and his friends had played tennis on the court beyond the shrubbery, or seen his mother, elegant in pink voile and creamy lace, inspecting the flower borders. They might have heard his father's Bentley crunching slowly across the gravelled forecourt, or seen one of the gardeners emerging from the kitchen garden with a trug filled with apricots, asparagus and strawberries . . .

All gone. The world had changed. For the better, it was said. There'd be decent houses for everyone now, jobs, schools, a free health service. There'd be an end to slums and lice, ignorance and malnutrition, and if it was true . . . *if* it was true, Leo could find it in his heart to be glad it was true. But he couldn't help mourning for the things that were lost forever.

In the dark cloud of grief that consumed him then, he knew he couldn't marry Lydia. Her money had been just a dream for him, like the vicar's dreams, of things that might be – if only. If only one had a right to them. He had no right. And no wish to marry anyone he didn't love. But he wished he *could* love her. It would make everything so easy . . .

He found his mother shelling peas on the kitchen doorstep. She'd changed out of her frock into a blouse and a skirt which, in the old days, she'd have deemed too shabby for the scullery maid. She seemed happy enough with the changes the war had wrought in her life, but she'd always been the adaptable type. His father had said she had tunnel vision, with hearing to match. Set her down in the middle of a battlefield full of screaming wounded and she'd see only the sunset, hear only birdsong . . . Neither Leo nor his father had thought this a virtue (virtue, surely, would acknowledge the wounded and tend to their needs?) but it was a marvellous mechanism for survival.

'Was the bus on time, darling?'

'Mmm.'

'When can she come again? She's a lovely girl, Leo. Beautiful complexion, glorious hair . . . And her figure!'

Leo smiled cynically. 'What figure are you thinking of, Mother? If it's the one that begins with three and ends with four noughts, I'd strongly advise you to forget it.'

As if he hadn't spoken, his mother smiled, closed her eyes and murmured blissfully, 'And hasn't she such perfect *manners*! Oh, what a treat!'

Leo's jaw dropped. Were they discussing the same girl?

'One doesn't expect it nowadays, does one? Especially with the young. Very much the thing in my day, of course, but I suppose Lydia's grandmother . . . It must make such a difference to be brought up by one's grandmother. She's skipped a generation, in a way, you see. She's more a Victorian than a truly modern girl. But I found it so *restful*, didn't you, darling? So calm and dignified . . . One just knew she wasn't going to put a foot wrong.' She sent him a

40

bright, birdlike glance from the corner of her eye. 'And she just loved Molliston, didn't she?'

Leo frowned and turned away. A Victorian? He hadn't thought of it quite like that, but in fact it explained a great deal. Calm and dignified ... Yes, looked at in a certain way – his mother's way – calm and dignified summed Lydia up very nicely. Leaving out her travel sickness at the start of the day (and she'd made the minimum fuss about even that) and her curiously passionate farewell, one *could* say she'd behaved as the old dragon had probably taught her. Oh ... Oh, dear. Had he misjudged the poor girl?

'Touch haughty, perhaps?' he demanded abruptly. 'A bit on the chilly side, would you say?'

'Shy,' his mother replied. 'Not the shrinking violet type, of course, but not entirely sure of herself either. Probably your fault, darling. You think too much and it can be rather daunting, you know.'

'Oh? Daunting? In what way?'

'Your father was the same. I used to catch him looking at me, sometimes, as if he'd like to take me apart, like a clock, to see how I ticked. Gave me the shivers.' As if to demonstrate the procedure, she shivered, her mouth tightening with irritation. 'I never wanted to know how *he* ticked,' she added, frowning. 'What difference would it have made? I couldn't change him.'

'But if you'd understood him a little better ...?'

His mother stood up. 'I wonder where Floral's got to?' she said brightly. 'She was meant to be fetching potatoes, but I'll bet you a fiver she's at those poor caterpillars again. She drops them in boiling water, you know. Ugh!'

Leo smiled and walked away, knowing he'd taken the conversation as far as it would go. He'd never had much insight into his parents' marriage; they hadn't got on, he knew, but they'd kept their differences pretty much to themselves and he'd seen the 'evidence' mostly in his own estimation of their individual characters. His father had been a serious, cultured man; his mother a creature who skimmed the surface of life, always looking for the easiest way rather than the wisest. He had something of her nature in his own – easier to marry thirty thousand pounds than to sell up – but he did have the sense to look a little deeper. A lot deeper. You couldn't marry a woman you didn't like: not just because it was cynical, dishonest and unkind, but because you might still be married to her thirty years later. His parents had married for love – the full works – and so as far as he could make out it had barely survived a full decade before something a good deal less romantic had set in. If you started out *without* love,

41

how far would you get before you were both thoroughly miserable?

He wandered towards the kitchen garden to see what had happened to Floral. She'd kept pretty much out of the way while Lydia was here, but he was sure she'd kept her eyes and ears open and would have something to say about it. Shy? Could Lydia have been shy? He supposed he *had* been rather daunting, but at least half of it had been self-defence, a guarded attempt to make her feel as uncertain as he felt. But he hadn't expected to succeed, and now that his mother . . . Oh, damn it! He was so bloody confused about everything! Why couldn't he pull himself together? He couldn't live the rest of his life like this, surely?

Forgetting Floral, he turned to gaze at the view and saw something small and grey running swiftly across the corner of one of the wheat-fields, making a beeline for Manor Farm. He thought at first it was a deer, but as it slowed at the fence, he realised that it was a child, one of Ray Duckett's boys going home. Late for tea and expecting trouble, he guessed, but where had he been? He seemed to be running from the direction of Molliston . . . Not pinching Floral's strawberries, he hoped. She'd have given him an earful if she'd caught him at it . . .

She chose that moment to give Leo an earful – by accident, and from behind an overgrown clump of laurel – but richly expressive for all that. Leo smiled and shook his head. Her voice – a cloyingly sweet purr, with the long vowels and rolling Rs so typical of the Bristolian dialect – was totally unsuited to profanity and she could make even 'Oh, sod the bloody lot of it!' sound like a lullaby for a fractious child.

She'd dropped the potatoes and was searching them out in the long grass, crawling about on her hands and knees, still muttering curses. She let out a gasp as he joined her. 'Oh, fank Gawd! I was coming to look for you when I went bloody flying. Lost me spuds, lost me caterpillars, lost me bloody temper . . .'

'Yes,' Leo murmured. 'So I heard.'

Floral chuckled. 'Johnny Duckett from the farm was just up 'ere. His dad's took bad. Malcolm's took him down the opstickle and Mary's going mental with the milkin', poor girl; don't know whether she'm comin', goin', nor haven't yet been. And *I* cassn't help. I never did know one end of a cow from t'other and cassn't stick the sight of either of 'em, so –' She sat down in the grass and grinned impishly up at him. 'So I told Johnny I'd send you down there,' she said. 'It's about time you done summat to earn your livin', ennit, my love?'

Leo narrowed his eyes, an exercise in self-restraint he felt rather proud of. A few weeks ago, before he'd grown accustomed to

Floral's impudence, he'd have turned crimson with rage, although he still felt like throwing her out by the scruff of her scraggy little neck. If he said she was four-foot ten he'd probably be exaggerating, yet she often made him feel as helplessly angry as if she was six-foot-six and threatening him with a cudgel. Not that it mattered. A few months from now she'd be out on her ear – as he would – and in the meantime . . .

'Ray's ill?' He frowned. 'What's wrong with him? What did Johnny say?'

'Said he passed out. 'Art attack, it d'sound like. Went all blue in the face and fell down in the muck like he been shot. They'd just started milking . . .'

Leo turned swiftly away and broke into a run, speeding downhill towards Manor Farm.

When old Mrs Westley was upset about anything, she looked exactly the same as when she wasn't: stately and upright, as calm as a judge. But she ran her words together, snapping them out like bullets from a machine gun: 'You-asked-him-to-lunch? What-on-earth-shall-we-give-him?'

After a day of living on the edge of her nerves, Lydia was exhausted and feeling almost blissfully numb. Leo had kissed her! He'd said she was wonderful! Ridiculous to feel so relieved after all they'd got up to at the Red Barn but still . . . She'd been so sure she'd lost him, been so certain she wouldn't be deemed good enough for such a man, such a family. But – clever girl! – she'd spotted his weakness for Molliston at the outset, played on it for all it was worth and, in the end . . .

'It doesn't matter what we give him, Gran. We're all on the same rations, after all.'

'You enjoyed your day, did you?' Gran was looking at her sideways, with a suspicious gleam in her eye which said something about hearts worn on sleeves, letting the side down, not conducting oneself quite as one should.

'Yes,' Lydia said firmly. 'It was all very pleasant. Mrs Chantry was charming. Leo showed me around the house and gardens. We had salad for lunch. Just lettuce, Gran, with new potatoes and some cold meat. Nothing in the least grand.'

'What-about-linen? What-about-silver?'

Lydia blinked and then burst out laughing. 'Gran, the place is a wreck! They've been overrun by evacuees, the roof leaks, there are holes in the floorboards and some of the windows are boarded up. You could serve lunch off a newspaper and Leo wouldn't notice!'

She smiled dreamily. 'It is rather beautiful, though. The house, I mean. It feels . . .' She sighed and stared off into space, wondering how it might feel to live in such a house, to make it her home. It felt wonderful, until she remembered that it would mean being married to Leo under the worst sort of false pretences – the sort that were found out in a matter of months. She was already seven weeks gone . . .

'I wish you wouldn't do that, Lydia. Unfinished sentences are just a form of laziness, you know. It feels what?'

'What?' Lydia jumped, wondering if Gran had read her mind.

'You said the house feels . . .?'

'Oh! Oh, that. Well, it feels very peaceful. Warm and contented. I had the feeling that everyone who'd ever lived there had died happy.'

'Hmph! Highly unlikely. Five hundred years must represent a good deal of trouble. Poor Captain Chantry's had enough to last his lifetime, and his mother, too, for that matter. The worry and grief that poor woman's suffered these past few years . . . Just the thought of it makes me shudder.'

'Yes.' Lydia closed her eyes on a prayer. 'But the feeling I had, Gran, was that it always works out all right in the *end*.'

When she opened her eyes again, she found her grandmother looking at her with a sad, wistful smile which was completely out of character for her. Hide your feelings, was her motto; they're nobody's business but your own. But her feelings were showing. She wanted Leo almost as much as Lydia did, albeit for different reasons.

'And did you take the impression that they liked you?'

Lydia swallowed and looked at her hands. 'Mrs Chantry was awfully sweet, but that could be good manners. And Leo kissed me when I left and asked when we could meet again, so I know he didn't hate me. Beyond that . . .' She shrugged. 'Who knows?'

The old woman turned away, her long, elegant hands stroking the edge of the kitchen table. 'We could kill a chicken, I suppose,' she murmured thoughtfully. 'Your father won't notice one missing.'

Lydia smiled. With Gran on her side, what could go wrong? Oh, a thousand things, ten thousand! But she had only to hold him for a few weeks before she told him she was expecting his baby. After that, it was all up to him. She almost added, 'And the Lord, in His mercy,' but had a feeling she'd be pushing her luck to expect help from that quarter. It was all up to her.

She had no notion, until Leo's letter arrived three days later, that her fate was in the hands of an unknown personage by the name of Ray Duckett. And Ray Duckett might have been surprised to know how bitterly an unknown young woman grieved for him as he struggled for life in his hospital bed.

'He's had a heart attack, Gran,' she sighed wearily. 'And Leo's running the farm for him. He can't come.'

Old Mrs Westley bit her lip and turned away.

In the two years that had been allowed him between Cambridge and the British Army, Leo had – or thought he had – run Manor Farm like a well-oiled engine, the cogs of the farmwork engaging neatly with the wheel of the seasons so that nothing – save nature – appeared to be going on. But things had changed since then. A gentle, unhurried workforce of ten men had become an overstretched gaggle of three. A few sleepy house cows had become a herd of thirty (with as many pigs to be fed and mucked out), the sheep had gone and their grazing land turned over to grain, and the harvest would be ready long before Ray Duckett would be well enough to reap it.

After only three days of taking his tenant's place on the farm, Leo felt ready to take his place in the hospital, too. He'd scarcely stirred himself enough to take a brisk walk since his liberation and now paid the price of sloth with aches in every muscle he possessed – and some he didn't. Yet, in spite of the aches, he felt better than he'd felt for years. Something to do with the fresh air, he supposed. Or perhaps just being useful. Or maybe it had something to do with giving orders again, being seen to be capable of taking the lead, even if, half the time, he hadn't a clue what he was doing. But he'd learned in the Army that knowing what you were doing wasn't half as important as being able to think on your feet, and he'd always been good at that. It was exciting to feel one's mind working at problems which *could* be solved rather than always grinding against the ones that couldn't. But he'd been working a week before it occurred to him that Ray Duckett's bad luck might, by a sad enough paradox, prove to be his own salvation.

Mary Duckett came home from visiting the hospital on Saturday afternoon to tell him that Ray would be 'resting' for at least six months. 'And the chances are,' she went on tearfully, 'that he'll never be well enough . . .'

As her teeth clamped down on her grief, Leo knew everything she was thinking. Manor Farm was the Ducketts' living and their home. To lose one would be to lose the other and that their loss would be Leo's gain was an irony his conscience could barely accommodate, let alone mention. 'Don't borrow trouble,' he advised Mary gently. 'I can keep things going until Ray's well enough to make his own decisions. I won't make them for him, I promise.'

Yet the truth was that he'd already made his decisions. Sell

Molliston, move to Manor Farm ... In his mind's eye he'd even planted a screen of trees along Molliston's boundary to hide his view of the prefabs ...

When he went home that evening he found a letter from Lydia waiting for him. It began with a typically formal expression of sympathy for Mr Duckett and his family and then – to his astonishment – launched into an account of old Mrs Westley's preparations for his aborted visit which included a description of her 'sneaking into the henhouse at dead of night to kill a chicken for your lunch'. She went on, 'Luckily for the chicken, my father heard the squawking and, thinking Gran was a fox, went out to scare her off with his shotgun. She was last seen bolting into the copse behind the Red Barn.'

The image this conjured made Leo shout with laughter and he read the rest of the letter far more eagerly than he'd begun it. She wrote very well, with a hint of mischief underlying even the more serious passages. One of her father's dogs was ill – 'probably been eating the laundry again' – and she'd been reading Tolstoy's *Anna Karenin*: 'which has given me a romantic urge to throw myself under a train. Perhaps it would be safer to stick with Jane Austen.' She ended, 'You are still invited to lunch, but I should warn you that a guard has been set on the henhouse lest Gran attempt another raid. Let us know when you are free and I'll see what can be done to capture a tin of Spam.'

She ended, equally surprisingly, 'With love', leaving Leo in something of a fix, because – if only in a small way – it reflected his own state of mind. He'd always loved women who could make him laugh. Lydia had seemed to him to be quite another kind of girl, but he had, very clearly, misjudged her. She was just shy and, like most shy people, could only trust herself to 'be herself' when she couldn't see the effect she was having on other people, as in her letter. Should he answer it? Did he want to? Wouldn't it be wiser, perhaps even kinder, to let her go? He certainly wouldn't have time, during the foreseeable future, to accept her invitation or even to invite her back to Molliston. Within another few weeks, the harvest would be in full swing, and after that he'd need to be thinking of selling Molliston ...

He could think of that quite calmly now and was rather proud of his calm until he remembered that he owed it to Ray Duckett's heart attack. What a thoroughly unpleasant person he'd become recently! He'd seriously considered marrying Lydia for her money and now was all set to evict the Ducketts from their home! And all because he was broke. Next thing he knew, he'd be hanging about on street corners, picking pockets!

No, he wouldn't write to Lydia. Keep himself out of temptation's way, that was best. He could convince himself that she was a perfect angel, that her arrogance was all shyness and her sore-throat voice as sweet as a bell, but when you came down to it – when you came right down to the nub of it – the best thing one could say about Lydia was that she was *rich*.

Lydia spent the next two weeks waiting for the postman. Her father and grandmother, if called to give evidence of her activities during that time, would have sworn that she'd done other things beside: exercising the horses, weeding the garden, collecting the eggs and washing the dishes, and although this was true, it was not true enough, for she hadn't been conscious of doing anything except wait for the postman. She waited most fervently between the hours of five and eight (in the mornings) and between one and three (in the afternoons), yet the minute the postman came and went without leaving a letter from Leo, she began waiting again. At each disappointment her heart became as small, as hard and as wrinkled as a walnut. At each renewal of hope it swelled up and throbbed until her whole body throbbed with it: her hands and knees, even her head, shaking with the effort of hoping, hoping, hoping . . .

She'd written three drafts of her letter to him and now read them again, time after time, searching out the paragraph, the sentence, even the single word that had offended him. She never found it. As letters went, it had been a perfect letter: light, gentle, kind and humorous. Not too long, not too short, not too intimate, not too formal. She'd sent her warmest regards to Mrs Chantry and polite good wishes to Floral. Her only possible error had been to sign off 'With love', but after the Red Barn, what else could she have done? No, the only answer was that he'd regretted the Red Barn, regretted ever meeting her and was just using Manor Farm as an excuse to avoid meeting her again. But that couldn't be true! How could he have kissed her, how called her *wonderful*, if he hadn't liked her? And, after all, it was Leo, not she, who'd asked for another meeting!

So . . . The trouble must not be with Leo but with Mrs Chantry. Behind all the kindness of her welcome, she'd been summing Lydia up and deciding that she was not good enough for her only son. Or had it had something to do with Uncle Avery? Some little thing Mrs Chantry had failed to mention? 'I sent him off with a flea in his ear . . .' But maybe she hadn't. Perhaps hers had been the ear with the flea in it. Maybe she'd been madly in love with him and had never forgiven him for choosing Aunt Catherine instead? Yes, that was a possibility . . .

But it hardly mattered now. Whatever her reasons, she'd persuaded Leo, and there was nothing Lydia could do about it. Time was running out and she knew she hadn't courage enough to do the decent thing – own up, face the music, watch her father's face, let alone Gran's, while she told them . . . Told them that everything they'd done for her, everything they'd hoped and planned for her, was laid to waste and shame.

Tomorrow she would go away. Tonight . . .

She sat at the little writing table in her room, dipped her pen in the ink and began, 'My dear Gran, my dear Daddy, by the time you read this, I'll be gone . . .'

An hour later, she stared down at an empty page. Beside her, the waste-paper basket was full of balled-up paper, lies and excuses. But she mustn't lie to them now; she had to tell the truth, if only to make them understand how greatly she blamed herself. But the truth was hard to tell. It seemed so cheap now, so utterly sordid. It hadn't been all that romantic in the back seat of the Austin Seven, either . . .

She couldn't even claim to have been swept off her feet. She'd *jumped*, knowing that for all his charm, his good looks, his blue uniform and gold braid, Nigel Marchant was no gentleman . . .

She raised her eyes to the mirror and smiled bitterly. 'And you, madam, are no lady,' she murmured. 'Oh, Lydia, Lydia, what the hell does it matter *now*? You've got one chance left! *Take* it!'

'Dear Leo,' she wrote. 'Appalling news. I'm afraid I've missed my monthly and can only suppose the Red Barn is to blame . . .'

Chapter Five

His mother always sorted Leo's post in the order she wanted him to open it: personal letters first, bills and tax demands last. Leo preferred to do it the other way around and, on ordinary occasions, would invert the pile and work through it backwards, but today he recognised Lydia's handwriting at the top of the heap and frowned at it wonderingly, his throat constricting with irritation. He hadn't thought of her at all during the past few weeks. He'd been certain that he'd done the right thing in ignoring her previous letter: the right thing for *her* as much as for his own conscience.

Thirty thousand pounds was too great a temptation for a man with such a need. It put Lydia in the position of a lamb tethered for tiger-bait, and she didn't deserve such treatment. Neither (as the tiger) did Leo. He wasn't – by nature – a dishonourable man and knew that if he took the lamb, the Great White Hunter of guilt would shoot him through the head immediately afterwards. He'd never be able to feel comfortable about it; he'd be apologising to her, in one way or another, for the rest of his life, and he couldn't bear the thought of that. Whatever else happened to him, whatever else he lost, he had to keep his self-respect. But why on earth was she writing to him again? For one so much a mistress of the proud gesture, it showed a distinct lack of pride!

Having observed the scantiness of the breakfast table (a bowl of wheat flakes and a slice of toast), he turned the pile of letters over and opened the buff-coloured envelope with 'On His Majesty's Service' stamped across it. His mother said, 'Oh, Leo!'

'What?'

'Why don't you read Lydia's letter?'

He smiled knowingly. 'Lydia's? Have you already steamed it open, then, Mother?'

'No! I recognised the handwriting! It's beautiful handwriting, isn't it? I noticed it the last time she wrote to you, darling. *Most distinctive.*'

Leo looked again at the envelope. Her writing was all right; very neat, evenly spaced, nicely rounded. It looked like a long line of swallows on a telegraph wire. Or perhaps a long line of noughts following a three . . . That aside, it had no distinction at all.

'Is there any more toast?' he enquired coolly.

'No.' His mother glared at him.

Grinning, Leo opened the letter. The first two sentences covered barely two lines of a small sheet of paper and Leo had read and fully understood them in the time it took to blink once. But he blinked more than once before he read the third sentence: 'I don't know what to do.' He closed his eyes and covered them with a shaking hand.

'Leo? What on earth . . .?'

I know it's my own fault, that I should never have taken such a risk and that I should not have let my feelings – or yours – run away with me.

Utterly dazed, Leo was still capable of admiring the immaculate diplomacy of an approach which put his own 'feelings' in a separate, almost blameless, clause of their own. Clever stuff. She'd dropped a ruddy great bomb on him and, in case that didn't finish him off, had added a poisoned dart for good measure.

You said at the time that you would not let me down and although I can't hold you to such a promise, which I'm sure you'll regret having made, I must ask you – beg you – to acknowledge this letter as soon you possibly can, so that I can be free to decide my next course of action.

'Leo?'

'Just a minute, Mother.'

'Is she coming over?'

'Loud and clear.' He began to laugh. Then, furiously scratching his head, he found that he was fighting against tears. Thirty thousand pounds! And they'd come to his hand like a tame little bird . . .

I don't imagine that this is the right time to say how much I care for you – were my feelings reciprocated, I think I should have heard from you by now – yet if you can, or think you must, respond as I hope, then perhaps it will help you to know that you may depend on my love and loyalty, with my most heartfelt gratitude, for the rest of my life.

There was just her signature after that: a sad, loosely written scrawl which trailed away hopelessly, with a little star-shaped blot of ink at the end. Leo swallowed. He felt rotten.

'What does she say?' his mother asked nervously. 'I can see it's bad news, darling. She hasn't ditched you, I hope?'

He tossed the letter across the table and sat with his head in his hands, going over it in his thoughts. You couldn't beat it for dignity. Or for tact. Or for humility, come to that. And yet he knew that if she were anyone else, he would not marry her. He didn't love her. He barely liked her. And honour had its limits. Marriages could and often did last fifty years and Leo certainly *hoped* to see his eightieth birthday, but the thought of living with Lydia for the rest of his life . . . No. He had wanted her for her money from the first, and he still wanted her for her money. It wasn't a thing a man could like himself for: doing the most honourable thing for the least honourable reason, but . . .

'Oh, Leo! Oh, darling! Oh, this is wonderful!'

He sent his mother a severe look. 'I've made a respectable girl pregnant,' he snapped. 'What's so wonderful about that? Her bank-balance?'

Peggy Chantry smiled as if butter wouldn't melt in her mouth and reached casually for the teapot. 'Ah,' she murmured softly, 'your father would be proud of you, darling. He was an old humbug, too, you know.'

Leo widened his eyes, with outrage at first, although he realised at once that outrage was inappropriate to the occasion. She was right.

'I wrote to Prue about Avery Moreton,' she said. 'Just to remark on the coincidence. But she knew all about it, darling, and so did you.'

Although – after a moment's thought – Leo conceded defeat, he couldn't let it rest there, couldn't let his mother think he was as mercenary as all that. 'You're right,' he said. 'But give me credit, Mother, for knowing that I was wrong, almost from the start. I really didn't want it to come to this. A marriage can last a long time and I don't *love* her – I barely like her. No matter how wealthy she is, her money isn't worth a lifetime of misery and regret.' He looked at his hands, sighing. 'Not that I have any choice, now.'

His mother was looking at him with a pursed mouth, clearly trying not to laugh. She didn't say a word, but he knew precisely what she was thinking. *Yes, you have a choice, and if Lydia was poor, you'd make that choice without a second thought.*

He squeezed his eyes shut and groaned. 'Oh, this is ridiculous! What's happened to me, Mother? I used not to be like this, did I?'

She didn't reply. When he raised his head to look at her, she'd turned to gaze from the window, her face as cold and sad as a tragedian mask. 'We're all like it,' she said quietly at last.

'A Chantry trait?' he murmured coolly, not believing it.

'A human one.' Smiling again, she collected the breakfast things into a precarious heap at her elbow. 'So cheer up, darling. She'll be as glad to have your name as you'll be to have her money, after all.' She leaned towards him, blissfully smiling. 'And, oh, darling, won't it be lovely to have a new *roof*!'

Leo was amazed. Until the very last word, he'd been sure she'd been about to say, 'a new baby'.

Lydia waited for the postman. The morning shift brought nothing and she spent the next few hours in a daze of misery, thinking – not for the first time – of all the most desperate measures known to woman for ending a pregnancy. Most of them didn't work, and the ones that did usually killed the mother as well as her child. Or crippled them both. And there was a part of Lydia – a small part, but essential – that wanted her baby. She couldn't help thinking of it as a curse, a punishment, couldn't help thinking of it with the same contempt she thought of herself (she'd even thought of calling it Austin), but sometimes, on the odd occasion when she wasn't thinking at all, she knew that she loved it and needed it as she'd never loved or needed anyone before.

She waited for the postman. The front garden at Priory Farm had been so thoroughly weeded and tidied while she'd waited during the past few weeks, she was now reduced to admiring the roses, checking for greenfly, trying to keep her stomach where it was meant to be, trying to swallow her thudding heart.

Jimmy Lessing had been 'invalided out' in '42, having lost an eye in North Africa, but the other one was still good enough to allow him to read everyone's postcards before he handed them over and to check who was writing to whom. 'One for your gran from America, Miss. One for your dad . . . Milk cheque, I'd reckon. An' one for you, Miss, with a Trowbridge mark. Durrible writing, though. Can't hardly read un.'

Almost fainting, Lydia took the letters. Leo's writing had surprised her, too, when she'd received his last letter: it was barely decipherable, like winter trees in a roaring gale: black, spiky and lacking the least sense of direction. But unmistakably *his*. She stared at the envelope – a long, pale blue one – in a moment of terrible hope and then closed her eyes, telling herself that it could contain nothing to help her. The best he would do would be to offer money and she didn't need money. She needed a husband.

Forgive me for not writing sooner. As I failed to explain in my last letter, my skills as a farmer leave several things wanting, biceps and pectorals not least among them. A strong backbone, if you know where I might find one, would be useful too. I became exhausted before noon – in fact before breakfast – on my first day at work and have only now regained strength enough to lift the pen.

Farming is hard to do and even harder to understand. I find that I know very little about cows and even less about wheat, although, for reasons I dare not investigate, I feel perfectly at home with pigs. My mother tells me that this is because they are intelligent, affectionate, discerning creatures, but I suspect she means to flatter me in flattering my friends.

As she read all this, Lydia's face turned cold and she leaned against the corner of the house, almost drowning in despair. He'd written this before he'd had her letter! It was all nonsense! That it was warm, friendly nonsense was her only hope. He hadn't forgotten her; he'd just been too tired and too busy to write, and although that was a relief, it was not relief *enough*!

He'd written on both sides of the paper and, as she turned the page, the mood changed. There was a report of Mr Duckett's progress and an indication that, if circumstances dictated, Leo might take over the farm on a permanent basis.

It will be sad for Ray, of course, but not for me. I need an occupation, if only to keep mind and body in good order, and my nature, being of an independent and stubborn cast (not forgetting 'intelligent, affectionate and discerning') could not be better suited elsewhere. I'm already feeling fitter and am sleeping more soundly than I've done in years. The pace of work is such that I am often harassed and irritable, but the reverse of the coin is that I have no time to be bothered much by melancholy. When dark clouds envelop me now, I generally find that my mother has burned the potatoes again.

Lydia had merely scanned this passage, racing through it at speed to confirm for herself that the letter was entirely meaningless. But suddenly she gasped and clapped her hand to her mouth with shock. He *had* had her letter!

It was good to hear from you again. I've missed your company more than you can imagine and wish I could spend more time with you than is, at present, possible, although I sometimes think that your time is better spent without me. I have so little to offer: raw bones and dark moods, an old house, an old name, but I offer them freely and would be honoured were you to accept and cherish them as I wish to cherish you.

Since the appalling day when Nigel had confessed he was already married, Lydia had shed scarcely a tear: her feelings had been too bad, too hopeless, too shameful for tears. But now she fell to her knees and sobbed like a child and didn't stop crying even when her grandmother touched her shoulder and demanded urgently, 'Lydia. What is it?'

'Nothing, nothing!' She groped in her pocket for a handkerchief and blew her nose. 'Leo . . . Oh, Gran! He's asked me to marry him!'

Even in a state of near-delirium, Lydia could have guessed her grandmother's response almost to the word: a controlled expression of pleasure, a gentle command that Lydia pull herself together, and then a wise reflection that 'fools rush in where angels fear to tread'. *You've known him such a short while, my dear . . .*

But Gran said none of it. She cupped her hand around one of the roses beside the path and murmured simply, 'I'm glad,' before walking regally away.

Strange as this was, it was not strange enough to divert Lydia's thoughts from Leo's proposal, his gentleness and generosity. Oh, what a kind, good man he was! He hadn't even mentioned the baby, hadn't written a word of complaint or criticism! It was almost as if he *wanted* to marry her, but how could he? How *could* he, poor man? She'd seen him three times! Just three times!

My mother of course is delighted at the thought of gaining another daughter, and although I don't expect your father to feel the same about losing you, I think I should see him as soon as it can be arranged. If you would walk with me for an hour beforehand, we can then decide how best to arrange things for the happiness of all. With all my heart I can tell you that your happiness is my first concern and if you make mine yours, we shall lack nothing.

Although he signed himself 'With love', the serious tone of this last paragraph touched Lydia more deeply than any romantic protestations could have done. But as she read the entire letter again, she realised that all of it had had a serious intention, so tactfully disguised with humour that she hadn't, at first, even noticed what he was saying. He'd drawn a character-study of himself, given her fair warning that she would be marrying not the lord of the manor but a busy farmer, a man subject to dark moods, irritability, tiredness and back-ache. He'd told her also (as if she needed telling after this!) that he was intelligent, affectionate and discerning, but also modest enough to compare his virtues with those of Mr Duckett's pigs! Oh, God, she didn't deserve such a man. She didn't deserve him!

Taking time only to put the other two letters on the kitchen windowsill, Lydia walked to the quiet little copse near the Red Barn, to compose herself and pull her thoughts into order. Leo's concluding sentence played repeatedly on her mind, and as the passion of relief began to fade, she understood how important a sentence it was. He was saying, really, that nothing else would matter so long as they put each other's happiness first, and he was right . . . Except that she'd already sacrificed his happiness – and her own. Six months from now, the entire house of cards would fall about their ears. Six months from now he would hate her. And yet she couldn't save him without sacrificing everyone else she loved . . . including her child. Her nameless child.

She sat among the roots of a beech tree, speaking softly to a God she had, until now, scarcely believed existed, although she'd sent him more prayers just lately than ever in her life before. He'd answered them. And now it would be churlish to ask for another favour, another miracle: that Leo wouldn't notice he'd been taken for a fool. No, she'd deal with that when it happened. Now, for the first time in a long time, she'd behave as she'd been taught. Thank God for his blessings and pray only that she could prove herself worthy of them. She'd be good to Leo – for six months. She'd make him happy – for six months. And after that . . .?

Three weeks of hard work, fresh air and glorious weather had done more to improve Leo's looks than he would have thought possible. He was still very thin, but he was beginning to build a few muscles in his arms and shoulders, and although they didn't quite show, they made him move differently, even breathe differently, so that he felt more generally human and much less like a bag of bones tied together with string. His hair had been very blond when he was a boy, and although its 'natural' colour now was a light, mousy brown, the sun had bleached it into pale gold streaks which nicely set off his tanned face and blue eyes. It was a relief in more ways than one. He'd never been – at least, he'd never *thought* he'd been – an especially vain man. He'd taken his looks for granted (much as he'd taken his father's wealth for granted) and hadn't realised how important such things were until they were gone. A decent appearance and a decent income were like a coat of armour against the world. They didn't make a man stronger, less craven or less selfish; but they made him feel less vulnerable to his weaknesses and more able to overcome them.

That was precisely what he wanted to do now: marry Lydia on his strengths, not his weaknesses. He did *have* a few strengths. He was intelligent and affectionate (he rather doubted 'discerning'), patient, courteous, humorous, and, within reason, fairly tolerant. He also had more than his fair share of common sense, and if only Lydia had as much of it as he did, perhaps they *could* make a go of it, or at least keep themselves on the right side of misery. There would, after all, be something they could share. Their baby . . .

God, what a strange thought! Fatherhood was an idea he had entertained hardly at all until now, but he found he rather liked it. It was like discovering a hidden talent, a new well of potential, a part of oneself one hadn't suspected was there . . . Yes, he'd enjoy having a child; and the child, too, was the best reason he could think of for making the best of a bad job. Bad job? *Rotten* job. He hardly knew her!

That he hardly knew her was the first thing on his mind as he went to see her and 'speak' to her father. But she, for a moment, didn't even *recognise* him!

'Leo?' she whispered. 'Oh, my goodness, you look so different!'

He smiled and bent to kiss her cheek, but withdrew at the last moment, realising that she'd changed too and certainly for the better. She looked softer, warmer, but at the same time more vulnerable, as if, while he'd been reclaiming his armour, she'd completely lost hers. It was the first time he'd looked at her and known without doubt that she was beautiful. Her mouth seemed fuller, more relaxed and inclined to smile. There was a soft bloom of colour in her cheeks. Even her eyes had changed. Either that, or he'd never really noticed them before. They weren't black at all, but a soft, chestnut brown, fringed prettily with dark, curling lashes.

He kissed her mouth. 'Shall we walk?'

She nodded. He gave her his arm and, having planned their talk to the last small detail, he found himself now with nothing to say.

'I want to thank you,' Lydia began softly.

'There's no need for that.' (Thirty thousand pounds, and she was thanking *him*?) 'We have to go forward now, Lydia, not back. Make plans, resolutions, sensible decisions. We have a marriage to think about and we hardly know each other. We have a child to think about and we don't know him, either.' He laughed. 'He could be a girl.'

'But don't you mind?' she asked incredulously.

'No. I've always been very partial to girls. Grown-up ones, mostly, of course, but I'm sure the small ones have their merits.'

'Oh, I don't mean that! I mean, don't you mind about the baby *at all*? It wasn't something you'd planned, resolved, decided! It was an *accident*!'

She'd pulled her hand clear of his arm. Leo reclaimed it and patted it into place, reflecting wonderingly that her voice hadn't sharpened as she became agitated but deepened to a throaty purr, with a rasping break where she emphasised the key words. He wondered what it would be like to have an argument with her, a real quarrel. Terrifying, probably . . .

'You've heard of happy accidents, I suppose?' he said.

Lydia looked at him doubtfully, and with good reason, for the 'happy' part of this accident wasn't the baby so much as the chance it gave him to save Molliston *for* the baby and, God willing, for a few more generations beyond. Complicated. But however complicated it was, it made him no less happy *about* the baby.

'Oh, I was a little – er – dismayed at first,' he confessed. 'But I've had some experience in "bowing to the inevitable", Lydia. As soon as you bow your head, you see the underside of the problem and realise that there's more to it than met the eye when you were standing upright. And I found, when I bowed, that I rather liked the idea of having a child. In many ways, you know, the past few years have been a kind of death for me, which is to say that I wasn't convinced I'd survived them. I came back safe, but I came back changed, to a changed world, and felt lost, rootless, completely out of touch. The baby has changed that. Because it's mine, a part of my flesh, it's put me back on course, somehow. It's given me a future if you like. It's made the future important again.'

He smiled and squeezed Lydia's hand, noticing with amusement that she looked totally horrified by his confession. 'Come on,' he encouraged gently. 'That's good, isn't it? That's why I wanted us to talk, you see: to get the future settled, to give ourselves something positive to work towards instead of seeing it all as a calamity. We could be married for a very long time, Lydia, and although it can't all be happy, I'm sure a great deal of it can, if we only think it over, talk it through.'

Lydia turned away to look at the view. 'There's no need,' she said. 'You've clearly given it a lot of thought and I'll do anything you say. We don't have to talk about it. Just tell me what you want and I'll do it, whatever it is.'

Leo was appalled. He stared at the back of her head, opening and shutting his mouth as the correct response continued to escape him.

But he thought of it at last. 'Love, honour and *obey*, is that the idea?'

'Yes.' She bowed her head, wrapping her arms around her ribs as she'd done once before. 'I owe you that much, don't I?'

She owed him nothing, and although it wasn't the time to tell her the precise balance of their account with one another, he couldn't bear for her to think herself so greatly in his debt. She wasn't made to be submissive. It didn't suit her. And it most certainly wouldn't suit him. It would bore him to tears, and there was nothing that terrified him more than boredom.

'Hmm . . .' he said. 'Well, all right. If you insist, I'll tell you exactly what I want. I want a partner, not a slave. I want a friend: someone to talk with and think with, and plan *with*, not *for*. You're not a child, Lydia. I refuse to tell you what to do, except to tell you to think for yourself. This is *your* life we're discussing. Your *whole* life. And if you don't take your share of responsibility for it, it's going to be a rotten life for both of us.'

She said nothing. She didn't even move except once, very slightly, to shake her head. Leo raised his eyes to heaven. 'Lydia, please. I'm trying to do the right –'

'I *can't*!' She was crying – as softly and discreetly as only Lydia knew how – and, as he realised it, Leo began for the first time to look at the situation from her point of view. She'd been, as the saying went, 'swept off her feet' by a virtual stranger and now, to all intents and purposes, was being forced to marry him. She was only twenty-two, was probably terrified out of her wits, and here was he doing his stupid boy scout act: *We're all in this together, chaps*, when all she needed was comfort and reassurance, someone to take control. *Leave it all to me, sweetheart. I know what I'm doing*.

He put his hands on her shoulders. 'It's all right, Lydia. I understand.'

'No, you don't!' She twisted away from him. 'I can't do it! I can't do it, I tell you! I've done something terrible to you!'

'No!' He caught her arm and pulled her around to face him. 'No, I've done something terrible to *you*, which is why . . .'

He halted, dismayed and confused, aware that his need to assuage Lydia's guilt was taking him into the dangerous territory of his own. But what, after all, did he have to feel guilty about? They were both of them getting exactly what they wanted. The account was squared.

'Oh, damn it all!' he said angrily. 'Come here, woman!'

She fought his kiss for a moment or two: wriggling and twisting, punching his shoulders. But he knew how to deal with this. Kiss harder.

The fight went out of her at last and he kissed her more gently, running his fingers through her hair until she began to kiss him back, tasting his mouth very tentatively, as if it were a strange foreign fruit and she not certain she liked it.

'Have a little more,' he murmured. 'It's good for the brain: like Marmite.'

She laughed tearfully. 'Oh, Leo,' she croaked. 'You're the sweetest, dearest man, but I –'

'Hush. You don't know what you're talking about.'

He kissed her again, and then wrapped his arms tightly about her, rocking her like a child. 'There,' he said. 'Don't cry any more, Lydia. It's all right. It's all right.'

'You really *want* to marry me?'

He was glad she'd laid the emphasis on 'want' rather than on 'me'. It meant he could answer without hesitation, 'Yes.'

But he'd make her happy. He'd make her happy if it killed him. He owed her that much, didn't he?

Chapter Six

Partly because they couldn't get married until the harvest was in, and partly because Leo had insisted on it, they confessed Lydia's condition that same night. Or rather, Leo confessed. Lydia merely sat with her hands in her lap, waiting for the rockets to go off. But nothing happened. Her father nodded gravely and sighed a good deal. Gran simply stared at the wall for a while and afterwards brought in the tea. Although she was relieved, Lydia also felt a little sad to think that Gran's strict moral code could so easily be put aside for a man called Chantry, when a Bloggs, Smith or Jones would have been lucky to come out of it alive. The others wouldn't have Leo's style, of course, his gentleness, decency and tact, but even if he'd lacked such qualities, his fine old name and his fine old house would have done the job just as well.

Lydia wasn't hypocrite enough to condemn her grandmother for that. She knew she had worse stains on her own moral escutcheon than mere snobbery. And after all, what would Gran have achieved by making a fuss? Nothing. Lydia had to marry someone, and that it was Leo was a comfort . . . At least for Gran. But as the time of the wedding drew nearer, it became less and less of a comfort for Lydia. He was a good man. He deserved the best woman in the world, not a liar and a cheat, a coward, an adulterer. He'd almost crucified her when he'd talked about the 'death' of the prison camp and told her that the baby had, in effect, restored him to life. She'd known then that she couldn't go through with it, yet here she was, about to kill him all over again! She kept telling herself that she'd *tried* to own up, kept telling herself that it was *his* fault she hadn't and that, by kissing her when he did – as he did – he'd somehow absolved her of all responsibility.

During the daylight hours, while she altered her frocks and skirts to make a decent – if rather shapeless – trousseau for the 'honeymoon' (they wouldn't be going away; Leo couldn't leave the farm), she could almost believe that he *had* absolved her. But at night, when she sat beside her bedroom window, watching the moon at play with the shadows on the lawn, she knew the truth about herself. At any time, before the kiss or after it, she could have said, 'It's not your child,' and let him go.

It was too late now. She'd been to Molliston several times since then – once with Prue – in an attempt to 'organise' the place to receive the blushing bride. They hadn't got very far. Mrs Chantry had been like a dog with two tails – so excited about it all, she'd given the impression that getting some girl pregnant out of wedlock was the best thing that could have happened to her son. It had confused Lydia utterly. She'd expected at least a measure of disapproval – some coolness, perhaps even resentment – and felt she could have coped with that a good deal better than she'd coped with all the approval that had come her way instead.

She'd mentioned this, as tactfully as she could, to Leo, on one of the snatched moments they'd had alone. Having failed to recognise him when he came to see her father, she failed to recognise him again at Molliston, although for different reasons. He'd been so caked in dust and sweat from the harvest fields, he'd looked like a coal-miner, with only his teeth and his eyes shining through the filth. And his sense of humour, of course. 'Darling, kiss me!'

It was difficult to find the measure of his humour, to know how to respond. She'd almost teased, 'I never kiss strangers,' but remembered the Red Barn and, embarrassed, had said, 'Don't be silly,' instead, which hadn't greatly pleased him.

'What's up?'

'Nothing. But I – I came to help your mother – er – rearrange things, and she doesn't seem to want to do anything. I don't know how anything works, or where I'm to put my things. I don't know what I'll be allowed to do, or be expected to do . . . And I do want to be useful, Leo. I don't want to just hang around being a nuisance.'

He had closed one eye and looked at her rather sternly with the other. 'Do anything you like,' he said. 'It's your home now, you know.'

'No, it's your mother's home. I can't possibly do anything without her approval. But I need her to *tell* me, and we're just wasting time . . .'

He'd laughed. 'Which is all you'll ever do if you wait for Mother to decide anything. She hasn't a practical bone in her body, Lydia. Go around the house on your own, make your own decisions, and then, if you like, ask her to approve them. She'll say yes without even giving it a thought, I promise you.'

He'd sounded so certain about it, Lydia had almost believed him, but the very idea of taking such liberties had shocked her rigid and she'd ended up with nothing done. She knew which bed she'd be sleeping in (Leo's), knew that the hot water system didn't work and that the bathwater had to be carried in pailfuls from the boiler in the scullery (which first had to be filled with pailfuls from the tap in the yard). She knew that the kitchen stove had 'revolutionary tendencies' and that the wireless in the parlour worked only if you kicked it. She knew that when it rained you couldn't hear yourself think for the syncopated beat of water dripping into buckets, that in winter none of the chimneys would draw and that, given the choice, she'd rather have all her teeth pulled out than live at Molliston.

With only two days to go before the wedding, which was to be as quiet and private as circumstances dictated, she looked around her grandmother's immaculate kitchen and, without feeling so much as a lump in her throat to give her warning, burst into tears.

'Oh, Gran!' she wailed. 'What am I to do? It'll be like living in a field when winter comes!'

'Work,' her grandmother said shortly. 'It's no good expecting Mrs Chantry to do anything. She's spent most of her life being waited on by servants, Lydia. She probably doesn't know *how* to work, even if she's willing to try.'

'But I can't mend the roof!'

'Find someone who can. Not *all* the men are away. There must be someone who can do it. Even if there are no materials to hand, a good plumber could at least patch the leads until they can be replaced. And, while he's at it, he can fix the hot-water boiler, too. You can't bring a new baby into a damp house, Lydia.'

'But if it were possible to find someone, Leo would surely . . .'

Her grandmother pursed her mouth. 'Leo's head isn't screwed on,' she said. 'Would he be in this fix if it were? It's up to you, Lydia, and if you want anything done, you'd better do it soon. It's August already.' She glanced from the window to a blue, cloudless sky. 'Thunder,' she predicted grimly.

Lydia's 'morning sickness' had worn off, but that didn't mean she didn't feel sick.

'What-about-this-Flora-person?' Gran demanded sharply. 'What does she do? Where does she fit in? What-kind-of-woman-is-she?'

'I don't know, Gran. I've scarcely laid eyes on her. I think she's avoiding me. Leo doesn't seem to like her, but apart from that . . . Oh, she does the garden. She seems quite good at it.'

'Well, that's something. At least she can work. And she must know the place inside out. Get her to help you.'

Lydia sighed, thinking of the tiny, gnome-like figure she'd seen at Molliston only from a distance – usually flitting out of one door as Lydia came in at another. Shy? Or scared? Or something else?

'She's probably mad,' she murmured wearily.

Mrs Westley turned on her heel, her eyes snapping with irritation. 'Then cure her!' she said.

Leo fell asleep, in a state of rare contentment, about twelve hours after his wedding. An hour later, having in the meantime completely forgotten both his wedding and his wife, he woke up again in a fright, convinced that there was a rat in the bed. It turned out to be Lydia, with her head under the pillow, whimpering, 'Oh, my Lord . . . Oh, my Lord . . .'

'What's the matter?'

'Thunder!'

It took him a while to work this out, but, having done so, he gathered her against him, composed himself to sleep again and murmured, 'S'all right, all right. Just God playing bowls . . .'

'I am *not* afraid of thunder.' Her voice sounded like a message from beyond the grave: deep, hushed and vengeful. 'I *am* afraid of *rain*!'

Leo opened his eyes, remembering all the tin baths and buckets he'd hidden in the gallery. Save for a few light showers, it hadn't rained since then. Now it was emptying down.

His mother had gone to stay with Prue for a few weeks so there was no hope that she'd be creeping around, saving the day, and there was never any knowing what Floral was up to. Groaning, he rolled out of bed and fumbled into his dressing gown. 'Well, well,' he muttered feebly. 'Isn't this romantic?'

'What are you going to do?'

'Set buckets. Go back to sleep.' He was groping for the door knob before he remembered to add, 'Darling.'

Still, the day hadn't been too awful, in the long run. He'd had a few nasty moments: a fit of blind panic in the register office when he'd had to imagine his shoes had been nailed to the floor to keep him from running away, and then a close shave with tears when the registrar had said, 'You are now man and wife,' as if it was a disease of the 'no cure' variety. Which it was, in a way. As far back as their history went, no Chantry had ever been divorced, which – if he and Lydia stuck with tradition – meant that at least one of them would not get out of this marriage alive.

Yet, in spite of the rain, he didn't feel as if he'd *quite* taken the road to ruin. She'd been . . . She'd been absolutely beautiful tonight: warm and passionate and alive. He'd been a bit shy – as much for her as of her – and had expected there to be more wooing, more romantic coaxing than she'd seemed to need. But whatever was frigidly Victorian in her daytime manners hadn't extended very far into the night. All she'd needed was love, and since that was exactly what he'd needed too . . . He grinned to himself in the dark. No, it hadn't been too awful. *Yet.*

A dark, spectral voice at his ear – 'Where are we going?' – made him gasp and clutch his chest just as Lydia stepped on his heel and made a grab for his arm.

'Lydia! What the hell are you up to? I thought –'

'I'm helping you.' Her teeth were chattering, and as the house came alive with a sudden flash of lightning, she jumped with fright and grabbed his arm again. 'Thought you might be scared of the thunder,' she added shakily.

'Thanks,' he said dryly. 'I feel braver already,' and was amazed to hear a wicked little chuckle echoing from the walls all around. Was this Lydia? Or one of Molliston's several – but usually discreet – ghosts? He was quite glad when he reached the light switch at the end of the landing, just to check he had the right woman clutching his sleeve. He did, and in spite of her tousled hair, bare feet and a dressing gown almost as ancient and motheaten as his own (she'd confided earlier that it was her father's: her clothing coupons hadn't quite run to quilted satin) she looked magnificent, like a wild woman on the rampage: head up, nostrils flared, eyes glowing like coals in the creamy white of her face. Thunder storms evidently suited her . . .

'The buckets are in the gallery,' he said. 'If you wait on the stairs, I'll pass them down.'

He opened the door at the foot of the stairs and heard a loud metallic clanking, which he recognised at once, although Lydia didn't.

'What on earth?'

Leo laughed. 'Floral's beaten us to it.'

'Floral? I thought she'd gone!'

'Gone where?'

'With your mother!'

He laughed again. 'Good Lord, no. She's like the woodworm – ever with us. All right,' he called out. 'Go back to bed, Floral, I'll see to it.'

'No, no.' With an orchestrated crash, she appeared at the foot of the stairs, stuck all over with metal pails, like a rock covered in limpets. Her gingery-grey hair was done up in curling rags, her feet in grey woolly socks, and the short bit in the middle hung with a stiff, brightly striped gown that looked as it if had once been a deckchair.

'Not on yer 'oneymoon, my love,' she crooned in her fruity, lullaby voice. 'You go off an' enjoy yourself while you – Ooh!' This last exclamation, accompanied by a frightened start, was in recognition of Lydia, whom she clearly had not expected – or wished – to meet, for she bit her lip, put her head down and clattered away down the main staircase without saying another word.

Leo rubbed his nose thoughtfully. Then he shrugged, put his arm around his bride's waist and whispered fruitily, 'Yes, let's go off an' enjoy ourselves, shall we?'

Lydia had parted with her virginity in a daze of excitement, curiosity, embarrassment and pain. She'd seduced Leo at the Red Barn in a daze of brandy-induced detachment, merely as a means to an end. But even then, she'd noticed the difference between Leo and Nigel and had wondered about it since, whether it had been a personal difference or just one of time and situation. It had been cold, cramped and squalid in the back seat of the Austin Seven; warm, clean and peaceful in the hay . . .

It had been different again in a soft feather bed, with Leo stone cold sober and a hot gleam of possession in his eye. Even while she still had her nightie on, he'd made her feel undressed. She'd half-expected him to dive on top of her in the next instant, but instead, to her amazement, he'd knelt at the foot of the bed and massaged her feet, his hands cool and firm, his long brown fingers contrasting sensually with the paleness of her own skin. She'd giggled nervously, 'What are you doing?' and the answer, 'Getting to know you,' had touched her heart, for he'd seemed to be memorising her body as he progressed along it, and she had a feeling, now, that there wasn't an inch of her skin he hadn't touched, observed or kissed. The sensations it had aroused in her had informed her, without a shadow of doubt, that he not only knew what he was doing but that he was doing it as it should be done, as if there were rules written down somewhere which he'd committed to memory long ago.

But she discovered, after their curious meeting with Floral (*was* she mad?) that if there were rules, they were very *complicated* rules, for now Leo embarked on another method entirely: rougher and more seemingly urgent, although it took just as long. When it was over she wasn't quite sure what had happened to her. It was as if every nerve in her body had screamed, shuddered and died happy.

She was beginning to drift into sleep when the noise began: a loud clattering on the stairs, followed by a prolonged ringing sound that went on ringing in her head even after it had ceased. Leo swore.

'What is it?' she whispered.

'Floral. Dropped the proverbial clanger. Sounds like a tin bath. I should have helped her.' He gathered her into his arms. 'But I had other things on my mind.'

'It's gone very quiet . . .'

'Mmm . . .'

'What if Floral fell, too?'

Leo was silent for a moment. Then, 'Oh, hell . . .' he groaned, and reached for his dressing gown.

He was gone scarcely a few moments, just long enough to look over the banister. 'No, she's all right. Her eyes are wide open, anyway.'

'*What*?'

He laughed. 'Just teasing. I think she's gone back to bed.'

'Where does she sleep?'

'I don't know. In one of the garrets, I think.'

'You don't know?' Lydia was appalled.

'Why should I know? She's nothing to do with me. According to my mother, she's nothing to do with her, either, but she won't ask her to leave. Bit of a puzzle, really. It worries me, to tell the truth. I sometimes wonder if there's something . . .' He sighed and seemed disinclined to finish the sentence.

'Something *wrong* with her?'

'Wrong in the head, you mean? No . . . But she has no status here. She's not a guest, not a tenant, not a servant. She's a complete anarchist, a law unto herself, and I don't find it at all comfortable.' He turned over and touched Lydia's nose with the tip of his finger. 'However,' he murmured, 'you are the mistress of the house now, and I think Floral knows it, judging from the way she looked at you just now. Sort her out for me, will you, darling?'

Lydia widened her eyes, knowing that he meant 'get rid of her', and knowing too that she could do no such thing. She liked Gran's idea better.

'Hmm,' she said thoughtfully. 'But she's like the rabbit in the Mrs Beeton recipe, isn't she? I'll have to catch her first.'

Leo had gone to the farm; it was raining again and, although not in the least cold, there was a clammy chill in the air which the *dink-plink* of dripping water did nothing to relieve. Except for the garrets and her mother-in-law's room, Lydia had toured the entire house and now knew that only three of the rooms – all in the west wing – were actually dripping with water; the others were just damp, as most houses were after six years of fuel shortages. If Leo had only thought of it, he could have done a good deal this summer to make the place more comfortable: had the chimneys swept, sawn up the dead wood that was lying all over the garden, pruned a few trees . . .

During all of her explorations she never once laid eyes on Floral, but eventually found her scuttling along one of the stony passages at the rear of the house, about to disappear up the back stairs.

'Oh, Floral! I wonder . . .?'

The little woman jumped, whirled on her heel, leaned against the wall and stared bleakly into Lydia's eyes. She smiled suddenly, and as suddenly ducked her head as if to avoid the cruel glare of a search-light. 'I'll be out of your way in two ticks,' she said. 'I was just –'

Embarrassed, Lydia smiled and held out a conciliatory hand. 'But I don't want you out of my way,' she said firmly. 'I want your company. And your advice. The kettle's boiled. Join me for tea?'

Floral squirmed uncomfortably. 'Oh, I dunno . . .'

'But you've lived here all through the war, and I've been here just twenty-four hours. I don't know anything, Floral. I can't find anything. I can't even make the stove work properly. Won't you help?'

'Oh . . .' Floral's head was still down, her small, boot-button eyes peering suspiciously from under a frizzled fringe of rusty grey hair. But again she smiled and brought her clenched fists together with a horrid click of bone on bone. 'Oh, well,' she said. 'All right, then. I s'pose that won't hurt.'

The stove, a fairly modern electric one, worked (as in fact Lydia already knew) by a method very similar to that used for the wireless in the parlour. Instead of kicking it, you gave the mains switch a hard thump with a wooden spoon and, if that didn't work, you thumped it harder. Lydia knew very little about electricity, but guessed she was taking her life in her hands with every thump.

'Is there no one in the village who'd know how to mend it?' she asked, and frowned with bewilderment as Floral turned away, muttering something about the roof.

'The roof?'

'Ain't no use,' she said. 'It's the water, Miss. Gets in the wires or summat.'

'So . . . Is there a man in the village who could fix the roof?'

Floral shook her head doubtfully.

'But we must get the roof repaired before winter. We must find someone, Floral. Haven't you any ideas?'

Floral shook her head, not so much from ignorance, Lydia guessed, as fear of saying something out of place. It seemed better to change the subject. 'You've done some sterling work in the vegetable garden,' she smiled. 'Do you enjoy it?'

Floral's expression relaxed slightly. 'I'd rather do it than go hungry, Miss.'

'And the house is remarkably clean, so I imagine you've had something to do with that? Mrs Chantry couldn't possibly have done it all on her own, I suppose?'

'Leo done it.' Floral sighed and folded her hands, which she gazed at intently, like a child reciting a lesson. 'We wuz all right,' she said softly, 'until he came back. I won't say we wuz friends azzackly, Mrs Chantry 'n me, but we done all right. Share n' share alike, like. When all the others went 'ome –'

'The others?'

'Evacuees, Miss. But I didn't 'ave a 'ome to go 'ome to, and Mr Chantry didn't want I to leave . . .'

'Leo?'

'His dad. He knew he was on his way out, see Miss, and I s'pose he knew Mrs Chantry wouldn't . . . No, I won't say wouldn't. *Couldn't.* She didn't have the stomach for it, Miss; she wasn't used to it, if you knows what I means. So I stopped here and helped him. And when he was gone, I stopped and helped her. But Leo don't like it, Miss. He wants I to go.' She smiled her bright, puckish smile for a moment before again gazing solemnly at her hands. 'I speck you wants it, an' all. Only natural, innit? Your house. Not mine.'

She drew up her shoulders and smiled again, a bright, childlike grin which Lydia was beginning to think must be some kind of nervous tic, for it seemed she had very little to smile about. Leo *did* want her to go, after all. But why did he? According to Floral, she'd nursed his father through his last illness. Surely she deserved better treatment than this?

'But what do *you* want?' she asked kindly. 'You say there's nowhere else? Were you bombed out?'

Floral nodded. 'It wasn't much of a place, mind. Mrs Chantry d'sometimes say this place ain't no better'n a slum, but she don't know what she'm talking about, Miss. She don't know she'm born.' She closed her eyes. 'It's lovely here, Miss. I thought when I first come I'd died and gone to 'eaven.'

'And you want to stay?'

Floral looked at her hands and said nothing. She didn't need to.

'Well,' Lydia said. 'I want you to stay. But only if you'll help me get this place straightened out. I can't do it on my own, and I can't live in it the way it is. What do you say? If I speak to Leo . . .?'

Floral opened her eyes as wide as they would go. '*You* wants I to

68

stay?' she repeated incredulously. 'Well, I'll be . . .' She laughed and jumped up from her chair to fetch the forgotten tea. 'Right,' she said as she poured. 'Where do we start, my love?'

Leo had expected to be doing most of the cooking while his mother was away (he did it the same as she did: throw everything into the pot and pray), but Lydia had claimed to be able to do it better than that, and on his walk home, he found that he was praying anyway. He hadn't expected her to be able to cook. He hadn't expected her to be so wonderful between the sheets. He hadn't expected anything except – if he ever dared to mention it – to be thirty thousand pounds better off. And to pay for it with a lifetime of regrets.

No regrets so far . . . Just fears and premonitions. He'd have to mention it soon. Winter was on its way, and if the house had to stand another six months of exposure to the weather, it would become uninhabitable and they'd *have* to move to the farm, which meant he'd have to evict the Ducketts. When he thought of that, Leo thought he'd rather die. Yet when he thought of telling Lydia he was broke . . . He'd rather die.

The rain had stopped, the sun had come out and the kitchen door was open. He stepped inside, expecting to find Lydia standing at the stove as he usually found his mother, in a panic of pots, plates, peelings and spillage; but the place was deserted. Not only deserted, but unnaturally neat and clean. She'd evidently been up to something, but cooking dinner wasn't it.

Puzzled, he wandered through to the old hall and, to his horror, saw her picking through the pile of rotting curtains he'd torn down and hidden in a chest before her first visit to Molliston.

'Damn,' he whispered, and immediately she straightened up and sent him a look of such icy contempt it froze him to the spot. He was on the point of explaining about the curtains, apologising, making excuses, but before he could speak a sharp spike of rage stopped the words in his throat and he found himself saying something else entirely, his voice very quiet, but throbbing with anger. 'I realise you wouldn't have married me had circumstances not dictated, but I quite fail to see why you should look at me as if I were dirt under your foot!'

Lydia's mouth dropped open and, after a long moment, closed again in a rueful little smile. 'Oh, dear,' she said and bowed her head. 'I'm afraid there's something I haven't told you, Leo.'

'What?' he snapped.

The rueful smile changed to an impish grin and she turned away, murmuring, 'I'm shortsighted.'

'*What*?'

She chuckled. 'I've got glasses somewhere, but I only wear them for driving. I heard you come in, but I couldn't see you. Still can't, actually.'

Leo had moved since he'd last said anything, but now, lifting her chin and peering into the shadows of the doorway, Lydia's expression changed once more to that contemptuous stare he'd come to hate so much.

'Like this?' she asked.

He let out a yelp of laughter. It was obvious now! She was as blind as a mole! Not despising him, just trying to see him! Still laughing, he moved along the hall until, at a range of about ten paces, he saw her eyes warming as they came into focus and she grinned again. 'Sorry,' she said.

He took her in his arms and planted a kiss on her mouth, remembering all the times she'd looked at him like that and hadn't seen him at all! 'Oh, hell,' he murmured. 'You're –'

'What?'

'You're a mystery,' he said. 'I hardly know you, and here we are – man and wife, with a baby on the way. I think we ought to talk a bit, don't you?'

'Yes . . . over dinner.'

'Dinner? There isn't any.'

'There will be. Have your bath first.'

He felt almost happy as he ran upstairs, reassessing her as he went, for almost all of his previous ideas about her had been based on 'that look'. And 'that voice', of course, but even her voice was beginning to seem quite attractive: the boyish huskiness and ladylike formality combining to create a strange sensuality which, when he thought of it, made him more hungry for bed than for dinner.

He was accustomed to taking cold baths: a quick plunge, a brisk rub-down with Lifebuoy and a loofah, another quick plunge and then out again. But he found the bathroom full of steam, the bath half-full of warm water and a topping-up bucket alongside which was still only a few degrees off boiling point. He could scarcely believe she'd done it. On the odd occasions when he'd indulged himself with hot water, the amount of work involved had made it barely worthwhile. It was, of course, a luxury he appreciated and, for long, pleasurable minutes, wallowed in. But in other ways there was nothing she could have done to make him feel more thoroughly uncomfortable. She shouldn't have done it. Carrying all those heavy pails through the house and up the stairs . . . She could have hurt the baby, for one thing, and, for another . . . Well, he couldn't tell her about the money tonight, that was certain!

He was going through the kitchen in search of his mysterious dinner (Spam salad?) when Lydia called him into the dining room, where she'd set a white cloth, silver candlesticks and a pair of silver chafing dishes he hadn't seen since before the war. (In fact, he'd been sure his mother had sold them.)

'Good God!'

'What?' She smiled and waved him into his chair. 'It's all ready. How was your bath?'

'Wonderful,' he murmured helplessly. 'Thank you.' He bent to kiss her. 'But you mustn't do it again, Lydia. It's too much like hard work. You'll hurt the baby.'

'Floral helped.'

'Floral?'

'Mmm.' She removed the lids from the chafing dishes to reveal a feast which looked remarkably like roast beef and Yorkshire pudding.

'Lydia,' he breathed. 'What is it?'

'Well, it's called meat loaf, but it's mostly carrots, onions and oatmeal. One of Gran's recipes. The secret is to fry everything until it's very brown and then bake it until it's browner.'

Leo stared at her, amazed. 'You really *can* cook!'

'Did you doubt it?'

He laughed softly, sorrowfully. 'What am I to do with you?' he asked. 'You're too good to be true.'

'No, I'm not,' she said. 'But I want . . .'

'What?'

'I want you to see my best side first, and good, plain cooking happens to be one of the things I can do quite well. I'm also a good housekeeper, but I can't do much about that until we get the roof mended, which we must, Leo, before the baby comes. But I need your permission –'

'No.' With only a mouthful swallowed, Leo lost his appetite and found his nerve. 'We can't get the roof fixed,' he said quietly. 'It'll cost a fortune, Lydia, and I don't have a fortune. As soon as it can be arranged, we'll be moving to Manor Farm.'

'Oh!' Rather callously, he thought, she helped herself to more roast potatoes. 'Is it big enough?'

'Big enough?'

'Big enough to house two families.'

'Ah . . .' He found himself turning pink, and there was an itch under his collar which, he'd discovered as a child, was the symptom of an uneasy conscience. 'The – er – Ducketts,' he said, 'will have to move out, I'm afraid. Molliston is a gentleman's house, Lydia. It requires a gentleman's income and I . . . no longer . . .' He sighed. 'I'm not penniless –' (he had ninety-two pounds in the bank) '– but I'm not rich enough to keep Molliston going. I'll have to sell up.'

Lydia said nothing. But for a woman who'd just discovered she'd married a pauper, she looked remarkably pleased with herself.

'How about a lady's?' she murmured at length.

'A lady's what?' he said, feigning innocence.

'I have a little money of my own. If I can find someone to do it, and if you'd allow it, I could afford to get the roof fixed.'

Leo clenched his teeth and pretended an absorbing interest in what was left of his meat loaf. How was he to manage this? He didn't dare refuse the offer in case she took him at his word, but neither could he accept it too readily in case she guessed that he'd been expecting nothing less.

'No, you don't understand,' he said. 'It'll cost a great deal, Lydia. It's not just a question of replacing the leads, you see. Half the timbers are rotten and the chimneys are positively dangerous: I daren't even get them swept for fear of –'

'How much would it all cost?'

'I don't really know. A few thousand, I should think.' He leaned across the table to take her hand. 'But that's not all, Lydia. With a house like this, you never reach the end – except of your money. Even if you could afford to re-roof the place, what then?'

Lydia grinned. 'Hot water,' she said. 'And new wiring.'

His heart thudding, Leo assumed a faint, wondering smile. 'You're joking, aren't you?'

'Were you joking when you asked me to marry you? A woman you hardly know? I owe you this, Leo. Let me do it, will you? It'll make me feel less . . . It'll make me feel better about everything.'

He stared at his plate, silently thanking God. And she was, after all, quite right. He *had* been rather decent to marry her when all was said and done, and yes, she did owe him . . .

But what the hell was he *thinking* of? He'd married her *precisely* for this!

He smiled, crinkling his eyes, charming the socks off her. 'Do you want to?'

'Yes, I do . . . On one condition.'

He sat back suddenly. This was it: the thing he had dreaded! And what would she want? The deeds transferred to her name? Separate beds? His head on a silver platter?

'Well?' he murmured coolly.

'I want Floral to stay.'

He stared at her, barely comprehending what she'd said because it was so completely different from anything he'd expected.

'Leo,' she said firmly, 'there are no such people as servants nowadays, and I need help. This is a big house and your mother, as you said yourself, isn't entirely practical. Floral wants to stay, and since she's offered to help . . .'

He laughed. 'But you can't pay her.' He meant that Floral wouldn't take any payment. He'd offered to pay her (if only for the right it would give him to sack her) and she'd refused outright to accept so much as a penny.

Lydia stood up and began to collect the plates together. 'I have fifty thousand pounds,' she said quietly.

'*Fifty*?' Leo gasped. 'But that's more . . .' He swallowed. 'That's – er – more than the entire house is worth! Why didn't you tell me?'

'I didn't realise you needed it.' She smiled. 'And even if I had, I'd have been afraid you were marrying me for my money. It's better this way, isn't it?'

'Yes,' he said feebly. (Marry her for her money? What a ridiculous idea!) 'Yes, I suppose it is . . .'

'And can Floral stay?'

'Yes,' he said again. 'Yes, yes, of course . . . If that's what you want.'

Fifty thousand! Where the hell had another twenty come from? Like Lydia herself, it was too good to be true!

But already he felt the crushing weight of guilt on his shoulders, the sour rage of dependency clutching his heart. He'd be skating on thin ice from now on, never knowing when she might turn her wealth against him, use it to threaten him, blackmail him, taunt and torture him . . .

And even if she didn't, even if she was an angel incarnate, he'd never, from this moment on, be able to call his soul his own. He'd sold it to the devil, for fifty thousand pounds.

Chapter Seven

In spite of Leo's embarrassed hesitations, Lydia experienced a few
moments of pleasure thinking that her money might save Molliston
for him. A new roof couldn't possibly repay him for giving her his
name – and it certainly wouldn't repay him for the name he'd be
giving another man's child – but perhaps it meant he wouldn't come
out of it thinking she'd robbed him of *everything*. His pride, yes; his
honour, yes; his child, yes; but not his home.

An hour later, however, she began to have doubts. Leo had been
very quiet since they'd finished dinner and, having said they must
talk, now seemed disinclined to say anything at all. She supposed
he'd been shocked to discover he'd 'married money'. Most men liked
to think they could support their wives and, in effect, she'd just made
it clear to him that he couldn't – not, at least, if they stayed at
Molliston . . . Oh, Lord, she'd done it all wrong!

'If you'd rather move to the farm,' she offered tentatively, 'you
have only to say so, Leo. I had no idea that you were considering it,
you see. It didn't occur to me that you might prefer it.'

He smiled stiffly. 'No, I wouldn't prefer it. I'd hate to have to turn
the Ducketts out. They've had enough misfortune. I doubt very much
that I'd be able to forgive myself if I made them homeless, too.'

They were sitting in the small parlour, which, as the sun began to
lower in the sky, was filled with a pale, rosy light. It was the most
comfortable room in the house, with a decent carpet and soft
armchairs: very much a place to relax in, although Leo looked far from
relaxed. He looked as if he was sitting on an ants' nest, the occupants
of which were crawling all over him. He'd washed his hair (which was
much fairer than she'd realised) and kept raking it out of his eyes,
scratching his neck, folding and unfolding his arms, tapping his foot.
Lydia walked to the window, sighing. 'But do you want . . .? That is,
do you think I've been . . .? Oh, dear, I don't know what to say.'

'About what?'

'Molliston. It's your home, not mine. I have no right –'

'It's *our* home, Lydia, not just mine. With your money or without it, that would still be true.'

She almost said, 'If it's our home, it's our money, too,' but managed to swallow the words before she could say them. Molliston wasn't her home. When she produced a full-term baby at seven months, she'd have no home at all – he'd show her the door, perhaps with the business end of a horsewhip – and it would be plain stupid of her to fetch up in the gutter with no money to call her own. But she wanted him to have as much benefit from it as she could give him in the few months that were left.

'Tell me what you want, Leo,' she said softly. 'As you've already said, we hardly know one another. There's no point my tip-toeing through your feelings until I know what your feelings are.'

He chuckled softly. 'The first thing you learned about me, Lydia, is that my feelings are in a state of chaos. I don't know myself any more, so how can you?'

'I can try, can't I?'

'Yes. But how on earth did you –? How can you be so –? Fifty thousand pounds, and no mention of it? Why didn't your father drop me a hint? Wouldn't that have been logical, sensible? He didn't even ask if I had the means to support you!'

Lydia shrugged. 'What would have been the point? I needed a husband, a name for my child. And since your name was probably the one he'd have chosen even if I *hadn't* been in a fix, why should he make difficulties about it? I needed a husband, Leo. I didn't need money.'

'But you don't *see*?' he cried. 'I could be a gambler, a thief, a drunkard! I could take you for every penny –'

Lydia laughed. 'If there were any danger of that, my grandmother would have known it the minute she laid eyes on you. She's an extraordinary judge of character. And *she* introduced us, if you recall.'

She frowned suddenly, recalling that fact as if for the first time. Gran *had* introduced them . . . Her frown deepened, recalling also that she had never in her life before introduced Lydia to an eligible man! Old men, yes. Respectably married men, yes. But not eligible. So was that fine judgement of character? Or just a finely tuned eye for a fine old name? And, if the latter . . .

'Are you a gambler?' she asked wryly.

Leo scratched his neck. 'No, nor a drunkard, and I hope not a thief, but if I allow you to spend your money on Molliston –'

'My home,' Lydia interrupted, smiling.

Leo nodded glumly. 'But Manor Farm would be cheaper.'

'Except for the Ducketts. And for your conscience, of course.'

'*Damn*!' He leapt to his feet, bared his teeth in a furious grimace and then fell back into his chair, laughing softly. 'Oh, God,' he said. 'My conscience is unlikely to survive this, whichever way I jump.' He turned pleading eyes to her face. 'Do you really want to stay here? Fix the roof and – and everything else you mentioned?'

Lydia turned again to gaze out of the window. 'All I want,' she said, 'is to be warm and dry when winter comes. If that's what you want too, I'll be glad, of course, but it's not essential. I have a regrettable tendency to put myself first, I'm afraid.'

Leo didn't reply and when she turned to look at him, he was lying back with his eyes closed and an almost blissful smile on his face.

He opened his eyes very suddenly and grinned up at her. 'Keep doing that,' he said.

'What?'

'Putting yourself first. It means you can be as generous as you like without putting me to any of the bother of being grateful. You can mend my roof, repair my wiring, fix my hot water pipes – and all I'll need to do in return is call you a selfish little madam. Is that right?'

Lydia smiled, but only because *he* thought he was joking. Selfish? She was robbing him blind. And the worst thing about it was that she had no regrets. Leo was a dear man, but not as dear to her as her own family. However bad 'losing him' might turn out to be, she could bear it. She *couldn't* have borne to lose them!

With the harvest over and the routines of the farm settling more easily around him, Leo often went home: for meals, mostly, but also – more reluctantly – to spend some time with his wife. Yet even ten days after the wedding he knew little more about her than he'd known ten days before it. He kept thinking – and sometimes saying – 'We must talk', but he was too confused to talk, and Lydia seemed content to live with a stranger, sleep with a stranger, make love with the stranger she'd married and knew next to nothing about.

Their love-making was the only escape Leo could find from the dull ache of his conscience, but even making love to her, when he thought of it objectively, was far from perfect. He *didn't* love her. He just *wanted* to love her – it was the only hope he had of surviving this marriage, after all – but a man can't love a woman just because he wants to. Love, whatever else it was, was a law unto itself, an independent force that caught one unawares, arriving out of nowhere, like poppies in a cornfield. You simply woke up one morning and found a great crimson flower growing through your heart . . . And all

Leo had growing through his were nettles.

But he couldn't complain. She didn't seem to want more than he could give her; in fact, seemed happy enough to be left to her own devices. Every time he went home she seemed to have done something else to make the place more comfortable, although he was never quite sure what these things were. A lightness and brightness he remembered from his childhood, a faint tang in the air of steam and soap-suds, a fastidious neatness about everything which had never existed while his mother was in charge. He liked it. He liked it very much. But it didn't help. He felt vaguely angry with her, in fact, for being so competent, so generous and uncomplaining. This was, after all, her honeymoon . . .

He'd take her out. Take her – where? To dinner, to the theatre – to a dance? Leo liked dancing. It brought out the courtier in him, the romantic side of his soul. (He visualised a girl with blonde curly hair and eyes that adored him as she floated in his arms . . .) Maybe the theatre, then.

He was on his way home to Molliston as these thoughts crossed his mind, and, as he emerged from between the shelter of the hedgerow, he looked up and saw three men on the roof. His heart leapt – she'd found someone to do it! – and then tightened like a clenched fist as he realised that the third man was Lydia. She was walking about like a practised steeple-jack, on a roof that might as well be made of tissue-paper for all the strength there was in it!

It was only then, seeing her there, that the child she was carrying became real to him. A baby, a person, a part of his own flesh. He broke into a run and didn't pause for breath until he found the open garret window they'd used as an exit to the roof – and in the same moment found Lydia calmly climbing in again. She had her hand flat across her belly as if to protect the tender life she held from being bumped against the window frame. Bumped! When she could have hurled him to his death!

Leo swallowed. He said, almost calmly, 'You shouldn't have done that. Go downstairs.'

Lydia's eyes widened. She laughed. 'I was perfectly all right.'

'Go downstairs,' he said again.

'But the men –?'

'I'll see to them. Go!' He found it quite difficult to convey all-out fury in a discreet whisper, but realised he'd managed it when Lydia's complexion suddenly paled and she hurried away, biting her lip.

One of the men on the roof called, 'We've found summat, Mrs Chantry!' and Leo pinned a smile to his face and called back, 'Just coming! What have you found?'

77

The technicalities of post-war roofing repairs (no time, no tools, no materials) took the best part of another hour before the men went away again, promising to return 'First thing Monday, zir' (which probably meant last thing Thursday). During most of that time they'd sat at the table in the great hall, sketching diagrams on the back of envelopes and totting up costings in a little red notebook. 'All right, zir?' they'd asked. And, 'All right, darling?' Leo had enquired of his graciously smiling wife. Then, when they were alone again, they'd both sighed and met each other's eyes across the dark oak of the refectory table. 'I'm sorry,' Lydia said, but there was a note of finality in her voice which seemed to add, 'And now shut up about it.'

'It's my baby, too,' he said icily. 'I almost went the way of Ray Duckett when I saw you up there.'

She turned scarlet and looked at her hands. 'But I couldn't have fallen, Leo. The parapet's high enough to –'

'You could have fallen *through*. The timbers are rotten. I've told you that before, haven't I?'

The colour in her cheeks faded again to a frightened pallor. 'I forgot. I just wanted to get it done.'

'Without consulting me? You knew they were coming and didn't tell me? Is that reasonable?'

'You're so busy. I thought –'

'When I'm too busy to be informed of what's going on in my own home, I'll let you know. In the meantime . . .'

'I really am sorry, Leo,' she said. 'It won't happen again, I promise.'

He knew she meant it. She looked as if she meant it and, after her fashion, even sounded as if she meant it, but her deep, lordly voice spoiled the effect of it, somehow. She sounded as if she was dismissing the gardener: 'I'm sorry, Briggs, I'm afraid we must let you go . . .' Proud and aloof. On her dignity. It made Leo feel furious all over again. He wanted to take her down a peg or two, teach her who was master in no uncertain terms. He'd learned in the Army that he could exert his authority most effectively when he kept his temper, kept his voice down and his eyes sternly levelled, but perhaps Lydia didn't understand such conventions. Perhaps she needed a good yelling at to set her straight?

Before he could decide on this course of action, she stood up, said, 'I'll see about lunch,' and exited gracefully to the kitchen: head up, shoulders back, hips swaying jauntily as if nothing at all had happened. And as the door swung closed behind her, Leo saw red.

'*Lydia!*'

He raced after her, jerked the door open again, and found the kitchen deserted. His conscience – ever present, like a dark cloud at the back of his mind – told him he was going too far, being unfair, asking too much. It also warned him that he was making a bloody fool of himself and might well live to regret it. But his temper had the upper hand. He marched outside and stopped as if he'd hit a brick wall. Lydia was leaning against the corner of the woodshed with her face in her hands, crying. As before when he'd witnessed her tears, she made no sound at all, but her shoulders were stooped and shaking with suppressed sobs. She looked the very image of heartbreak.

Yet the first thought to cross Leo's mind was one of weary cynicism: *Woman's secret weapon?* before his conscience reminded him that she'd come out here to hide her tears, not turn them against him. He also recalled that the 'Army method' had, in its time, reduced grown men to a powder, and that he should have known – he *should* have known – that it would do the same to Lydia. He'd bullied her shamefully, yet he wasn't by nature a bully. So what the hell was wrong with him? Why had he done it? Did he hate her so much?

No, his conscience whispered. *You hate yourself.*

Even three hours later, as she watched Leo hurrying back to Manor Farm to get the milking done, Lydia still felt as if she'd been run over by a tank. He'd apologised fifty times over, poor man, as if it was *his* fault she'd made such a tactless, stupid hash of things, frightened the life out of him, made him so angry. And it *wasn't* his fault; it was hers, all hers! She'd been so intent on getting things done before her time ran out, it hadn't even occurred to her to ask him about it. Fool! Stupid fool!

The trouble was, of course, that *she* knew they had only a few months together and *he* thought they were building a marriage, laying the foundations of 'mutual respect and cooperation' on which to raise a family, the next noble generation of Chantrys. Ha!

Oh, God, he was going to kill her when he found out the truth! She'd thought of this before, of course, but it had always been a rather remote idea, to be faced when the time came. It wasn't remote now. He'd been, he'd said, only a *little* annoyed with her today – yet, without losing his temper, without even raising his voice, he'd very nearly skinned her alive. It was true that at least one of the knives he'd used to skin her had been her own guilt (*It's my baby too, you know,*) but there'd been far more to it than that, and at least half of it, she guessed, had nothing at all to do with her. He was angry about everything: the war and his years of imprisonment, the house, the farm, his parents, Floral . . . Lydia was just the last straw on the camel's back, but she'd seen the entire weight of his burden in those smouldering blue eyes of his: a white-hot volcano of rage, capped by the thinnest crust of self-control. *Terrifying* . . .

''Ave he gone?' Floral appeared at the corner of the terrace, her head on one side, like a sparrow checking the garden for cats.

'Yes . . .' Lydia sighed and looked at her feet. 'Are you afraid of him, Floral?'

'Nah!' The little woman laughed. 'He'm not the type.'

'What type?'

Floral sat down on the edge of the terrace, kicking her feet like a joyful child. 'He've got more spark in 'im than his dad 'ad, I'll grant you, but they'm azzackly the same underneath. Wouldn't hurt a fly. He could've chucked I out a dozen times – asked I to go, told I to go, put his boot under me ask-ya-father and kicked I five miles down the road – but he never.' She plucked a stem of grass from between the flagstones and chewed the end of it. 'I don't say I trusts 'im wiv me life, mind,' she said thoughtfully. 'There's a fred runnin' through 'im I haven't quite found the end of . . . But, there, I could say the same about his ma, and she haven't chucked I out either, so there you are. What about the roof? Can they mend it?'

'They can patch it and rebuild the chimneys, but there's no hope of a new roof just yet. No lead, no slates, no wood . . .'

No time. The patches wouldn't last very long; a few years at most before the rain came in again. And then what would Leo do? He might, by then, be taking a decent living from Manor Farm, but it wouldn't be enough to save Molliston. Yet if she couldn't give him a new roof, what else could she do for him? No matter how much money she had, she was scarcely any richer than Floral, for there was nothing in the shops to buy. She couldn't even lay in stocks of coal for the winter . . .

But she could start gathering some wood together. That wouldn't kill her.

'Have we got a saw, anywhere, Floral?'

'A who?'

'A saw. Or an axe. Or both.'

'Oh, I dunno about that,' Floral said. 'You barely bin married a fortnight, my love. Give 'im another chance, eh?'

Peggy Chantry returned to Molliston three days before she was expected. Leo came home for dinner one night, expecting one of Lydia's culinary miracles, and instead found his mother, in a welter of pots, peelings and steam, doing the honours instead.

'Where's Lydia?'

'Mother, darling,' Mrs Chantry prompted cynically. 'How wonderful to see you.'

'Ah, yes . . .' Leo sketched her kiss. 'Where's Lydia?'

'I've told her to lie down. She's worn to the bone. I should never have gone away, I knew I shouldn't. But you would insist. Some kind of honeymoon that poor girl's had! I'm ashamed of you, Leo. But you're all the same.' She tipped a boiling vat of cabbage in the rough direction of a colander, missed, and scooped the soapy overspill back into the pan. Leo winced.

'Gerald been getting you down?' he enquired dryly.

'I could *quite* easily kill him. Arrogant, odious little . . . I couldn't bear to stay a moment longer. My smile *ached* so. But Prue seems happy enough, so who am I to judge? I've had my hair done.' She patted it smugly. 'What do you think, darling? Ten years younger? And look at this kitchen.'

Leo looked. In the space of a few hours she'd turned it into a bomb site.

'She's cleaned out all the cupboards, polished the floor, washed the *ceiling*! The entire house is immaculate. And have you seen the woodshed?'

'The what?'

'No, I thought you hadn't. You haven't seen the shadows under her eyes either, I suppose. Your father was the same. If it wasn't a horse or a cricket match, he went completely blind.'

Leo smiled knowingly. 'That had its advantages, I'm sure.'

She laughed. 'You may be right. But at least he noticed me on our honeymoon. Didn't have me chopping wood the entire time, anyway. She's your wife, darling, not a skivvy. In love or out of it, you should never forget that. We must ask the Westleys over, by the way – before she dies of overwork.'

'Hmm . . .' Trying to look unhurried about it, Leo hurried out to the woodshed, which – as he'd begun to suspect – was stacked to the rafters with firewood. He recognised some of it from his own good intentions: the old pergola, a collapsed trellis, the dead wood from the orchard and several quite sizeable tree trunks, sawn neatly into logs. He told himself precisely what he knew Lydia would tell him: that Floral had helped – done most of it in fact – as if she was six foot tall and built like a tractor.

Warm and dry . . . Lydia had said it was all she cared about, and he should have taken note, should have done something about it. He pulled a face of despairing amusement. No wonder she'd fallen asleep at the theatre . . . He'd turned himself inside out to get the

81

tickets, arrange an evening off from milking, find enough petrol to get them to Bristol, and she'd been away with the angels halfway through Act One! He'd spent the rest of the evening rearranging her head to stop her snoring . . .

He re-entered the house through the main door and ran upstairs, half-expecting to find Lydia snoring again. In fact, she was standing by the window with her arms wrapped around her ribs which – he was beginning to learn – meant that she was agitated about something: probably her mother-in-law.

'I thought you'd been told to lie down,' he said, in what he thought was a fair mimicry of his mother's voice, although Lydia didn't notice the difference.

'I'm not a sheepdog,' she said without turning around.

Leo set one knee on the windowseat beside her and affected to look at the view. 'Tell me exactly what you're thinking,' he murmured. 'I'll probably agree with everything you say, and even if I don't, I'll do my best to understand.'

She turned her head suddenly, her eyes wide with surprise, and Leo took the opportunity to check the shadows under her eyes, which, he realised now, had always been there. He'd noticed them – without really making a note of the fact – after their fateful ride to the Red Barn. He remembered thinking how vulnerable she'd looked, and those shadows had been a part of it. Now, with her pregnant state beginning to be obvious, she looked even more vulnerable, for the clear line of her jaw and the delicate shaft of her neck were somehow emphasised by the growing swell of her breasts and belly. It was rather touching, in fact. She seemed so aloof, so self-contained, he often forgot that she was scarcely more than a girl.

'Peggy's ideas and mine are so different,' she said. 'I don't see how . . . I don't see how a compromise . . .' She turned away again, uttering a gasp of bitter laughter. 'It doesn't matter.'

'Yes, it does. And I think I can help. She's a bit excited just now. Gerald's stretched her patience beyond its limits and she's letting off steam, that's all. I'm sure if she guessed how cross you were about it, she'd be appalled.'

'I'm not cross. I'm –' She bit her lip.

'You're frightened,' Leo said, only just realising it. 'You've built a warm, dry nest for the baby, and Mother breezes in and starts pulling it apart. Is that right?'

She'd been standing there with her back as straight as a ramrod. Now she slumped and walked wearily to the bed, sighing.

'Not quite,' she said huskily. 'The truth is, I suppose, that I can't bear to live in a muddle.' She smiled wanly. 'I can't bear to be treated like a child, either. I've lived with myself for almost twenty-three years, Leo. I know my own strengths, know what I'm capable of. Collecting the wood with Floral was easy. It was fun.' She flicked him a wary glance under her eyelashes. 'She did most of it, of course.'

Leo bit back a smile. 'Fun?' he prompted doubtfully.

'Yes, like camping out with the Girl Guides. I haven't laughed so much in years. Floral can climb trees like a monkey, you know. How *old* is she?'

'I haven't a clue.' He was surprised by a sudden pang of jealousy as he imagined the pair of them running wild about the garden, dragging home tree limbs and lengths of pergola, joking and laughing like children. He'd never known Lydia to laugh like that. A chuckle now and then, a smile, one of her husky, bedtime giggles. But she'd never really laughed. Something to do with him? Or just something to do with Floral?

'She's extraordinarily capable,' Lydia added softly. 'She even knew how to sharpen the axe. I wish she'd let me pay her, but she says she's never been anyone's servant and if I pay her she'll be mine. Yet she does everything I ask. She's never once said no. Isn't that odd?'

'What on earth does she live on, though?'

'Her savings. Did you know she used to be a milliner? Nothing exclusive – I doubt it was much more than a sweat-shop – but she saved virtually every penny she earned to buy herself a cottage for her old age – and then she was bombed out and came here. She can't buy the cottage now, of course. She never did save enough. And now . . .' She turned sad, pleading eyes to his face. 'Let her stay, Leo?'

He laughed. 'Haven't I said she can stay?'

'Yes, but . . . But if . . . if anything happens to me . . .'

'Don't be silly!' He crossed the bed and sat beside her. 'What can happen to you? You're not worried about young Lionel, are you?' He patted her belly. 'I know he kicks a bit, but he won't kill you. As you said, you're strong and healthy.'

'Lionel? That was your father's name, wasn't it?'

He smiled. 'And his father's, and his grandfather's – and as far back as we can trace. Family tradition for first sons.'

'So why are you Leo?'

'I had a brother who died.' He patted her stomach again. 'Not in childbirth, however, so I'd advise you to forget that little anxiety and get back to the big one. My mother.'

'Hmm,' Lydia said.

'My own policy is to listen to everything she says and then ignore it. *Most* of it, that is. She often – usually by accident – says something very sensible, which we'd be foolish to ignore. You really do need more rest than you're getting.'

'No, I –'

'Hear me out? If you'll promise to go to bed for an hour every afternoon from now on, *I'll* promise –' He pulled his mouth down at one side. 'I'll promise to *try* to convince her that you are not a sheepdog. Will that serve?'

Lydia smiled and thought about it, one finely drawn eyebrow dipped to express her (quite understandable) doubts. Then, to his surprise, she caught his hand and kissed it.

'Thank you,' she whispered.

'Now, now. I only said I'd try . . .'

'But you're too good to me, Leo, and I don't –'

'Nonsense. I've been far from good enough.' Abruptly, he kissed her temple and then, thoroughly embarrassed, hurried away to have his bath. Too good to her? He wished it was true. The fact was, however, that he'd done nothing for her. He'd given her a night at the theatre she could well have done without, a few compliments about her cooking, and a good telling-off that had made her cry.

His mother was right. He was just like his father. But his father had had good reason for being 'blind' to his wife (it was either that or take a whip to her) and Leo had no such excuse. Lydia was a damn good woman: responsible, patient, capable and – under the frosty Victorian veneer – as soft-hearted and generous as any man could wish. But even now . . .

Gritting his teeth against the cold-water plunge of his bath, Leo dived in and experienced a sudden revelation. It didn't matter that he didn't love her! Even if he had loved her – as his father had once loved his mother – the feeling would wear off with time, and then what would he do to keep things going? Pretend?

Pretend!

Chapter Eight

The chops were charred, the cabbage a pulp and the gravy a grey gelatinous slime that Lydia couldn't bear to look at, let alone eat. And all of it had come to the table as cold as November.

'Where are the chafing dishes, Mother?'

'I've put them away, darling. Silver needs so much cleaning. One needs an army of servants to do it, and since *our* army is still *in* the Army, so to speak . . .'

'Two chafing dishes do *not* need an army to clean them, Mother. And they keep the food hot, which is far more important – especially when *you're* doing the cooking.'

Lydia blushed and looked at her wedding ring, twirling it frantically as she awaited Peggy's outraged reply. But it didn't happen. She just laughed. 'Beggars can't be choosers.'

'But we aren't beggars,' Leo said smoothly. 'Or, if *we* are, Lydia certainly isn't. She's accustomed to eating good, hot meals, Mother.'

'Oh, please,' Lydia murmured, 'there's no need . . .'

'On the contrary.' He sent her a beaming smile and a wink to take the sting out of his next words. 'I know precisely what we need. We need order and comfort, a hint, at least, of civilised living. I suggest that you see to the cooking in future, Lydia, and you, Mother, can clean the silver. Does that seem fair?'

'Yes,' said Lydia hurriedly.

'No,' Peggy said, still laughing. 'You wouldn't know "fair" if it hit you on the nose, Leo. Lydia's worked quite hard enough. For the rest of her time, she's going to sit with her feet up and –'

'Starve,' Leo said. 'Look at her plate, Mother. Has she eaten anything? And if she hasn't, can you blame her?'

Lydia thought she would die of embarrassment. She'd never witnessed anything like it before and hoped never to do so again. Her father had never spoken to *his* mother like this – Gran would certainly have killed him if he had! That one deferred to older women was bred in Lydia's bones, and if Peggy wanted no chafing dishes, if she wanted to serve pig-swill for dinner, if she wanted to drive her daughter-in-law crazy with frustration and boredom, that was her privilege. How could Leo speak to her like this? He was right, of course, but that wasn't the point!

'The point is,' Leo said, as if he'd read her mind, 'that Lydia knows what's best for her, Mother, and you only think you do. Just because you could lie around eating grapes when you were expecting –'

'Ooh! That's not fair!'

'Or, if not eating grapes, doing precisely what you liked –'

'That's fair,' Peggy chuckled. 'But Lydia *also* needs to do precisely what she likes, and –'

'And Lydia would like to do the cooking, wouldn't you, darling? She'd also like to run the house as she thinks fit. And Floral helps.' He grinned. 'In fact, Floral does most of it, so there's no need to worry, is there?'

'You're talking complete nonsense,' Peggy said. 'No woman – no woman in her right mind, at least – wants to work her fingers to the bone! You're thinking of your own comfort, Leo, not Lydia's. And I can assure you that Floral does no more to *help*, as you put it, than she needs to do to help herself.'

'Oh, no,' Lydia murmured. 'She's been wonderful, Peggy. I couldn't have done anything without her. And Leo's quite right: I really don't want to put my feet up. I'd be bored rigid.'

'Oh, well . . .' Peggy seemed to lose her sense of humour suddenly. She pursed her mouth and said dismissively, 'As you like.'

'Oh, but I do appreciate –' Lydia began, and then stopped as Leo's hand clamped her wrist like a vice.

'Good,' he said silkily, 'that's decided then. What's for pudding, Mother?'

As autumn turned to winter, Leo discovered that in pretending to be in love with Lydia, he was becoming quite fond of her. At least, he was taking a good deal more notice of her, and had not, so far, found anything much to dislike. Her relentless seriousness continued to irritate him, not for its own sake, but because she seemed to use it to hide her true feelings, which he sometimes glimpsed, like moths, flitting across the darkness of her eyes. Tiredness, irritation, even laughter, came and went with a single bat of her lashes, rarely reaching her mouth or changing her voice, so that had he not known otherwise, he'd have thought she had no feelings at all.

But he caught her unawares one Sunday morning in November. Her people were coming to lunch and, as on previous occasions when her grandmother was expected, she was as tense as a stretched wire, wanting everything to be perfect. Had Mrs Westley been anyone else, Leo would probably have found this amusing, even silly, but the old girl had the same effect on everyone, himself included. She was like royalty (even looked like Queen Mary, with her ramrod spine and high Edwardian collars). When she came on the scene, everyone stood to attention and tried to look virtuous.

Lydia was standing with her back to him, arranging evergreens in a vase on the refectory table, seemingly lost in the task. He opened his mouth to speak just as his mother called through from the inner hall, 'No need to sweep the parlour, Lydia! I've just done it!'

Lydia's head went up. She gripped the edge of the table until her knuckles whitened. Then she said, 'Oh, thank you, Peggy,' very smoothly and, 'God, I'll die!' in whisper so desperate it made Leo's spine tingle with fright.

'What's the matter?' He kept his voice low and steady, almost as if she really was dying. 'Are you ill?'

'Oh . . . Oh, hello, Leo. You're home early.'

'Yes. Are you ill?'

'Er – no. No, I'm not ill. Thank you.'

'But something is the matter.'

Lydia looked at her hands and said nothing.

'It wouldn't be my mother, by any chance?'

She sighed. 'I swept the parlour before breakfast. And dusted and polished.' She sighed again. 'Now everything will be covered with dust again . . . and I don't have time . . .' She swallowed, straightened her spine and produced a weary smile. 'But it doesn't matter. She means to be helpful, I know.'

Leo wasn't so sure about that. He knew his mother *did* have good intentions, chief among them a desire that everyone should be happy, but she wanted everyone to be happy as *she* defined it rather than as it best suited *them*. She didn't like Lydia's way of being happy; she didn't understand it and, because of that, Leo would not put it past her to demonstrate how pointless she thought it all. *There, all that time you've wasted making the place clean, and now it's filthy again. Give it up, read a book, enjoy yourself!*

'Where's Floral?' he asked casually.

'Standing guard in the kitchen,' Lydia said. 'I really couldn't bear to be helped . . . to cook lunch.'

With one hand pressed to the back of her waist and the other sheltering the mound of her belly, she eased herself gently into the

87

carver chair. 'Give me a minute and I'll make some coffee.'

'I don't want coffee.' He smiled more to comfort than to charm her. 'I'm hoping your grandmother will bring a small gift of the real thing from America. Think she might?'

'How could she not? She knows the way to your heart.' It wasn't much of a joke – a feeble tease, accompanied by an equally feeble smile – but her eyes filled with tears as she spoke, and she blinked and looked away, regaining her composure so quickly, Leo could almost have thought he'd imagined it. She didn't use tears as some women did. Prue could cry at the drop of a hat – when she was tired, when she was bored, when she was thwarted – but they were a sign of real emotion with Lydia, which meant she was in trouble she could barely handle.

'Young Lionel bothering you?' he asked gently.

'Mm.' She stroked the bulge, her narrow hand splayed wide as if to catch the little blighter, should he fall. 'He's probably twins.'

'I was beginning to wonder, I must say. Aren't you a bit big for six months?' He frowned, recalling that since it wasn't yet December, she still had a week to go for six months. Poor kid, she'd be lumbering around like a hippo before her time was up.

'I suppose I'm carrying a lot of water . . .' She could scarcely breathe and the shadows under her eyes had darkened to violet. A few more months of this, with his mother thwarting her at every turn, and she'd be too weak to cope with the birth. She'd booked herself into a good clinic; she'd have the best possible care . . . But still, there was a long way to go yet. She needed a rest.

'I've just had a very expensive idea,' he said. 'So if it won't help, for the Lord's sake tell me.'

She chuckled dryly. 'What sort of expensive idea?'

'The worst kind. It involves sending my mother to London for a few weeks.' He screwed up his face in terror, only half of which was feigned. 'Christmas shopping,' he whispered – and flinched.

'Is there anything to buy?'

'If there isn't, she'll have a wonderful time hunting for it. And, if there is, we'll have a wonderful Christmas. She adores shopping – especially when it's *my* money she's spending.'

'Or mine?'

'No, not this time. But – will it help?'

Lydia smiled and closed her eyes. 'Oh, yes . . .'

Although Leo was already counting the cost of his offer – two weeks' hotel bills, train fares, cab fares – he deemed it money well spent just to see the lines of tension melting from Lydia's face. She'd learn in time that there was nothing to be gained from trying to understand his mother. She simply *was*, as the rain was, and there was no point at all in asking it why. You just had to be a duck and let it run off your back.

'And while she's gone,' he said, 'slow down a bit, will you, darling?' He cupped her ear with his hand (she loved having her ears touched) and felt her lean into the caress, as trustingly as a child. He crouched beside her. 'I love you, you see,' he said softly.

It was only half a truth, the other half a lie – and yet, just for that moment, he could barely see the join.

The bedrooms at Molliston weren't arranged as in other houses, with every room opening to the landing. Leo's and Lydia's room was connected to another three rooms; Peggy Chantry slept in a warren of four more. Some of the rooms could only be reached by walking through another; some opened into bleak little hallways or narrow passages that seemed to echo with the history of the house: clash of swords or clipping of horses' hooves, the creak of a spit turning over a hissing fire.

Partly in hope, but mainly for the sake of appearances, Lydia had made the smallest of their own three rooms into a nursery for the baby. Floral had helped with the application of whitewash and had scrubbed and polished the floorboards. The chest of drawers was packed with Lydia's official quota of nappies and baby clothes, and there was a shawl her grandmother had knitted long ago when Lydia was a baby. She'd acquired a cot – an ugly wooden crate with a Utility Mark stamped underneath – but no crib. If she was allowed to return here after the birth (which she doubted and, in a strange way, almost dreaded) she could line a drawer for the first few months of the baby's life; and if she couldn't return . . . Well, wherever she was, there would be a drawer.

She tried not to think about it, to think of none of it, because all of it was terrifying. If Leo threw her out, would Gran take her in? And if not . . .?

She'd cope somehow. She knew she'd cope, for the baby's sake, but even the baby couldn't save her from the grief she was feeling now. She had the most appalling feeling that she was falling in love with her husband, and an even worse one . . . that he was falling in love with her. She hadn't meant it to happen. Hadn't wanted it. She'd been happy to let him *make* love to her (while she could; those nights had gone), because, like the repairs to the house, she'd needed to give him something in return for everything he'd given her. But she hadn't meant either of them to *fall* in love. She'd kept herself detached from him, made no demands on him, filled her days with work not so much to be of use as to keep herself from going crazy with guilt. And fear. Fear of his rage at first. Now . . . fear of his grief.

Christmas had passed in a black daze of work and exhaustion as she'd tried to be seven months pregnant when in fact her time had almost run out. Now she was two weeks overdue and beginning to hope that if she could last another week she might get away with it. She'd been told that the size of her stomach might bear no relation to the size of the baby and, if it was a small one, if she could convince everyone it was *really* premature . . .

But the thought of living with the deception for the rest of her life filled her with such revulsion and self-hatred, she almost began to hope that the baby would be enormous, for she had no faith at all in her strength of mind should he be tiny. She wanted to stay here! Even if she wasn't exactly *in* love with Leo, she certainly cared enough for him – honoured him, trusted him – to want to be with him for the rest of her life. The dark moods and irritability he'd warned her of, although they certainly existed, hadn't amounted to much: he was too much of a gentleman to let them. And he had a bossy streak (especially with his mother) that made Lydia shrivel up inside, making her wonder what he might be like when he was really angry. But, for all that, he was a good man, kind and appreciative, generous and supportive. If she travelled the world, she'd be lucky to find another to equal him.

But she'd done all she could to repay him. Every inch of the house was clean (every inch she could reach, at least) and as comfortable as she could make it. Even at her worst, Peggy would take a year, at least, to undo it all, although even she had rallied to the new boiler behind the parlour fire. Hot water in the taps made everything so much easier, as did the new mains cable for the kitchen stove.

Yet the house was still as cold as a tomb, and as the weather grew worse – it was snowing now – life at Molliston was narrowing to the kitchen, the parlour, and as few shivering trips to the bathroom as Lydia's tormented bladder would permit.

She was returning from one of these excursions when, in spite of the cold, she felt a sudden need to check the baby's room and plodded through, holding the ache in her back. She'd already packed a case and left it open on the top of the chest of drawers. Now, to her bewilderment, she found the case closed on the floor. On the chest stood a crib, quilted in white, edged with flounces of snowy lace and embroidered with silken rosebuds.

It was the sort of thing one barely dreamed of after long years of war and hardship; the sort of thing that might have existed in another time, another world. With one hand at her throat, Lydia touched it with gentle fingers, her eyes wide and blinking with amazement. Who on earth? How on earth? The work in it was extraordinary . . .

'Like it, my love?'

Floral sidled in from the back stairs, her familiar, mischievous grin softened with shyness.

Lydia almost wept. 'Oh, Floral, Floral,' she whispered. 'Floral, I can't . . .'

She couldn't bear it!

'Did *you* make it?'

'Warn't no different from makin' a hat, my love. Bigger, o'course, but no different. There's a tin bath inside there somewhere, but 'tis wadded thick enough; the baby won't know 'tis there. I got all me stuff still, see. Me waddin', me silks, me bits 'n' pieces. I wanted to give thee summat, my love, just to say . . . Well, fanks for everyfing.'

'For what? I should be saying thanks to *you*, Floral! And I do! But –'

'They'd have turned me out if you hadn't come, my love. One day or another . . . Mrs Chantry told I *you'd* get rid of I, and you never. And I appreciate it, my love. That's all.'

'*Peggy* said I . . .'

'She'm a tricky one.' Floral grinned. 'Winds us round 'n'round, she do, gettin' s'all in a tangle. Good as gawld, o' course . . .' She put her head on one side and waited, bright-eyed, for Lydia either to agree or deny it. Lydia hadn't yet decided what her mother-in-law was made of. She suspected, however, that it wasn't gold, although she'd certainly glittered a good deal since her trip to London. Hotel life had reminded her (too well) of what life had been like before the war, and now she spent most of her time sitting graciously by the fire, waiting for someone to deliver tea on a tray, and little sandwiches with the crusts cut off. But at least she'd stopped complaining about the chafing dishes.

'Nerves,' Floral said. 'That's what 'tis, my love.'

'Yes, I expect you're right.'

'Give you a bit of advice, my love? You don't need it – you'm as straight as a die, I knows – but if you wuz ever to get in a tangle wiv Mrs Chantry . . .'

'Yes?' Lydia prompted warily.

'Be straight,' Floral said. 'Never tell her a lie.'

When Floral had gone, Lydia went on standing there, watching the snow drift past the window. She wasn't really thinking about anything, but the words, 'Too late,' kept blowing across her mind, as cold and cheerless as a blizzard.

* * *

Leo stepped out of the warm kitchen at Manor Farm and tipped his face up to the snow, his teeth bared in a grin of pure pleasure. Ray Duckett, home from hospital but only slowly regaining his strength, had surrendered his farm lease, voluntarily, and without a word from Leo to hasten his decision! Until now, Leo had been taking a manager's wage for his work. Now . . . God, what a relief! He was solvent again, or at least knew that he had the means, the *right*, to be solvent, if only he worked hard enough and thought things through.

It was odd: he'd cared about his own solvency much more since he'd married Lydia than he'd cared about it before. Then it had been an aching worry, a gnawing pain that he'd never felt free of. Now it had become an almost passionate *desire*; not to be rich for its own sake, but to regain his pride; to be, if only in a small way, his own man again. Make plans . . . Make decisions . . .

He made his first decision as he hurried across the yard to the milking byre: Lydia could spend her money on Molliston. He would provide everything else: her clothes, her food, everything she needed.

'Cap'n Chantry!' With her head and shoulders draped in a shawl against the snow, Mary Duckett waved to him from the door he'd just left. 'Cap'n Chantry! It's yer mother, zir! On the telephone!'

Solvency didn't matter so much, he thought later, when one had survival to worry about. Lydia had gone into labour six weeks too soon; poor young Lionel would almost certainly die and Lydia certainly might. They all might, for Ray Duckett's rickety old Morris was barely equal to a blizzard (and was almost out of petrol) and if they got stuck halfway to the clinic, they'd all freeze to death.

He'd wrapped Lydia in two blankets and an eiderdown, but she'd shaken them off before they'd got out of the village and now was kneeling on the floor, between contractions talking as calmly as if they were off on a summer picnic. 'There's a stew on the hob and a meat loaf in the larder, Leo. Tell your mother to cut it in half before she heats it up. It should do for two meals. After that, she's on her own.'

'Right,' he said, having heard almost none of it.

'If this weather goes on, you'll need extra blankets. They're in the small chest in the – are you listening? – small chest in the bedroom. But air them before you put them on the bed. They're probably damp.'

'Yes, fine, fine.' The windscreen kept icing up; first inside, then out. He stopped, got out, scraped, got in. Drove a hundred yards and stopped again. He was shuddering with terror, shuddering with cold. His wife was dying, his child was dying, he had thirty cows queuing up in the yard waiting to be milked and his cowman had gone home to bed with the 'flu.

'And the coal should be delivered tomorrow,' Lydia said calmly. 'But we'll be lucky to get more than a hundredweight. *Do* tell your mother to be careful with the wood, Leo. The shed's half-empty already and it's still only January.'

The windscreen wiper jammed. Leo swore. Lydia put her hand on his knee and said quietly, 'Hush. Calm down. You've been through worse than this, haven't you?'

'It doesn't matter what *I'm* going through!' he yelled. 'It's *you* I care about, damn it!'

And that was true. It was true. If she died out here, in this bitter cold, they could drop a bomb on him afterwards and he'd be grateful. She didn't even *sound* scared, let alone look it, and here was he . . . Calm down. He couldn't change anything, couldn't help at all except by keeping the blasted car going. So that was precisely what he'd do, even if he had to push it the entire ten miles.

He produced a shaky smile and a shakier lie. 'Nearly there, darling. Won't be long now.'

It took another hour, during which time Leo gave up scraping the windscreen and drove – or skidded – the rest of the way by hanging sideways out of the open door, reminding himself that it had often between twenty degrees colder than this in Germany, although in fact he was too cold to tell the difference. There were no other cars on the road. The only vehicle he saw was an ambulance, its bell urgently clanging, hurrying towards St Martin's at a death-defying lick of fifteen miles an hour.

Leo was close to tears by the time they reached the nursing home. A nurse in a blue cape rushed out with a wheelchair and bore Lydia away to the warmth of the hall. Leo carried her case inside and knelt beside her, holding her hand. Oh, God, if she should die, he'd never forgive himself! 'Lydia,' he whispered urgently, 'there's something I must tell you –'

'There's no time!' She snatched her hand clear and laid it over her mouth. 'If you want to help me, you must go home. Look, there's still some daylight left. If I know you can make it in daylight, it'll save me worrying about you. Please, Leo? Go now?'

'You're the bravest girl –'

She smiled. 'Go, Leo.'

He bent to kiss her, but his lips barely made contact with her mouth before the nurse pushed the wheelchair away. Lydia didn't look back. As he drove home, his hands frozen to the icy metal of the steering wheel, the thing that hurt him most was that she hadn't once looked back. Yet he was glad he hadn't told her. It had been a stupid

– and very selfish – impulse, a need to assuage his guilt, no matter what suffering it caused her. *I'm no good. I'm a louse. I don't deserve your respect, your concern, your patience and generosity. I married you for your money.*

'Know what you are?' he asked himself wearily. 'You're a bastard.'

'It's a boy!'

He weighed eight and a half pounds and had a thick, spiky cap of black hair, which continued in a line all the way down his back. 'Don't worry about that,' the midwife said, 'It'll rub off in a few days.'

Lydia wasn't worried. As she held her son in her arms for the first time, gazing in amazement at his pouting, crumpled-up little face, they'd have had to bring Hitler back from the dead just to make her blink, let alone worry. Eight and a half pounds made a pretty big baby, yet everything about him was so tiny it almost broke her heart with wonderment. Hands like little rosebuds . . .

'Feet like plates of meat,' the midwife informed her unfeelingly. 'He'll be a whopper. How big's his daddy?'

'Six foot two,' Lydia said, and didn't realise until later that she'd been thinking of Leo, not Nigel. She could barely remember Nigel. Didn't want to. In many ways, she didn't want to remember Leo, either, but would have to . . . Any minute now.

But it was gone seven in the morning before they wheeled her to the telephone in the hall. Leo – if he'd survived the journey home – would be milking at Manor Farm, and it wasn't fair to expect him to wait for news until he went home for breakfast. It would be easier for everyone – for Lydia especially – just to leave a message with Mrs Duckett.

'It's a boy,' she said. 'Tell Leo we're both fine, and tell him not to visit us until the snow clears.'

Oh, but it wasn't fair, not *fair*! She must give him *some* warning!

'Tell him,' she said, 'that I want to call the baby Richard. Not Lionel. Can you hear me, Mrs Duckett? *Not* Lionel.'

She woke from a deep, dreamless sleep soon after eleven to the sound of her own baby, crying for his first feed. It wasn't as easy as she'd expected – she kept checking to make sure he hadn't been born with a complete set of teeth – and when the nurse took him away (crying just as loudly as when he'd arrived), Lydia wanted to cry too, like a baby, for someone (Gran, for preference) to come and take the pain away, stick a poultice on her entire miserable life and promise, 'There, now you'll be better.'

But her grandmother didn't come. When the door opened again, it was to admit Peggy Chantry, as bright and breezy as only she knew how to be. She was wearing the tweeds she'd worn to London – tailored for her in '38 and still as good as new, although reeking of mothballs – a hat she'd bought in London (dark green, with a brown feather) and black rubber boots, still rimmed with snow. And she was smiling.

'Darling, how are you?'

'Fine,' Lydia mumbled, blushing. 'How did you get here? You shouldn't have, Peggy. The snow –'

'The roads are almost clear. I came on the bus. Leo will be here later, if he can get some petrol. If he can't, darling, you can move over and I'll stay the night. You look like death. Was it awful?'

'Apparently not. They said it was all very straightforward.'

'Hmph. They would. Not *quite* like cracking an egg, though, is it?'

Lydia sighed and turned away, biting her lip on self-pitying tears. Any minute now, Peggy would ask to see her grandson. Any minute now, she'd *know*. She'd had two – no, three – babies of her own. Nothing would convince her that the little heavyweight Lydia had produced was six weeks premature.

'Here we are, Mummy! Here we are, Granny! All changed and burped and happy again!'

The nurse bent her knees to deposit the little bundle in Peggy's lap, but she reared away, laughing nervously, 'Heavens, *I* can't hold him. I'm hopeless with babies. Put him in his cot, for goodness' sake, and let him sleep.'

She didn't even look at him, except as one might look at a spider in the bath, and when the nurse had gone away, gave him a second look, peering cautiously over the sides of the hospital crib as if he might suddenly jump up and bite her.

'Had nannies for mine, of course,' she explained brightly. 'Scarcely set eyes on them when they were tiny and as little as possible thereafter. Trouble with babies –' she lifted her behind from the seat of her chair and peered at the baby again, wrinkling her nose '– is that they never come when you want them.' She sat down again, her eyes as wide and as brilliant as sapphires. '*Do* they, darling?' she added mischievously.

Although she'd been expecting it, Lydia turned pale with shock. Her mouth was a dry as tinder. She couldn't swallow, couldn't speak. Couldn't think of anything worth saying.

'Who was it?' And still Peggy smiled. 'Anyone we know?'

Lydia turned her stunned gaze to the window and was surprised to see that the sun was shining, melting the snow. It seemed years ago

– could it have been only yesterday? – that she'd stood in the nursery at Molliston, watching it fall. *Be straight*, she heard Floral saying. *Never tell her a lie.*

'Naval Commander,' she croaked, and immediately felt the warmth returning to her face and a feeling of peace to her heart. It was over. Like an illness. And, oh, God, she was glad it was over! 'Married,' she added softly. 'I didn't know.'

'Hmph,' Peggy snorted. '*Men*.'

She stood up and went to the baby's crib, not bending over it as most women would, but leaning away, just stretching out one finger to tweak the shawl from his chin. 'Hmm,' she said, and sat down again, pulling her mouth to one side.

'I doubt if Leo knows what a premature baby looks like,' she said. 'Come to that, I doubt if he knows what *any* baby looks like. Want to risk it? I will if you will.'

Lydia stared, blinked a few times and stared again, her heart thudding like a drum. She knew that Peggy had said something wonderful, but she knew also that she'd said something terrible and hardly knew which thought to deal with first. She was right. Lydia could go on deceiving him for the rest of their lives together, and he might never know a thing about it. But Lydia would. And Peggy would . . .

Never tell her a lie. She winds us round 'n'round . . .

'I don't think you can mean that, Peggy,' she said. 'You couldn't deceive your own son, or let me –'

'Deceive him?' Peggy laughed. 'In what way? There's no need to *say* anything, darling. Men are so blind. He'll never even think about it, let alone ask questions. All *we* have to do is keep mum.' She stood up and strolled to the window, leaving little grey puddles of melted snow all over the pale green lino. 'He should be here soon . . .'

She meant 'decide now', which meant there was no choice. Lydia knew she was being tested, knew that if she chose the lie Peggy would despise her, 'wind her round and round' in the coils of her own deception, and perhaps, in the end, even tell Leo the truth.

'No,' she said firmly. 'I won't lie to him any more, Peggy. Not even by omission. Although you can't condone it, I'm sure you understand my motive in lying to him in the first place, but I regretted it from the beginning and have regretted it more and more as I've got to know him. And he doesn't deserve it. The truth will hurt him, I know, but only for a short time. The lie might hurt him – hurt us all – for the rest of our lives, and I won't do that to him, Peggy. I won't do it.'

She didn't look Peggy's way as she said all this and yet somehow sensed that her words had been received rather differently than she'd anticipated. Surprise? Shock? Whatever it was, her next words shocked Lydia to the core.

'Don't be a fool,' she said, and she wasn't smiling any more. 'What possible good can you do by telling him?'

Lydia didn't know. She didn't know. As far as she could see, she could do no good at all. And yet the harm she could do – to herself, to her baby, and to Leo himself – was as plain as day. A lie of seven months' duration had turned her soul to poison, sucked the life out of her, made her examine every word she uttered for fear of saying something out of place. She would have no more of that. She couldn't bear it.

'If you tell him,' Peggy warned, 'I don't know what he'll do. I don't know him any more, you see. The boy who went away to war did not return, Lydia.' She scratched a nub of loose wool from the lapel of her coat and sat down again, sighing. 'War changes people,' she said. 'They never get over it – the killing, the fear of being killed. And for all I know, Lydia, he might kill *you*.'

She had thought the same thing, many times, but now as Peggy voiced the thought, she found she didn't believe it. She also, for a moment, hated her mother-in-law for even suggesting that her own son might be capable of such a thing. But maybe this, too, was a test?

Lydia lifted her chin and met Peggy's eyes with what she hoped was a cool, unflinching gaze. 'I'll risk it,' she said.

Chapter Nine

For reasons he didn't bother to analyse as he hurried down the corridor to Lydia's private room, Leo imagined he'd find her looking as happy as he felt, transformed into the woman of his dreams: flushed and fragile, sweetly smiling, her elegant, ribbon-like hands softly cradling the baby at her breast.

Mother and son both doing well! Mary Duckett had rubbed her hands at the news, watching his face until she knew he'd understood it, and then hugging him, like the good soul she was, so that she should not see his tears. But even he'd been amazed at the joy he'd felt, the relief. *Mother and son . . .* It sounded so beautiful!

But it looked dreadful, and in any case one of the happy pair was missing. Lydia's hair had been dragged back from her brow in a way which did not become her. Her face was white, puffy, bruised-looking, and strangely grim. Her plain white flannelette nightgown had a stain on it where milk had leaked from her breast. There was no sign of the baby. Just Leo's mother, fiddling nervously with her gloves.

He smiled into Lydia's eyes. She lowered her eyes. He turned his gaze to his mother, who went on fiddling, reminding him of Nero and the burning of Rome.

'What's wrong?' he asked softly. 'Is the baby . . .?'

'The baby's fine!' His mother jumped up and stood over the crib beside the bed which – for some reason – Leo hadn't noticed. 'Dear little thing,' she said brightly, 'Look, Leo. Isn't he adorable?'

He should have been relieved, yet knew something was wrong, that nature itself had gone amiss somewhere, for surely Lydia should be looking at the baby, or at him, not gazing at her folded hands as if she was already bored to death with the entire thing? She looked so *ill . . .*

He stepped closer, ran a gentle finger over her ear. 'Are you all right, darling?'

'Yes, I'm fine.' Her voice, as firm and formal as ever, was nevertheless pitched so low it seemed to have issued from under the bedclothes. 'But I need to talk to you, Leo.'

He slid his gaze to the crib, but could see nothing more than a neat little hump of hospital blankets. There was something wrong with the child. He knew there was something wrong.

'Can't I see him?' he asked warily.

'*Yes!*' his mother said. 'Look, Leo, he's –'

Lydia caught his hand. '*No.*' She directed a violent look in his mother's direction and said coolly, 'You'll find a waiting room just down the hall, Peggy. I think it's the third door on the right, but if I'm wrong I'm sure you'll find someone to ask.'

Had Leo been in his mother's shoes, he'd have obeyed on the instant. It was Lydia as he'd first perceived her: icy and compelling, with a strong hint of Queen Mary in the lofty set of her jaw. But Peggy didn't move except to shrug and walk to the window. 'Oh, that's all right, darling,' she said sweetly. 'I'll be quite comfortable waiting here.'

'Mother!' He glared at her, outraged, half-expecting her to laugh as she usually did when he was annoyed with her. Instead, she turned to Lydia, her eyes narrowed and blazing, saying silent, desperate things to her that Leo scarcely dared guess at.

He marched to the door, held it open and swept his arm towards it in a manner his mother couldn't possibly misinterpret. But she still hesitated, stretching her spine as he'd often seen her do with his father, as if gathering strength for yet another round of futile battle. Lydia closed her eyes and sank back against her pillow with her hand at her throat, panting slightly, as if her heart was giving out. Peggy looked at her once more, then set her mouth in a grim line and marched away without meeting Leo's eyes.

He closed the door. He returned to Lydia's side and stroked her hair. 'All right,' he said gently. 'She's gone. What's going on?'

'Sit down, Leo, please.'

He sat. 'What's wrong with the baby?'

'Nothing.' She raised her head, looked at him for a long moment and then closed her eyes again. 'Except that he isn't yours.'

Leo blinked. The skin on his brow tightened and something cold trickled through his chest as if his blood was turning to ice. He couldn't speak. He wasn't entirely sure he'd heard her, understood her. Not *his*? *Not* his? How could that be?

'I – cheated you,' Lydia murmured. 'Deliberately, callously, cruelly . . . and in absolute desperation. I loved my family, Leo. I didn't love you. And now that I do love you –'

'Be quiet,' he whispered. 'Don't say another word.'

He tried to stand up, to get as far from her as he could without actually running away, but his legs had turned to jelly. He couldn't move. *And now that I do love you . . .*

Oh, God, he *hated* her!

But he was too shocked . . . too shocked even to be as angry as he should be. He wanted to cry, and he couldn't even do that . . .

'Leo . . .'

'Be *quiet*!' He leapt up and went to the window, clinging to the sill to keep his own impetus from hurling him through the glass. Oh, she'd killed him, destroyed him! He couldn't think! *She wants to call him Richard, Cap'n Chantry*. Dear God, she'd actually given him a clue! And he'd thought, *anything you like, darling. As long as you're all right, nothing else matters.*

'Who is the father?' he muttered.

'A Naval Commander.'

'Ha! And he ran off back to sea, before you could nail him?'

'Back to his wife. At least, that's what he said.'

'And then . . . *I* . . . came along.' He heaved a sigh and then another, but his lungs wouldn't fill. He was suffocating. Panicking. Trapped! He covered his face with his hands. God, he'd walked out of one prison, straight into another! She'd . . . she'd . . .

The words 'Double-crossing little bitch' came to mind, but he didn't dare say them. In moments of great stress, he was inclined to get his tongue in a tangle and, ever aware of this disability and deeply ashamed of it, he knew that 'bubble-washing little ditch' would be the end of him, cover him with more humiliation than he could stand. He had to think!

Hush. Be calm. You've been through worse than this. Yes, he had. Far worse. This was nothing by comparison. But she *was* a double-crossing little bitch! In fact, a *double*-double crossing little bitch, for even while he'd thought he was tricking *her* . . .

Oh, dear God, he'd married her for her money! She'd had him in torments of guilt for the past six months because *he* was marrying *her* for her money! And, all the time, she'd been tricking *him*!

He laughed out loud and immediately covered his mouth with his hand, wondering if he'd gone crazy. But he hadn't. No, he hadn't, because . . . because if one looked at it objectively, nothing very much had changed. He'd always known she'd married him for his name. Only that. And the fact that she wasn't entitled to it was neither here nor there. He wasn't entitled to her money, either. So . . . perhaps they were even? And back to the beginning, marrying for convenience, with no love – *no* love – to complicate matters on either side.

Deliberately, callously, cruelly . . . He blew out his breath from the side of his mouth. Yes, he could say the same about himself and excuse himself as she had: *I loved my house. I didn't love you. And now that I do love you* . . .

But that wasn't true any more and might never be true again. What little love he'd had for her had been too fragile to survive this, and perhaps too contrived, for he hadn't so much fallen in love as marched into it with his eyes wide open: she's my wife, so I'll love her . . . But no, not even that. She's my *rich* wife, so I'll stay on the right side of her. And it hadn't been too difficult. After all, she had her good points . . .

The baby began to cry: a thin, snuffling little wail, and as Leo turned towards the sound, he saw Lydia turn too, and smile into the crib, stretching out a hand to ease back the shawl. He'd never seen her smile like that, so sweetly, so warmly, so . . .

She made to get out of bed and before he could think what he was doing he said, 'All right. Stay there, I'll get him.'

She went rigid. It was only then that he remembered she didn't know. She thought she'd robbed him, and she hadn't; she'd *paid* him and would go on paying, damn her, for the rest of her natural life. After all, what kind of fool would throw fifty thousand pounds away? What kind of fool would divorce her?

Oh, but she didn't *want* him to touch the baby . . . Her eyes were wide with fear and her lip was trembling. In her white flannelette nightie, she looked like a little girl caught out in wickedness and sent to bed with no supper. Well, it wouldn't hurt her. For a while.

He stooped over the crib and gently lifted the wailing little bundle, resting it in the crook of his arm, tweaking the shawl from its chin. He was surprised to see the shock of black hair and tiny arched brows, the dark tangled lashes. There was even the remote look in his eyes that meant he couldn't yet focus . . . Just like Lydia.

'You look like your mother,' he muttered. 'Not a bad thing, I suppose. In the circumstances.'

He'd never actually seen a baby at such close quarters. He'd smiled into a few perambulators, tickled a few chins, said (from a safe distance), 'He looks like his mother,' while in fact thinking, *He looks like a turnip.* But this little one didn't look like a turnip. He looked like his mother, which meant . . . It meant that Leo need never have known! She needn't have told him! So why in the devil's name *had* she told him? She couldn't want a divorce – old Mrs Westley would no more countenance that than an illegitimate child! But then, how was he to know what Lydia wanted? Perhaps his name had been her first concern after all, and to hell with her grandmother's feelings. Well, she had a nasty shock coming if divorce had been her plan . . .

He laid the child in Lydia's arms and saw her eyelids flutter with relief, her teeth clamp down on a sob which, as usual, went no further. She'd never tormented him with her tears. She was a brave girl. He had to grant her that.

He sat down and, with some difficulty, smiled. 'You want to call him Richard, I understand?'

'Yes,' she whispered.

He heaved a sigh, trying to take pleasure from her misery and finding none, trying to take comfort from his part in the double-cross and finding none of that, either, for it was like trying to take nourishment from a rotten apple. Yet he could find hope – a little of it – in knowing that he owed her nothing. They were even. The account was squared.

He smiled again. 'Oh, well,' he said. 'Let's call the next one Lionel then, shall we?'

Still shaking, hardly daring to breathe, Lydia stared at him, knowing exactly what he'd said but not believing it. She swallowed and bent her head to look at the baby, who was screwing up his face to cry again. Poor little thing . . . What a terrible welcome he'd had to the world . . . She slipped the tip of her finger into his mouth and immediately felt him begin to suck and saw his face smooth out with the onset of sleep. Oh, dear Lord, what kind of life was he going to have after a beginning like this?

Let's call the next one Lionel . . . She still didn't believe it. She didn't even believe that Leo was sitting here, smiling at her as if she'd *given* him something, not taken everything away. He should have killed her. For a minute or two she'd been convinced that he would, and then . . . She'd been just as convinced that he'd kill the baby – just pick him up and hurl him at the wall – and the most terrible thing was that she'd been too frightened to stop him. She'd been paralysed with fear. But he'd been so gentle.

Let's call the next one Lionel. It must mean something else, something worse than being killed! A woman couldn't do this to a man without being punished! It wasn't natural! His first reaction to her revelations had been very natural indeed – she'd never seen anyone so helplessly, so *passionately*, angry. He'd looked as she imagined a man might look who'd swallowed a live octopus, something so big, so ugly and violent, it couldn't possibly be contained. And yet he'd said almost nothing. Neither, for that matter, had she. When Leo Chantry said, 'Be quiet,' in that tone of voice, you began to think you'd never speak again.

'The n-next one?' she stammered at last. 'What do you mean?'

Leo raised his eyebrows. 'What could I mean? This one's yours. I want a child of my own, now.' He blinked a few times as if listening to his own words and finding them as surprising as Lydia had. 'Well, not exactly *now*, of course. Mustn't rush you, must we?'

There was bitterness in his voice and a cynical curl to his mouth which cut Lydia to the heart. Yet . . . he meant it. He wasn't going to kill her. He wasn't going to throw her out. But what the devil was he going to do instead?

'I . . .' She swallowed another lump of terror. 'I thought . . . I thought you'd want a divorce.'

'Hmm.' He was still very agitated. He kept rasping his teeth over his lips, drumming his fingers on his knee, looking from left to right, up and down, as if trying to find something he'd lost long ago. 'The Chantrys have never divorced,' he said. 'It isn't done.' He narrowed his eyes. 'I believe one of the Littons did. My father had it all written down somewhere, but I've forgotten most of the details.'

'The Littons?' she echoed weakly.

'They were at Molliston before the Civil War. Cromwell drove them out and . . .' He looked at the ceiling. 'Well, they just disappeared. Then, when Charles the Second took the throne, the first Lionel Chantry laid claim to Molliston because his mother . . . or was it his wife? Anyway, someone related to him . . . was also related to the Littons.' He stared at the wall above Lydia's head. 'There's never been a divorce since then. It would be a shame to start now, wouldn't it?'

'But how can we *live*, Leo? You must hate me so!'

He dragged his hand over his face. 'It's true that I'm not as fond of you today as I was yesterday,' he said slowly. 'But – to be frank – I wasn't all that fond of you to start with. We married for necessity, not love. But because yesterday I was fond of you –' again he stroked his face '– there's always a chance I might be so again. And since that's just about the only chance we have, we'll just have to hope for it, shan't we?'

He stood up, walked to the door, opened – and shut it again. 'However,' he said quietly, 'this deception, as you must realise, must serve you the rest of our lives together. If you ever lie to me again – if you cheat me of so much as a farthing – I'll make your life such a misery you'll wish you'd never been born.'

Any other man making such a threat would, Lydia guessed, have raised his voice, bared his teeth, pounded his fist on the table. But

Leo's voice had grown softer, until he was barely moving his lips. It was the voice of a man who was too ill to speak, who'd been crushed to the bone, and might never be the same again.

'Do you understand that?' he asked.

'Yes, of course. And, oh, Leo, I promise I'll never . . .'

'Don't promise me anything, Lydia, because I won't believe you.' He bowed his head and muttered. 'I'd better go.'

Again he opened the door. And again closed it. 'My mother knows?'

'Yes.'

There was a long, breathless silence while he stared at his feet. Then, 'Why?' he murmured. 'Why did you tell her?'

'Because premature babies don't weigh eight and a half pounds, Leo. Richard does, and to anyone who knows anything about babies, it's very obvious that he does.'

'Ah . . .' he said. 'And did she – by any chance – suggest that you shouldn't tell me?' His mouth slanted in a cold, weary smile. 'Merely to protect my feelings, of course.'

'Yes, she did.'

'So why *did* you tell me? Do my feelings mean nothing to you?'

Lydia had been on the edge of tears since she'd first seen him come through the door, but now she wanted to howl, scream, beg him for forgiveness. Her grandmother's training was all that stopped her. *Never cry when you've hurt someone else, Lydia. Your tears will hurt them more.* Tears in such circumstances were also a form of leverage, even of blackmail, a way of forcing forgiveness from someone who could not willingly give it, and she couldn't do that to him. Even if she ruptured her throat to keep herself from weeping, she *wouldn't* do that.

'Your feelings mean a great deal to me,' she said at last. 'I told you the truth, Leo, because I was sick of lying, because I couldn't drag your mother into the same deception and . . . and because I thought it would do you less harm to know it now than later, when perhaps . . .'

'Go on.'

'Oh, Leo!' she wailed. 'If you'd thought he was your son, you'd have *loved* him!'

He looked bewildered, utterly uncomprehending. 'But wouldn't that have been better than *this*, Lydia?'

'Only if you never found out! But if you did . . . If Peggy told you the truth when he was three, or six, or ten . . . Oh, I know you think I've broken your heart, but this is nothing compared to that, Leo! It would have killed you!'

He nodded, sketched her a wry, twisted smile. 'Yes. Yes, I see.' He took a deep, steadying breath and closed his eyes. 'Thank you.'

Thank you. Thank you. The words seemed to score themselves on her mind as if they'd been etched with acid. She had to squeeze her eyes shut against the pain. When she opened them again he was gone.

Then she wept.

They'd been driving a good five minutes before Leo's mother spoke to him again. 'Well?' she demanded sharply.

'Wells are deep and dark, Mother,' he said. 'Best to keep away from them, I think.'

Another minute passed. 'You can't just say that!' she spluttered furiously. 'What did she tell you?'

'About what?'

'About the baby!'

'Oh . . .' He glanced at her sideways. He'd never been sure how his mother's mind worked. It certainly wasn't predictable, except insofar as she usually (perhaps always) put her own needs first. She could be very generous, very kind, but there was usually a self-serving motive involved in it somewhere. Most people were the same, of course, but most people were fairly frank about it and Peggy never was. The principle, 'I'll scratch your back if you'll scratch mine,' was one she operated on but never acknowledged. He wasn't sure why. The truth was, however, that she'd never given him anything without making him think, *What does she want?* which was unfortunate, because if she'd *said* 'I'll give you this if you'll give me that,' he wouldn't have minded at all.

'Well?' she said again.

'She wants to call him Richard,' he said. 'I don't really like breaking the Lionel tradition, but on the other hand . . . So long as he's healthy, what does it matter what it says on his birth certificate?'

The lightness of his voice had cost him an effort, but as he glanced at her again, the effort paid off. He hadn't really been aware that she'd been sitting bolt upright, with every nerve and muscle strained to its limits. But now she went as limp as a popped balloon, and, although she didn't say anything, he knew she was thinking, *Oh, thank God, she didn't tell him!*

But what else was she thinking? *I know something you don't know?* He wouldn't leave her with that idea for very long. Just long enough for him to think things through and regain his balance. She was probably just relieved to know that there was no divorce in the offing, for although she hadn't seen so much as a penny of Lydia's money, she reaped the benefits of it (as he did) every time she ran a hot bath or walked the house without carrying a brolly. But Lydia had brought them both more benefits than mere money. The comforts of a clean, well-run home, decent food and a peaceful, ordered atmosphere, had done Leo more good than all the rest of it put together. And maybe it was *that* his mother couldn't bear to lose – the idea that someone else would bear the brunt of cruel domesticity. She'd never been any good at that side of things.

The morning's thaw was beginning to freeze again as they reached home. Leo ran upstairs to change into his farming gear and found Floral waiting for him on the landing, grinning her wide, impish grin.

''Ow's Lydia!?'

'Fine.' He turned towards his room.

'And the baby?'

'He's fine too.'

'Oh, come on,' she laughed. 'Thee can do better'n that!'

Leo sighed. She always gave him the idea that she was mocking him, that she 'had something on him' he wouldn't want a policeman to know. And while he had nothing like that on his conscience, he wasn't entirely sure his mother didn't. There was no knowing what might have happened between his father's death and his own return home. He knew she'd sold a great many things: the horses, the Bentley, paintings and the like. Nothing wrong with that on the surface, but a lot depended on who'd bought them and how much Floral knew about it. He wouldn't put blackmail beyond her . . .

Floral chuckled and brought clenched fists up to her chin. 'I bin worryin' meself sick,' she said. 'She were ever so scared, see, Leo. It's not easy, havin' a baby, is it?'

He almost laughed. (*That* wasn't why she'd been scared!) But Floral evidently *had* been worrying. And why not, after all? Lydia had been good to her. Probably too good.

'No,' he conceded. 'I don't suppose it is. But she's all right. And the baby – er – weighs eight and a half pounds, if that means anything to you.'

Floral's jaw dropped. 'Ooh,' she said. 'A gurt big 'un.'

'And he looks like his mother.'

'Aw, bless his little heart,' she cooed. 'And if he'm as good as his ma in his ways, you'll 'ave a son to be proud of. Best day's work you ever did, marryin' 'er, Leo.'

He turned into his room and closed the door, leaning against it with his eyes shut. Best day's work? God, if she only knew! But it was no good blaming Lydia. It was his fault, too. *All* his fault, for she certainly wouldn't have caught him so easily had he not been so busy

106

catching her. He'd taken the wrong road – deliberately, callously, cruelly – and now was paying for it, precisely as he should. He'd cheated her and she'd cheated him. They were even. But he still felt betrayed. Yes, betrayed. It had never crossed his mind that she'd be capable of pulling such a filthy trick. She'd just *used* him, as if he was *nothing*! And yet, what else was he?

He'd taken the wrong road. But even wrong roads have turnings. Lydia had already demonstrated that in making her confession – a confession she *needn't* have made. He didn't trust her motives for making it – perhaps she *had* wanted a divorce – but even if her motives were wrong, she'd certainly made the right choice. A secret like that, shared with his mother . . . She'd never have had an hour's peace from it.

He stared at the head of the bed and saw Lydia, white and terrified in her hospital bed, telling him the truth. He might have killed her! Or killed the child. She wasn't to know he wouldn't. Indeed, she *hadn't* known it, poor girl; been terrified that he would. And yet . . . He'd never known a woman so brave. Her eyes had filled with tears on at least three occasions, yet she'd controlled them. Her voice had choked a few dozen times, yet she'd swallowed the lump and gone on as calmly as before. And the only time she'd raised her voice . . .

If you'd thought he was your son, you'd have loved him!

Yes . . . She'd saved him from that.

The wrong road. But where was the right turning? Oh, he knew, damn it! Tell her the truth, restore the balance, give them both a chance to start again. If she wanted a divorce she could have one. He'd never loved her, anyway.

He changed his clothes and ran downstairs to get warm by the parlour fire, where his mother was already settled, winding wool from a pale blue skein.

'Blue for a boy,' she said brightly. 'I found the wool in London; clever me.'

'What if it had been a girl?'

'I found some pink, too.' She laughed and patted her temple. 'Oh, you can't fool me.'

'Evidently.' Leo turned his back to the fire and gazed dreamily at the opposite wall, pretending to be deep in thought. 'Oh,' he said. 'I've just remembered something else Lydia told me, Mother.'

She looked up with a smile, all unsuspecting.

He snatched his coat from the back of the chair and made for the door. 'He's not mine,' he said. And left.

It snowed, off and on, for the next five days. The sixth was dark and freezing. Lydia felt as if she'd been walled up in a harem. Gran couldn't get here. No one could. She'd never been so miserable in her life. Even the baby gave her little joy. She couldn't feed him. Even without teeth, he'd chewed her nipples raw. Every time he howled for food, she howled with despair and didn't care who heard her. She'd never in her life wept so much or felt less guilty about it, for she was angry, angry with the whole damn world: the nurses, the government (breast feeding had become a patriotic duty), her grandmother, her father and the narrow, bigoted, hypocritical society they stood for, Nigel (God rot him), Peggy Chantry . . . and herself.

But not Leo. She'd hurt him too much to hate him. She respected him, admired him, pitied him (what had he ever done to deserve such trouble?), but most of all she feared him. Not for anything he'd said or done and not for anything he might do, but just because she was so ashamed. The very thought of seeing him again made her blush, moan – yes, and weep. The thought of Leo seeing *her* again was even worse. She looked appalling. Her eyes were red, her hair like rats' tails, and she'd broken out in spots. Even if he had loved her, he wouldn't love her now.

But – to be frank – I wasn't all that fond of you to start with. God, how that had hurt! And still hurt, even though, compared with some of the things he could have said, it was nothing. She didn't deserve such a man.

He came at last when Richard was nine days old, but as soon as he walked through the door she burst into tears.

'Lydia!'

He didn't say anything else and she couldn't stop crying. He took her hand and patted it. He stroked her hair, but his gentleness only made her cry harder and after a few minutes he went away again. She'd thought, until then, that she was as miserable as she could get, but his leaving seemed to break yet another dam of tears, until she thought she'd die of weeping.

The clinic laundry had starched her hankies – it was like blowing her nose in a newspaper – and while she was in the middle of this painful procedure, Leo came back and said firmly, 'Get dressed. I'm taking you home. They're fetching – er – Richard from the nursery.'

Having been meant to stay a fortnight, Lydia could only stare. Her eyes were swollen to slits, but she could actually see her own nose, a scarlet, throbbing thing, which sat in the middle of her face like a grilled tomato on a plate. Her mouth was open, as were the buttons of her pyjama jacket, and she could tell from the pained look on Leo's face that he'd never seen anything more hideous in his life.

'It's going to snow again,' he said. 'I might not be able to get out of the village for another week, and I'm not leaving you here like this.' He smiled stiffly. 'There's nothing to be afraid of, Lydia. Don't cry any more.' He averted his face, as if he couldn't stand the sight of her and added, 'Please,' with a note of faint desperation.

Lydia blinked and tried to think about getting dressed, going home, but it was all too complicated, too difficult. Too frightening. Virtually the only good thing about living in a snowed-up harem was that nothing happened, and that it went *on* not happening, day after dreary day.

Leo sat on the bed and took her hand in a firm grasp. 'I've never seen you like this. I know it's my fault . . .'

'Oh, no!'

'But this isn't the time to discuss it. I just want to say – and to know that you believe – that so far as I'm concerned, this episode is over. We were both . . .'

Without letting go of her hand, he covered his face with the other, thought for a few moments and then smiled. 'We were both fools,' he said. '*Both*, you understand. But we don't have to go on being fools, Lydia. God willing, we have long lives ahead of us and must do what we can to live them happily and decently from now on. What do you think?'

'Oh, Leo, Leo.' The tears flowed again. 'How can you be so kind to me? I've hurt you so much, taken everything . . .'

'No. You've given quite as much as you've taken.' He turned away, hunching his shoulders as though fighting some dark, internal battle which Lydia guessed was between the angel he almost certainly was and the devil he could be, if only he let himself. But he would never let himself. He was a gentleman, through and through.

'Can you imagine what Molliston would have been like now if you hadn't taken it in hand?' he asked ruefully. 'We'd have frozen in our beds, Lydia.'

She smiled, loving him, knowing that he was lying only to make her feel better. He'd have moved to Manor Farm, been as warm as toast under the thatch. She might have saved the Ducketts from eviction, but she'd done virtually nothing for Leo.

Yet, as if he'd read her mind, Leo added thoughtfully. 'I couldn't have evicted the Ducketts. Every time I thought of it . . . well, I couldn't; but it was largely because I couldn't leave Molliston – not, at least, until it collapsed about my ears. You've saved me from *that*, Lydia . . .' Again he turned away to resume the battle with his *alter ego*, clenching his hands, clenching his teeth, wrestling with anger and disappointment until the fight was won and he smiled again.

'We're square,' he said. 'No debts outstanding on either side. If you'll go on helping with Molliston, I'll do all I can to help you and the baby. Does that seem – fair?'

He spoke tentatively, almost as if he doubted the extent of his own generosity or feared she might ask for more.

She tried to say, 'I'll build you a palace,' but the words wouldn't come. She tried to say, 'Thank you,' but couldn't say that, either. In the end, she just nodded and hoped he'd understand. But, oh, dear Lord, she'd build him a *palace*! Just as soon as she stopped crying.

Chapter Ten

Leo blamed it all on Lydia's tears. He'd walked into her room with his confession all prepared, fully expecting it to be received as he'd intended to present it: with dignity, good sense and philosophical calm. Instead . . . Well, he'd barely recognised her. Even in the moment before she'd burst into tears, he'd known she'd been crying for a week, at least. Crying alone. He hadn't meant to leave her alone all that time. He'd been snow-bound, cut off, unable to dig himself out of Manor Farm, let alone out of the village. The telephone wires had been down. Even the post hadn't come in (or gone out) for four days. Yet he'd spent every day of that time in a frenzy of hard, physical work (the most healing medicine he knew of) while Lydia . . . He knew how it had been for her. He'd been through it himself: feeling trapped and helpless, having nothing to do but wait, seethe, turn the agony over and over until you knew every part of it and still couldn't find a way out.

It was clearly no time for confessions. He had to take her home while he still could. At least, that was what he'd told himself. The truth was, however, that he'd wanted to confess as much as he wanted to lose Molliston and, when she'd cried, she'd given him the excuse he'd needed to 'think it over' one more time. He hated himself for it; but that wasn't his only problem and he knew that time would reveal more. When he'd thought she was carrying *his* child, he'd found Lydia beautiful, desirable even when she was too pregnant to make sex more than a happy memory. But as the exhausted, tearful mother of another man's child, she left him cold.

It had something to do with the weather. The small parlour was the only warm room in the house, and even there 'warm' was a relative term. Bundled up in two cardigans, knee-socks and woolly slippers, Lydia looked about as desirable as a block of wood.

Yet when she spoke to her baby she acquired a radiance she had

111

never once shown Leo. The sheer warmth of her smile as she cooed motherly nonsense of the 'ah-diddums' variety astonished him utterly. Her face lit up, her eyes glowed. And she'd somehow acquired a crescent-shaped dimple at the corner of her mouth which Leo had *certainly* never seen before. He found it all rather fascinating, almost hypnotic. It seemed rather strange to him that this little lump of unbaked dough, this puking, whimpering, bawling bundle, could have caught her heart and fished it out, raw and quivering, for the whole world to see. It raised a question he hadn't considered before: did she love the baby so much because she'd loved its father? Had *he* known Lydia as she really was?

Peggy found Lydia's motherly feelings a little disturbing, too. The whole thing irritated her; she kept saying it wasn't normal, wasn't right, wasn't *done* for a woman to be so involved with her offspring. 'I had nannies for mine,' she said, as if Lydia had had the choice and turned it down. 'Never changed a nappy in my life.'

'Neither had I until a few weeks ago,' Lydia said, and then, jutting her chin, raising her eyebrows, showing her teeth in a brilliant smile, she tickled the kid's fat little belly and added, 'Had I, sweetheart?' as if he knew all about it and might be expected to say so.

'You really love him, don't you?' Leo said wonderingly during one of their rare private moments together.

Lydia looked at him, her eyebrows quivering as if she wanted to laugh and didn't dare.

'Did you love his father?'

'No.'

'Then . . . I don't understand. He has no personality. He can't talk. All he does is eat, sleep, and – and leak. My mother –'

'It was different for your mother. She was accustomed to having servants to do everything for her, but her feelings weren't any different, Leo. When you carry a child inside you for nine months, you aren't – at this stage of his life – loving him so much as loving yourself. He's a part of you.'

'A *part* of you? Like a sort of – third foot?'

Lydia laughed, but then drew back in her chair as she might to put distance between herself and a madman. 'You really don't understand?'

'No, I don't.' It was only when he heard the snap in his voice that he realised he was angry. But he didn't know why. Reason told him that he wasn't jealous of the baby, or of its father, but the feelings he'd had when he'd learned that the child wasn't his had come back in force. He felt *cheated*.

Lydia sighed. 'Your feet are attached to you,' she offered

112

tentatively. 'Your own nerve-endings tell you when they're cold, dirty, damaged or in danger; and you can respond to that without even thinking about it. You can't feel a baby's pain or discomfort. You have to anticipate it, think about it constantly. In a way, you're a slave to his needs, and I think . . . I think, just to make your slavery endurable, nature forges your chains with love. If I didn't love him, Leo, I wouldn't care for him. And if I didn't care for him, he'd die.'

'But my mother . . .' His mouth had gone dry and his heart was pounding uncomfortably close to his throat. Why was he so angry?

Lydia snatched his hand suddenly and squeezed it between both of hers. 'That was different,' she said. 'And it would be different for me, Leo, if there were someone I could trust – trust *absolutely* – to do the job for me. Your nanny was probably an old family retainer, someone your mother knew as well as she knew herself. Someone like Gran is for me; someone she knew would *never* let her down.'

'Yes,' Leo murmured. 'I see.' And he did see. He saw very clearly, remembered it all, partly from hearsay, but also from experience. He'd had at least four different nannies and two different governesses before, at seven, he'd been banished to prep school. No one – least of all his mother – had ever been a slave to *his* needs. So perhaps in a way he *was* jealous of the baby . . . Lucky little brat.

It was a miserable, filthy, exhausting winter: a tightrope Lydia walked with ten kinds of danger lurking on either side should she lose her balance and fall. The cold was the worst of them. Her carefully garnered stocks of firewood were disappearing faster than a national shortage of coal could replace them. They lived in a twenty-room mansion and might just as well have been living in a one-room slum, for they couldn't keep more than one fire going and the small parlour had become all things to all men: sitting room, dining room, laundry (where else could she air the eternal washing?), nursery – even bedroom. She didn't dare let Richard sleep in his own nursery. There were icicles on the insides of the windows, a damp, icy bloom on the furniture on which one could write 'death' with a fingertip and still see it there the next morning. She knew she was dicing with another kind of death when she slept on the sofa and sent Leo to bed with only a hot brick to warm him, but she had no other choice. The baby came first.

But the cruelty of that bitter winter was softened by a single kindness. They were cut off by snow often enough and released from it rarely enough to make visits to and from Lydia's family well-nigh impossible. She'd spoken to her father and her grandmother on the telephone, but they still thought Richard had been premature and by the time they saw him . . . Well, they'd be amazed at how well he'd thrived. But they wouldn't know.

In fact, it was desperately hard to care for a tiny child in such conditions and that Richard thrived at all seemed as miraculous to Lydia as it would be to her grandmother. Leo and Peggy seemed to be of the opinion that the correct way to raise a baby was to put it in a cupboard for a few years and let it out only when – by some magical process – it had learned to walk, talk and use the lavatory. Lydia was aware that this was not just a matter of background. It was mostly because Richard wasn't theirs. They didn't care about him. They couldn't understand what all the fuss was about.

Lydia made as little fuss as possible, but even that had its dangers. She couldn't leave Richard to cry, even for a minute, when at his first wail Peggy put her fingers in her ears! Yet if she dropped everything and ran to him, she ran the risk of spoiling him, or worse – of letting the dinner burn. If it hadn't been for Floral, who adored him and entertained him during his waking hours with a purring recitation of absolute drivel – 'Ooda booda liddle boy, den?' – Lydia would have run away, run back to Gran, thrown everything away – past, present, and future – just to be certain that Richard was safe.

She knew that Leo was unhappy – as was she – and probably regretting ever having laid eyes on her. But he kept his eyes on her far more than was comfortable, especially when she was with Richard. Was he jealous? Or just hating her for so wickedly destroying his life? She told herself she wasn't *entirely* responsible for the miseries that were besetting him: the one-room dwelling, the lack of privacy or comfort, the bitter cold. Surely half his grief was to do with his memories of happier times, when there'd been fires all over the house, servants to supply his every need? True, he'd run Manor Farm before the war as well as after it, but he'd been a gentleman farmer then, a director of operations, wearing warm tweeds and fine leather boots, not the collection of rags and darns which were all that protected him now. No, it wasn't all Lydia's fault. Just . . . most of it.

The spring came so slowly, so painfully, she scarcely noticed it happening. The ice retreated from the house, but not from the garden. Six-foot snowdrifts thawed an inch at a time until one day, the heavy pall of cloud that had hung over the world for so long brought rain instead of snow, and the last of the ice disappeared. The sun came out, the temperature soared. Lydia flung the doors and windows open, washed every rag in the house and hung it *outside* to dry, watching the sheets dance and billow on a fresh westerly wind as if they were a host of angels.

'Oh, Floral,' she said tearfully. 'God save us from another winter like that one!'

Life felt more like life after that. Floral went back to her gardening, Richard to his nursery, and Lydia, more tentatively, to Leo's bed, where he kissed her on the cheek and said, 'Goodnight,' exactly as he'd done when she was sleeping on the sofa. A little pain, like a prodding finger, jabbed at her heart, but she'd spent the day spring-cleaning the parlour and fell asleep soon afterwards, forgetting the pain entirely until the next night. And the next.

Blinking against tears, she murmured, 'You said we should try to be happy . . .'

'Yes,' Leo said dully. 'But I'm afraid it was *easy* to say.' Then, turning his back on her, he beat his pillows into shape and went to sleep.

Lydia visited her family the next day, feeling like a washerwoman, with a shawl-clad Richard straddling her hip and an oilskin bag, full of his nappies, bibs and feeds, banging her legs. Her father met her at the bus stop and carried Richard home. He said, 'You look worn out, darling. What a winter, eh?' and then chatted to Richard as if his daughter wasn't there.

Mrs Westley was more tactful, but only just. She said, 'How are you?' and sighed as if to say, 'Don't answer that.'

After a tour around the farmyard Richard fell asleep, his grandfather went back to work and Lydia and her grandmother drank coffee in the kitchen. For a while, save for the clinking of china, they were silent.

'Why didn't Leo bring you?' the old lady asked at last.

'I didn't ask him. He's very busy.'

'And what do you want to ask me?'

The question had been fully felt, but only half-formed: *Can I come home?* but now, as she met her grandmother's eyes across the table, she knew she couldn't ask. By Gran's standards, marriage was for ever. One made a choice. One made vows 'until death' and such vows were not to be broken.

'I don't want to ask anything, Gran. I just wanted . . .' She smiled. 'I just wanted to see you. It's been such a long winter. How have you coped?'

'Well enough. And you?'

'It has been difficult,' Lydia confessed. 'If Peggy's said, "I had nannies for mine," once, she's said it a thousand times. She's never touched Richard.' She was about to add, 'She never touched her own babies, either,' by way of explanation, but before she could go on, her grandmother interrupted.

'Does that surprise you?' And then, sighing, 'Oh, Lydia, I wasn't born yesterday, my dear.'

The hair at the nape of Lydia's neck rose. She swallowed and stared, mesmerised with horror, into her coffee cup. Gran knew!

'I probably knew before you did,' Mrs Westley said. 'Your face changed. Your skin changed. I knew the signs, my dear. And I know you.' She smiled ruefully. 'I knew even when the fellow turned you down. Who was he, by the way? One of those silly Naval officers, I suppose? Uniforms, uniforms . . . Tch!'

Lydia closed her eyes and tried to catch her breath, but it kept escaping from lungs so compressed with panic she began to think she'd never breathe again. She couldn't believe it! She couldn't believe . . .

'But if you knew all along . . .' she gasped. 'Gran! How could you let me do it!'

'How could I not? You had to marry someone.'

'But – but what about morality? Right and wrong?'

'Your father doesn't know,' Mrs Westley said. 'And when *you* have the choice of breaking your own son's heart or that of another woman's son, you'll understand that there's no right and wrong, only the best of a bad job. And I had your son in mind, too. Leo is a gentleman, Lydia. He might never forgive you, he might make your life a misery, but he'll give your boy a home and a name . . . And that's all that matters. You *don't* matter any more. You made that child in selfishness and wickedness and you must pay for it, whatever the price.'

'But Leo's paying, too!'

'More than he needs to pay, to judge by the look of you. Your hair's a mess, your clothes are a disgrace. And have you run out of lipstick or only of pride?'

Rage struck Lydia's breast like a hammer blow. She wanted to cry out, 'If you'd been through everything *I've* been through . . .'

But that wasn't fair. Gran had had hard times too. She'd suffered grief, illness and privation. She'd worked like a dog. Yet never once had she let her shoulders sag or her hair escape its neat prison of pins. *Hide your feelings. They're no one's business but your own.*

Gran was right. Pride wasn't just a matter of keeping one's temper and hiding one's tears. It was more a matter of –

'Seeming to win,' Gran said, 'when you are losing, is the best method there is of actually *winning*, Lydia. It can't be guaranteed. But it's the best chance you have.'

'Pretend, you mean?'

116

'Pretend?' The old lady smiled. 'Yes, I suppose I do. It's just a game, after all. *Life!*'

Although they'd given up the farm, the Ducketts had kept their lease on the farmhouse. Ray had renewed his lease on life and, as the weather warmed up, he returned to work.

It was 'mornings and light duties only' at first, but even so, it was remarkable what a difference it made to Leo. He felt he'd spent the winter trapped in a horrible treadmill of darkness, cold and hard, unremitting labour in which the miseries of his life at Molliston had been . . . Not unimportant, but peripheral, something he'd deal with later, when there was time.

As the weather softened and the treadmill slowed, he found that he had time to think about Lydia and the child, but found also that he didn't want to think about them. He wanted to forget them. He wanted them to go away. It was easier to forget them now that the house had opened up. They no longer awaited him, like a recurrent nightmare, in the sealed box of the small parlour. He often had no idea where they were, or what they were doing, and didn't care. When Lydia found a carpenter to repair the roof timbers and the hole in the library floor, he found he didn't even care about Molliston any more. He listened to the man for an hour or more and was bored stiff. He almost said, 'Do what you like – I don't care,' but heard the words in his mind before he could utter them and was shocked to silence. Had he sold himself for nothing?

Later, as he walked back to Manor Farm, he turned to look at the house, its leaded windows glinting in the brilliant light of a glorious Maytime, and tried to imagine it as a heap of rubble, tried to imagine a cluster of prefabs or council houses in its place. Yes, he still cared. But only just. And not for himself so much as for all the Chantrys who'd cared for it before: generation upon generation of them, perhaps none more happy than he was now. Most of them would have had arranged marriages, have slept with strangers for one reason or another: for money, for power . . . Rarely for love or in hope of love. And the babies had been put out to wet-nurses in those days . . .

He didn't quite realise that he'd absented himself from his feelings – put them to sleep, in a way – until, in the first week of June, as he walked home to lunch, they woke up again, shaken into life by a motor car, a Naval officer, and, oddly enough, by a white frock printed with red roses. Lydia was wearing it, but he'd never seen it before and even with his eyes skidding over the other parts of the

117

tableau, Leo knew she looked wonderful in it. The Naval officer was a fine figure of a man, too. His car was a dream: a smart Riley tourer in British Racing Green . . .

Leo's teeth snapped shut. His heart leapt with . . . it leapt, but he didn't know why until Lydia saw him coming, and with a deft twirl of her hips dumped the baby into the sailor's arms and ran across the grass towards him. 'Dumped' was the operative word. Except for Floral, no one had held that child since Lydia had first brought him home. She'd never let him go. Until now. Surely she hadn't had the impudence, the *insolence*, to bring her lover here? And she was *smiling*, damn her!

'What the devil's going on?' he hissed. 'Who the hell . . .?'

'It's Mr Day's nephew. I met him just now, when I went to the rectory, and he wants –'

'*Who*?'

'Mr Day! The Rector! He's been posted to Hong Kong and he wants to sell –'

'*What*?'

She said it all again, but Leo wasn't listening. He'd worked it all out as soon as he'd seen them standing there and now only wanted the details filled in so that he could be absolutely sure whose nose he was punching – and give his Riley a bloody good kick while he was at it. The only trouble was, the details didn't match the story. Why was the Rector going to Hong Kong? And what did his journey have to do with Lydia's lover?

'– and he wants to sell the car!' she concluded at last.

'What?'

Lydia laughed suddenly and caught his hand. She looked . . . She looked as she'd never looked before. Excited and happy, flushed and pretty. And her lipstick exactly matched the roses on her frock.

'Come on! He's going back to London tonight, so if you want it, we'll have to decide now. It's a super car, Leo. Old, of course, but it *goes*!'

Still confused, but beginning to catch her drift, he allowed himself to be led back to the house, although he still didn't know who the sailor was, and was under the impression that the *Rector* was going to Hong Kong. He hesitated again, was again overwhelmed with doubt as the Naval chap lifted Richard over his head, rocked him from side to side and said, 'Boo!' as if they were the best of friends, renewing an old acquaintance.

'Lieutenant Robert Day,' Lydia said, 'this is my husband, Captain Leo Chantry. Lieutenant Day is the Rector's nephew, Leo . . .'

Leo blinked, did the appropriate thing with his right hand, and blinked again as the fellow bumped Richard over his shoulder, like a sort of kitbag, before shaking hands.

The sailor grinned. 'You look as confused as I feel, Captain Chantry. I thought I was joking when I asked your wife if she'd like to buy the old bus, but she was certain you'd want to take a look. I've been posted to Hong Kong. Likely to be there a while, so I'd like to know she's gone to a good home. What d'you think of her?'

Leo thought 'she' was marvellous. Virtually any car not an absolute wreck would have been worth looking at, for the production of new cars had entirely ceased during the war years and everyone who still had a pre-war car was hanging on to it for grim death. But the Riley was a beauty. Not much tread left on the tyres, but there was no canvas showing through, which was more than could be said for Ray Duckett's Morris. And the engine was as sweet as a nut . . .

As the conversation became more technical, Lydia took Richard back to the house. But a second later she popped out again, calling, 'Don't go back to the farm for your cheque-book, Leo. Lieutenant Day's expected back at the Rectory for lunch.'

Leo smiled nervously, acknowledging her tact with a wave of his hand and his dependency on her cheque-book with a sigh. But he wanted the car. And so did she. Even with petrol shortages, it would make such a difference to their lives.

Later, with the deal done and his hair still ruffled after a blissful 'spin' around the village in his new toy, Leo went home for his lunch at last and found Richard all alone in the kitchen, strapped safely in his high chair with his gums clamped hard around a crust of bread. Leo frowned. Richard withdrew the crust and presented it, soggy end first, to his nominal father, saying, 'Ga!' rather decisively and then, 'Goo-oo,' on a sing-song note, which seemed to mean, 'It's good. Have a bite.'

'I was hoping for something more substantial,' Leo said tentatively, and was astonished when the kid chuckled and dropped the crust on the floor. 'Ooh!' He leaned sideways from the chair, his eyes widening with astonishment to see the crust now so far from his reach.

'Well, that was a silly thing to do,' Leo said. He picked it up and gave it back. Richard smiled, said, 'Whee!' and threw it down again, laughing like a drain.

Only an idiot would have failed to see that he was being fooled with, and Leo did see it. In his mind's eye, he also saw Lieutenant Day throwing the child about, playing with him, smiling at him. Did a six-month-old child really have the wit to play games, to see a joke? It seemed impossible, and yet . . .

He picked up the crust again and pretended to eat it. Richard widened his eyes, smiled, and held out his hand, wriggling his fingers with a certain authority, as if to say, 'No, not like that. Give it back, and I'll show you how it's done.' His smile was of the sort to charm birds off the trees, the look in his eyes not just innocent but intelligent, as if he'd played the same game before and knew all the rules. Leo gave the crust back and Richard held it out, grinning, as if to drop it again, a wicked sparkle in his eyes that made Leo laugh with astonishment.

In the cool, windowless passage between the kitchen and the dining room, Lydia stood with her fingers crossed, listening to every word, every chuckle. This was the first time Leo had spared the child more than a passing glance. He'd never spoken to him like this, never played with him, never acknowledged him as a person in his own right. Now . . . Oh, Lord, was the tide turning at last?

Richard let out another chortle. Lydia didn't know what he was doing – she'd tried peeping through the door-hinge but the dresser was blocking her view – she knew only that Leo was liking it, whatever it was, although he was doing his best to sound peeved. 'Hey, you're wearing me out! Are you trying to tell me something? You don't like bread, is that it?'

'Whee!'

'Well, don't blame your poor father, old man. I'd have steak on the menu if it was left to me. Speaking of which . . .'

There was a long pause, a whisper and a series of happy gurgles. Then, 'Come on, let's go and find my lunch and I'll throw it at *you* for a change.'

He'd taken Richard out of the chair! Lydia tiptoed away and turned at the end of the passage to make it seem as if she was just arriving, biting her lip as she heard the echo of the words, '*Don't blame your father*'. In the instant that she began to walk back to the kitchen, Leo appeared in the doorway with Richard in his arms. Richard had a grip on Leo's nose and was shouting, 'Gaga! Gaga!'

'I will be before long,' Leo said. 'Ah, here's your mother, come to rescue me at last. He says I've gone gaga. Think he's right?'

Lydia laughed. 'He's probably just trying to say Daddy. How was the car?' She didn't offer to take Richard from him and he didn't offer to pass him over. And he hadn't flinched at the name 'Daddy'.

'Seems fine. Really? Would he really be starting to talk at this age?'

Lydia smiled. 'Trying, anyway. They begin to learn to almost as soon as they're born.'

'No . . .' He frowned.

'Well, yes, in a way. That's why I talk to him all the time. He can't learn to speak if no one demonstrates the language, can he?'

Over lunch, when Richard had gone upstairs for his nap, Leo began to 'demonstrate the language' as he hadn't done since Richard's birth. He talked almost non-stop: first about the car, then about Ray Duckett and Lieutenant Day, and then, with his mouth full of rhubarb crumble, 'Why did you go to the Rectory, anyway?'

'I didn't. I was just passing and they were in the drive, looking at the car. The Rector . . .' She glanced under the table to hide the expression in her eyes. 'He asked me when we'd be having Richard christened. But he introduced me to Lieutenant Day before I could – er – think of an answer, and you know the rest.'

'No, I don't know the rest. When *are* we having him christened?'

'I – I don't know. I meant –'

'But he'll have to be christened, won't he? How do we go about it?'

'Oh, we'll have to throw a party!' Peggy said. 'How exciting! Who shall we have for godparents? And we'll need a cake, a christening gown . . . I've still got yours upstairs Leo, but its full of moth and anyway it'll be too small for Richard. You were done at two months. We had eighty-odd people here; the church was packed. But then, it was usually packed, in those days. That was the first year of the Great War, Lydia, when there were still a few men around. By the time poor Prue was christened, we had just a handful of widows and spinsters and nothing to eat. And here we are again.' She laughed shortly. 'Like being on a merry-go-round, isn't it?'

A tense silence fell. Leo was fingering the edge of his plate, apparently deep in thought. Lydia was thinking, too, but could scarcely get a grip on one idea before another crowded it out. Could they really have Richard christened? During the winter, they'd gone to church scarcely at all, and although he hadn't remarked on the fact, the Rector had given Lydia a very meaningful look when he'd asked about the christening, which had made her blush to the roots of her hair.

'Yes, but it's stopped,' Leo said.

'What has?'

'The merry-go-round.' He stood up and gave Lydia a look which reminded her uncomfortably of the Rector's, making her blush again. 'Come on,' he said. 'Walk back to the farm with me and we'll talk it over.'

He put his arm around her shoulder, the first time he'd touched her – except for those silly goodnight kisses – since Richard was born.

They went out by the front door and stood for a moment to admire the little car on the forecourt. Lydia's thoughts were still all over the place, jumping with excitement, apprehension and hope. But Leo was thinking clearly. His voice was firm and steady, his eyes bright, a little smile hovering at the corners of his mouth.

'My mother might be right,' he said. 'Maybe we are on a merry-go-round. But it's better to travel in circles than just sit and pine, isn't it?'

With her heart in her throat, Lydia nodded, thanking God.

'And you're too pretty to spend all your life at a standstill.' He kissed her and, as he drew away, grinning, with a smear of lipstick on his mouth, Lydia laughed, thanking Gran.

Chapter Eleven

Leo had been saying they must talk almost from the first, but somehow they'd never got around to it. There'd been no time, no privacy, and, on one side or the other, no inclination. They'd both, for their own reasons, been afraid to talk. But the subject of Richard's godparents opened a kind of sluice-gate on a river of words which continued flowing through Leo's mind even when Lydia was elsewhere, so that he spent most of his time making mental notes of the next thing to say – or to ask – when he saw her again.

They'd been married nearly ten months and he'd only now learned that she had friends! One in particular, an old school-friend who'd joined the Land Army and married a Hampshire farmer's son, was her choice for Richard's godmother. 'But I haven't written to her for ages.'

'Why not?'

'It's difficult to know what to say when you can't tell the truth about yourself.'

'Not even to your closest friend?' He narrowed his eyes, hating the thought.

She shrugged. 'My privacy is your privacy, too. And Rose has never been any good at keeping secrets.'

'I'd understand it better,' Leo said, 'if I knew . . . This Naval chap. You say you didn't love him, but . . .'

'He was a fantasy, Leo. I was bored. He was glamorous and full of fun. He took me dancing. I love dancing . . .'

'*Do* you?' He laughed and suddenly understood everything about the Naval chap, for when you dance with a well-matched partner, the sex act has already begun: an intoxication of mind and body, a merging of two minds, two bodies, in a union which, when it ceases, quite naturally leads to more.

'And I suppose I was curious,' Lydia went on despairingly. 'I was sixteen before I discovered that babies don't come from under a gooseberry bush and eighteen before I knew where they *really* came from. But Gran . . . She didn't encourage me to have boyfriends and when I did . . . Well, you know Gran. When I had my twenty-first birthday I decided to kick over the traces, enjoy myself . . .' She laughed dryly. 'And nothing happened. By the time Nigel came along I was like an over-ripe apple on a tree. He didn't have to pick me; just catch me as I fell. But I hardly knew him. I certainly didn't love him.' Lydia glanced at her husband, turning her mouth down at the corners before looking swiftly elsewhere. 'No happy memories, I assure you.'

'And it happened – how many times?'

'Once. In the back of an Austin Seven.'

'My God. How on earth . . .?'

'With his feet out of the window.' She turned to look at him again, half-smiling, dipping her head so that she viewed him through a screen of dark, curling lashes. The shadows had gone from under her eyes and her cheeks were the colour of wild roses. Leo realised suddenly that the reason he'd never before seen her like this was that he'd never before seen her *well*. She'd been pregnant, cold, tired, worried and over-worked. And, since Richard's birth, unloved and unsupported. Yet she'd pulled through it all and now . . .

'Do you hate me, Leo?'

'No,' he said softly. 'Not at all.'

'And can you really accept Richard? As if he were –'

'Mine? I don't know. He raises questions I've never asked before; never even thought about. Nothing to do with you or with him, but about . . . Well, myself. When you said you were enslaved to him, when you said he'd die if you weren't . . .' He sighed.

'Are you thinking about your mother?'

'Hmm. And my brother. *He* died. Did I tell you? I don't know much about it. My mother's never discussed it and my father . . . I did ask him, once, but it embarrassed him and he mumbled something about a chest infection. Pneumonia, I suppose, and just some ignorant nursemaid to look after him while my mother . . .' He sighed again. 'Oh, dear. This is deep water.'

'Your mother was there,' Lydia said firmly. 'She was with him, Leo. I know she was.'

He blinked. 'She's told you?'

'No. But if he was ill, she wouldn't have left him. I know she wouldn't. It would be impossible, an agony she couldn't bear. How long before you were born did he die?'

'Four years.'

'And doesn't that tell a tale? Of her grief, Leo? And if she never talks about it, surely that tells the same tale? Oh, if anything happened to Richard!' She turned away.

'But that's just my point. Nothing *will* happen to Richard, because you love him too much to let it.'

'Love is no match for pneumonia, Leo. Look, if you think I love Richard more than your mother loved you, it's an illusion, created by circumstances. When you were tiny, the house wasn't cold and damp; there was plenty to eat and someone to cook it and quite a few others to fight off all the dirt that can threaten a baby's life. I've had to *work* to keep him healthy. Your mother didn't. But that's the only difference, Leo, I promise you.'

He could see the sense of that and could almost believe her. But somehow didn't. His mother didn't like babies. She'd never even touched Richard. But then, neither had he, until he'd seen Lieutenant Day fooling with him, throwing him about, making him laugh. And that hadn't been anything to do with Leo's not *liking* babies. Just not understanding them. Perhaps that was his mother's difficulty, too.

Yet as soon as he told his mother that the christening was 'on' and that he'd written to ask two of his friends (one from his schooldays, one from prison camp) to stand godfather, he understood her difficulty precisely and wondered why the hell he hadn't guessed it before. She'd been sitting on the fence, waiting for him to decide which way he'd jump before committing herself. Almost within minutes of his picking the child up with the words, 'Come to Daddy,' *she* was suddenly the adoring 'Grandmama' who'd brought up two children of her own and knew *exactly* how it was done.

He should have known. She'd always been the same, yet somehow it always shocked him. She'd done the same thing with Floral. It had only gradually dawned on him, since Lydia had 'adopted' Floral, that his mother couldn't possibly have managed without her during the years after his father's death, that she'd been a tower of strength, not the alien parasite he'd thought her. Yet in the instant she'd registered his displeasure at Floral's presence in the house, his mother had denied all knowledge, just shrugged Floral off as being none of her business. 'If you don't like her, darling, tell her to go.' She'd probably known he wouldn't, but even so . . . Had she *no* sense of loyalty?

He felt inclined to warn Lydia not to trust her, before laughing at himself and shrugging it off. How could he say such a thing about his own mother? Had he *no* sense of loyalty?

Lydia understood Peggy scarcely better, after a year of knowing her, than on the day they'd first met. That she had depths – dark ones, at that, for what is darker than the death of one's firstborn? – was something Lydia had learned at second-hand. From the evidence Peggy herself gave, she existed entirely on the surface of life, rarely saying or doing anything of real use or importance. She'd begun knitting a matinee coat for Richard on the day he was born and, eight months later, she was still knitting it, although she was now saying it would do for Prue's baby, which was due in November. During the winter, she'd also worked part of a hearthrug, embroidered part of a tablecloth and sewn herself a new skirt, perfect in every particular except that it was two sizes too small.

The sheer waste of all this effort – not to mention precious materials – made Lydia grind her teeth, as did Peggy's profligate use of virtually everything else that was in short supply. Even when she offered to help – peeling potatoes or washing dishes – she did it so badly it was better when she didn't. Lydia sometimes suspected that she made a complete mess of 'helping' so that she wouldn't be expected to help again, but that was unfair; she was simply inept and in fact did many things to help which needed no skill at all. She and Floral took turns to queue at the shops, for example, a time-consuming, back-breaking procedure which Lydia was so grateful to be relieved of, she could forgive everything else.

And it was easy to forgive a woman who was so forgiving. Since that first day at the clinic she'd never uttered a word to Lydia of censure or blame and, even in ignoring Richard, seemed to bear him no ill-will. She wanted to enjoy life, regardless of its many griefs and sorrows, and although Lydia couldn't agree with her view that nothing was worth taking seriously, she appreciated it – and learned from it. In a way, Peggy was taking Gran's advice: *seeming* to win when in fact she wasn't running the race and didn't even know where the starting post was, let alone the finish!

'*Why* can't we have a party for the christening? It's just what we need, Lydia! Fun, company, conversation! And dancing. I adore dancing. So does Leo, but I suppose you've got two left feet?'

'No, I've the full complement of right and left, thank you.'

Peggy laughed and added in an aside to Floral, 'I can never tell when this girl's joking, can you?'

'But it'll be difficult enough to feed and house the godparents for the weekend, Peggy. What do we do about food and drink? Crockery and glasses? Or music, come to that. You can't dance without music.'

Peggy smirked. 'There's a string quartet in the village. Quite dreadful, of course, but *marvellously* funny. And there's a suite of

Waterford crystal and three dinner services in the cellar. Lionel put them there when war broke out.'

'Three *dinner* services? I've been wrestling with five cracked plates all this time and there are three dinner services in the cellar? Why didn't you tell me?'

'I'd quite forgotten them, darling. And as for food and drink, if you've plenty of the necessary . . .' She widened her eyes and rubbed her thumb against her fingers to indicate her meaning. 'Such things *can* be acquired, you know.'

A short hiatus followed this, while Lydia, first widening her eyes, then narrowing them, then blinking and looking at the wall, tried to think of a way of catering for a party *without* dabbling in crime. There wasn't one.

'You don't,' she said hollowly, 'by any chance, mean the black market, do you, Peggy?'

'Why not, for heaven's sake?'

'B-b-because . . . Because it's criminal!'

They were having tea on the terrace. Richard was sitting in his pram close by, bashing a small knitted teddy-bear with a large wooden rattle, at every bash letting out a wicked laugh that made him sound more like a lewd old man than a babe in arms.

Peggy reached out to rock the pram, smiled lovingly and said, 'No one's perfect, darling.'

Lydia's heartbeat quickened with a sickening lurch which made her aware of every pulse in her body. It wasn't because Peggy was turning the moral thumb-screw, but because she was doing it so cleverly, so subtly: simply changing her line of view from Lydia to Richard, saying, without saying anything in the least offensive, *After what you've done to me and Leo, you have no right to criticise.*

'We just want a little party,' she said now to Richard. 'Don't we, precious? We just want a little fun, don't we? What's so dreadful about that?'

Floral had wandered off, but Lydia clearly heard her saying, 'Be straight. Never tell her a lie,' and, for the first time, began to understand what it really meant. It didn't mean that Peggy was too good to tolerate lies. It meant that she'd use them as ammunition, shoot you down with them, tie you up with them, 'wind you round and round' until you were helpless to do anything except do as she said. A party. On the face of it, it wasn't much to ask. But the black market was illegal and, with food shortages worse than they'd ever been during the war, it was getting more illegal by the day.

'You could go to jail for it,' Lydia said.

'Nonsense. Who'd know?'

Lydia frowned. Who'd know? Was the woman crazy? She'd already dreamed up a guest list of fifty (not to mention the string quartet!) and she was asking who'd *know*?

But it didn't matter. Peggy's income didn't run to black-market prices and the only reason she was consulting Lydia was because she wanted her to cough up. But almost as soon as this thought crossed her mind, Peggy gave her another dig.

'I'd ask Leo – he adores parties – but wouldn't it be lovely to surprise him, darling? He'd be thrilled. It would make up to him for so much . . .' She smiled sadly. 'His poor father's death, Germany. Everything . . .' Her gaze turned again to Richard.

'How much?' Lydia asked softly.

Peggy shrugged. 'Fifty pounds should do it.'

Richard was beginning to grizzle and, silently thanking him for the distraction, Lydia unfastened his harness and took him out of the pram. 'Oh, you're wet, poor little soul . . . Won't be a minute, Peggy.'

He *was* wet, but not very, and as soon as Lydia had gained the house by the front door she left it again by the back, speeding around to the kitchen garden in the hope of finding Floral.

It took scarcely a minute to tell her the problem and only a second to hear the answer.

'Ask Leo.'

'She wants to surprise him.'

'Ask him.'

Lydia asked him as soon as he came home. He stared at her for a moment with narrowed eyes, inspected the kitchen ceiling for cobwebs and the floor for crumbs, blinked a few times and sighed, 'Where is she?'

'Laying the table.'

'Stay here a moment.'

He wandered through to the dining room. He left the doors open at both ends of the passage and Lydia tiptoed about her business with twitching ears, hoping to hear something that might tell her which way the wind blew. If Leo wanted to dabble in the black market there was nothing much she could do to stop him, except refuse to pay, and that would only create more trouble.

But she didn't hear a word and when, an hour later, they all sat down to supper, the subject wasn't raised. Peggy talked about some woman in the village who'd reupholstered her sitting-room furniture with marine canvas – twenty yards of it at ninepence a yard, off ration – which she'd dyed in her kitchen boiler. Lydia began to suspect that a plot was being hatched between mother and son that would exclude her entirely.

She spent the rest of the evening in a state of deep agitation, her feelings veering between hurt (which she had no right to feel), fury (likewise), and fear. She'd thought that she and Leo were at last reaching an understanding, getting over the worst. They'd talked more, this past month, than ever before; Leo had begun to take notice of Richard – and of Lydia. They'd even made love once or twice, rather tentatively and without much satisfaction on either side, but at least it was better than nothing. She'd *thought* it was better than nothing, but now wasn't so sure. Perhaps Leo and Peggy . . .

When she thought of the hurt she'd done them, Lydia could see that she had no right to expect anything of them but vengeance and, had they come straight out with it, she could have *coped* with vengeance. But Peggy was always so sweet, Leo always so gentle . . . She could suspect them until the cows came home, but without proof that they were working against her, she could do very little to defend herself. Or Richard . . .

It was still broad daylight when she went to bed at ten o'clock. Leo was hogging the bathroom, as usual – he took a solid five minutes just to clean his teeth – and, while she waited her turn, Lydia sat at the dressing table, brushing her hair. As he came through to the bedroom she saw him reflected in the glass; saw him shrug off his dressing gown to reveal a bare chest, furred down the middle with long, red-gold hair and a rib-cage which no longer looked like the picked bones of a rabbit. He was still as slim as a reed, but he wasn't skinny any more. His stomach was flat rather than hollowed out and the hard knobs of bone which had given his shoulders the look of a rustic coat-hanger, were now lightly padded with muscle, over which his skin shimmered like satin.

'You're gaining weight,' she said.

'Thanks to you.'

He laid his hands on her shoulders, gently stroking the back of her neck with his thumbs. It was a possessive, masterful caress, delicious when there was nothing else to think about, but disconcerting in the extreme when Lydia already felt under threat. 'We *could* have a party, you know,' he murmured. 'Might be a good move.'

'Oh?'

'Mother's bored. And when she's bored . . . She's like a child, Lydia. She gets mischievous. Doesn't mean any harm; just can't help it.'

Lydia turned to look at him.

'That party you threw for the vicar . . . I forget his name. You had plenty of food for that, didn't you? How did you get it?'

'Not on the black market,' Lydia said warily. 'Everyone brought something: sandwiches, cakes, jellies, cups and plates and spoons. It's . . . the way it's done nowadays.'

'Then why couldn't we do it that way?'

Lydia sighed. 'Have you seen Peggy's guest list? I don't think she's included the Royal Family, but everyone else . . .' She sighed again. '*Can* you ask Lord and Lady Moreton to bring their own sandwiches?'

Leo laughed and dived into bed. 'Why not? I was at school with Eddie Moreton. He's human, darling. And his sandwiches will probably be bloater-paste, like everyone else's.'

Lydia smiled at last. 'That's true.'

'And it'll be fun. We need some fun, Lydia. Come on, darling.' He patted the bed invitingly, crinkling his eyes as he hadn't done for months. 'Let's start now, shall we?'

It was an invitation Lydia couldn't resist.

When Leo met Douglas White from the train in Trowbridge, his life – or, rather his mind – fell into order for the first time in eighteen months. Douglas had changed a good deal since Germany; like Leo, he'd gained some weight and looked generally healthier, happier and more relaxed, but as their eyes met and their hands clasped in the age-old gesture of friendship, it was as if no time had passed at all. They understood each other and, in understanding that, Leo knew that half his problems – in fact, most of them – had arisen from loneliness. He and Doug – and quite a few other men – had dwelt together in a unique corner of hell which could not be imagined by, and certainly not discussed with, anyone else. Now, for the first time, he felt that he'd really come home.

'You've moved fast, old man,' Douglas teased as they drove back to Molliston. 'A wife and child, the farm, a motor car . . . Nice little bus, too. You found your feet before I'd even caught my breath.'

'Good Lord, I haven't exactly organised it, Doug. It just . . .' He took his hands off the steering wheel to mime the effect of being bombarded by falling rocks. 'It just happened.' It was against the rules of civilised conduct to say that Lydia – and everything that had come with her – had been a mistake he would rue all his days, but he didn't need to say it. Douglas understood.

His worst fear was that his friend wouldn't like Lydia; that he'd think her cold and – worse – unwelcoming. He didn't much care if Lydia didn't like Douglas, but if she showed it . . . Oh, she wouldn't exactly *show* it. She was too polite for that; but she was so damn good at hiding her feelings, it would amount to the same thing in the end. And if she made Douglas feel unwanted, if she made him feel he couldn't come to Molliston again . . . One thing Leo had always been able to expect from his mother was a warm, uncritical welcome for his friends, but Lydia was different. When a woman has cheated, disguised herself as effectively as Lydia always had, one couldn't depend on her for anything.

They talked about Doug's job – he was an engineer – and about Leo's work at Manor Farm for the rest of their short drive home, but even while he was explaining the finer points of pig-keeping, Leo's heart was racing with a strange kind of terror. Doug was here to stand godfather to a child he thought was Leo's, and if Lydia didn't show him the honour and respect he deserved . . .

'My God!' Doug gasped as they crunched (rather too speedily) up the drive. 'This is Molliston? You said –'

'What?'

'You said it was small! Leo, it's wonderful!'

He couldn't have said anything more soothing, and since he went on saying it – in several different ways – for the next few minutes, Leo's heartrate had almost returned to normal by the time Lydia came out to meet them. She was smiling and wearing Leo's favourite dress: the white one with red roses which, with her dark hair and eyes, made her look like a Spanish dancer.

'This is Lydia, my wife.'

He'd fully intended to make the proper introductions, but before he could continue, his wife took his friend gently in her arms and kissed his cheek. 'Douglas, how lovely to meet you.' Her voice was as husky as ever, but there was a warmth in it which almost broke Leo's heart, so that, had he not laughed, he was certain he'd have cried. Strangely enough, he felt rather proud of her. Even more strangely, he felt an odd pang of jealousy, for Lydia was actually flirting with Doug, showing off that crescent-shaped dimple at the corner of her mouth which, so far, had been Richard's exclusive preserve. She was never this warm with her husband.

And yet it was absolutely the right thing to do. Although in many ways tougher than Leo, Douglas was deeply sensitive to hidden undercurrents and had Lydia played it any other way, he'd have spent the entire weekend on the alert, working things out and, ultimately, realising that things weren't as they should be. It was the last thing Leo wanted. The two men had talked so much about their ideals – of happiness, of morality, of everything they wanted to aspire to (including, in Leo's case, a blonde wife with curves!) – and it would

131

be more than he could bear if Douglas were to know he'd turned his back on all of it.

'How's he treating you?' Doug teased now, in response to something Lydia had said which Leo hadn't quite caught. And again Lydia said exactly the right thing.

'*Horribly.*' With a delicious chuckle. 'But I'm getting used to it. Now, come indoors and meet your godson while I put the kettle on.'

Everything went well after that, although Leo was aware throughout the rest of the day that he was seeing his wife through Doug's eyes, assessing her as he might a complete stranger, in fact, assessing her exactly as he assessed Rose Hutchinson, a blonde with curves and big, innocent blue eyes: the girl of his dreams.

She arrived in time for tea, complaining about standing room only on the train, complaining about the weather, and then, to Leo's displeasure, saying that Molliston was too big, too old-fashioned, too difficult to keep clean. Lydia had produced an extraordinary tea of tiny oatmeal buns, cucumber tarts and fresh raspberries in jelly, and Rose spent the entire feast complaining about the bread ration. (Tea wasn't tea without sandwiches, apparently.)

Lydia smiled through it all, graceful, gentle and humorous. She was efficient, brisk and capable. She was intelligent and well-informed, discussing politics with Doug, gardening and poultry-keeping with Rose, literature and music, history and motor mechanics, horses and cookery . . .

'How do you know all that about the Labour Party?' Leo asked as they crashed, exhausted, into bed that night.

Lydia smiled and closed her eyes for sleep. 'I read a book once,' she mumbled.

'What was it called? *Everywoman's Guide to Every Damn Thing?*'

'Oh, you read it, too?'

He reached out to stroke her hair. 'You were wonderful. I was proud of you.'

She didn't reply and, after waiting long enough to be sure that no reply was forthcoming, he hoisted himself up on his elbow to kiss her goodnight. Her face was wet with tears.

Lydia had been exhausted even before the weekend began. Even with only two guests in the house, the difficulty of providing sufficient food, comfortable beds (thank God it was too warm for anyone to need more than one blanket), hot water and a few dozen other comforts, had run her ragged with work and anxiety. She didn't mind too much about Rose who, in spite of her tendency to find fault with everything, was in fact too easy-going to think anything truly *wrong*.

She could have been housed in the woodshed or the best guest room at Windsor Castle and still found *something* to complain about.

Douglas was different. He was Leo's friend and must be treated with the utmost care and consideration, not really for his own sake, but just *because* he was Leo's friend. Lydia knew very little about male friendships, but guessed that this one was extra-special just because they'd been thrown together in the worst of circumstances – as prisoners-of-war – supporting each other when they'd each been at their lowest ebb. A kind of love, perhaps; and Lydia knew that if she loved – or at least tried to love – those whom Leo loved, there was a chance, ultimately, that Leo would love *her*.

But it was hard work. Douglas was a sweet man, but too quiet to be easy, and Lydia's skills as a hostess had been learned more from her grandmother's book of etiquette than from practical experience. Also, she'd been a guest herself, and remembered how many odd little things could make the difference between feeling comfortable or wanting desperately to go home. Hunger was the worst of them, and with the bread ration cut to one slice per person per day and the meat ration almost non-existent, it was the hardest one to avoid. But Floral's fruit and vegetable garden was in full production and there were rabbits and mushrooms aplenty. Leo shot the rabbits. Floral picked the mushrooms, dug the potatoes and picked the fruit and vegetables. All Lydia had to do was to work like a donkey and try not to act – or look – like one.

She had no real idea – was too tired to judge – how well she was doing until, on the first night, Leo said he was proud of her – and then she wanted to hit him for his rotten timing. She'd been feeling quite strong, and then she just melted inside and dissolved into tears of relief, gratitude, and a resolution to do even better the next day. The worst day. Richard was being christened at three o'clock (lunch at one), with tea and cake to be served immediately afterwards to Rector, godparents and family. At four, the rest of the guests would begin to arrive with their 'picnics', and after that ... After that, Peggy would have to take charge. Lydia hadn't a clue how to organise a party!

She went through her own part in the day's proceedings in a state verging on trance, following the lists of instructions she'd written for herself to the absolute letter, noticing nothing except that nothing much went wrong. Her grandmother sat with Richard when he went upstairs for his post-christening nap. Lydia washed, changed, did her hair and make-up and then, trembling slightly, went downstairs, wishing she could run away and hide until it was over.

As she went through to the great hall, Leo walked in from the terrace, wearing his demob suit (which looked much better now that he had real shoulders under the shoulder pads), a white shirt, starched collar and his regimental tie.

He tipped his head to one side, apparently inspecting her outfit, an ancient frock of silk georgette in a dull pink called 'Ashes of Roses'. Floral had made a new collar for it in cream satin cut from an equally ancient petticoat, and a string of pearls, in Lydia's opinion, had finished it off quite nicely; but when Leo tipped his head the other way, dipping a critical eyebrow, she began to have doubts.

'What's wrong?' she asked nervously.

'You took the words out of my mouth.'

'The dress?'

'Is lovely. So why do you look so scared? The worst is over, surely? You've done everything that needs to be done.'

'I suppose I'm shy. You'll know everyone and I . . .'

Peggy was settling her string quartet in the drawing room with a horrible caterwauling of tuning which, by a miracle, suddenly developed into the opening bars of the 'Skaters' Waltz'. Leo grinned. He said, 'May I have this dance, Mrs Chantry?' and drew her into his arms. He danced beautifully, gliding on his toes, holding her in an embrace at once so firm and so gentle it was as if he'd melted her bones. They danced through the hall, the kitchen, the dining room, the inner hall and back again to their starting point, by which time they were both laughing, and the guests had begun to arrive.

'Still shy?' Leo grinned.

No, Lydia wasn't shy. She had a funny feeling that this was going to be the happiest night of her life.

Chapter Twelve

In the frosty days of November, Leo spent most of his spare time sawing wood. He'd thinned the stand of conifers behind the tennis court as soon as the harvest was in; Floral had denuded the felled trees of twigs and small branches and tied them (with a little help from Peggy) into 'faggots' for kindling, and now Leo was stacking logs against another winter. The woodshed was full; there was a stack of logs almost as big again in the garage and a ton of coal, accumulated gradually during the summer months, was still virtually untouched. Even if they had another hard winter, they would not be as cold as they'd been last year.

Still, it was already getting chilly and despite his work with saw and wheelbarrow, Leo was glad to go home to get his hands and feet warm and grab a cup of tea before milking. He found Lydia in the parlour, knitting a small greyish-blue thing he vaguely recognised as being one of his mother's projects.

'What's that?'

'Your mother's knitting. She finished it last night. One of the fronts was twice as long as the other, so I'm re-making it. It was either that –' she shuddered '– or burn it.'

He laughed. 'Wouldn't that have been wiser? It's filthy.'

'It can be washed. And Prue's baby's due any day now. It'll be nice for Peggy to give her something she's made herself.'

'Wasn't it meant to be for Richard?'

'He grew out of it before she'd finished casting on.' She smiled down at her fast-growing son, who was sitting at her feet, happily beating a cushion with the back of a wooden spoon.

Leo stooped to ruffle his hair – 'What's that poor cushion done to you?' – and stretched out in an armchair to warm his feet by the fire.

'What's happening about tea?' he asked idly. 'I'll have to go in half an hour.'

'Peggy's doing it. It's a swap for the knitting. She wouldn't take no for an answer.'

'Oh, dear . . .'

Lydia chuckled but, typically, said nothing else. That Peggy sometimes stretched her patience to its limits was a fact Leo recognised, and that Lydia rarely mentioned it was a blessing he appreciated, for there was nothing he could do about it. His mother was over sixty and too old to change.

He closed his eyes, wiggled his toes and listened to the peaceful sounds of Sunday afternoon: the click of knitting needles, the hiss of resinous logs burning in the grate, the solemn tick of the long-case clock in the corner. He didn't notice a dearth of other sounds until Lydia whispered, 'Leo, look . . .'

He opened his eyes. Richard had abandoned his attack on the cushion and was now standing up, creeping slowly sideways along the padded front edge of the couch. He looked rather solemn, frowning, his mouth pursed with concentration. Only last week, Lydia had been worrying that he was showing no sign of wanting to crawl: put him on the floor and he just sat there, as if he'd been glued to the rug. But now, to all intents and purposes, he was walking!

'Walk to Daddy,' Lydia said calmly.

'He's done this before?' Leo asked incredulously.

'He's never got this far, before. Call him. Hold out your hand and see if . . .'

Leo reached out his arms and called softly, 'Richard. Here. Come to Daddy.'

Richard laughed and sat down very suddenly on his well-padded behind.

'Oh, dear,' Lydia soothed. 'Try again, darling. Go to Daddy.'

Richard tried three more times, but eventually, grinning, he pushed himself off from the couch and took two tottering steps into Leo's outstretched arms.

'Hey! You walked!' He swung him through the air, planted a few kisses on his head and sat down again, holding him on his knee. 'You'll be playing cricket next, I suppose,' he joked, and suddenly saw a picture of a school cricket ground with Richard (much taller than he was now and minus his nappy) leading the batting. 'I'd better put his name down for school,' he said thoughtfully. 'Daren't leave it too late.'

Lydia laughed. 'He's only ten months old. Give him a chance.'

'Most people do it as soon as they're born, darling.'

'Only for places like Harrow and Eton, though, surely?'

'And Winchester.' He tickled Richard's ribs, making him scream

136

with laughter. 'Want to go to Daddy's school?'

Peggy came in with the tea-tray and the subject of Richard's education was forgotten. Forgotten entirely by Leo, but, as he realised as soon as he got into bed that night, not at all by Lydia.

'Did you mean what you said about Richard?'

'What did I say?'

'School.'

'Oh . . . Yes. If you remind me tomorrow night, I'll –'

'I don't want to send him away to school. There are plenty of good schools nearer home where he could be a day boy.'

Lydia was still sitting at her dressing table, doing the things she did before bed: brushing her hair, creaming her face and hands, peering intently into the glass as if in search of changes in her physiognomy which might have occurred since the last time she'd looked.

'It depends what you call a good school,' he said. 'A *really* good school gives one rather more than a sound grounding in geography, darling.'

Lydia's chin went up. 'Nevertheless, it's not what I *want* for Richard. I want –'

The emphasis she'd placed on the word 'want' annoyed Leo, opened up wounds he'd been trying very hard to heal.

'And what you want you get,' he said quietly.

Lydia's head snapped around, her eyes wide, her lips parted as if to gasp for breath.

'But you can't have it all ways, Lydia,' he went on steadily. 'You wanted me to accept him as my son. I've done that. And now, as his father, *I* will decide how best to educate him.'

'That's not fair! Even if he *was* your son, I wouldn't want to send him to boarding school! It's nothing to do with –'

'Me?'

'No! I was going to say it's nothing to do with who his father is! All right, he's your son, but he's mine, too! Don't my opinions count?'

This was the nearest they'd ever come to a real quarrel, and it was exactly as Leo had imagined it would be. Lydia's eyes were blazing, but her voice was pitched even lower than usual, her diction more clipped and precise. She was furious, yet in perfect control of herself, while Leo – with thudding heart, a tremor in his stomach and the eternal threat of getting his tongue in a knot at the critical moment, was not at all sure he could hold out for victory. Yet he was aware that their whole lives depended on his winning this argument, somehow. *She* could insist that Richard went to a day school just because *he* hadn't the means to send him elsewhere, and the same would be true of their next son: *his* son. Well, he wouldn't stand for that.

'Of course your opinions count,' he said, 'if they're informed opinions. But in this case your opinion can't be informed. You were never a boy and you didn't go to a boarding school, so how can you know anything about it?'

'I was never a boy,' Lydia conceded. 'As for the rest . . .'

'Boys need different things, Lydia. They need –'

'Love and security!' she snapped. 'The support of their family! And you, of all people, are informed enough to know *that*!'

This, Leo decided, was 'knife in the back' stuff (he should never have mentioned his doubts about his mother) that could only be countered with more of the same.

'The support of your family is something you've always been able to depend on, I suppose? Being educated at home gave you that, did it?'

'Yes!'

'Then why did you need to marry me?'

Lydia's mouth closed very suddenly and she clamped her teeth over her bottom lip to keep it from trembling.

'They'd have disowned you, wouldn't they?' Leo asked softly.

She bowed her head. 'That's not the point.'

'Yes, it is. It's the basis of your entire argument, and it's let you down dismally. Sorry, darling.' He turned over, giving his pillows an extra-hard thump by way of punctuation. 'My sons go to Winchester.'

'You can't just –!'

'Yes, I can. Love, honour and obey, remember?'

'You said you didn't want that!'

'I've changed my mind.'

A long and extremely tense silence followed, during which Leo pretended to compose himself for sleep while fully expecting Lydia to throw something at him. Or, worse, ask him how he proposed to pay for 'his sons' to go to Winchester at a fee, per son, which would consume his entire annual income.

Nothing happened. She sighed. Then, in a small, submissive voice, 'How old will he be?'

'What?' He turned to face her and found her looking at him with a smile which had very little of 'submission' about it and a fair amount of mischief. And she was right, of course. How old would Richard be when he went to Winchester? Thirteen. And today he'd walked his first steps at exactly ten months old!

Leo bit his cheek to suppress a grin. 'That's beside the point,' he said. 'Start as you mean to go on, that's my policy.'

'Evidently.' She turned her head to hide her smile in the lapel of her dressing gown, exposing her throat and the tender line of her jaw. She looked beautiful: young, pale and fragile, yet curiously strong. Wise, too, for she knew that any damn thing could happen during the next twelve years. Winchester – and Molliston – could have been blown off the surface of the earth by then. It wasn't worth arguing about.

Leo laughed. 'Oh, all right,' he said. 'I will put his name down, but if you still feel the same twelve years from now, he can go to a day school. How's that?'

Lydia slid into bed beside him and ran a seductive thumb over his lips, her hand over his chest and, deliciously, her fingers under the loosely tied knot of his pyjama cord. 'Seems to cover everything,' she said. And turned off the light.

At eighteen months, Richard could scale the bars of his cot, his playpen and the staircase. Take your eyes off him for a minute and he'd next be found in the coal cellar or halfway up the stairs. Although he could say 'Mummy', 'Daddy', 'Gamma' and 'Floral' (which he pronounced 'Fofo') and a few dozen other words which only Lydia knew from Double-Dutch, his favourite word was 'No', or, if pressed, 'No, sanchoo.'

'Eat up your porridge, darling.'

'No! No, sanchoo.'

'Time for bed, Richard.'

'No, no, no! No!'

He ran her ragged. He tested her energy and her patience further than she'd ever thought either could go. He was as tough as old rope: rarely cried (if he did, he was either ill or furious) and laughed a good deal more than he had any right to – usually when he'd done something to frighten the life out of his mother. She realised very quickly that he was clever and that half of his mischief was the result of boredom, but keeping him entertained and out of danger was more than she could manage if she was also to keep Molliston running at its usual steady pace.

She and Floral had devised a system for ridding the house of its dirt on a monthly basis, with the main rooms and stairs cleaned in a weekly routine and the kitchen and bathrooms getting a daily once-over. Laundry and ironing, cooking and shopping, had also to be fitted in, as had the tending of the kitchen garden; but on the day Richard climbed out of his playpen for the first time, the entire system went to blazes and chaos reigned. Leo, who always came

139

home ravenous, waited hours for his meals, turned out the laundry basket (with a bewildered, almost tearful expression on his face) in search of a clean shirt, searched the house for his car keys (which Richard had hidden in his toy-box), and finally, for the first time in Lydia's experience, lost his temper. With his mother.

It began calmly enough with his asking Peggy what she was doing to help – and when she replied, truthfully enough, that she was re-making the drawing-room curtains (which, having removed the rotten bits, she'd been doing all summer), he hit the roof. He said something about the ironing (which was dear to his heart), something about the cooking (even dearer), something about the total irrelevance of drawing-room curtains, and something else about knitting and the French Revolution, which neither Lydia nor Peggy understood. During this diatribe he said 'damn' three times and 'bloody' twice, which was upsetting enough, because he so rarely swore, but when he roared, 'You cheat Diggler like a double slave and I won't slander it!' and stormed out of the house, she guessed he was pretty well beside himself and that something would have to be done.

Peggy went on sewing. Except to explain about the curtains, she hadn't said a word in reply to Leo's accusations, but now she remarked idly, 'You're both utterly stupid.'

'What?'

'I knew as soon as you began that you'd live to regret it. There's only one way to survive in a house like this without a proper staff, and that's to maintain the lowest possible standards. Cobwebs don't kill you. Neither does dirt, within reason. And when food is hard to get and harder to prepare, it should be a means to stave off hunger, not the ridiculous meal *you* make of it. I have not treated you like a slave, Lydia – if that's what he was trying to say – I've let you go your own way just because I knew it was futile to try to stop you. But now you've set the standard, the least you can do is find an easier way of maintaining it. You're like your husband, I'm afraid: all brawn and no brain.'

'Oh!' Still reeling from Leo's explosion, Lydia was in no state to cope with this, which seemed a trifle unjust, to say the least.

'There are women in the village,' Peggy said. She seemed to say it apropos of something else, but then she sighed and wandered away, leaving her curtains, typically, in a heap on the floor.

She was gone for almost three hours. When she came back, she had company. Her name was Doris Lodge. She had three children and a husband disabled by leg ulcers. She lived two miles outside the village and had worked, until recently, in a factory in Trowbridge, but the demands of husband and family had made her late for work once too often and now she was three weeks behind with her rent. In spite of all these problems, she was dignified and precise and clearly intended to stand for no nonsense from Lydia.

'I've got me bike,' she said firmly. 'An' if you lets me come and go to suit Mr Lodge and the kiddies, I can give you six hours a day, five days a week. I can clean, wash, iron, sew and plain cook. I'm strong an 'elfy. I keeps meself to meself – an' I wants three pound ten a week, with overalls. So?'

Weak with relief (and shame: why hadn't *she* thought of this?), Lydia smiled and said, 'So when can you start?'

Throughout this rather one-sided interview, Peggy had kept very quiet, leaving everything to Lydia, but when Mrs Lodge had gone (promising to start tomorrow), she smiled, tipped her head to one side and said softly, 'I sometimes forget you're just a child.'

'I'm twenty-four!' Lydia said indignantly.

'Quite. I'd . . . had a baby when I was twenty-four, but I'd never done anything else.' She closed her eyes. 'You're so capable, darling.'

'Oh, Peggy . . . Peggy, I didn't complain to Leo, really I –'

'I know. But you seem to do everything so well, and the best things you've done, although I doubt if either of you realises it, is to make yourself indispensable to Leo. You've made him feel safe. I suppose that was why he was so angry. Disorder frightens him, while I barely notice it and would be quite as happy to live in a slum as in a palace. It broke his heart to come home from Germany and find everything . . .' She put her fingers to her mouth. 'My fault.'

'Nonsense,' Lydia said softly. 'I was brought up to work. You can't do what you've never been taught, Peggy, and *I* wasn't taught to hire servants, so you've done something marvellous for me today. It hadn't even crossed my mind.'

She'd kissed her mother-in-law only once – on her wedding day, when kissing appeared to be the done thing, bearing little relation to how one truly felt – but now she really wanted to kiss her, and did: a light peck on the cheek, a little hug, a warm: 'Thank you.' But Peggy seemed upset. She patted Lydia's arm and hurried away, muttering about the curtains.

Once she'd found her way around, Mrs Lodge solved a great many problems and created only one, although it kept itself under wraps until, on a fine day in October, Lydia found Floral weeping over the last of the autumn digging.

'Floral! What on earth is the matter?'

She sniffed, wiped her nose on the sleeve of her jersey and said, '*Well* . . .!' as if that explained it all. She carried on digging but there

141

was a furtive look about her, as if she half-expected someone to sneak up on her from behind.

'It's that Doris,' she said at last. 'Her an' her . . .'

'Her what?'

Floral sniffed again. It sounded dreadful, like three gallons of soapy water spiralling down a drain. '*Wages*!' she cried.

'Oh! But you said you didn't want to be paid! Oh, Floral, if you want to be paid, I'll . . .'

'I don't! It's not that! It's just . . . Well, I fought I wuz earnin' me keep, helping you wiv the house, and now . . .' She bowed her head. 'What use am I now?'

'Oh,' Lydia said, thinking on her feet. 'I didn't realise you liked the housework so much, Floral. I thought Mrs Lodge would free you for more important things.'

'What important things? Once I've dug this over, there won't be nothing to do till March!'

'But I've got millions of things to do. Cleaning out the gallery, making loose covers, preparing for Christmas, planting a new orchard. How can I possibly do it all without you? And you know we've never yet turned the library out. I'd hoped you'd help with that.'

Floral swallowed and leaned on her spade. 'Really?'

Except for the loose covers (the marine canvas idea had stuck in Lydia's mind ever since she'd heard of it) the bulk of all this 'important work' had come out of nowhere, shocking Lydia almost as much as it had surprised Floral. True, it all needed to be done, but she'd hoped to put it off more or less indefinitely. Now she couldn't.

'Loose covers first,' she said. 'We'll need a sewing machine, which is rather like saying we need a hundredweight of diamonds. Think we can find one?'

'We can try,' Floral grinned.

As she walked back to the house, leading Richard on his walking rein and stopping at every third step to inspect grass, woodlice, sticks, stones and everything else that existed at ground level, Lydia wondered what Floral had meant with her impassioned cry of: 'Wages!' Money must be a problem for her. She had board and lodging provided, but still needed a few dozen other things to keep body and soul together and seemed to be acquiring none of them. Her clothes were next-door to rags, her shoes in holes . . .

'Hmm,' she said. 'Come on, Richard. Let's talk to Fofo again.'

They sat on the remains of an old stone bench, Lydia with her hands in her lap, Floral pleating her skirt nervously with tiny, dirt-engrained fingers, Richard at their feet, trying his hardest to tie Lydia's shoelaces together.

'It's a matter of mathematics,' Lydia said.

'Oh, Gawd, I never could do sums.'

'Neither could I.' Lydia smiled. 'But I had a sudden brainwave. It was what you said about earning your keep. You've always done a good deal more than Mrs Lodge does for her three pounds ten a week. Cleaning, gardening, shopping, nursing . . . If you'd been paid for it, you'd have earned four or five pounds a week.'

'Nah!' Floral shrieked with laughter.

'Oh, yes. But even if it had only been three pounds a week, with board and lodging deducted, I'd still owe you thirty shillings a week, wouldn't I?'

'You'd never!' But as Floral's eyes brightened at the thought, it was as if the past six years of work and insecurity fell away from her, ironing out the weather-beaten lines from her face so that she looked almost young again. For the hundredth time, Lydia fought down the urge to ask, '*How* old are you?' (Forty-five? Sixty-five?) But smiled instead and said only, 'That's settled, then. Come on, Richard. Time for lunch.'

It was extraordinary what an enormous difference a little money made. A few pounds here, a few pounds there, and suddenly Leo lived in a spotless house, with a beautiful wife, a happy child and glorious meals served dead on time. Perhaps 'glorious' wasn't quite the word to describe mock-fish (otherwise known as parsnips), mock-steak (haricot beans) and mock-figgy-duff (prunes), but since there was plenty of it and it tasted fine, Leo had nothing much to complain of.

The only thing he still, at times, absolutely hated about Lydia (and hated himself for hating) was her way of taking everything so seriously. She was the absolute antithesis of his mother, and while Leo had no wish at all to be married to someone like his mother, he would have preferred a happy medium: someone who did the best she could to be organised and responsible without thinking it the end of the world if some little thing went wrong. Not that she ever made a fuss (he'd have preferred it if she had); she just seemed to retreat into a state of concentrated calm which reminded him of men going into battle, their every thought and feeling centred on getting the job done and, with any luck, coming out of it alive.

The household accounts were a case in point. Leo gave Lydia sufficient cash to pay for food, fuel and clothing and trusted her to use it as she saw fit, without ever needing to mention it again. But on the last Sunday of every month she brought him her accounts, with every damn thing set out fair and square ('1 yd elastic . . . £0-0s-2d')

143

and neatly totalled at the end. He could have coped better with this if she had not also presented him with Molliston's accounts – the expenditure of her *own* money which, in spite of the difficulty of finding anything to spend it on, she still, somehow, managed to spend in amounts that made his toenails curl. He didn't want to know. He *told* her he didn't want to know.

'Nevertheless,' she'd say firmly, 'I'd rather you did.' And then sit with him and explain away every confounded penny as if its mysterious disappearance would bring down the government.

Many of the things she did for Molliston were things to make life safe for Richard: gates at the top and foot of the main stairs, a new lock for the door of the cellar, bars at the window of the nursery. To be fair to her, Molliston was not an especially safe playground for an adventurous child: there were death-traps everywhere you looked and Leo was especially concerned about the stone baluster at the edge of the terrace which needed a month's work from a master stone-mason to make it safe (and no stone-mason could be found with that much time to spare). But Lydia's understandable anxiety about these things was also carried over to the *little* things, things that could matter only in a perfect world: a sprig of parsley to make a parsnip look more like a haddock, a button missing so low down on his shirt-front that, even before it fell off, he'd never bothered to fasten it. She carried a little notepad around with her and wrote endless lists of things to do, to buy, to make enquiries about, or even to transfer to other notebooks, other lists.

Leo suspected that at least half of it was his own fault. He'd been too appreciative of her efficiency and – on one embarrassing occasion – too obviously displeased when it failed. Even now, he didn't really want her to be less efficient, just less serious about it. Life had never seemed worth living, to Leo, if one couldn't see the funny side of things. Lydia was by no means a misery: she smiled her polite little smile, laughed at Richard's antics, at Leo's jokes, and (more rarely) at comedy programmes on the wireless. But she couldn't laugh at life's little ironies – rain, power cuts, Richard wetting his pants just when she thought she'd got him toilet-trained – and without that ability she created an atmosphere of tension which Leo and, more especially, Peggy, found hard to live with.

About a week before Christmas (which Lydia had organised down to the last paper-chain, sage-leaf and currant), Leo came home to supper as usual, went upstairs for his bath as usual, and was met, not at all as usual, by his mother, who was standing in the shadows on the landing with a finger pressed guiltily to her lips.

'Ssh,' she whispered, and then, 'Eddie Moreton rang. He wanted you, but since you weren't here, we talked ... And before I knew what I was doing I invited them here for Christmas! What am I going to do, darling? I can't possibly retract the invitation, but on the other hand ...' Her face fell into a despairing grimace.

'Have you told Lydia?'

'No! She'll attack me with a hatchet!'

He raised an eyebrow. 'Has she done that sort of thing before, Mother?'

'There's a first time for everything. And four extra mouths to feed ...'

'*Four*?' Leo howled.

'Oh, *hush*! Yes, there's Helen, Eddie and his mother ... and Helen's brother's staying with them. They can't leave *him* behind, now can they?'

Imagining the look on Lydia's face when she heard all this, Leo could only groan, 'Oh, Mother, Mother, what on earth made you *do* it? Don't you ever *think*?'

'I did think, darling, but not – quite – beyond the haunch of venison. It's all they've got, poor things.' She smiled wickedly. 'That and a cellar full of burgundy, of course.'

Leo stared at her, torn between laughter and tears. Lydia had invited her father and grandmother (who'd bring a chicken and a cake), with Prue, Gerald and their baby daughter (plum pudding and elderberry wine), yet even with these contributions added to Lydia's carefully garnered store of provisions, it threatened to be a rather thin, drab sort of Christmas. A haunch of venison ... burgundy ... And Eddie Moreton, even without the burgundy, would certainly hone the conversational edges of old Mrs Westley and bloody boring Gerald ...

'Right,' he said. 'Leave it to me, Mother.'

She chuckled softly. 'Now don't be too masterful, darling, or she might attack you with a hatchet, too. Break it to her gently. After all, *she'll* have to cook the venison.'

Lydia had had two pretty dreadful Christmasses at Molliston. For the first she'd been too pregnant (and terrified) either to cope or to care, and for the second too inexperienced to make the proper preparation. But this year, for more than one reason, it was going to be the best Christmas *ever*. In a few small ways she'd been preparing for it since August, when she'd begun to squirrel away her scant rations of dried fruit and sugar for a bonanza of cakes and puddings. In September she'd gathered hazel-nuts, sweet chestnuts and a marvellous crop of walnuts from the tree behind the barn. She'd collected poppy seed-boxes and teazles for decorations, identified where the best holly trees grew and where to find mistletoe. And there was a Christmas tree . . .

She felt wonderful about the Christmas tree; not only because it would be such a treat for Richard, but because Lydia had never had one as a child. Gran thought they were messy and worse than messy – *pagan* – just as the holly and mistletoe were. Lydia couldn't deny it, for they were also magical, and Gran had never had much time for magic. Duty, dignity, patience . . . All good things, but oh, they did need a little *magic* to brighten them up!

But there was more magic about this Christmas than a mere bunch of greenery could supply. Lydia had missed two periods. She was expecting Leo's baby; and although the new jersey she'd knitted him would be a nice enough gift, the baby was going to be her real Christmas offering. Gran already knew. She'd known before Lydia had and, this time, had given her the cure for morning sickness as well as the diagnosis! All you needed to do was to eat a little breakfast before you brushed your teeth, which, when you were feeling queasy on an empty stomach, was the equivalent of putting a finger down your throat.

'Gran! Why didn't you tell me that the first time?'

'You didn't ask.'

Fair enough . . . But her happiness at the idea of being pregnant had been too much for Gran to resist, and she'd asked Lydia an unprovoked personal question for almost the first time in her life.

'Do you love him, my dear?'

'Yes. It's not . . . At least, I don't know what it's like to be *in* love; I don't know if it's *that* . . . But I do love him. He's been so good to me, Gran. If I live a thousand years, I'll never be able to repay him. And he's so sweet with Richard. He plays with him and cuddles him and teaches him – when he'll sit down long enough, that is. And if he can love Richard so much, how will he be with a child of his own? He'll be so happy, Gran.' She'd positively smirked when she thought of it. 'Oh, Lord, I'm going to make him *happy*.'

But she had to get this Christmas organised first. She'd ordered a goose from Mrs Duckett, who'd been fattening three – one for the fox! The presents were all wrapped. She still had to pick the holly (Floral would help), and get the spare bedroom aired for Prue and Gerald. But apart from that . . .

There was stuffed marrow for dinner, with salted runner beans and roast potatoes. Leo had finished most of his before he asked, 'How are the Christmas preparations going, Lydia?'

'Fine.'

'Everything ready for our guests?'

'More or less. I'll have to bring the mattress down to air it, though. I thought – if I light a fire in the inner hall – I could hang it over the banister. The warmth might penetrate upstairs a little, too. Think so?'

'Mm-hm.' He sighed. 'God, three days with Gerald . . . How will we survive? And he's so cock-a-hoop about young whatshername –'

'Jennifer, darling,' Peggy supplied dryly. 'Pretty name. Might be worth remembering, since she's your niece and all that.'

'Yes, but you'd think he was the first father on earth! He's such a bore, Mother! I've only ever heard him say one thing – albeit in ten thousand different ways – and that's, "Aren't I clever?" Well, the answer's no, not very.'

Lydia smiled. Although he'd expressed it a touch forcibly, Leo was right about Gerald. She hadn't taken much notice of him when she'd lived at Priory Farm, but since he'd been 'family', he'd bored her to tears. In fact, he *was* fairly clever; his main problem was that his ego was bigger than his brain and he could never stop talking about it. The emphasis in all his statements was on the words 'I', 'me', or 'mine', which were words Leo hardly ever said. He was more likely to say, 'we' or 'us', not because he was especially modest, but because he saw himself as *part* of a family rather than the most important person in it.

'What we need,' he said now, 'is a spot of light relief: someone to brighten the group up a bit. I don't mean to criticise, Lydia – you know I think the world of her – but your grandmother is never quite the life and soul of the party, is she?'

'And Daddy's rather quiet . . .'

'True. He's good on the subject of farming, of course . . .'

'But we have enough of that from you,' Peggy said sweetly. 'Why don't we ask the Moretons over? Eddie would make mincemeat of Gerald, darling. He's so witty. And Mrs Westley took quite a shine to Helen at the christening, didn't she? Such a sweet girl. She'll be company for you, too, Lydia.'

Lydia smiled, smelling a rat. When Peggy started talking about other people's comfort, she was usually up to something designed solely for her own. To be fair to her, she did find Gran rather oppressive company, and Prue would be fully occupied with her baby (Peggy, much to Lydia's astonishment, was no more interested in Jennifer than she'd been in Richard when he was tiny), and Eddie *was* good fun. If he could be persuaded to bring his gramophone, they might even have some dancing. Food would be a problem, but the larder was full of 'stretching' provisions and there were still enough sprouts, leeks and parsnips in the garden to feed an army . . .

'I can't possibly feed three extra people,' she said firmly.

In the second that passed between that statement and her next, she saw Leo's eyebrows quirk with dismay and Peggy's teeth nip her bottom lip. They were like children, the pair of them, and by no means as dissimilar as Leo liked to think. He was just like Peggy in some ways: once the possibility of a little fun cropped up, he virtually foamed at the mouth to get his share of it. And why not? Like chocolate, there was barely enough of it to be had these days, and she did so want him to be happy . . .

Wanting very much to laugh, Lydia pulled her face straight. 'They'll just have to bring their gramophone,' she said. 'And sing for their supper.'

Chapter Thirteen

It was the best Christmas ever. Leo spent the entire three days of it either laughing himself to tears or fighting off tears of another kind, the kind that wring one's heart. Household accounts aside, it explained every one of Lydia's notebooks, her months of battle-calm, for she'd planned it down to its smallest detail: every walnut, every bauble, every hard-won ribbon, carol and candle-flame. For his own part, Leo had hunted down a Christmas tree, a bottle of sherry and a few necessary presents. But Lydia had bribed the church choir to come calling on Christmas Eve. She'd invited the tenants for mince-pies and mulled ale. The windows were all wreathed with greenery, great logs burned in the hearth of the great hall. The entire place smelled of cloves and oranges and, although many people cried, 'Oh, Lydia, Lydia, how did you *do* it?' only Leo knew just what it had cost her. There were shadows under her eyes again.

But even this was explained on Christmas Day when, mellow on Eddie's burgundy and a delicious excess of *real* figgy-duff, they'd all sat around the tree and opened their presents. Lydia had knitted him a jersey and bought him a pair of cuff-links. With the cuff-links had come a little card: '*I am expecting your baby. With all my love, Lydia. Happy Christmas.*'

He'd given her a fountain pen. As he'd stared at that card, swallowing more emotion than he'd felt in a decade, that ruddy fountain pen seemed . . . It wasn't even studded with diamonds, let alone bound with gold. Inadequate. Cheap. A poor return for all she'd given him . . .

He couldn't even thank her properly with old Mrs Westley and bloody Gerald looking on. But later they'd danced, alone, on the uncarpeted stone floor of the inner hall, and he'd thanked her then, body and soul.

'You're wonderful, d'you know that?'

Laughing, blushing, floating in his arms, she was like another woman, so happy and seemingly carefree, he barely recognised her. The Moretons, even when she discovered that they were four extra mouths to feed, rather than the three she'd complained of, hadn't bothered her at all and he doubted that any of his friends had ever received a warmer welcome. He was so proud of her . . .

'Why don't you laugh more often, sweetheart?'

'I've been saving it up. For tonight.'

'And tomorrow?'

'Yes, of course. I might well collapse after that, though!'

She had, too. When everyone had gone, the extra fires had withered to ashes, and the remains of the Christmas meats had been boiled up for soup, Lydia put her feet up and read a book. Leo had a slight turn when he noticed it was a gardening manual.

'You're not thinking of tackling *that* next, I hope?'

'No. It was just the first book I put my hand on. Quite interesting, though, and we'll have to do something about it, eventually, so I might as well find out how it's done. I didn't realise gardens had to be designed, I thought they just happened: dig a bit, plant a bit, dig another bit . . .'

Leo was about to tell her that the original plan of the garden was still in the library when he noticed she'd fallen asleep. He'd been rained off the afternoon's work at the farm (it was hammering down) and wouldn't be needed again until milking. He was about to close his eyes for a much needed doze when he heard Richard, screaming, 'No, no, no!' from the drawing room, where he'd been playing quite happily with Peggy. Peggy didn't have a great deal of patience with him. She was all right until he got bored and mischievous, but then, instead of distracting him with something new, she gave up and handed him back to Lydia, saying, 'Blowed if I know what the little perisher wants. Why can't he speak English, like the rest of us?'

Leo tiptoed away, closing the door softly behind him, just as Peggy emerged from the drawing room clasping Richard's hand in a vice-like grip. 'Let's find Mummy,' she said, and then, her eyes brightening, 'Or Daddy. Look, here's Daddy!'

'Ssh,' he hissed. 'Lydia's asleep. Come on, Richard. Let's go upstairs.'

He picked him up, marvelling as always at the wiry lightness of his body and the lightning-quick workings of his mind.

'*No* up-airs! *No* bed!'

'All right, all right. Don't jump to conclusions. We'll play skittles in the gallery, shall we?'

Richard widened his eyes. 'Diddle!'

'Oh, no. I'd never diddle you, darling. Not until you diddle me, anyway.'

The clearing out of the gallery was something Floral had done in the autumn. She'd chucked out a good few heaps of old rubbish, sorted through much of the rest and stacked the remains very neatly along the inside wall. This left a good forty-foot length of open floor where Richard could drive his little pedal car on rainy days or, as now, play skittles. It was cold, gloomy and dank, and since Richard couldn't yet be trusted to play alone, he hardly ever came here. Lydia couldn't stand the cold, Peggy couldn't be bothered, and Floral was negligent about safety and would let him play with razor-edged tin boxes, things with nails sticking out of them, anything to 'keep the poor little mite happy' – just until the poor little mite killed himself.

The skittles set was a child's version with a soft ball, and since it was one of Richard's Christmas acquisitions, he hadn't yet got the hang of it and spent most of his time chasing the ball rather than hitting the skittles with it. He was an extraordinarily nimble child whose bones, apparently, were made of india-rubber, for he ran, fell, bounced up and ran again, without seeming to take any hurt at all. He laughed as he ran, laughed as he fell, laughed when he knocked the skittles over (with his feet, not the ball) and laughed when Leo set them up again. And while his energies seemed limitless, Leo's were not: within an hour he was exhausted and getting cold and bored.

'Let's go and find Mummy,' he said. 'An hour's quite long enough for her afternoon nap!'

In fact, Lydia's nap had ended when she'd heard Richard shouting, 'Diddles!' (which any fool would know meant 'skittles') and, after lying there for a little while, staring drowsily into the fire, she sat up and began to read again. Having never been more interested in gardening than duty demanded, she found herself quite seduced by the thought of it now. Bourbon, damask and musk roses, lilies and delphiniums ... The very words were a kind of poetry, conjuring images of warm summer evenings, the air drenched with perfume and dew.

Keeping a large old house in good order had its satisfactions, but it gave one very little tranquillity, which Lydia found she wanted now – and felt she'd earned. It had been a fair old battle, in one way or another, but she'd won it at last. Molliston was more than a house now. It was a home. This Christmas had made it a home. It was still shabby and, more than a yard from the fire, still cold and draughty, but there was nothing she could do about that until the dratted 'shortages' lengthened a bit. The garden, on the other hand ...

151

No, not with Leo's baby on the way. Pregnancy and heavy digging didn't go together, and after her experience with the roof, during her first pregnancy, she didn't think Leo would take too kindly to any risk-taking with *this* one. This very special one . . .

Peggy came in, sighing, and picked up her knitting: a cardigan for herself which seemed to be making quite steady progress.

'Pahhh,' she said. 'The longest – Oh, Lord.'

'What? Dropped a stitch?'

'No, a brain. I was about to remark that January's the dreariest month of the year. And then I realised it's still December. It all seems so *flat*, doesn't it? Do you know, I'm even missing *Gerald*? I quite enjoy deflating his ego, you know.'

'Yes, I noticed. I'm not sure it's the right thing to do, though. He just tries harder to prove you wrong.'

'Yes, but that's the part I most enjoy. Do you think I'm *perfectly* dreadful, darling, or only partially?'

Lydia laughed. 'Only partially.'

Peggy pretended to pout. 'Oh, well, I'm obviously not trying hard enough. What's Leo doing with that child? Killing him?'

Lydia frowned and came up from her deafening pile of cushions to listen. 'Er – no,' she said. 'That's a chasing-up-and-down-having-fun scream. I'd have thought you'd know the difference by now.'

'No.' Peggy turned her knitting and began a purl row. 'It's all Chinese to me. Still, he's miles more advanced than Leo was. He didn't say his first word until he was two and a half, and Richard's not two yet.' She smiled. 'He's a dear little boy, Lydia. I know I don't . . .' She fluttered her fingers over her knitting. 'I know I don't show it much, but I *am* rather fond of him, you know. And Leo adores him. You've done a wonderful job, darling.'

Lydia squeezed her eyes shut on a sudden rush of gratitude. 'I've tried to. I owe him – and you – so much.'

'Oh, nonsense. Is there any cake left? I want my tea.' She seemed almost embarrassed by the exchange and hurried away to put the kettle on, leaving the door ajar so that a chill draught crept into the room, fidgeting annoyingly around Lydia's shoulders. Leo and Richard were still playing chase, but not, as Lydia had first thought, in the great hall. They were on the landing. Leo was pretending to be a bear, to judge from the ferocious growls he was producing. Richard was just being Richard, laughing and shrieking, his little shoes making a thunderous patter on the floorboards as he ran away.

It was lovely to know they were so pleased with each other . . . Lydia just wished they'd be pleased with each other somewhere else, somewhere safer. If Leo hadn't closed the gate at the top of the stairs and if Richard fell just there ... He often fell when he got too excited, and although he hardly ever hurt himself, he'd never yet fallen down a flight of uncarpeted stairs (although not for want of trying).

She should go and see. But she was too tired to move. Leo, anyway, *would* have closed the stair-gate; he was almost as safety-conscious as Lydia was. And after four months of non-stop work, it was so blissful just to sit and do nothing. At least, it would have been, if Peggy hadn't left the blasted door open!

Shivering, pulling her cardigan more closely around her, Lydia sighed and strolled out into the inner hall, smiling sleepily up at the two playmates on the landing. Leo was on his hands and knees (a tiger, then, not a bear) and Richard, biting his lip on giggles, was tip-toeing towards him, his hands making little fists of excitement. Leo growled, Richard screamed and ran away. Lydia's eyes followed him safely past the stair-gate (which *was* shut) before she called out cheerfully, 'Hey, you two! What's all the row about?'

Richard spun around to look at her in mid-flight, lost his footing and fell against the wooden struts of the banister. Even as he fell, Lydia saw him, in her mind's eye, curl into a ball and jump up again, to run on just as nimbly as before. He almost never cried when he fell. He nearly always jumped up again as if nothing had happened. But something went wrong. There was a crack of splintering wood and a strange, bird-like cry as he went on falling, reaching out his little hands to save himself before he screamed and crashed to the cold, stone floor, fifteen feet below.

It took two seconds. It took two hours. As the banister rail snapped, Lydia leapt forward to catch him, but it was like running through a swamp, through a nightmare. She ran until her heart burst with the effort, and yet, when Richard's body hit the ground, she found she hadn't moved an inch from the spot.

And he was so quiet, so still ...

Her face a mask of rage and terror, she turned to Leo (who had barely dragged himself upright) and screamed, 'You fool! You fool! *You've killed my baby!*'

It took a moment. It took an hour. And even as it happened, Leo cursed himself for being a tiger. Had he remained a bear, had he stayed on his feet, he might, in that moment, that hour, have lunged out and caught Richard before he fell. But he couldn't move! He couldn't move; and yet it all happened so slowly, as in a dream. Richard ran, Lydia called out, 'Hey, you two!' and, as on so many previous occasions, the child whirled around, lost his balance and fell. Even as he fell he curled in on himself so that his little shoulders struck the railings first. He should have jumped up, unhurt, still laughing. Instead, the rail broke and he tumbled through, his legs slipping after him, slowly, almost as if to give Leo time to save him. But his scream went on and on, echoed by Lydia's screams: 'You fool! You fool! *You've killed my baby!*'

'*No!*' Leo roared. 'No, *no*! We were all right until *you* –!'

But the look on her face silenced the words in his throat, choked him with horror, cut off his breath.

'He might be all right,' he whispered. 'Oh, God, oh, God, make him all right.'

He felt his way down the stairs on legs that would barely hold him, praying as he'd never prayed before. But Richard was dead. Leo had seen dead men, dead animals, dead birds – a dead child – and, in them all, death had looked the same. There was no mistaking it. It was as though death were a creature in its own right – grey and cold, utterly indifferent – which laid its own mask upon its victims so that they were no longer themselves. Richard had gone.

Yet Lydia hadn't realised it. She knelt over him, stroking his hair, whispering to him softly as the tears rolled down her face. 'Come on, Richard. Wake up, darling. Mummy's here. Mummy's here.'

Weeping, Leo knelt beside her and put his arm around her. 'Lydia . . .'

She shrugged him off and went on chanting her hope, her disbelief, her prayers. 'Come on, Richard. Come on, darling. Call the doctor, Leo, *quickly*. He must have bumped his head. Wake up, Richard. Wake up, darling. Mummy's here.'

'Lydia, don't, my love. He's –'

'*No!*' She screamed like an animal in a trap, throwing her head back so that the cry echoed from the walls all around. Then she pulled Richard into her arms and rocked him, rocked him, her voice changing to a low, rhythmic moan that filled Leo's heart with ice. He had seen death many times before, but he had never seen – or felt – such grief.

The doctor came. Mrs Westley came. Lydia allowed them to touch Richard. She allowed them to touch her and to speak their cold, dry words of wisdom and consolation. But she wouldn't let Leo near her. The pain of it was one pain too many and he went quite numb, afterwards, doing everything Mrs Westley told him to do, thinking nothing.

It was two in the morning before he realised he hadn't seen his mother since, a few minutes after Richard's death, he'd told her to call the doctor. Floral crying, and as white as a wraith, had been very much in evidence, scuttling here and there at Mrs Westley's bidding. But where on earth was Peggy?

He'd been sitting alone in the small parlour. Now he went upstairs, wanting to go to his own bedroom if only to see that Lydia was asleep, in some kind of peace, but instead he turned left, past the gap in the banister (woodworm: a stick of celery would have been stronger), to his mother's room.

She was sitting in a chair by the window, still fully dressed but with neither blanket nor fire to warm her. She was as still as a statue and didn't even turn her head when he spoke to her.

'Mother?' One side of her face was palely lit by the moon (the rain had ceased and thinning clouds were flying on a brisk, north-easterly wind which penetrated the leaded casement like razors) and, perhaps because the other side of her face, like the moon itself, was in darkness, he didn't recognise her. She didn't look like his mother at all. Although not an essentially beautiful woman, her frivolous mind and mischievous nature had lent her a bright animation, an almost unfailing pleasantness of expression, which Leo had come to think was her greatest, perhaps only, real virtue. But that animation had gone and taken her virtue with it. Had he not known that she was in the cold clutch of grief he would have said she looked . . . evil.

He took her hand, which was icy and as unresponsive as stone. 'Mother, you're freezing. Come downstairs and sit with me. Come on.'

When she didn't respond, he gave her a little tug to jolt her into action. She snatched her hand away and curled both hands into fists which she held defensively against her chest. 'I wasn't there,' she said, her voice small and frantic, shuddering as a sudden paroxysm of shivers racked her body. 'I was ill! I couldn't move!'

Lydia had said much the same thing: screamed it, rather, as her grandmother tried to comfort her. 'I was paralysed! I couldn't move! Oh, God, I could have caught him! I could have caught him if only –'

It wasn't remotely true. None of them could have caught him, for although it had seemed to take an hour, it had only taken a moment, and they'd all been too far away: Lydia perhaps four yards, Leo three, and his mother . . . He hadn't even realised she'd been there, but since she'd been out of his range of vision, probably as much as six yards away. No one could cover that distance in a *moment*.

'None of us could move,' he said. 'It's not your fault, Mother. It's not anyone's . . .' His voice broke on tears. Oh, yes. It was *his* fault. All his fault. He'd put Richard down at the foot of the gallery stairs and when he'd run away, grinning back over his shoulder to coax

155

Leo to chase him, the idea of danger had actually crossed his mind! But he hadn't thought of woodworm. He'd known the house was riddled with it; he'd been worrying about it for years, yet hadn't even thought . . .

'No,' his mother muttered strangely. 'It wasn't *my* fault. *I* didn't do it.' Her teeth were chattering, fragmenting the words so that afterwards, even though they'd made his hair stand on end at the time, he wasn't absolutely sure she really said what he'd thought she said: 'The girl did it! I wasn't *there*!'

'Go to bed, Mother. Please, darling. You aren't making sense. You aren't well.' And oh, God, who could blame her? A shock like this was enough to turn anyone's mind, and she'd never been very robust in that respect. She'd never been able to face harsh reality, only escape it, whichever way she could.

But without exerting force to shift her from her chair, he couldn't persuade her to move and, in the end, hoping to keep her alive if nothing else, he stripped the blankets from her bed and carefully wrapped her, cushioning her feet with pillows to keep them from the draught.

He went downstairs again and dozed for a short while in his armchair by the fire. When he woke – soon after four – he found old Mrs Westley sitting opposite him, a crumpled, frail little thing with red-rimmed eyes who now bore little resemblance to dear old Queen Mary.

'My dear,' she began gently, 'I don't know how to help you.'

His heart went out to her, for she'd been like a rock tonight, a hard rock in a raging sea. He opened his mouth to say, *You are helping. What would we have done without you?* But before he could speak, she went on softly, 'Lydia's lost the baby, my dear. The doctor's with her now.'

While they buried Richard Chantry in the churchyard at Sinden St Michael, Lydia slept a drugged sleep and, a few days afterwards, went home with her grandmother to Priory Farm. She didn't want to be at Molliston any more. She didn't want to be with Leo. She didn't want to be alive, to be aware, to be made to care for anyone's grief but her own. Some small, thorny remnant of conscience informed her – when she allowed it – that this was not right, not good, but it couldn't make her care. What was Leo to her, after all? She hadn't wanted to marry him; she'd barely known him; his only function had been to give Richard a father, and Richard was gone. It was all meaningless, now.

'Nothing is meaningless,' her grandmother told her. 'Everything has a purpose, Lydia. Our grief is only in not knowing what that purpose is, until –'

'Too late,' Lydia finished acidly.

Her grandmother sighed and turned away.

'Oh, I know,' Lydia said. 'I know it's a punishment for what I did to Leo, but it's – oh, it's not *fair*, Gran! I did *everything*, everything I could to make it up to him, and I thought the baby, *his* baby . . .'

Tears. More tears and more. They scoured her hollow, until she thought she could never – if only for exhaustion – cry again. But there were always more tears. And more.

'It's not a punishment,' Gran said gently. 'It's just part of a pattern, my dear, like a piece of lace made from a single thread.'

She went to the linen drawer and fetched out a tablecloth she'd made before the war: a piece of Irish linen with triangular fillets of lace at each corner. It was a beautiful piece – Gran's last before failing eyesight let her down – and although it was all worked in white, every flower, bee and butterfly of the pattern was clearly delineated. Roses, lilies, daisies, iris; red admirals, swallowtails and little holly-blues.

'The roses were the hardest,' Gran said. 'I kept losing my place. But I loved doing the butterflies, and since they were the last part, I could only do them if I first did the roses. Do you see what I mean, my dear?'

Lydia bowed her head. 'I'm afraid I can't believe there are any butterflies for me.'

'No, of course you can't. And there won't be any, unless you work through the roses, my dear.'

Work, work, work. It was Gran's cure for every damn thing, but it couldn't cure death! It couldn't bring Richard back, or the baby he'd taken with him! It couldn't mend a marriage that had lost all its purpose. Gran meant well and, if you believed her, she had an answer for everything. But Lydia didn't believe her any more. The only thing work did was to make you *tired*.

For almost three weeks she slept and cried, slept and cried, and, in the few hours that existed between times, pottered around the house like a zombie, noticing sometimes that it was raining and thinking it would rain for the rest of her days, that the sun, like her children, was dead. And then, one day at the end of January, it proved her wrong, and as it shone down on her from a blue, frosty sky, she knew she'd go mad if she didn't do something.

Her father had sold her gelding to Libby Dent at the far end of the village, so she took his hunter out instead, riding through the muddy lanes in a wide circle which drew her – inevitably, although at the time it seemed fateful – to the Red Barn.

Leo had been to see her several times, which was rather like saying she'd had toothache several times: the relief was wonderful when it went away. His last visit had been three days ago, but then, as on the previous visits, she'd scarcely known him. He hadn't looked very different, but he'd lost all his edge, that mildly masterful, faintly *amused* air which had always made Lydia think of sandpaper (for some reason) and made being with him such a challenge. He was afraid now. Afraid of saying something out of place, of making her cry. Afraid, as she was, of the barrier of blame that lay between them.

She closed her eyes and saw again that dreadful scene at Molliston, heard again Richard's terrified scream and Leo, shouting, 'We were all right until you –' *Interfered? Distracted Richard? Made him fall?* He might have said something else too. *How many times have you dusted the banister? How many times have you seen these struts peppered with woodworm and thought: I must see to this?* Yet she'd accused *Leo* of killing Richard!

Poor man. Poor, poor Leo . . . From the first, from their very first day at the Red Barn, she'd made him take the blame for all of her sins. It was no good pretending that she'd paid – in work, money, patience and love – for when you came down to it, she'd done it all for *herself* and had still failed to do the one thing, the *one* thing that might have kept Richard – and Leo's baby– alive. *She* hadn't been able to live in a state of dirt and disorder, *she* hadn't been able to live in a cold, damp house, *she* hadn't been able to live without decent food in her belly, the comfort of Leo's arms around her, his pride in her, the hope of his love. *His* love? No, just love, for when you marry *any* man who will not divorce you, you have a lifetime to look forward to which is – which must be – unendurable without love.

Unendurable. Yes. She might have lived with the grief – after all, she wasn't the first to suffer it and would not be the last – but she couldn't live with the guilt, the knowledge that she'd both created and destroyed her own son in wickedness, selfishness and cruelty. *You killed by baby!* No. Leo had given him everything, given without stint: a home and name, love and laughter. *You killed my baby!* No . . .

She'd write to him. She'd leave him in no doubt that all the wrong and the blame belonged to her. And then she'd set him free.

Although Leo had been appalled at Lydia's decision to go home with her grandmother, he'd realised too that it was the right thing to do. She needed all the comfort she could get and, as the architect of her grief, he was in no position to comfort her. He'd driven over to see her several times, but even that was an agony neither of them could bear. He could never think of anything to say. And even when he did, she didn't hear him. *Don't think this is the end, Lydia. We still have our lives before us; we're still young* . . .

But he felt as old as the earth and often wished he could be a part of it, incapable of feeling anything, ever again. Somewhere along the line, and without knowing much about it, he'd come to love Richard as if the child were his own. The house was so empty without him. So silent, so still. Every time he crossed the threshold – even when he warned himself in advance that it wouldn't happen – he expected to be greeted by a small, adoring whirlwind who shouted 'Daddy!' and hurled himself (in absolute trust of being caught) into Leo's arms. *In absolute trust of being caught* . . . Dear God.

But something else had happened during this past year that he'd had little idea of until it was too late. He'd fallen in love with his wife. And it had happened for precisely the reason he'd so often thought he hated her. As she'd knelt on the stone floor of the inner hall, screaming, moaning, beside herself with sorrow, he'd known that everything he held most dear depended on her, and that he'd lost it all before he'd even known he'd gained it. She'd given him peace. She'd brought order out of chaos. And her money had had almost nothing to do with any of it, for she'd spent very little; there was too little to spend it on. The investment she'd made had been an investment of steadfast labour, thought and patience. And, he realised now, of *hope*. He'd thought she'd been holding Molliston's *past* together – patching up history – but she hadn't been; she'd been building a *future*. And he'd let it go; just watched it . . . slip away.

And now, in quite another fashion, he was letting Lydia slip away. Thanks to him, her life was in ruins and she must be allowed, now, to salvage what she could of it, in the way *she* thought best. He had no hope – none at all – that he would be a part of it. Any affection she'd had for him had died when he'd let Richard die. So . . . he wouldn't see her again until she asked to see him. And if, then, she wanted a divorce – so be it.

He'd made this decision the last time he'd seen her, three days ago, and since then had been quite sure that it had been the right decision. But for some reason he doubted it today. He was busy, taking advantage of the frosty ground to get some much needed muck on the fields, breaking his back to get it done before the thaw. But Lydia kept trickling over his mind like the sweat that trickled over his ribs, tickling, irritating, turning to ice within moments of his stopping to take a rest. Turning to ice. Turning to ice . . .

Her life was in ruins and she must be allowed to salvage what she could . . . But there was nothing to salvage! She'd lost everything!

Ray Duckett was driving the tractor, Leo shovelling manure from the trailer behind, but with the average speed of muck-spreading being less than five miles an hour, it was easy enough to jump off and overtake Ray on foot. 'Ray, I've got to go out. Go back to the yard and get Malcolm to finish this, will you?'

Forty minutes later, still stinking of the midden, he drove into the yard at Fred Westley's farm and, for the first time in his married life, marched into the kitchen without knocking.

'Oh, hello, Leo.' Mrs Westley said calmly. 'I wasn't expecting –'

'Where's Lydia?'

'She's gone for a walk, my dear. You've only just missed her.' She frowned suddenly. 'Well, that's rather strange. She's left a letter here for you, but –' She put a hand to her mouth. 'Oh, dear Lord,' she whispered. 'Leo, for God's sake, open it!'

It was almost dark when Lydia reached the bridge over the river for the second time. She was no happier than when she'd reached it the first time, but at least now she knew she wasn't going to throw herself in. She stood there for a while nevertheless, gazing into the muddy torrent, listening to the roar of it, imagining the depth and force of it, knowing without doubt that it would have killed her in seconds.

It had been raining since Christmas, and although the river hadn't burst its banks, its functions as a drain had almost ceased. The fields all around were inches deep in ice-skinned water and the banks strewn with the detritus of flood: dead tree boughs, heaps of grass and reeds torn from their roots, a broken packing case with *Home & Colonial* stamped on its side, a bent bicycle wheel and a laundry basket. All thoroughly uninviting. And yet the deafening roar of the water combined with the breakneck speed of its passage under the bridge had a strangely compelling quality, rather like those enormous bonfires on Guy Fawkes Night whose very danger seem to lure one closer.

She put her feet on the base of the parapet to get a closer look – and in the same instant was dragged away, held tightly in a warm embrace which smelled, rather comfortingly, of pig manure.

'Oh, Lydia! Lydia! Oh, thank God, I found you!'

She laughed. It was mostly shock (she hadn't heard the car, although he'd parked it right behind her), but mostly a curious sort of relief that someone cared – that *Leo* cared – enough to . . . To weep for her!

'Oh, Leo,' she whispered. 'Don't. Don't cry, *please*! I wasn't going to do it. I was just looking.'

He hadn't heard a word. He bundled her into the car, drove half a mile up the road and pulled the car into a gateway before laying his arms on the steering wheel and hiding his face.

'I wasn't going to do it, Leo! I – I meant to . . . But – but someone thwarted me, and now . . .'

'Thwarted you?' He sniffed, slid the sleeve of his jacket under his nose and gazed blankly at her through the dusk with wide, bewildered eyes. 'What do you mean?'

'I met an old lady. She lives in a cottage on the far side of the bridge. She asked me to carry her shopping and I –' She laughed again, wryly, fighting off tears. 'I didn't have the heart to refuse. Ridiculous, isn't it? She asked if I could spare the time and I said, "Yes, I wasn't doing anything important," and then realised how true it was.' She sighed and covered her eyes with her hands. 'I suppose she was sent by the Great Lacemaker in the sky.'

Leo didn't ask what she meant. He just held her hand and, as the silence lengthened, Lydia had another thought which hadn't occurred to her before.

'But where did *you* come from?' she asked. 'We weren't expecting you, were we?'

'No,' Leo said thoughtfully. 'The Great Muck Spreader sent me. He gave me a clout with his shovel and told me to bring you home.'

Chapter Fourteen

In fact it was March before Lydia came home to Molliston. Her grandmother took ill with influenza and, before she was halfway better, Lydia was felled by the same thing. If it hadn't been for Prue – and, latterly, good old Floral – they might both have died: Mrs Westley because she was too elderly to fight it off without aid and Lydia . . . Lydia just because she had no interest in living. Once the pain and fever of the early stages were over, she lay staring into space like a rabbit into the headlights of an oncoming car. She said, 'I'm alive only on the outside. Everything else is dead, Leo. I can feel it all rotting inside me.'

Prue, run off her feet with young whatshername – Jennifer – had insufficient time to give Lydia the care she needed and Peggy wouldn't go near her: she'd always had a dread of illness which no amount of familial duty (if she acknowledged such a thing) could overcome. Leo didn't press her. For one thing, she'd be virtually useless at all the practical things Lydia needed done for her and, for another, the shock of Richard's death was still with Peggy, as it was with them all, and in her usual attempt to pretend it hadn't happened, her behaviour (while perfectly normal for *Peggy*) left something to be desired for everyone else.

Because he'd seen her on the night of the tragedy, almost literally frozen with grief, Leo could tell himself that she was being brave in her attempts to laugh it off, but it both looked and sounded tasteless, flippant, even cruel. One wrong word from her and Lydia might well find strength enough to get out of bed, but it would be a complete waste of effort if all she had to look forward to afterwards was being hanged for strangling her mother-in-law.

Eventually, and without much hope that she'd agree (she'd always been terrified of Mrs Westley), Leo asked Floral to go over there for a few days. 'You won't have to do anything for the old lady,' he coaxed. 'She's up and about now, a bit weak on her pins, but . . .'

'I dussn't mind what I does for either on 'em!' Floral fired up indignantly. 'I'da gone weeks ago, but nobody asked I!'

'Then why didn't you say so, Floral? Good Lord, I've been worried out of my wits all this time! If you'd only –'

'It ain't my place to say!' she stormed. 'I'm only the bloody lodger, en I?'

In other circumstances Leo might have said (in fact, probably *had* said) much the same thing about her, but now, suddenly, he saw her in a quite different light. His difficulty in perceiving her as she really was had been partly a matter of class (she was as common as thistles and who gives a damn about thistles?) but also of physical stature. It was so easy to overlook someone who existed so close to the ground, skidding about like an abandoned roller-skate, belonging nowhere and to no one. He'd once thought she'd claimed squatter's rights to Molliston, taken it for her own, and perhaps that was true. But she'd also claimed 'ownership' of everyone there: Richard had been *her* baby, too, and Lydia was the love of her life. She'd do anything for Lydia. She'd die for her if dying were asked.

'I'll go and pack me bits,' she muttered now, but Leo reached out to stop her, grasping her shoulder (a bony, unyielding shoulder) to turn her gently into the curve of his arm.

'No,' he said. 'You're not the bloody lodger. You're family now, Floral, and we love you.' He attempted to drop a kiss on her forehead, but since her forehead came barely halfway up his chest, he missed and had to make do with a hug instead. But as his arms closed around her she burst into tears and clung to him like a child, her entire, skinny little body shaking with sobs that found a treacherous echo in Leo's heart.

'Hey, hey,' he said frantically. 'Don't, Floral, *please!*'

She tore herself away from him and blew her nose on a frayed rag that Leo recognised as a duster, complete with stains of Brasso and brick-coloured Cardinal polish. 'Well,' she muttered angrily, 'it's yer own bloody fault, you soppy gurt lummox! Whatchya wanna go and say *that* fer?'

Leo smiled. 'Because I meant it. And who are you calling a soppy gurt lummox? *I'm* not the one crying my eyes out, am I?'

'Huh! I can call thee whatsoever I likes,' she said defiantly, and produced a wide, watery smile to tease him. 'I'm *fambly!*'

Floral's arrival at Priory Farm came as a relief to Lydia, not because she wanted or needed anything from her, but because the only feelings she'd had, since she'd fallen ill, had been vague stirrings of

163

guilt about her grandmother. She was ill, too, and her too-frequent trips up the stairs with 'tempting' trays of soup, Bovril, toast or stewed fruit, exhausted her and made Lydia feel a good deal worse, not better. She didn't want to eat. Her mouth tasted like a midden, as did most of the food she put in it. If she'd been left alone all day with just a jug of cold water, she'd have been grateful just for the release from being *grateful* all the time.

Floral didn't need or expect gratitude. She took everything for granted: Lydia's foul manners included. 'Oh, go *away*, Floral! I don't *want* anything to eat!'

'Oh, I knows, my love. I *knows*. Leo's dad was the same, but he had a growth in his stomach, poor soul, and you just got 'flu, so be grateful. Ooh, the agony that man went through . . . Don't go tellin' Leo mind. Peggy told un' he died of 'art failure.'

'Oh? Why?'

'Well, you know Peggy. She couldn't hardly bear to think of it, let alone write it down. She'm not daft, that one, but she were brung up wrong. Cruel, really.'

'Cruel? What do you mean?'

'Well, unnatural. Her and her sisters – she had three, all dead now – wasn't allowed to cry when they was little. Their mum and dad wanted 'em to be 'appy and smilin', so when they cried their nurse used to lay into 'em with a stick. And if they cried for that, she'd lay in harder. It was easy to be cruel to kiddies in them days, see. The rich folk used to go off for months on end – South of France, Indial, Africal, all over the flamin' place – and never know what was happenin' to the little 'uns. And just so long as they was 'appy and smilin' when the parents come 'ome again, why should they care, or ask any questions?'

'But that's terrible!'

'Not so bad as it could've been – the woman left when Peggy was seven and they had someone more decent after that – but that sort of thing sticks, my love, which I s'pose is why I'm telling you. She'm not as foughtless as she do seem, see, Lydial. She *do* care about you. She *do* care about Richard. She cared about Mr Chantry, too, yet she never went near him when he were dyin', nor even when he were dead. She got to be 'appy and smilin', see, my love. She *got* to be 'appy and smilin'.'

Appalled, Lydia stared into Floral's eyes, thinking things she didn't dare utter; but when Floral went away the thoughts didn't, and later she did pluck up courage enough to ask, 'And when her baby died, Floral? Couldn't she cry . . . even for him?'

'I don't know, my love. She've never spoke of it, not even when she were tiddly, which she *was* when she told I about that nursemaid of hers. Mr Chantry mentioned the baby once or twice, but he were ramblin' a bit by then, and I couldn't quite catch what he were on about. I took the idea that she . . . Well, I'm not sure: went a bit funny wiv her nerves, I s'pose. Bound to. If you cassn't cry, see, Lydial, what else *can* you do?'

Lydia couldn't imagine it: not being able to cry for Richard, yet that night was the first she didn't cry for him. Floral's revelations had worn her out, and she had her first truly restful night's sleep since the day he died.

Floral 'wore her out' the next day, too, filling her in on all the Sinden gossip she'd heard in the butcher's queue. 'Old Mrs Dibble's popped off at last, Lydial. 'Er couldn't walk, 'er was stone deaf, stone blind and never had a toof in 'er 'ed, an' everyone's still sayin' "Ninety-free, and all her faculties to the last!" He'm tryin' not to show it, but Leo's over the moon about it, o'course.'

'About – her faculties?'

'No! It's the only property he got left not tied to one o' the farms, see, Lydial, an' what wiv the Admiralty in Bath and housin' so short, he can get a good rent for it now. Mrs Dibble bin payin' the same rent since her old man died, in '32. Five bob a week. He can get as much as three pound for it now, he do reckon. Oh, and you remember me sayin' he got a fred runnin' through 'im I 'adn't caught the end of? Well, I caught it now. He'm daft, he'm soppy, he'm soft as summer butter, an' if you don't get 'ome soon to sort him out, he'll go right off the rails, I'm warnin' you.'

Lydia blinked and was surprised to discover that her heart-rate had quickened, almost as if she cared.

'What on earth do you mean, Floral?'

'I means . . . Well, he'm like a kid in a way, Lydial. He do need a lot of comfort an' cuddlin', especially now, wiv fings so sad an' upsettin' an' topsy-turvy. He 'ad his arms around some woman t'other day, to tell the trufe. Nothing *in* it. I'm not sayin' *that*. She wasn't his type. A very *low down* sort of woman, I'd 'ave said. But I s'pose if a man's desperate, he has to take it where he can find it, don't he, my love?'

Lydia stared at the wall for a moment, too shocked to speak. Even when she caught her breath, she could only croak, 'Who?'

Floral grinned. 'Me,' she said. 'Lovely it was, too. He've got a surprisin'ly gentle touch fer such a big man, 'aven't he?'

Lydia subsided against the pillows, wanly smiling. 'Beast,' she said and then, even more wanly, 'Thanks, Floral. I needed that, didn't I?'

'You needs him, too, my love.'

Yes, she needed him. She wanted to go home: to lie in his arms and hear him say, yet again, 'It wasn't our fault, darling. We can blame ourselves all we like, but we'll never bring him back. So we must live as if he were still here, and do all we can to give him a home and a family to be proud of.'

She couldn't imagine it. She couldn't bear the thought of holding a child in her arms who was *not* Richard. But she knew it was right. Not yet, not yet, but in a year or two, when the grief had softened a little . . . Yes, she would give him a home and a family to be proud of.

Although she was good at so few things, Peggy was very good indeed at keeping servants up to the mark and she'd kept Mrs Lodge ticking over perfectly while Lydia was away. The house could not be made immaculate until a team of decorators was let loose in it, but as Leo did a tour of inspection, the day before Lydia's return home, he conceded that it was as immaculate as it *could* be.

His mother shrugged when he thanked her for her efforts, which worried him more than a little. She'd always been more inclined to preen herself when compliments came her way: a trait which had irritated him in his youth; he'd despised that sort of vanity, although he understood it better now. Preeners aren't so much proud of their talents as ashamed of their lack of them, taking comfort for the lack wherever they can find it.

'What's wrong, Mother?' he asked now. 'Not looking forward to Lydia's home-coming?'

She arched her brows and looked away. 'Dreading it, if you must know. Comfort for the bereaved is not my best suit. Every time I think of it I feel like slapping her. Hardly fair. But true.'

'*Slapping* her?' he repeated incredulously. 'Why, for heaven's sake?'

She shrugged again. 'I don't know.'

Even at her saddest and most defensive, Peggy was rarely without a smile on her face, but the smile she wore now was one he recalled from his childhood – a miserable summer holiday when, to the best of his knowledge, his parents had spoken scarcely a word to each other they hadn't first dipped in acid. As smiles go, it was the nearest she could get to a sneer without actually sneering.

'Look,' he said gently, 'if you're unhappy, Mother, you'd better tell me about it now, while I can do something to help without affecting Lydia. We'll be skating on thin ice after tomorrow, and you must realise that I can't – won't – let anything worry her until –'

166

'That's the whole point,' his mother said icily. 'It's no fun being a dowager at the best of times, but if I have to watch every word I say, skate constantly – as you put it – on thin ice from now on . . .' She closed her eyes. 'I think perhaps you should let me have the Dibbles' cottage, darling. I'll be happier there, out of the way. Floral can come with me if she likes.'

Shocked, Leo looked at his hands and tried to think this over, but it was more difficult than it seemed. He'd already disposed of the Dibbles' cottage – in his imagination, at least – and even if he did let his mother have it, he was pretty certain Floral would not 'like' to go with her. And Peggy certainly couldn't go on her own. She'd live in squalor, never eat . . .

'Let me think it over, will you, darling?' he said kindly at last. 'I – er – quite see your difficulty –' (in fact, he didn't; not at all) '– but it might be a good deal easier than we anticipate. Lydia's a sensible enough girl. She won't burden you with her feelings if she can possibly avoid it. You know that, don't you?'

His mother laughed and, in a sweetly mocking voice, echoed his own. 'If you're *unhappy*, Mother, *do* tell me about it, darling!' Then she left the room, adding, just as sweetly, 'Don't say you weren't told, will you, Leo?'

It sounded very like a threat. Or perhaps just a warning . . . Something to think about, certainly – and very seriously – if only he knew where to start. But he couldn't let her go to the cottage just because that was what she *wanted*. His mother's wants were legion, her needs few, and she rarely spared much thought for either of them: just took the first (when she could) and ignored the second, with no regard at all for the consequences. There was, very obviously, something deeper involved here, something to do with Richard's death and the burden of grief they were all carrying. But surely Peggy could see that Lydia's burden was the heaviest? She'd experienced the same thing, after all!

Every time I think of it, I feel like slapping her.

But *why*, for God's sake? *Why*?

The end of March was dry, windy and cold and Lydia spent as many daylight hours as she could walking the fields and lanes around Molliston, walking until she was exhausted and thoughts of a chair and a cup of tea were thoughts of heaven, even if they existed in hell. And Molliston *was* hell. She'd expected it to be bad, of course, but not as bad as this! Richard was *everywhere*. She'd known she'd 'see' him on the landing, on the stairs, lying dead on the floor of the inner hall or, white and straight (at rest . . .) in his cot in the nursery. But he wasn't just *there*. He waited behind every door to jump out at her as she walked through it, shouting, 'Boo!' He played under the table in the small parlour, so that, when she sat there, she was careful of her feet, lest she kick him. Every time she fetched a hod of coal from the cellar, she searched the place with her eyes, afraid of shutting him in. Every time she served a meal she put out a small plate for Richard, or thought of it, or scraped a carrot especially, because he wouldn't eat cabbage. But worse than all this was the silence, the constant expectation she had of something that would never again happen. Waking up, listening for his voice and – hearing nothing.

There were other difficulties, too, that she hadn't anticipated. Pitying looks from the women in the village, pitying words that filled her with rage, for although they all said it, hardly any of them could possibly *know* how she felt! And the one woman who did know, the one woman she truly wanted to pity her (no, not pity; just *understand*), hardly spoke to her at all. Wouldn't even look at her. She couldn't have believed that Peggy could be so *skilfully* evasive. She reminded Lydia of a skater on a frozen pond: just when you thought she was coming towards you at last, she whizzed by, and was suddenly speeding away just as fast as she'd approached. On the rare occasions when she was pinned down, she talked incessantly – usually to Leo – about pigs, winter wheat, opera, dogs, daffodils, Princess Elizabeth, Mr Lodge's leg ulcers and Helen Moreton's jewellery.

No one else would have noticed anything wrong. She smiled and joked; she spoke Lydia's name almost as often as she *seemed* to look at her. But she never looked except at her brooch, her ears, over her shoulder, or sometimes at all three with a bright, trance-like stare that saw nothing at all.

'She blames me,' Lydia confided to Leo at last. 'She might not know it, or want to admit it, but I'm sure that's what it is, Leo.'

'*No*, darling.' Kind and protective as he was, even Leo's attempts at comfort fell wide of the mark. He was like his mother, in a way, more inclined to escape the bad things than to confront them outright, and Lydia knew that her only salvation was in facing up to things, sorting them out, seeing them through.

'Look at it from her point of view,' she said now. 'Richard wasn't her grandson, but she accepted him, loved him after her fashion and lost him, in a tragedy which *must* have reminded her of her own loss, brought it all back . . .' She sighed. 'I don't *know*, Leo. All I know is that if I hadn't tricked you into marrying me, none of it would have happened. She *must* blame me. It was my *fault*, after all.'

'No, no.' He wrapped his arms around her and rocked her gently

168

against him. 'It wasn't anyone's fault, Lydia. It just *happened*.'

'Oh, I don't mean that! I mean that you could have married someone else, Leo, or not married at all. Either way, none of this trouble would have happened to you, or to her!'

He stiffened suddenly, sighed. Sighed again. 'No, even that wasn't your fault. I – I . . . I *wanted* to marry you, Lydia, and – and . . . And I *would* have wanted it, even if I'd known that Richard wasn't mine. You see, I –' His embrace tightened, he buried his lips in her hair. 'I love you,' he whispered. 'You mean everything to me and I can't bear for you to be always blaming yourself like this. I *must* tell you –'

Lydia had been fighting tears all day, but this was too much and she broke down and sobbed, clinging to him, almost clawing at him to bring his love closer and closer until she suffocated in it.

'Oh, Leo!' she wailed, 'I don't deserve you! You're so good, so kind, so . . .! Oh, Leo . . . what would I do without you?'

'Hush,' he soothed gently. 'Hush, hush . . .'

He released his breath into her hair, letting it go very slowly, as, once again, he swallowed the confession that might cure – or kill – her. *It's not your fault. None of it's your fault. I married you for your money.* But now that he loved her, it wasn't so simple. Yes, it might ease the burden of her guilt, but it might also destroy the one thing that was keeping her going – a marriage that still had some hope in it. Hope stained, hope wounded, hope limping along on a wing and a prayer, but hope, nevertheless. So he couldn't tell her now. One day, perhaps, but not now. He'd have to think of something else.

'Do you know what I think is really wrong with Mother?' he mused softly. 'I think she's jealous.'

'*Jealous*?' Lydia gasped. 'Of *me*?'

'Hmm – perhaps envious would be a better word. She told me once – not very long ago – that it was no fun being a dowager. She was actually asking me if I'd let her have the Dibbles' cottage and although I didn't understand it at the time, I'm – beginning to. You and she are as different as two women can be, Lydia. She's a butterfly: always flitting from one thought to another, from one diversion to another, finding her nectar where she can. And you're a flower, firmly rooted, self-sufficient, asking nothing that you can't make for yourself.' He stroked the tears from her cheeks. 'If you were a butterfly, wouldn't you envy a flower, Lydia, and perhaps find the contrast a little painful, now and then?'

He paused, biting his lip, remembering how painful he had once found Lydia's seriousness, her attention to detail, her determination to do everything just so, as if to fail in any particular would be to bring the wrath of the gods down upon . . .

Under the shelter of darkness and the bedclothes, he bared his teeth, for he'd realised only now that that was *precisely* what Lydia had been doing: trying to cover her tracks, trying to be perfect, so that the gods might forget how grievously she'd sinned against them . . . But the gods forgot nothing; they exacted their own price for services rendered and there was never a 'never-never' plan to make the payment any easier.

'You mean she wants to get away from me?' Lydia whispered now.

'No . . . But maybe she wants to be alone, to be herself, for once. She's never been allowed that, you know, except – perhaps – between my father's death and my return home. I've thought about their marriage a great deal recently and I think . . . in fact, I'm pretty sure he . . .'

'What?'

Leo had been going to say, 'he despised her', which was probably too strong an expression for Lydia's ears, however true it might be.

'He wasn't happy with her,' he amended carefully. 'And she isn't stupid, Lydia. She isn't nearly so insensitive as she seems. I'm sure she tried to make him happy, to make us all happy. But she has tunnel-vision, Lydia. She can't understand anything beyond her *own* ideas of happiness, so perhaps it would be kinder to let her find that, on her own.'

'I wish I could talk to her,' Lydia murmured. 'But she won't let me near. I thought we'd be closer now. I thought, because of Lionel, she must know how I feel . . .'

Her voice had slowed with weariness and before much longer he felt her sag against him as she drifted into sleep. But Leo went on thinking. *Because of Lionel, she must know how I feel.* Yes, of course, that was it. Peggy knew, and didn't want to know. She didn't want to be reminded. And who could blame her? Once was enough for any woman, let alone a woman like Peggy. She couldn't go through it again.

He told her the next day that she could have the Dibbles' cottage – under certain conditions.

'Oh? What conditions?'

'That you come to eat with us at least twice a week, that you find someone to clean for you before you move, and –'

'Oh, nonsense! Floral can see to all that!'

'– and that you don't ask Floral to go with you.'

'*What*? Why on earth not?'

'Because I've already asked her, and she doesn't want to go.'

As he'd anticipated, his mother paled slightly. He'd known she'd depended on Floral to go with her, which was why he'd asked Floral first, putting the case as fairly as he could – as he was certain Peggy would not if the asking were left to her. She wasn't above a little emotional blackmail. All she ever wanted was to have her own way, as her next words clearly indicated.

'Puh! Who is she to say what she wants and doesn't want? She wouldn't have a home at all if it weren't for me!'

Leo lifted his chin, realising as he did it that he was mimicking Lydia at her most determined. 'Take it or leave it,' he said coolly. 'I'm not going to make it easy for you, Mother. I'd rather you stayed here. This is your home, for God's sake. You *belong* here.'

'I hate it,' she said.

He sighed and closed his eyes, knowing, for the first time in his life, that he hated it, too. After all, it was only a heap of stone and wood. Ancient and beautiful as it was, it wasn't worth a tenth of the suffering it had caused. The worry of it had probably killed his father, just as the decay of it had killed Richard and blighted poor Lydia's life. They should have sold it years ago when the Depression had first begun to hurt: cut their losses, moved to Manor Farm. True, it would have broken his heart *then*, but it was breaking his heart *now*, so what was the difference?

As the remnant of winter warmed into spring, Lydia's long walks through the countryside became more painful, her thoughts more bitter, angry and desperate. Everywhere she looked she saw signs of life renewing: celandines gleaming in the sun, huge clumps of primroses buttering the hedgerows, dark spikes of bluebell leaf thrusting through the deep mould of the woods. Hawthorns set a starry sprinkling of green against virgin blue sky; blackthorn hedges were drifts of white blossom; blackbirds and robins sang songs of love and carried tufts of dry grass to their nests. It was all so beautiful. And so cruel, for Richard could see none of it – and none of it *knew*, or cared.

The worst thing, for Lydia, was being rational enough to know that it was totally *irrational* to hate a blackbird for singing and utterly *wasteful* to hate the beauty of the world which should fill her only with hope . . . And with gratitude that she, at least, was still alive to see it. But try as she might, she couldn't be grateful. Try as she might, she felt no hope, only a stagnant pool of stubborn resilience (either inherited from, or pounded into her, by her grandmother) which kept up a dreary chant at the back of her mind. 'You *will* get through this, you *will* get through.'

Most of her walks took about two hours, the last fifteen minutes of which were the worst, when she saw the chimneys of Molliston, tall

171

and ominous against the sky, reminding her that *it* was the reason for her misery, the centre of her grief, the hard stone of the bitter fruit she must taste for the rest of her life. She hated every hour she spent in it. Even exhausted and longing for tea, she never saw it without wanting to turn around and walk for another two hours. Anything, rather than go back.

At the end of one of these walks, she took a stone in her shoe on the last few hundred yards, and although she managed to limp half the distance, she eventually sat on the ruined wall of the kitchen garden and took off her shoe.

'Well, for one thing it got no garden,' she heard Floral say reasonably, quite close to her back, although the wall divided them. 'I can't do wivout me garden, see, Peggy. I never 'ad one before, an' now I got one . . . All the work I put into it over the years . . . No, I can't do wivout it, an' that's that.'

'You can come back and do it,' Peggy said sharply. 'For heaven's sake, Floral, we'll only be a few hundred yards down the High Street!'

'I'd feel trapped,' she said. 'It've only got two bedrooms, see, Peggy. Come winter, us'd be caged up like a pair of eggbound canaries, an' I've *had* all that. I knows what it's like: no space, no privacy, nowhere to keep me bits. Us can come an' go as we please, here, see, Peggy. Be wiv one another or apart, upstairs or down, in or out . . . An' anyway, you don't know what I means about the garden. It's 'avin' it right on the doorstep that matters, see, my love. You got to *live* wiv a garden, keep yer eye on it all the time. Dig a bit here, plant a bit there, weed n' water, potter about . . .'

Her voice drifted away as she 'pottered' to the far end of the plot, beyond Lydia's hearing, but Peggy laughed and in softly venomous tones said, 'My God, you've got a nerve. Anyone would think you had a *right* to –'

'I have got a right, my love,' (Floral had evidently pottered back again), 'and *you* got no right to deny me. Your right was to turn me out afore Leo came home, and you never. Now it's *his* right to turn me out, but if he do, Peggy, I still shan't come down Dibbles' wi'thee. I 'on't be tied, my love. I 'on't be told.'

'I didn't tell you – I asked you!'

Floral produced a delighted little chuckle. 'Aye, an' I said no, an' *then* you told I. An' now I shall tell thee: go to Dibbles' if you wants, but you 'on't find what yer lookin' fer, Peggy, 'cos it ain't damn well *there*!'

An hour seemed to pass before Lydia's heartbeat slowed to normal. She wasn't certain why it had raced so hard, fluttering and struggling in her breast as if she was in some terrible kind of danger. Guilt, perhaps. She'd been eavesdropping, after all and, like most eavesdroppers, hadn't liked what she'd heard. It had frightened and confused her; not just because Peggy had seemed so angry, but because Floral had been so sure of herself, so strong. And what had she meant when she'd said Peggy wouldn't find what she was looking for at the cottage? What the hell *was* she looking for?

Lydia stood up and wandered through to the garden where Floral remained, watering an empty trench of carefully tilled soil.

'Oh, hello, my love. Had yer walk?'

'Mm.'

'You looks wore out.'

'Mm. Floral? I heard what you said to Peggy just now. About not finding what she's looking for. What is it?'

Floral smiled. 'Same as what you're looking fer, my love. Peace.'

'Hmm. So where *do* we find it?'

'I dunno, my love. I found it right where I am now: messin' about wiv me spuds and cabbages, doin' summat useful, summat natural and quiet . . . The Lord do speak to I when I'm gardenin', see Lydia! I don't yer his voice, mind, an' he don't yer mine, but – ooh, we 'aves a quiet little fink, sorts fings out between us . . .' She looked up, her smile widening to a bright, puckish grin. 'An' he'm ever so nice when you get to know him.'

Hot tears filled Lydia's eyes. 'Is he?' she asked bitterly. 'Then why? *Why*, Floral, *why*?'

Floral bent again to her work. 'I dunno, my love. Ask him yerself, that's the best. You'm in the right place fer it, see, entcha?'

'What do you mean?'

'Six ruddy acres of nettles and brambles? If you don't find the answers amongst that lot, you ain't lookin' proper! Walkin's all right, see, my love, but it ain't no *use*; it don't make summat outa nothin'; it don't *give* you nothin', bar blisters, an' you can get them anyway, if you wants 'em so bad.'

Lydia said nothing, thought nothing, felt nothing – except an awful weariness, a dread of the awful, relentless, inescapable *cure*. Work, work, and *more* dratted work!

She shrugged and turned away, as disappointed by her interview with Floral as Peggy had been with hers. And yet . . . apart from the minimum necessary to stay alive, Peggy had never done a hand's turn, and *she* wasn't cured.

Lydia turned again and watched Floral carefully sprinkling seed into her watered trench.

'I wouldn't know where to start,' she said dully.

173

'In the farthest corner,' Floral said, without looking up. 'As far from the 'ouse as you can get, my love, some place secret, where no one can find 'ee.'

It sounded . . . good.

'Thee dussn't 'ave to fink of doin' it all at once, see, Lydial. Just a bit at a time, slow, but sure. Make a little garden for Richard, my love. Just him and you . . . An' the earth . . . An' the Lord.' She looked up at last, grinning mischievously. 'An' the flamin' rabbits, o'course, but nuffin's perfect, is it?'

Chapter Fifteen

During that summer, although he'd never set eyes on the place Lydia called 'Richard's Half-acre', Leo came to love it almost as much as she did. This was partly because she looked so wonderful in breeches – and, later, in shorts – but it was mostly because, for the first time since he'd known her, she was happy. She'd worked out her rage with weapons of vengeance: sickle and scythe, axe and mattock; and wept out her grief claiming it was backache. But as spring turned to summer and her white skin turned to gold, all the agony left her and she was like a girl again. Like a girl, in fact, for the first time in Leo's experience, for when he'd met her she'd been very much a woman – enough, at least, to surprise him when she'd said she was only twenty-two. She was twenty-five now – and sixteen. Leggy and slender, quick and bright and – when she sprawled on the couch or lay on the rug, eagerly sniffing the herbacous borders of her precious gardening books – as relaxed and unselfconscious as a child.

She said it was partly because Peggy had moved out, which also surprised him. Until Richard's death, he would never have seen his mother as being capable of constraining anyone into *good* behaviour (leading them astray, perhaps), but Lydia said it wasn't because Peggy was *Peggy*; it was because she was Leo's *mother*.

'There's a difference?'

'There is, for me. It was the way I was brought up. One defers to older women *whoever* they are – Floral and Mrs Lodge included.'

(Yes, he'd noticed that and, quite unconsciously until now, admired it for its tact and gentleness.)

'But the greater the woman's status – and there's no status higher than "mother-in-law" – the more necessary it is to defer to her. Peggy didn't expect it, I'm sure, but I always felt I should be on my best behaviour with her. I think it would have been easier if she'd been more like Gran: more demanding and critical. It would have given me a perimeter to work within. It's a good deal easier to toe the line when you know where the line is, but I never quite knew where I was with her.'

'You and a million others,' Leo said.

'So the safest thing was to keep toeing the line I knew: Gran's line. The trouble is that with Gran I can cross the line occasionally – let myself go – just because I *know* she'll push me back to the right side of it. But if I'd let myself go with Peggy, I wouldn't know where to stop. I'd fall off the edge and –'

'Kill her?'

'Possibly. I've been so angry about Richard, I could have killed anyone who got in my way.'

'Are you still angry, darling?'

'Yes. Oh, yes. But it's different now. I'm using it to make "summat outa nuffin'", as Floral put it, and it helps.'

Against all his expectations, Peggy, too, was making 'summat outa nuffin". She was making a home and loving every minute of it. True, she'd got someone else to rid the walls of seven layers of wallpaper, plaster the cracks and slap on the paint. She'd got someone else to scrub the floors. Hard labour aside, though, she'd done a great deal to turn the place from a rustic labourer's cottage into a smart little 'dower house' which was all frills and roses, as different from Molliston as chalk from cheese.

She'd never before lived alone, but didn't seem to mind it and was far from being lonely, which knocked one of Leo's arguments against the move very squarely on the head. She said living *in* the village was quite different from living beside it and set apart, even if the difference was only a matter of a minute's stroll. Molliston's boundary wall kept people out more in a visual way than a physical. At the cottage she saw the neighbours passing, just as they saw her watching them pass. From there, it was just a matter of putting one's head out of the window to say hello, talk about the weather . . . And from that point, apparently, all manner of curious things could happen. There were few things *more* curious than Peggy joining the Women's Institute, sitting on committees, raising funds for the refugees . . . But if it was what she needed, who was Leo to judge?

It was June of the following year before Lydia finally showed him the garden she'd made. It shocked him so much and for so many reasons he didn't know what to say. The first – and strangest – reason (although he realised the logic of it later) was that she hadn't so much created a garden as *re*-created one, restored it to an almost perfect representation of the way it had been before the war. It wasn't, she said, the exact site she'd originally chosen. Having cleared her first half-acre and begun to dig, she'd found the edge of a paved circle and wouldn't rest until she'd found the whole of it. Having found it, she'd then realised that it must form the centre of her garden, which meant she'd had to clear yet more ground to establish a symmetry. Perhaps that very symmetry had dictated the rest of the design, but still . . . There was something rather eerie about it which made Leo shiver, for it was, as it had always been, a garden without colour. A standard of white roses stood at each corner. Everything else was green or grey: ferns, plaintain lilies, sage – and a few dozen other things whose names he didn't know.

In its original version, it had been surrounded by yew hedges, but Lydia had found even those and chopped them almost to the ground. Now she told him (for the second time, he recalled) that they would grow again, in time, a strongly as before.

'Is there meaning in that for you, Lydia?' he asked, almost harshly, for it was eighteen months since Richard had died and he wanted another child, wanted it so badly it hurt.

'Yes,' she said quietly, and then, even more quietly, 'Don't you like it, Leo?'

'Of course I do. It's beautiful.' But that, at least in part, was a lie. In many ways it was like a graveyard, peaceful and still, almost too tranquil to be borne. It needed . . .

'Why are there no colours?' he asked tentatively.

'I don't know. I meant there to be. When I first imagined it, it had lots of colours, but they . . .' She turned away. 'You *don't* like it.'

'But they what?'

'They seemed inappropriate, that's all!' She whirled to face him again, her eyes burning with unshed tears. 'He doesn't need them! He's asleep!'

'Yes.' He pulled her into his arms and stroked her back, her shoulders, her hair. 'It's a perfect garden – and totally appropriate, Lydia. I was just a bit taken aback. Not just taken *aback*, but actually taken *back*. My father used to sit here, you know, in a garden . . . a garden very like this. There was a birdbath in the middle and a seat at the far end – I believe we burned the remains of it the winter before last.'

'A birdbath,' she echoed dreamily. 'Of course. *That's* what it needs. I *knew* there was something.'

She knew. Yes, she knew, and since it was impossible (wasn't it?) for her to have been visited by the ghost of a garden, Leo decided she must have found the old plans of the grounds and, perhaps unconsciously, been influenced by them. But when he mentioned them later, she swore she hadn't seen them, hadn't even known they existed. At her insistence he went to find them and then wished he hadn't. She went crazy with excitement and wanted to do it *all* – the rose-walk, the knot garden, the whole bloody lot!

'You can't!' he laughed. 'Lydia, we used to have five gardeners to keep it all up! It's impossible, darling. You'd kill yourself, and I don't want . . . Oh, Lydia, isn't Richard's half-acre enough? Isn't it time we thought about having another child?'

'No.' A small, thin voice, not at all like hers. A frightened, evasive glance which darted to his face and then away again, to settle longingly on the old garden lay-out. 'No, not yet. Please, Leo. It's . . . too soon.'

He had an idea that it would always be too soon, that she'd never want another baby. The last time he'd mentioned it (which had also been the first), she'd accused him of wanting to replace Richard, which wasn't true at all. Richard had had his own identity, and that was as true of him dead as it would have been alive. Leo didn't want a replacement – the very idea appalled him. He just wanted *another*, a brother or sister for Richard, just as he and Prue had been for Lionel. They'd never known Lionel, after all, yet Lionel had always been their brother. But Lydia couldn't accept that. She was afraid.

'All right,' he said at last. 'But we can't leave it too long, Lydia. We'll give it another year, will that do?'

He still had some qualms about her tackling the rest of the garden, however, and when, a few weeks later, a young boy came to the farm to ask for a job, Leo took one look at him and thought, 'gardener'. Since the men had come home from the Forces he had enough labour to work the farm and the boy looked respectable enough, spoke quietly and sensibly . . .

'What did you say your name was?'

'Alec Digger, sir.'

Leo laughed. It was a good local name, a good local family, but, just at the moment, it seemed too good to be true!

As soon as she set eyes on Alec Digger, Lydia fell in love. She didn't know it. Almost until it was over, she never knew it, for he was only fifteen and a woman of twenty-five doesn't expect (and doesn't want) to fall in love with a boy so young. The trouble was that he didn't look fifteen. He was a few inches taller than Lydia and as perfectly proportioned as only the very young are: as straight as a sapling, as strong as a tree. He had darkly curling hair and pale, blue-green eyes which in laughter, sorrow or anger could change through all the colours of the sea. He was beautiful.

His beauty was one of the most terrifying, fascinating, bewildering things that had ever happened to her. It made the blood rush through her veins like wine, so that she always felt mildly drunk when she was with him, wanting to talk, laugh, sing and dance – and not daring to do any of them in case she made a fool of herself. She'd thought some small, nameless part of her had died when Richard had died, but Alec brought it to life again (that, and a few other nameless parts, which had *never* before been alive). He made the sun come out on a world grown dark. While Alec was there, she needed nothing else, thought of nothing else. She'd never been so happy.

Neither had she been so shy, so unsure of herself, so fragile. He was her employee, a gardener, an ordinary country boy from a poor country family whose historic relationship with the Chantrys had gone no further than a bow, a scrape and a tug of the forelock; but she couldn't have given him orders to save her life. She could barely look at him for fear of being blinded by the green fire of his eyes.

They pored over the old garden plans together and Lydia stammered, 'I thought of tackling the rose-walk next. What do you think?'

He thought it unwise, but didn't say so; she just knew.

'Or do you think we should carry on where I left off? There was a shrubbery there. No, here – behind the yew hedge. If we can clear it before October we could get it planted and –'

'Can we get the glasshouse repaired, Mrs Chantry?'

'The –?'

'We'll need a glasshouse to bring stuff on through the winter. No sense buying stuff in when you can grow it on from cuttings.'

Lydia had read about cuttings, but hadn't believed that she could perform the miracle they seemed to demand. Only expert gardeners could take cuttings and have a hope they'd survive. But if Alec could do it ... 'Right,' she agreed nervously. 'I'll get the glasshouse repaired then, shall I? And what next?'

Next they cleared the ground for the shrubbery. Having already won the battle for Richard's half-acre, Lydia thought she knew all there was to know about brambles, bindweed and nettles, which, in high summer, could grow almost as fast as she could clear them, giving her the idea that, like King Canute, she was trying to turn back the sea. But Alec went through them like a knife through butter, clearing more in a day than she could have cleared in a week, the easy swing of his shoulders weakening her knees with strange, inexplicable tremors.

There was a terrible tenderness in his strength which arose, she knew, from its all-too-recent acquisition. Two years ago (although she hadn't known him then) he'd been a little boy, still at school,

179

scrumping apples, playing football. Now, to all intents and purposes, he was a man, full of a man's strength and power yet still cocooned in the raw silk of childhood. Silk on his arms, his hands, his smooth, golden throat, silk on his face . . .

A few weeks passed before she began to realise that there was more to Alec Digger than met the eye. They'd stopped for a much needed glass of orange squash and, seated comfortably on a previously buried, rather dilapidated stone wall, he asked suddenly, 'What date is she? 1590?'

'Er –?'

'Molliston.' He spoke the name in a dreamy murmur, as if 'she' were a woman he loved. 'She's Elizabethan, I know, but late, and James I succeeded in 1603, so . . .' He slanted Lydia a sweet, sideways smile. 'Don't say you don't know the date of your own home, now, will you, Mrs Chantry? It's one of the best –'

'*Small,*' Lydia chanted wryly, 'Elizabethan manor houses in England. I know that, at least. It's not small to live in though, Alec. It's not small to keep clean and warm. History has its drawbacks, you know.'

'Everything good has its drawbacks. It's beautiful. That's enough for me. Do you know who built it?'

'I'm afraid I don't. I'm sure Mr Chantry must have told me – and the date – but I'm afraid I've forgotten. Why are you interested?'

'I'm interested in all kind of buildings. I'd have been an architect if . . .'

'An *architect*! Really?'

'You need money for that sort of thing, though. I could have gone to a decent school: I passed the scholarship all right, but there was no money to send me. My mum couldn't wait for me to leave school and start bringing home a pay-packet. Education comes last at our end of the High Street, Mrs Chantry. Do you know how many books we've got in our house? Three – and one of them's about how to tell people's fortunes.'

'What are the other two?'

'The Bible and Longfellow's poems. I go to the library when I can, but you can never learn enough by yourself. You need teachers, someone to guide you along the right track, give you ideas, that sort of thing. They didn't have real architects when this place was built, of course. Most of the builders were stone-masons, working from pattern books of other people's designs. Even Sir Christopher Wren –'

'St Paul's Cathedral,' Lydia interspersed, merely to prove she wasn't a total ignoramus.

'He started out as an astronomer, not an architect.' Alec scratched his ear and sent her another sideways glance. 'So there's hope for me yet, eh, Mrs Chantry?'

His voice had the soft local lilt of rolled R's and muted T's, but he didn't drop his aitches and his grammar was excellent, considering his background. It seemed a terrible irony to Lydia that he should have been born just a few years too late to take advantage of the free secondary education the post-war government had introduced. He was much too intelligent to be just a gardener's boy.

Over supper that night, she asked Leo all the relevant questions about Molliston – built between 1586 and 1598, probably by Arnold (a stone-mason, just as Alec had said) who'd also built Montacute House and Wadham College, Oxford. Leo wanted to know why she was so interested suddenly, and, afraid he might laugh at Alec's ambitions, she said, 'Oh, I just thought it was about time I learned something about it. It's my home, after all.'

A few months later, when he found her studying an entire book about Elizabethan and Jacobean architecture, which she wanted to read before loaning it to Alec, she was beginning to be interested in the subject for its own sake and was wondering how to modernise the place without detracting from its great historic value.

'Those new windows we had made,' she said. 'They're all wrong, Leo. I ought really to find an old-fashioned glass-blower and get the panes re-made to match the old ones.'

Except to approve this idea (and to doubt her chances of finding such a man) Leo didn't say much about it, but he regarded her with a warmth in his eyes which made her feel deeply uncomfortable. She hated it when he looked at her like that, for it meant only one thing: that he thought she would soon be ready to have another baby. Well, he had another think coming. Another year, he'd said, and even that would be too soon. She didn't want another baby. Not now, not ever. All she wanted was to restore the gardens with Alec and restore Molliston *for* him. Or get *him* to restore it! After all, he didn't really need to be *trained* to do it. It all came quite naturally to him, as it had to whatsisname . . . Arnold.

'Arnold wasn't a real architect, you know,' she told Leo firmly. 'He was just a stone-mason, working from patterns.'

He laughed. '*Just* a stone-mason meant something quite different in those days, darling. It's rather like saying Michelangelo was just a man who painted ceilings.'

'Oh, really?' She frowned.

'Of course. When a house has stood for five hundred years, you know it was built by a master, and it makes no difference whether he was a master stone-mason, architect or ballet dancer. That the house stands and continues to function is qualification enough, surely?'

He was hectoring her as he often hectored Peggy, enjoying himself, but clearly wanting an argument. Lydia didn't want an argument. Arguments about neutral subjects could turn, all too easily, into arguments about other things, and Lydia could see precisely where *this* argument might lead. For although Molliston was still standing, it *wasn't* really functioning any more. It was like an abandoned beehive, empty and sad . . .

When it was first built for the Littons, in the late-sixteenth century, it would have been bursting at the seams with people: Lord and Lady Litton, their sons and daughters, nurse, cook, clerks (and their various minions), grooms, gardeners and ploughboys, all packed in and jostling for space by the fire. It was meant to be a *family* home, not this echoing, rattling barn of a place with only three people in it. Lydia sighed, realising suddenly that she'd just argued herself into a corner, without Leo's even opening his mouth to help her along.

Oh, she knew, she knew! But she didn't *want* to know. Children were thieves. They stole your heart, your soul, your mind, every sensitive, quivering part of you so that, when you lost them, you lost everything worth having. She *couldn't* risk that again! And anyway, she was too busy. With Alec.

Lydia's fascination with young Digger was something Leo noticed only gradually, and at first with a vague admiration that she should concern herself for his welfare at all. Later, when she began talking about sending him to Technical College, he began to feel a little anxious, although on the surface of things he could see nothing wrong with the idea. Everyone with more than the dimmest glimmer of intelligence was getting educated these days, so why not Digger? Leo was thinking along the lines of a basic evening class in horticulture. Lydia, it turned out, had something more ambitious in mind: a diploma in draughtsmanship and engineering.

It was the basis of their second serious quarrel, although, when it was over they both knew that their first hadn't been serious at all. It started out calmly enough, with Leo pointing out that the boy had parents of his own and that it was their place, not hers, to decide what was best for him. She pointed out that they were too poor to decide anything beyond the best way to spend his wages. He reminded her that there was pride in poverty and that her interference might not be seen in as rosy a light as she imagined. Even if they were glad to be offered such a chance (which he doubted), it would set off repercussions elsewhere in the village, bewilderment and envy, enmity and gossip.

'You're being ridiculous,' Lydia snapped. 'All I want is to give a good, intelligent boy a decent chance in life!'

'Yes, but he's not the only good, intelligent boy in the village, is he, Lydia? What about the rest of them? Are you planning to send them all to college, and if not, why not? Why should Digger get all the luck and Tom, Dick and Harry none at all? They'll say it isn't fair – and they'll be right. They'll mutter about favouritism and ulterior motives. They'll wonder if you'd have been so kind to Digger if he'd had buck teeth and a squint, like their Harry.'

Lydia had listened to him so far in a state of icy calm which had made him nervous enough; but when she leapt out of her chair and said, 'How *dare* you?' he was scared out of his wits. Being scared was the best way he knew of losing his temper (which scared him even more), but since she'd already lost hers, there was nothing else for it but to let rip and hope for the best.

'I *don't* dare!' he roared. 'But they *will*! That's what I'm trying to *tell* you, you idiot! And I'll tell you something else, too! They'll make *Digger's* life a misery, not yours!'

'You're wrong! He wants an education more than –'

'No! That's what you *think* he wants! But you're *not* thinking, Lydia! You're playing bloody stupid games with other people's lives, and until you realise –'

'Don't you swear at *me*!' She was shaking like an aspen leaf in a hurricane and so, when he came to think of it, was Leo. He sat down suddenly, biting his knuckles, muttering an apology about the swearing but adding firmly, 'I retract nothing else. I know these people. I know what I'm talking about, Lydia.'

'You don't know Alec!'

'Neither do you. He's an ordinary country lad, Lydia, not – Einstein!'

He'd almost said, 'Not Richard', which, he suspected, was at the root of her fascination with Digger. She'd lost one son and adopted another, older, stronger and less vulnerable but (in her eyes at least) just the same. Richard had been as bright as a button, and his intelligence would have been nurtured to its limits until *he'd* become an architect – or whatever else he'd wanted to be. But Digger *wasn't* Richard. Richard was dead, and the best thing Lydia could do with all her spare mother-love was to produce another child of her *own*, not go about stealing other people's!

He didn't dare say any of this to her. True as he thought it, the truth could sometimes be too cruel. But, without saying it, he found himself with nothing useful to say, and their quarrel turned into a nasty, pointless spat which ended only when Leo forbade the entire venture and Lydia stormed away in tears.

They never kissed and made up, just pretended it hadn't happened, which, for Leo, was too reminiscent of his parents' quarrels to be comfortable. But to say, 'I'm sorry; I was cross; I didn't mean all I said,' would also involve reminding Lydia of the things he *had* meant, and she didn't want to know, didn't want to listen.

She never mentioned Digger again. She spent the best part of every day with him, but when Leo asked about their progress in the garden, she told him precisely what he'd asked to know and not a single word more. The shrubbery was complete and the rose-walk – two months ahead of time – was ready to be planted.

This, after scarcely more than a year's work, seemed to Leo a remarkable achievement, for the original shrubbery had covered more than an acre and the rose-walk a good hundred yards. It wasn't possible to inspect the work from a distance and, in the absence of an invitation to view it more intimately, Leo eventually wandered down through the remaining acres of wilderness to take a closer look.

The original garden had been laid out on four levels, the largest and lowest of which had since been taken over by Manor Farm for grain production. The shrubbery and Richard's Half-acre were on the next level, the rose-walk and the still unreclaimed knot garden above that. But there was not – and never had been – a point from which one could see it all. It was a garden of surprises which – even in its heyday when every inch was under cultivation – always gave the impression that it was keeping a few secrets to itself.

It hadn't changed in that respect, for as Leo came to Richard's Half-acre, he found much to surprise him: a stone seat where the old wooden bench had been, a bird-bath in the centre and a bright new growth on the yew hedge, already clipped to shape. There were also a few small touches of colour: lavender bushes encircling the rose trees, clove-scented pinks edging the grass. He felt rather hurt that Lydia hadn't mentioned these changes. Small though they were, they'd given the place a quite different air, a feeling of vitality and growth. Of healing, perhaps . . .

As this thought crossed his mind, he heard her laughing. She was some distance away, beyond the shrubbery (neat as a pin, but still too sparsely grown to be worthy of its name), but as he walked towards the sound, expecting it to cease, she went on laughing in such a way that he began to wonder if it really was her, or someone else, a young village girl perhaps, come to visit young Digger. Whoever she was, her funny-bone had been tickled half to death, for she went on laughing. She couldn't stop.

He saw them before they saw him. They'd scythed the long grass which was all that remained of the old knot garden and Digger was stuffing handfuls of the resulting hay down the back of Lydia's blouse. It was an innocent enough game, locally called 'grass salad', which Leo had played quite a few times in his youth. But with his youth some distance behind him, he knew the game was not as innocent as it seemed. It was an expression of unidentified longings, unrecognised hungers, passions one felt without knowing what they signified. Grass salad, in short, was a boy's first taste of forbidden fruit. And Alec Digger, God damn him, was getting *his* first taste from Leo's wife!

Rage struck him speechless for a moment (a lucky moment, he realised afterwards, because if he'd spoken he'd almost certainly have spluttered, 'Fake your girty hands off my knife!'). But he took a step forward, his eyes blazing, and Digger looked up, turned white and dropped Lydia like a hot brick.

Still happily chortling on the ground at his feet, she scrabbled (quite wantonly, Leo thought) inside her blouse to fish out itchy handfuls of grass. 'You beast!' She laughed huskily. 'I'll get you for that, Alec Digger.'

The boy nudged her shoulder with his knee. An awful silence fell, during which, Leo noticed, Lydia's face went red and Digger's a sick shade of green. Leo suspected that his own complexion was probably purple, partly with rage, partly with the effort of controlling it and partly with the difficulty of saying something – anything – that would come out the right way around.

In the end, and rather to his surprise, he said, 'Telephone, darling. Queen Mary. It sounded rather urgent, so I thought I'd better find you.'

'Gran?' The colour drained from her face. She jumped up, tweaking the hem of her blouse to shake out the remains of the grass. 'Did she say what was wrong?'

'No, but I think you should call her back as soon as possible.'

They walked back to the house together, Lydia almost running, and Leo striding beside her, not letting her advance an inch out of arm's reach. After its enforced pause for breath at the scene of the crime, his temper had double-declutched from roaring first gear to cruising top; he could feel it roaring in his ears, ruffling his hair, filling him with an almost exultant awareness of his own power. He was going to wake her up, sort her out, show her who was boss! Just let him get her behind closed doors and he'd wipe the floor with her!

Lydia knew she'd done something dreadful – and knew why – in the instant she saw Leo standing there, all tensed up and blazing like a torch, as on the day she'd told him that Richard wasn't his. And yet, as on that occasion, he'd spoken almost in a whisper, so calm and controlled, she could almost hear his sinews cracking under the strain.

He had a lot more sinews to crack, now, of course. Four years of hard work and good feeding had done wonders for his physique, although she hadn't quite realised the extent of those wonders until now. He stood six feet two in his stockinged feet (a good inch taller in his boots), and although he could still be judged a slender man, the only raw bones that were evident now were his knuckles.

His news of her grandmother's phone call had frightened her (if Gran sounded urgent she must be frantic about something!) but as she ran back to the house to return the call, she knew that at least half her fear was of Leo – or, rather, of her own thoughts concerning him. She wanted to be on her own for a little while to sort things out in her mind, but every time she thought she'd escaped him, a glance to her right always revealed the toe of his boot, keeping pace, just one step behind her.

Oh, dear Lord, what had she done? What had she *done*? Had she been Leo Chantry's *daughter*, had he found his *daughter* rollicking about on the grass with the gardening boy, he'd have been well within his rights to have walloped her halfway to Kingdom Come. But Lydia wasn't his daughter. She was his wife!

That was part of the trouble, of course, that she didn't *want* to be his wife. She loved him dearly (oh, yes, dearly), yet had never felt for him as she'd felt for Alec – so full of life and love and . . . Oh, hell . . . So full of *lust* she hardly knew where to put herself when she was with him. Lust? *Lust*? Really that? A desire for his body and nothing else?

No. A desire for his youth. A desire to be sixteen again, to have known no grief – and no regrets – beyond the lack of a good education. He'd given her that, that brief return to careless youth, for she had until now almost believed they were the same: two children playing on the brink of – *adultery*. Yes, just playing, for Lydia was certain the bubble would have burst before her stupidity had led her further, but that was no excuse! She should have known better!

Molliston's great oak door (which weighed half a ton) stood wide open and as she hurried through to telephone her grandmother, it slammed behind her with an almighty crash. She halted, shuddering, biting her lip on terror, knowing precisely how much strength – how much fury – Leo had needed actually to *slam* a door of such dimensions.

But what could she say to him? What could she do? She'd never be able to explain it, not in a million years, and even if she tried he wouldn't listen, for he had right on his side, and she had no excuses. A married woman of twenty-six had lost all her claims to innocence. A married woman of twenty-six is culpable and has nothing left to do but . . . face the music.

She turned to face him, gritting her teeth to keep them from chattering, and saw a man she barely recognised: tall and powerful and so grim of countenance he'd have scared off an army, let alone an erring wife.

'Your grandmother didn't call,' he said softly.

'Oh . . .' She squeezed her eyes shut on despair and muttered shakily, 'I'm sorry, Leo.'

'Yes, so am I. I've been a bloody fool. But not any more.' He covered the distance between them at such speed she could do nothing to save herself. His hand gripped her elbow and snatched her against him. The breath left her body at the contact, but nothing happened to Leo. Even his stomach didn't give. He was as hard as nails.

'Leo!' she wailed frantically. 'Please! *Listen* to me!'

'No.' His voice was so soft, so terrible, it made Lydia's hair stand on end. 'You listen to me, madam, and listen well.' He shook her, quite gently. 'And look at me while you listen, because I'm the only man you're going to see from now on and you'd best get accustomed to the idea.' He shook her again. 'Look at your *husband*, Lydia.'

She looked and was amazed to find him smiling down at her, almost lovingly, almost sweetly. It was the smile of a man planning torture.

He steered her firmly towards the inner hall, his hand on her arm like iron. Lydia dug her heels in, but it made no difference at all. He walked, she walked. She clawed at his hand, twisted to free herself, cried out frantically, 'Stop, Leo! *Please*!' But it made no difference at all.

'Will you walk upstairs?' he asked pleasantly. 'Or shall I carry you? Fireman's lift, I'm afraid, nothing fancy. I have to conserve my strength for the rest of the day's exertions.'

Lydia's stomach performed a swooping somersault. She searched his eyes for a clue to his intentions, but found only a hard, icy glitter which promised nothing but the worst. She heard an echo of his voice from long ago and far away: *If you cheat me again, I'll make your life such a misery, you'll wish you'd never been born.* She hadn't believed it then. She believed it now.

'W-what are you going to do?' she whispered.

His smile softened. His voice hardened to its usual authoritative rasp. 'I'm going to do what I should have done a long time ago, Lydia. I'm going to give you a baby.' He pulled her into his arms, planted a laughing kiss on her mouth. 'So grit your teeth and think of England,' he chuckled. '*I'm* hoping for triplets.'

Part Two

Chapter Sixteen

At eighty, old Mrs Westley looked scarcely different than she had at sixty-nine, when Leo had first met her and privately called her a dragon. He no longer thought her a dragon. He respected and admired her, might even be said to love her, but he'd never been able to bring himself to call her 'Gran' (which had always seemed to him to be beneath her dignity) and, after some early experimentation with other forms of address, he now called her 'Ma'am,' teasingly linking her with the regal lady she so closely resembled.

As she poured his coffee at breakfast and kept a beady eye on the children's table manners, he scanned the Announcements page in *The Times* until he found what he was looking for.

'Got it,' he said. 'Here we are, Ma'am – "Lionel David Ranolph, a brother to Dinah, Charlotte and Julia".' He passed the newspaper to Mrs Westley, but his smile turned in another direction, to the two flaxen-haired little girls seated on heaped up cushions at the table and to little Julia (who'd pronounced herself 'Zula'), in her highchair.

'There you are, girls,' he said. 'It's official. You've got a brother. It says so in the newspaper, so it must be true.'

'We already *know* that,' Dinah said. (She was five and knew it all.) '*We've* known for ages.'

'And we don't like it,' Charlotte added severely.

None of Leo's daughters greatly resembled their mother in looks, but Charlotte was so like her in character she kept Leo in a state of near-constant fascination and amusement. She was three: healthy, well-fed and loved half to death, yet somehow she gave the impression she was carrying the world on her shoulders and was about to expire under the strain.

Floral, who was trying to feed Zula her porridge (without much success), said, 'Wadja mean, you don't like 'im? Your own darlin' little bruvver? 'Course you likes 'im!'

191

'We don't, then,' Dinah piped up bossily. 'For one thing, in case you don't know, Floral, he cries all the time and, for another, we don't like his name.'

'David,' said Mrs Westley, 'is a fine old name. A name from the Bible, Dinah. You've heard the story about David and Goliath, haven't you?'

'So why,' Dinah asked, 'are we calling him Linoleum?'

Leo laughed, inhaled a crumb of toast and put himself out of action for the next few minutes. By the time he'd recovered, the conversation had moved on a little and Mrs Westley was explaining about the Chantry tradition of calling first sons Lionel. Out of respect for Peggy (or perhaps for Richard) Lydia had suggested that they christen the child Lionel and call him David, which seemed simple enough to Leo, although the girls couldn't make head or tail of it.

He'd taken the two older ones to visit Lydia in the nursing home, but it had worried them more to see her there than not to see her at all. Charlotte kept asking what was wrong with her and was Leo *quite* sure the doctor could make her better? And David, who'd scarcely stopped crying since he was born, five days ago, had frightened them all – including Leo. Although he'd been pronounced perfectly healthy, he screamed like a soul in torment and rather looked that way, too.

It was sad for Lydia to have had such an uncomfortable start with him, for he was the only one who looked like her – and thus like Richard. Zula was like Richard in nature: mischievous, energetic and always laughing (she drove the other two crazy), but David was the spitting image of Richard, even to the ridge of silky black hair which ran the length of his spine. Still, Lydia's skills as a mother were now so well developed she complained of nothing but tiredness. 'Probably just colic,' she'd said. 'It'll go.'

Leo hoped she was right. With the children coming at such regular intervals (at Lydia's insistence, not Leo's, although she'd also insisted that David would be the last), they'd had barely a year's quota of unbroken sleep during the past five years. Even before his son's birth, Leo had been dreading the upheaval a new baby would bring. He wished to God Lydia would get a nanny to help her, but he'd put her off the idea, years ago, when he'd complained of his mother's 'neglect' of her offspring.

He was pretty sure, now, that he'd imagined that neglect. True, Peggy wasn't at all keen on small babies, but once they could walk and talk she seemed to find their level as no one else could. Lydia said it was because she'd never grown up, which was true enough. True of himself, too, in a way, for he was rarely happier than when he was with his own children and he was already looking forward to teaching his son to play cricket. It would take a few years, perhaps, but what were a few years? He could recall the day of Dinah's birth as if it were yesterday, and it still *felt* like yesterday. The years since then had flown like the wind, and although that wind had brought its fair share of miseries, they couldn't have been very important, because he could scarcely remember them now.

With breakfast over and the family dispersed about the house, Leo stood for a few minutes at the dining-room window, staring thoughtfully out into a misty November drizzle. They'd mis-timed David's conception. After Richard's arrival in the teeth of a blizzard, Lydia had sworn she'd never again have a winter baby. Yet here it was, November. Cold nights for feeding, wet days for washing. Poor Lydia.

The door creaked behind him and he turned to see Charlotte standing there, regarding him with large, solemn grey eyes as she said anxiously, 'Daddy? When will Mummy come home?'

'Two more days, darling. Not long now.'

She frowned. 'And does she *have* to bring that baby with her?'

'Well, yes. He's not just *that* baby, you see, darling. He's *my* baby. As you are. What would I have done if Mummy had left *you* behind at the nursing home?'

'Was *I* at the nursing home?'

'Of course you were. So were Dinah and Zula.'

'No.' She frowned again. 'Zula wasn't. You said you bought Zula in Woolworth's, for ninepence.'

Leo sucked his cheek. 'I was just teasing, sweetheart. We got her at the nursing home, really, where all the *best* babies come from.'

She thought this over, as was her habit, standing on one leg with her finger in her ear. She wasn't a sad little girl – let loose to play with the others, she laughed as much as they did – but when she had something serious to consider, she gave it her all and wouldn't rest until the problem was solved.

He picked her up and sat her on his hip, rocking her back and forth. 'So what's the difficulty?'

'I don't know,' she sighed. 'I never had a brother before.'

'Ah, I see.'

'Mary Woolton's brother frows stones at her.'

'Good Lord, does he? Well, that's rather different. Such things don't happen in our family. We're kind to one another, aren't we? And if you are kind to David, I'm sure he'll be kind to you.'

She thought about it again before whispering desperately, 'But what if he *isn't*?'

'I'll deal with him,' Leo said. 'Don't worry, darling, you're quite safe with me.'

He knew he'd said the right thing, because as soon as the words were out she wriggled to get down and skipped from the room without sparing him a backward glance.

He was no nearer understanding children then he'd been when Richard was a baby, but Charlotte had given him more insights into his wife's character than he'd ever had before. He'd often felt crushed by Lydia's aloof severity, her lordly manner, her total inability to smile at a problem until it was solved. But he'd discovered from Charlotte that it was all a front. They were both most on their dignity when they were most insecure, worried or frightened. It was rare for Lydia actually to *look* frightened or in need of comfort, but he knew now that when he was too terrified to approach her, that was exactly the right time to approach. *Don't worry, darling. Leave it to me. I'll deal with it.*

He laughed. Thank the Lord she didn't believe him!

Insofar as Lydia could be cured of the death of her firstborn, she thought her three little girls had cured her, filling her life with so much love, laughter and – of course – work, there was little space left for grieving. But David brought the grief back. Not, as Leo, imagined, because he looked so much like Richard, but because, almost before he was born, she'd been certain she would lose him.

Having the girls had been like laying eggs (Zula had missed being born in the car by only forty minutes), but David hadn't wanted to be born; he'd fought every inch of the way and, even two months later, still hadn't forgiven her for bringing him into the world. She'd never known – never even heard of – such a miserable baby. He cried even while he was feeding and rarely slept more than an hour before his screams tore her own sleep to rags. They said there was nothing wrong with him (and Lydia saw to it that 'they' included two of the best paediatricians in England), but *she* knew there was something wrong. He was her fifth child and when a woman has raised five babies there's nothing she doesn't know about soothing and comforting, easing their pain. Wind, colic, constipation, nappy rash, chills, fevers and teething troubles; she knew it all. But she didn't know what was wrong with David. She just knew there was *something* wrong and was certain it would kill him.

As the weeks passed without any noticeable improvement, Lydia became so tired she almost ceased to care. Almost. The worry, like every other thought, failing to find accommodation in her benumbed, sleep-starved brain, found another, deeper, lodging (somewhere between her stomach and her spine) where it acquired teeth and ate her hollow. Having always prided herself on her patience and good manners, she became snappy, irritable and overbearing. Leo scarcely dared speak, let alone do anything to help her. Dinah, having asked her mother the same question three times and received no answer, cried, 'For heaven's *sake*, Mummy!' and discovered, for the first time in her life, how it felt to be smacked and sent to bed.

For an hour after that, Molliston was almost as wet with tears as it had once been with dripping rainwater. David was crying as usual, Dinah with a sore leg and a broken heart, Charlotte and Zula in sympathy and Lydia just because she'd tried everything else and, anyway, couldn't stop. Floral made her a cup of tea and tiptoed away to comfort the girls. Leo came home to comfort Lydia in the only way he knew how – he lost his temper.

Lydia was afraid of very few things. She could pick up worms, toads and large, hairy spiders, thumb her nose at Leo's Hereford bull and walk undaunted through dark country lanes without sparing a thought for escaped lunatics and murderers. But when Leo lost his temper, she was afraid. It wasn't because he'd ever hurt her, or even that she feared he might. It was just that he always, *always* did it when she was feeling too guilty, stupid and inadequate to defend herself and could only think, 'I deserve it. Do your worst.'

His 'worst' on this occasion was to stand over her while she wrote out an advertisement for a trained nanny. Then, with blazing eyes and a quivering index finger pointing resolutely upstairs, he hissed, 'Now go to bed – and stay there until *I* tell you otherwise!'

While she slept, the family ate fish and chips from newspaper parcels, the girls went to bed unwashed and Leo walked the floor with David until five the next morning.

Ten hours of uninterrupted sleep did wonders for Lydia and so, rather strangely, did that advertisement for a nanny: a *trained* nanny who might, with even wider experience than Lydia's, guess what was wrong with David and know what to do about it. But the course of advertisements ran slowly. Two weeks passed before she received the first letter of application and by that time she was as weary and desperate as she'd ever been and Leo, who'd started sheep farming again after the hiatus of the war years, was in the middle of lambing and could no longer help her.

The only time David really 'slept like a baby' was when he was in his pram and the pram was moving. This wasn't a great deal of help. The weather was generally awful – either snowing, raining or blowing a gale (sometimes all three), and even had it been fine, Lydia was too tired to walk very far and the girls too small to walk v

They could be left with Floral, but not for very long. She adored all three of them, but Floral's idea of adoration meant letting them do what the dickens they liked. This was fine when they wanted to play with their dolls. It was terrifying when they wanted to make toffee.

Nevertheless, on the first day afternoon that presented itself (when David had been crying for four hours without cease), Lydia put him in his pram, issued stern warnings to Floral and the girls, and set off to snatch an hour's peace in the lanes. David screamed the full length of the gravelled drive and then, with a last tormented sob, fell silent. He never fell silent without Lydia's needing to check that he was still alive. That done, she walked like a zombie for the next half-hour and didn't begin to think again until she was on her way back, within sight of Peggy's cottage.

Guilt (one guilt among thousands) churned in her stomach. David was eleven weeks old and, except at Christmas, she'd seen Peggy only twice during that time, both times at Molliston. Peggy's last visit had been very brief (David had cried throughout), but it had been long enough for Lydia to have noticed that her mother-in-law was not at her best. She'd been giggly and nervous, talking more quickly than usual about nothing at all. She'd also been in something of a sartorial pickle – wearing a knitted tea-cosy instead of a hat. True, her taste in winter hats rather tended *towards* the tea-cosy mode, but she'd never before hit it spot-on, wearing the hole for the spout (complete with tea-stains) bang in the middle of her forehead.

She was only seventy. Too young to be addled, but by no means too young to be lonely. Lydia stopped walking for a moment and heaved a sigh. Could she – *must* she – worry about Peggy, as well as everything else? Could she – *must* she – care?

She must, of course. Peggy said she'd always wanted to move out of Molliston and had only been waiting for the right place to turn up, but Lydia had never believed it. She'd moved out, at least partly, because of Richard's death, but even before that she hadn't liked living with Lydia. She'd once said, laughing as usual, 'Oh, darling, why do you have to be so po-faced about everything? You spoil all the fun!' It was true – Leo had said quite similar things at different times and, usually, for different reasons – but Lydia couldn't change herself. For her, having fun was something you were allowed to do only when all the work was done and, since the work was *never* done, she must be wrong, Peggy right. Yes, it was her fault Peggy had moved out, her fault she was alone when she could, at this moment, be at Molliston, 'having fun' with Floral and the girls . . .

She'd better call in, then. Just long enough for a cup of tea and a chat. If David would only stay asleep that long . . .

She left the pram under the kitchen window, made her usual check that he was still alive and then tiptoed inside, smiling, her finger pressed to her lips. Peggy welcomed her warmly, asked after everyone and put the kettle on. The hem of her skirt had come unstitched at the back and there was a stain on the front of her otherwise immaculate blue twinset. Such things worried Lydia – her fingers itched to put them right – but it worried her more when, after the relevant enquiries, Peggy said she'd resigned from her beloved W.I.

'But why?' Lydia asked. 'You've always enjoyed it so much!'

'Oh, not really, darling. I enjoyed it at first, when I thought I was doing something useful, but . . . Oh, I don't know. Put a crowd of women together, and all you've got is a gossip factory. You don't realise it, of course, until the crowd disperses into little gaggles, each being as vicious as they can about the next.' She produced her bright, devil-may-care little laugh. 'That's when you begin to wonder what they say about *you* behind your back and since I'm –' Her mouth tightened and she turned away to make the tea.

'You're what, Peggy?'

'Hmph!' She darted a curiously venomous look over her shoulder. 'It's no good *you* sounding so innocent! You're like the rest of them, so ruddy perfect it's sickening!'

'*Perfect*?' Lydia laughed, and felt like weeping. 'Oh, Peggy, if only you knew!'

David started to cry just as Peggy poured the tea and as his preliminary snuffling wail turned to a full-throated scream, Lydia lay back in her chair, closed her eyes and said wearily, 'There. That's how perfect I am, Peggy. I can't stop him crying. I don't know what's wrong with him. It's driving me *mad*.'

She sat up and opened her eyes. Peggy was sitting opposite her, bolt upright, chewing her lips, her eyes darting hither and yon as if to pursue the flight of an out-of-season moth. David's cries were clearly disturbing her as much as they disturbed Lydia, but there was little point in going to fetch him. He cried as much when he was picked up as when he was left alone, and for a mother who wants only to give comfort, that's worse, far worse, than giving him no comfort at all.

'Oh, Peggy,' she sighed. 'What can I do? What can I do?'

'Smother him,' Peggy said. She laughed as she said it, but it was a strange laugh, accompanied by a mischievous glance from the corner of her eye which made Lydia's hackles rise. Some jokes were too tasteless for words. Peggy meant no harm, of course, but surely she could tell how desperate Lydia was? She needed a word of

197

reassurance, not damn silly jokes!

The walk home wasn't long enough to soothe David again and, as his screams echoed from the grey stones of Molliston's high boundary wall, Peggy's words echoed ominously from the grey wall of Lydia's mind. *Smother him.* Detached from the influence of Peggy's laughter, the words acquired a different sense, a different feeling. They were as deep as a well, as dark and empty as a dreamless sleep, as peaceful as . . . death.

Ray Duckett had retired and returned to his home village on the far side of Trowbridge, leaving the house at Manor Farm empty and ripe for conversion into two decent-sized dwellings for Admiralty personnel.

The post-war years had been good ones for farmers and Leo no longer considered himself a poor man. But he wanted to be richer and, since David's birth, had wanted it more than ever. After three midwives had told him, 'It's a girl,' Leo had largely lost interest in continuing the Chantry line and he'd long since forgotten his passion for Molliston. But David had brought it all back. David was the heir, now. Molliston was his. And, if he loved it only half as much as Leo once had, he'd want to keep it for his own son, and perhaps . . . Good Lord, imagine it surviving a thousand years and still having a Chantry in residence!

But it would all cost money. Lydia had given the house an entirely new roof the year Dinah was born, blinking at the enormous cost and informing Leo (more in wonder than resentment) that she could have bought a *brand-new* house for the same money. A very much smaller house, of course, but easy to keep clean, easy to keep warm . . . For all her studies of history and architecture with young Digger (who'd joined the Navy on his National Service call-up and never been seen since), 'easy to keep clean and warm' was still her idea of heaven.

Over the years she'd also repaired or replaced a good few other crumbling corners – the landing balustrade first among them – and now wasn't half as wealthy as she had once been. She'd never been what Leo would call a spendthrift, but she was getting positively *careful* now, worrying about the children's futures, their education, even their *weddings*, for heaven's sake! She was right, of course. One couldn't be too careful with children. But that was precisely why Leo wanted to contribute his own two-penn'orth to the family coffers and the rents from Manor Farmhouse should do it rather well.

He'd had to install a new kitchen at one end, a new bathroom at the other, and get the two halves separately re-wired, but the division of the two dwellings had cost next to nothing, involving only the bricking up and plastering over of three internal doorways. All it needed now was a lick of paint and a few tenants – and by the time David attained his majority he'd be a wealthy man.

If he survived that long. He might not, if Leo accepted the care of him again (which he never would). How Lydia could stand it day after day, night after hag-ridden night, was beyond him. It was torture, the worst part of which wasn't the back-ache, the weariness, the dread of falling asleep on your feet and dropping the child on his head. The worst part of it was *wanting* to drop him on his head.

No. The worst part of it was loving him and knowing that in spite of everything the doctors said, the child was in agony. Doctors didn't know every damn thing! There were all sorts of ailments they knew nothing about until a child failed to develop at the proper rate. When he was two and couldn't walk, when he was three and couldn't talk ... Oh, dear God. And in the torment of that endless night, when there was nothing to do but imagine the kid's pain and be able to do *nothing*, nothing at all to help him ... how could you not want to put him out of his misery?

It was the worst thing Leo had ever contemplated and, once it had crossed his mind, it had been all he'd been able to do not to run upstairs and drag Lydia out of bed – 'Take him, quick, before I kill him!' But David had quietened soon afterwards and they'd both slept for an hour on the couch in the parlour. Nevertheless, Leo wouldn't risk it again. They'd have a nanny before much longer. Until then, Lydia must bear the brunt as best she could. It might kill her – poor, tired little Lydia – but at least it wouldn't kill David.

Lydia interviewed two nannies. She thought the first one best (older and more experienced) but chose the second – a plump little Welsh girl called Mary Preece – just because she could start sooner. She was very sweet with the girls but saw David at his best (asleep), and Lydia would have been happier if she'd seen him at his worst, giving everyone within a range of five miles a death-wish and a splitting headache. But when Lydia mentioned that he wasn't always so good and that she'd *sometimes* (she didn't say always) wondered if there was something wrong with him, Nanny Preece said something wonderfully comforting, just because it was the thing Lydia had first thought of.

'Some babies just don't like being born, Mrs Chantry. And who can blame them? It's a hard old life, isn't it? But he'll get used to it.' She'd bent over the crib and smiled into his face which, even in sleep, bore signs of his waking torment. 'And with a lovely family like yours, Mrs Chantry, I think he might even learn to like it.'

Almost three months of sleeplessness had made Lydia more than usually emotional, even a bit mawkish, and it was all she could do not to fall into the poor girl's arms and sob, 'Thank you! Oh, thank you!' But she controlled herself, shook hands instead and said, 'We'll see you in a fortnight, then.'

A fortnight. For all the relief it offered it might have been forty years, but it was the best that could be done, and Lydia had always maintained that the best was good enough. But oh, God, it *wasn't* good enough! She needed help *now*. If only Gran weren't so old! If only Peggy weren't so . . . everything. If only Leo weren't so busy with his lambs! And if only Mary Preece could sleep under the table, without needing the whole house turned inside out to receive her . . .

The difficulties of turning the house inside out, even with Floral's help and that of the faithful (but rheumatic) Mrs Lodge, turned out to be the straw that broke the camel's back. Heaving heavy furniture about, even in good health and strength, had never been Lydia's best suit, but with the children asking questions about it at every turn, David screaming in the background, Mrs Lodge saying, 'It's no good, Mrs Chantry, I'll 'ave to sit down a minute,' just as Lydia had 'taken the weight at her end', it was all too much to be borne.

When it was all straight, scrubbed and polished, she fell asleep on the couch and woke up, soon after eleven, to a deathly silence. Leo had gone back to his lambs after dinner and wasn't likely to be home until gone midnight, when one of the men was due to relieve him. David, who'd been crying when she'd dropped off, was fast asleep in his carry-cot.

She never knew how she managed to get him upstairs without waking him, but she remembered for the rest of her life how much the effort had hurt. Her spine felt as if it had crumbled to hot dust, her shoulders and elbows shrieked with the strain, her legs were molten iron. Yet David slept.

Lydia stood over him for a moment, her hands clasped in prayer. Just a few more hours. Just a few, please, God. She thought of a bath, a blissful hot bath, but at times like these bathing was a luxury she couldn't afford. She kicked off her shoes, stripped to her petticoat and fell into bed like a rock.

Since lambing had begun, she and Leo had been sleeping in different rooms in hope of snatching their few hours of rest without risk of disturbing one another and her last thought before she fell asleep was one of blissful gratitude that they'd arranged it that way. *Nothing* would wake her now.

She learned later that she'd slept for three hours which, taking David's feeding pattern into account, was no less than she could have asked. But when his screams woke her, she thought she'd been sleeping only minutes, for she seemed to emerge not from the dark well of oblivion she'd longed for, but from the dappled shadow of mere drowse. She'd scarcely put her foot across the borders of heaven. Now she was back in the wild, shrieking torment of hell.

Aching in every limb, sobbing with rage and disappointment, she stood over the cot and watched narrow-eyed, while her son, dimly lit by the night-light on the landing, writhed and roared, his clenched fists lashing the air, his eyes squeezed to slits, his face darkened to purple. He was a goblin, a demon. He wasn't her son, but a changeling sent by the devil. She *hated* him!

Smother him!

No, no, she loved him! She loved him so much, so *much*! But what more could she do? She'd tried everything, done all she could to ease his suffering, yet knew . . . Knew that his suffering would last all his days. There was something *wrong* with him!

Smother him. Put him out of his misery, put an end to his pain . . .

She was not aware that she'd already taken the pillow from the bed. Had there not been a mirror behind the door she might never have known it, but as she raised the pillow to press it to his face, her own movement reflected back to her and, thinking Leo had caught her in the act, she whirled to face him – and faced only herself. She looked like a lunatic, wild-eyed and demented, murderously insane.

Lydia screamed.

How *that* scream woke him when none of David's had, Leo never knew. He didn't even know he had woken until he was halfway down the landing. He'd gone to bed in his skin and was still wearing only that and one sleeve of his dressing gown when Lydia (in her petticoat) ran to meet him and threw herself into his arms, sobbing, 'Help me! Help me! I nearly killed him!'

From a state of shock and nerve-jumping terror, Leo was suddenly overtaken by a strange feeling of calm, which he later recognised as relief – that he wasn't the only one to entertain murderous thoughts about his own flesh and blood. At the time, though, calm was all he felt and all he needed. While Lydia clung to him, with difficulty he tied the sash of his gown and carried her back to his own bed, murmuring, 'Hush, hush, it's all right, sweetheart, I understand.'

'No! No, you don't! I was going to suffocate him! I had the pillow in my hands!'

'Better than dropping him on his head, as *I* once contemplated.'

'What?'

'It's only natural, darling. We're worn out – you more than me –

but if I couldn't stand it in one night, why should you, after ninety? The important thing is that we both stopped ourselves in time. He's not dead yet, is he?'

Lydia stared at him, amazed. Then, her gaze sliding to the clock beside the bed, she began to cry again, weakly, covering her face with her hands. 'Oh, God, it's two o'clock! Oh, poor David! He's *hungry*!'

'Go to sleep. I'll see to it.'

'But you've scarcely been in bed two hours . . .'

He smiled and stroked her hair, loving her more in this moment of weakness than he'd ever loved her in her strength. 'Ssh. Go to sleep.'

David was still crying, but Leo didn't go to him. He covered Lydia with the blankets, tucked her in and went on stroking her hair until she relaxed, closed her eyes and curled into sleep. Leo tiptoed to the door.

'It was your mother,' she murmured drowsily. 'It had never crossed my mind until she said it.'

'Said what?'

'*Smother him* . . . Joking, of course. Always joking . . .'

The next day, after waving a few pound notes under a few noses at Manor Farm, Leo reorganised his working life to ensure Lydia some sleep. Four days later, as he marched David up and down the great hall, reciting huge tracts of Shakespeare to keep his mind from the screams, the screams suddenly ceased. The silence which followed made Leo feel dizzy. His ears rang with it. He shook his head as if to shake it off, but it went on . . . And on.

'"Oh, sleep",' Leo quoted breathlessly, '"Oh, gentle sleep, how have I frighted thee that thou no more wilt weigh my eyelids down –"'

David frowned up at his father, blinked a few times and frowned again.

'"– and steep my senses,"' Leo whispered, '"in forgetfulness?"'

David made a little 'oo' shape with his mouth. With bated breath Leo watched him, sensing that something had changed, that the pain – whatever it was – had gone and that David, like his father, could scarcely believe it. He looked so surprised! He turned his head and stared intently at the button on Leo's waistcoat, then reached out his hand to grasp the gold watch-chain which looped around it.

He'd been fed an hour ago and had cried ever since. Now, his frown clearing, he smiled for the first time in his life – and fell asleep. He was still asleep when Leo went to do the milking, four hours later.

Chapter Seventeen

It seemed a terrible irony to Lydia that David stopped screaming a few days *before* Mary Preece arrived to relieve her. She couldn't believe it at first. Every time he fell asleep (often for six hours at a stretch, as if to make up for lost time) she gazed at him without comprehension, hovered over him to check that he was still breathing, waited – her nerves stretched like electric wires – for him to wake and begin crying again. He *did* sometimes cry, when his nappy was wet, when he was hungry or windy, but when she answered his needs (uttering prayers), he soon settled again to gaze up at her with that wondering, healthy-happy baby look which seemed to say, 'I know you, don't I? But I can't quite place you.'

Lying naked on his towel, while she disposed of a soiled nappy and reached for a clean one, he began to play with his feet and to burble to himself as a baby should, trying out his voice with sounds other than the full-throated roar she had come to dread. 'Ga-ga-bo-boo, goo-goo-goooo.'

When the girls had been at the same stage, Lydia had answered these conversational gambits with burbling drivel of her own: 'Did you, darling? And what happened next?' But she couldn't think of a thing to say to David. Except, perhaps, 'Sorry'. She'd wanted to kill him, had been within inches of actually doing so! And, now that it was over, she knew that it had been not to put him out of *his* misery, but to put *her* out of her own. Leo had said he'd felt the same, but she didn't really believe him. He'd said it only to comfort her, she was sure, because how else could he have sounded so casual about it, so easy of mind? *He's not dead yet, is he?* He wouldn't have been able to say that if he'd felt as guilty – as appalled – as Lydia felt! She'd been within *inches*! And been saved only by her reflection in a mirror . . .

Ever since she'd tricked Leo into marrying her, Lydia had been driven by a need to make it up to him, make him happy, almost in spite of her. Now she felt the same about David – so much so, that for the first few weeks after Mary Preece's arrival, she could scarcely bear to let the poor girl near him. She felt as if she was convalescing from a long illness, and that – like regular doses of tonic wine and calves-foot jelly – David was the only hope she had of getting back on her feet again. She had to *show* him how much she loved him, had to *feel* that love, *convince* herself of it. Mary helped enormously by learning to know the girls while Lydia learned to know her son, and although she'd been told, originally, that she'd been engaged for David's sake, she tactfully said nothing to remind Lydia of it.

On the first fine afternoon in March, Mary took the girls out for a much-needed walk and Lydia, still feeling a little weak and unsure of herself, wandered around the garden, with David in her arms. Although it had never been fully restored to its pre-war condition, it was a lovely garden now. The top lawns, which Leo had once used as an extra hayfield, were edged by wide herbaceous borders. The rose-walk and the old knot garden were thriving as of old. It was all maintained now by a trained man – one Wilfred Sparrow – and his strong but 'innocent' brother-in-law, Dandy. Lydia hadn't been too happy about Dandy's innocence at first: his drooping eyes and sagging mouth had been a little off-putting, to say the least. But he was as good as gold and as sweet-natured as a child. And although he understood very little else, he understood about Richard's Half-acre.

'Daz Miz'z Chaahnry's corner,' she'd once heard him tell the girls. 'Wer she do zet all by 'erzelf an' watch the birdies.'

'Watch the birdy' was a phrase which went with 'Say cheese' when Leo was taking family photographs, and for ages afterwards Dinah had been convinced that Lydia went to Richard's Half-acre to have her photograph taken. But she didn't. She went there to find peace. To think things over and, with luck, to find some way of forgiving herself.

In her good tweed coat, green felt hat and gloves, she sat on the stone seat with David on her knee and told him the names of the flowers. Violets and primroses, tiny wild daffodils, windflowers, celandines and almond blossom. Flowers of the spring. Flowers of rebirth. Flowers of hope.

'Your daddy's right,' she said at last. 'It's no good grieving about the things we can't change. Richard's dead, but you're still alive, sweetheart, and that's all that *really* matters, isn't it?'

At four months, David was already mastering the art of blowing raspberries through copious streams of dribble. He was also learning

204

to be proud of his achievements, to chuckle and preen himself just as Richard, at the same age, had done. Lydia laughed and kissed him.

'You don't care, do you?' she teased gently. 'Every day's a new day for you. I wish I could be the same . . .' She sighed and looked about her, noticing that from the hatchet-scarred stumps she'd once made of them, the yew hedges had grown up tall and straight again – five feet in only seven years. She remembered Leo asking *Does that have any meaning for you?* and it had, it *did*! But the yew hedge had nothing on its conscience and Lydia had so many things on hers. A woman couldn't renew herself; she couldn't start afresh; she could only learn from her mistakes and hope to grow old gracefully with the wisdom (please, God!) she acquired along the way.

Grow old gracefully . . . The thought put her in mind of Peggy, who was *not* growing old gracefully – just lonely. She hadn't been to Molliston in weeks and Lydia – for obvious reasons – hadn't quite pined for her company in the meantime. Poor woman . . . Although Lydia had blamed her a thousand times in her mind and even now felt a few stirrings of resentment, it hadn't really been Peggy's fault. A joke, that was all.

'But it's too late to do anything about it, today, David.' (His eyes had glazed and were beginning to droop with sleep.) 'We'll go and see her tomorrow.'

A Captain Markham and a Mr Williams, with their respective wives and families, had taken the tenancies at Numbers one and two Manor Farm. Leo's land agent had seen to all the necessary business, leaving Leo with nothing more onerous to do than say hello, if he felt sociable, and, since Leo generally felt a good deal more sociable than his circumstances allowed, he said hello.

Mr Williams, a civil servant, was a thin, balding chap, terrified of his wife (equally thin and almost equally balding) who, in her turn, was terrified of living in the country. She asked Leo what she should do if she met a fox. Leo said that if she met one there'd be a fair chance it was dead, so the best thing to do would be to take no notice. She asked him what she should do if she met a bull or a poisonous viper. His own bull was of the type known in farming circles as 'a funny bugger' – thus rarely let loose to make social calls – and the vipers had been cultivated out of existence years ago. He advised Mrs Williams to keep to the roads until she felt more at ease with the local fauna. Then, smiling rather more broadly than was his wont with complete strangers, he went next door to say hello.

Captain Markham, a submariner, had performed the devilishly clever trick of hiding under the Atlantic Ocean while his wife was moving house. She was still in the throes of it when Leo called, her face flushed pink, blonde curls peeping from beneath a jaunty little turban with a bow on top. Her blouse had departed the waistband of her skirt and was bursting its buttons in a manner Leo found delightful, as was her frank little chuckle when she confessed to being 'a terrible sight'.

A terrible sight indeed. It made Leo quite weak at the knees, all that lushly bulging female flesh, those laughing blue eyes, that wide, happy smile with the rapacious eye-teeth which (he imagined in a daze of confusion) might sink into his throat and inject him with a wild contagion of careless youth. If she was twenty, it was all she was, while he, heaven help him, was forty-two and ageing fast.

'Settling in all right?' he asked dreamily. 'Anything I can do?'

She asked him to show her where the stop-cock was, and he had to think about it for the best part of half a minute before he understood what she meant. Her name was Angela. Angela, Angela. It tasted of ambrosia . . .

He spent the rest of the day in a state of restive depression, unable to think of anything but his age and the sneaky way it had crept up on him. It seemed only yesterday he'd been liberated from prison camp – on his thirtieth birthday – and although the time had passed so quickly since then, he seemed to have spent every minute of it trying to make up for lost time, trying . . . Trying to get *started* again. The start had always been delayed by something or other: marrying Lydia, having Richard, losing him, getting over it, having some more. They'd kept saying they'd have a holiday – as soon as Dinah was toilet-trained, as soon as Charlotte was walking, as soon as Zula could sleep through the night, as soon as David stopped crying. They'd kept saying they'd have the decorators in, throw a garden party, go up to Town for a week's shopping and theatre-going . . . But none of it had happened. They'd worked, wept and worried enough, certainly. But they hadn't *lived*! They hadn't even *started*! And here he was, forty-two, and on the way back again!

After dinner, while Lydia sat smocking the front of a new summer frock for Dinah, Leo watched her over the top of his newspaper – and found her wanting. Since rationing had ceased, she'd bought herself some new clothes: all 'good', all sensible, all suitable to her station in life and as drab as jute sacking. No, that wasn't fair. Her twinset *was* red (she'd always looked her best in red) – but it was the dullest red in the spectrum, the colour of house-bricks – and it made her face look so white, her eyes so lifeless and tired . . . How old was she now? Thirty-four? A woman couldn't give birth to five babies and at thirty-four still look twenty. And Lydia *didn't* look twenty. Yet she was still slim, still upright and graceful, and her hair was still untouched by grey. Save for a few crows' feet around the eyes, she *could* have been twenty. But wasn't. Even in repose she looked serious, dutiful, responsible. There'd never been much joy in her.

He sighed.

'What?' Lydia asked.

'What?'

'What were you thinking about?'

'Er – I was wondering what *you* were thinking, actually. Now that things have smoothed over a bit, I'd have thought you'd feel happier, but you don't look it. Aren't you satisfied with Mary?'

'Yes, she's marvellous.' She smiled, teasing him. 'I can't think why you wouldn't let me get a nanny years ago.'

Leo shrugged. 'Sheer cruelty,' he confessed. 'So what *were* you thinking about?'

'I don't know. Everything, nothing. Your mother mainly, I suppose, I keep meaning to call in on her, but . . . Seen her today?'

'The usual.' He popped in at the cottage most mornings, usually just long enough to say 'Everything all right?' before popping out again. Given her head, his mother could talk for a week and, at the end of the week, still have said nothing remotely worth hearing. Even she wasn't as much fun as she used to be. She bored him to tears.

'Tell you who I *did* see today,' he went on brightly. 'Our new neighbours.' He wanted to talk about Angela, but dealt with the Williamses first, making Lydia laugh. Any other woman (his mother, for example) would have drawn blood from the joke, worked it to its limits, but Lydia just laughed, stopped laughing and added depressingly, 'Oh, poor dear. We'll have to be kind to her, won't we?'

'Will we?' Leo demanded in a pained voice. 'Why? I was thinking of setting the bull on her.'

'Beast.' Lydia snipped her embroidery thread and held the work up for her shortsighted scrutiny. 'What about the other people? Captain Mottram, was it?'

'Markham. Now *he's* a man after my own heart. I liked him enormously; think I could learn something from him, in fact.'

'Oh? What?'

'How to disappear when my wife's moving furniture. In short, he wasn't there and isn't likely to be for the next five months. His wife's the one you should be kind to, poor girl.'

His eyes suddenly went hot and he hid behind his newspaper, pretending to scan the fat-stock prices. 'Why don't you ask her to tea one day?' he murmured, still hiding. 'Nice girl. Clergyman's daughter. She's got a little boy. Eighteen months. Someone for Zula to play with, perhaps?'

'Mm,' Lydia said. 'Sounds fun.'

Mmm, Leo thought. It did.

Lydia was strolling down the drive with Zula, both on their way (at last) to visit Peggy, when Angela Markham, with her little boy in his pushchair, walked up it. Lydia knew she was Mrs Markham only from Leo's off-hand description of her. ('I didn't really notice, darling. Fairish, plumpish. A bit like your friend Rose, I suppose.')

Without saying anything at all, he'd said rather a lot about their new neighbour. He hadn't cared much for Rose. And when they'd met Howard, Rose's husband, Leo had been rather sniffy about him, too. Lydia hadn't actually minded Howard's mildly suggestive jokes, his one lapse into 'language not fit for a lady's ears'. (She'd been too busy to listen, and anyway had heard it all before.) In her view, Howard had been a perfectly normal, well-intentioned and – on the whole – quite decent, countryman. But Leo, being a perfectly normal country *gentleman*, evidently expected higher standards.

Lydia quite saw his point, of course. He'd even forbidden any swearing on the farm lest his wife or – worse – one of his daughters happened by, and he'd never been able to tolerate salacious or smutty jokes. Sex was private. Sex was sacred. Funny as it sometimes was, its humour was not a thing one bandied about in company. So Howard wouldn't do . . .

Leo hadn't forbidden Lydia to invite them to Molliston again; in fact, he'd taken great pains to say she could, but there'd been little point and, after Richard's death, the friendship had fallen completely by the wayside. They just sent Christmas cards now.

But Leo was right about Mrs Markham. She didn't really look like Rose, but she had something of Rose about her – a free and easy, frank and fearless look, which, for Lydia, had a certain charm. It seemed such a *sensible* attitude to life. She'd always wished she could be the same, but had never learned how. There was always so much to worry about.

'Mrs Chantry?'

Lydia smiled. 'Mrs Markham?'

'Heavens, how on earth did you know?'

'My husband said you had friendly blue eyes.' (He hadn't, of course, but 'fairish, plumpish' wasn't really quotable, and she *did* have friendly blue eyes.)

They introduced each other to their respective children (the young Markham was called John) and then attempted to introduce the children to each other, laughing when the only courtesies to result took the form of shy, rather hostile stares.

'But I see I've come at the wrong time,' Mrs Markham said. 'You were on your way out. Going somewhere nice?'

A depressing image of Peggy's dusty little cottage flitted through Lydia's mind. So did yet another pang of guilt, but Mrs Markham's friendly blue eyes soon quenched that. 'No,' Lydia said. 'Nothing that can't wait. Come and meet the rest of the tribe and have coffee with me, won't you?'

Lydia knew for a fact that this exchange took place at ten o'clock in the morning, because she'd looked at the church clock and heard it begin to strike in the instant before she'd seen Angela Markham. The next thing she knew, it was half-past twelve, and she knew that for a fact because Leo walked in for his lunch (a cold one, fortunately, but not even thought of, let alone ready) and caught the pair of them in fits of giggles on the drawing-room sofa.

The first thing Lydia noticed, before her own face turned red, was that Leo had gone red in the face too. He was too well-mannered to complain of his missing lunch, Lydia too well-mannered to explain it and make Angela think she'd overstayed her welcome. The only thing to do was to look calmly at her watch and invite Angela to eat with them.

As she was meant to, Angela said, 'No, no, I simply must *go*.'

As he was *not* meant to (the remains of the roast beef had certain limits), Leo laughed and said firmly, 'No, no, you simply must *stay*. We insist, don't we, darling?'

Her anxiety about the roast beef aside, Lydia had rarely felt so grateful to him for anything. She'd discovered that she and Angela had been to the same girls' school in Bath. There'd been a nine-year gap (Angela was twenty-five), but they'd shared the same sadistic games mistress and the same half-crazed music teacher; they'd walked the same green-tiled passageway with books balanced on their heads to correct their 'carriage'. Absolute hell at the time. Hilarious now. And it was lovely to share something so basic – and so unimportant – with another woman. As once before, with Alec Digger, Lydia felt she was clawing back pieces of her youth from Angela, sticking them, like flesh-coloured plasters, over the wounds of life, so that she began to feel whole again.

Mary Preece had given Lydia a similar feeling, but not the same. A close intimacy was impossible, anyway, with someone whose salary you paid and Mary was as aware of that as Lydia was. She was always friendly, always kind and cooperative, but the professional distance between them was a kind of no-man's land which neither dared cross. Angela was different. Angela could be a *real* friend.

'I didn't realise I needed a friend so much,' she told Leo when they went to bed, 'until you invited her to stay to lunch. And you liked her, didn't you, Leo? You won't mind if she comes again?'

He laughed, a little uncomfortably Lydia thought, so that she began to wonder if his apparent liking of Angela had been *only* good manners. But he called her a dope, told her Angela could move in if it would make Lydia happy.

'I *want* you to be happy,' he said roughly. 'Can't you get that through your head? I *want* you to be happy.'

He made love to her then, more passionately and pleasurably than he had done in years. When it was over, and Lydia burrowed into the curve of his shoulder to sleep, her penultimate thought of the day was, 'I *am* happy.'

But there was another thought, too: 'Damn it. I *still* haven't seen Peggy . . .'

Angela's half of the farmhouse was the one nearest to the farm driveway. Virtually every time he went by, Leo saw her hanging washing on the line, pulling weeds in the garden, adjusting her sitting-room curtains, or walking down the drive with John in his pushchair. As often as his self-control permitted, he only waved and hurried by, but it hurt every time. He wanted to talk to her, look at her, touch her. He felt like a fish, with a hook in the most tender part of its mouth, knowing that the pull of the line was irresistible, yet resisting it for all he was worth.

It wasn't, he realised, because she was so very beautiful. Her eyes were gorgeous, as was her hair, but her nose was too large, her neck too short, her hands too broad and excessively freckled. No; the real attraction Angela had for him was that she really *was* the girl of his dreams, the one he thought about when Lydia was pregnant, or recovering from being pregnant or, as in David's case, *not* recovering from being pregnant. (He had no such excuses now, but that was by the by.) The things he really dreamed about were Angela's curves: her straining brassiere, her tight-packed corsets, her thighs bulging wickedly from their (imagined) suspenders and stocking-tops. Lydia scarcely filled any of her underwear: there was always a tiny – but disappointing – space between the skin and the lace which was elegant, certainly, but not entirely appetising. He wanted to eat Angela and go on eating until his hunger was sated.

And apart from all that (when he could drag himself away from it), she was such a happy, carefree little soul. She'd made Lydia laugh. She'd made Lydia forget *lunch*, which, in a way, was the same as making the Pope forget God. And, when lunch had finally happened, nearly an hour late, they'd talked about silly, feminine things he'd assumed Lydia had thought rather beneath her, although she'd seemed to know all about them. Paris fashions, French films and French literature, nail varnish and rock-and-roll.

Rock-and-roll. The little he'd heard of it Leo hadn't greatly liked – partly because he couldn't make head or tail of it and partly because it belonged to another generation: the new generation of a new world in which he had no place. The farm, Molliston, Lydia and the children; they were like anchors, holding him down, keeping him fixed to the same dreary spot. *Security*. He'd wanted it once. He didn't want it now. He wanted excitement and romance. He wanted freedom. He wanted *Angela*, and he couldn't damn well have her!

He knew he couldn't have her. He was married, she was married. The twain could never meet. Every time his desire for her caught him unawares, he reminded himself of that, and his desire turned to a sour pain in his gut which ate him raw, like an ulcer.

Lydia was almost as much in love with Angela as he was, and he wasn't sure what to make of it. He often found them together at Molliston, talking art, religion or philosophy, playing boisterously with the children ('boisterous' suited Angela down to the ground) or strolling about the house planning a new 'decor'. They were an ill-matched pair, the one so dark, the one so fair, the one so contained and the other . . . brimming over. The contrast did nothing for his 'ulcer' and even less for his common sense. If he couldn't have Angela, he wanted Lydia to be more *like* Angela, but short of force-feeding her on butter and dunking her head in peroxide he had no idea how to go about it.

He didn't want to be old and disappointed. He didn't want to be his father all over again – married to the wrong woman.

Lydia spent the best part of the hundred-yard walk to Peggy's cottage rehearsing her apologies. The first fifty yards produced a frank, no-nonsense, 'Sorry it's been so long. The time just seems to fly, doesn't it?' but by the time she arrived she'd added a few fibs to make it easier – settling the new nanny in, a few juvenile head-colds, problems with the new tenants at Manor Farm. Lydia hated telling lies. After her first and worst one, when Leo had told her it would be her last, even the smallest venture into the realms of untruth had given her palpitations. She had them now: an awful, guilt-driven thump of her heart which made her more inclined to turn around and go home again than take the last few steps up Peggy's garden path.

Peggy was on her knees when she walked in, turning pots, pans

211

and kitchen china out of the cupboard. 'Oh, hello,' she said brightly. 'Won't be a minute. I'm just looking . . .'

'I'm sorry it's been so long,' Lydia began. 'I'd have come sooner, but –'

'Sooner? Good Lord, how could you? You were here only yesterday.'

As Peggy burrowed deeper into the cupboard, Lydia caught her breath and stared at the floor, wondering if she'd misheard, misunderstood or simply imagined it. *Yesterday*?

'Er – can I help?' she asked tentatively. 'What are you looking for?'

'The best china. I've a suite of Spode somewhere; I know I have. Haven't seen it for years. Lionel put it away when –' She stopped talking very suddenly and began shoving everything back into the cupboard. 'No,' she muttered. 'No, I remember now. I left it at Molliston.'

She had a little difficulty getting up off the floor, but when Lydia took her hand to help her, it felt like dry twigs wrapped in dry leaves. She'd lost weight, and hadn't been overly plump to begin with. But she behaved quite normally after that, seeming to realise that she hadn't seen Lydia yesterday, because she asked all the appropriate questions. How was the new nanny settling in? How were the girls? What did Lydia make of the new people at Manor Farm? She didn't ask about David and when Lydia mentioned him, she seemed surprised, as if she'd completely forgotten his existence. Fair enough, Lydia supposed. She never had been interested in babies.

Although her cottage was one of the best in the village, with a bathroom and two good-sized bedrooms upstairs (many of the others had no bathroom at all), there were only two rooms downstairs, one of which – now the living room – had originally been the kitchen. Before the war, Leo's father had added a little kitchenette at the back, just big enough to house the sink, the stove and a tall kitchen cabinet, the modern equivalent of Molliston's huge, old-fashioned kitchen dresser.

When Peggy absented herself to this little cubby-hole to make a pot of tea, Lydia looked around the living room with a vague feeling of distaste. Peggy lived like a hibernating hedgehog, in a warm nest of litter: heaps of newspapers, heaps of clothing, abandoned tangles of knitting and sewing, shopping baskets, boots and shoes. There were crumbs under the table, cobwebs in the corners, dead flies on the windowsill and ashes in the hearth.

It was all such a shame, because underneath the mess was a cosy and very pretty little room which demanded no more than an hour's

212

work each day to keep it fresh and neat. Leo had said, right at the start, that it would come to this. He'd made 'conditions' to keep it from happening, but of course Peggy hadn't honoured them. Her regular, Wednesdays-and-Sundays visits to dinner at Molliston had fallen by the wayside the year Dinah was born. Since then, she'd come to dinner only when she was formally invited and since the invitations had always come from Lydia, not Leo, she hadn't been invited just lately. Oh, God . . .

Peggy came through with the tea and a plate of biscuits. There was no milk. Peggy said she'd lost her taste for milk in her tea: it was much nicer without – Lydia should try it. Smiling, she said she'd rather not and went to fetch the jug. The jug was empty. Or, rather, not quite empty, for the milk still lurking in its base was solid, stinking and covered with a pale green fur. Appalled – and suspicious – she opened a kitchen cabinet. It was empty save for two tins of peas. Another smell, that of mouldy bread (just a crust, but as green as a leaf), emanated from the enamel bread-bin.

Lydia drank her tea without milk and said nothing about it. She didn't quite know *what* to say. This was her fault; entirely her fault, for she'd known all along that Peggy had no idea how to take care of herself. And here she was – just as Leo had predicted – starving. Even the biscuits were limp.

It was Wednesday. They usually had liver for dinner on Wednesdays, but now Lydia composed another menu: a nourishing vegetable soup, roast lamb, and a buttery sponge pudding with a three-egg vanilla custard. 'Come to dinner tonight,' she said, 'and meet Mary Preece. I'll ask Angela Markham, too. You'll like her, Peggy, she's *fun*.'

'Fun,' Peggy echoed wistfully. 'That sounds lovely, darling.'

But she failed to arrive, and when Leo went down to fetch her, he found her in bed, with (she said) a splitting headache. Lydia worried about her for the rest of the evening, anxiously noting that Leo and Angela, well-nourished on iron-rich burgundy and three-egg vanilla custard, scarcely spared poor Peggy a thought.

'She's your mother,' Lydia reminded Leo later when they went to bed. 'We can't just leave her –'

He groaned. 'For heaven's sake, Lydia. She had a headache, not the ruddy plague!'

'Yes, but –'

'And she's a grown woman, living exactly as she chose to live. She left of her own free will, remember, without the slightest encouragement from either of us. We advised her not to go. What else could we do – lock her up?'

213

'Yes, but –'

'And there's another thing you might consider – we haven't neglected her half so much as she's neglected *us*!'

Lydia bit her lip. It was true . . . in a way. Leo called in on her almost every day to check . . . but what was the use of checking if you found her in a muddle and did nothing about it? She was thin and hungry! She was living in squalor!

Leo gave his pillows a more than usually thorough thrashing and turned away from her, apparently having forgotten their usual goodnight kiss.

'Sleep well,' Lydia murmured, a trifle acidly.

'And the same to you,' Leo said.

Chapter Eighteen

As soon as the family had breakfasted, Lydia began again, cooking eggs and bacon for Peggy, with hot toast and a flask of coffee. Floral had already gone to the cottage with cornflakes, milk and butter and, with the hot things carefully stowed in a basket, Lydia followed as fast as she should, wearing her best 'gosh-what-fun' smile to soften the edges of what Peggy might see as a patronising act of charity.

Her smile disappeared when she saw Floral waiting for her at the open cottage door, looking as sour as the dregs in Peggy's milk-jug.

'What's wrong?'

'She'm bard!' Floral's sour expression collapsed into a trembling spurt of tears. 'I found 'er on the floor, very near froze!'

She was lying on her bed when Lydia ran upstairs. Floral had picked her up and helped her (heaven knew how; Peggy was twice her size), but she was indeed very 'bard': conscious but rambling, picking frantically at the bedclothes with icy, trembling fingers.

My fault, Lydia thought as she hurried to call Leo and the doctor.

'It's all my fault!' Floral said later. They were waiting for the doctor, performing a quick spring-clean while they waited, which Lydia couldn't help thinking of as a covering up of the evidence. Evidence of neglect which verged upon the criminal. There was no excuse. Peggy lived only a few hundred yards from her nearest and dearest and they'd let her come to this!

'Of course it's not your fault, Floral,' she said.

'It is! She took I in, didn't she? And then, when she asked I to move in wiv 'er 'ere, I wouldn't! Selfish, no-good, ungrateful . . .' She burst into tears for the third time in an hour, her thin, knobbly little shoulders shaking with remorse. 'I knew she wouldn't look after 'erself, see, Lydia! I knew 'ow much she needed I! But I couldn've lived with her; not in this tiny little 'ole!'

'Of course you couldn't. I quite understand.'

'No, you don't.' Floral blew her nose and went on guiltily, 'Trouble is, my love, I can't stand bein' wiv 'er night and day. I'm ever so *fond* of 'er, but . . . I don't really *like* 'er, Lydial. She . . . she do get on me *nerves*, so.'

It was hard to hold Floral, even to comfort her. Lydia had tried it before, but it was like holding a cat in a sack, a leaping frenzy of bones, with nothing to get a good grip on. She patted Floral's shoulder instead and, for want of anything better to say, quoted Leo. 'There's no sense blaming yourself, Floral. She *chose* to come here, and she's a grown woman –'

'No,' Floral said. 'No, she ain't grown. Not inside, she ain't. She don't understand nuffin' see, my love. She'm like a kid. Tell 'er all you like the fire's hot, but she cassn't see the sense of it till she've got burned.' She smiled a watery smile. 'Not like you, is she, my love?'

Lydia smiled too, recognising the truth of this and knowing that, in its way, it was almost as bad. *She* knew the fire was hot even before she lit it. Her whole life seemed to revolve around her fear of being burned.

'Should we have stopped her, Floral?' she asked now. 'Should we have refused to let her have the cottage?'

'No.' Floral shook her head. 'She'da gorn mad, Lydial. After Richard . . . She couldn've stopped at Molliston no longer.'

Leo and the doctor arrived soon afterwards. When the doctor diagnosed, 'depression, exacerbated by starvation,' Leo put clenched fists in his pockets and stared at the ceiling as if trying to keep a hold on his temper.

Much later, when Lydia returned, exhausted and miserable, from settling Peggy in at the clinic, he said only, 'How is she?' in a bored tone, which seemed to indicate that he wasn't at all keen to hear the answer.

'She seems better already. Much brighter. The ward sister was very nice. She said a couple of weeks rest and regular meals would put her on her feet again, and Peggy said it was like the Dorchester, all the fuss they were making of her.'

'Hmph,' Leo said.

'Why are you so annoyed?'

He sighed and scratched his head. 'Oh, I don't know. It all seems so unnecessary. When you come down to it, she just wants someone to make a blasted *fuss* of her.'

'Leo, she's lonely!'

'Why is she lonely? Did you ever make her feel unwelcome here? Did I? Good God, Lydia, even if she didn't like our company, the

216

house is quite big enough for her to have avoided us when she chose! She didn't *need* to move out, and I absolutely refuse to take responsibility for it!'

He spoke as if Lydia was blaming him, although she guessed that in spite of his absolute refusal to do so, he was blaming himself. They were all blaming themselves. But Leo had been right the first time: it was no one's fault. Peggy had made the decision for herself.

'Oh, well,' she said. 'She'll have to come home now. The doctor said she shouldn't live alone again. He said . . .'

'What?'

'He said she's always been prone to depression. Did you know that?'

He shrugged. 'I suppose so . . . But I also know what "prone" means.'

He meant that Peggy had simply lain down and let it happen, but that wasn't true. She'd tried very hard to make a life for herself in the village. She'd made friends, joined the W.I. . . . All right, the experience had 'burned' her and, knowing Peggy, she'd misjudged her new friends and been more shocked than she need have been when they'd failed her. But she *had* tried. Leo was being unfair. At least, Lydia thought he was being unfair, but who was she to judge? He'd known his mother a good deal longer than Lydia had and knew things about her that Lydia could only guess. Peggy had never been a confiding person. She talked a lot, but never about anything significant and the only part of her life she'd told Lydia about had been the good times, the 'fun' times, most of which had taken place between her sixteenth birthday and her wedding. She'd been a debutante, been presented at Court. She'd worn silk, lace and cashmere, furs and exotic perfumes. She'd eaten caviare and drunk champagne and danced until dawn. Happy and smiling . . .

Leo's exasperation with his mother lasted only long enough for Lydia to begin to feel exasperated on her own account. After two days of being well-cared for, fussed over and waited on hand and foot, Peggy was as bright as a button again. Lydia drove in to visit her every day, taking fruit, books and clean nighties and, after warmly thanking her, Peggy invariably said she'd prefer chocolates, or that she'd already read the book, or that she never wore that particular nightdress because the lace scratched her neck. When Lydia took chocolates, Peggy said she preferred fruit.

These visits somehow stole three hours of every day: hours Lydia could not afford to lose. She still had four children to care for (Mary Preece was marvellous, but she couldn't do it all), a big house to run, shopping to do and meals to prepare. And it was spring: the busiest

217

time of the year in the garden. Everywhere she turned, she found someone waiting for her, wanting her to do something, decide something, or even (especially in the children's case) simply to stop being busy and pay attention.

Angela Markham disappeared to London for a few days in the middle of all this, having left baby John in Bath with her mother. She came back with a fashionable new hairdo, a lavish summer wardrobe and a complexion expensively glowing with the after-effects of a 'facial'. Although she had no time to spare for something as trivial as envy, Lydia somehow managed to fit it in – usually in the car, while driving to and from her visits to Peggy. She wore her glasses for driving, which didn't help a great deal. Every time she glanced into the rear-view mirror, she saw a grim, bespectacled, white-faced *thing*, which reminded her (and, no doubt, Angela) of the half-crazed music teacher they'd been giggling about only a few weeks ago.

In keeping with Gran's instructions, Lydia never presented herself to the world in any condition less than immaculate. Her hair was always clean and neat (but old-fashioned), her clothes likewise (but serviceable) and she *never* failed to put her lipstick on. Trouble was, she chewed it off again within minutes, leaving only a pallid pink stain which made her look more washed-out than ever, like an under-nourished vampire, she thought, wondering where its next meal was coming from.

At the beginning of Peggy's second week at the clinic, Lydia told her she'd be wise to give up the cottage and move back to Molliston. Peggy refused. She said she'd enjoyed her independence and wouldn't give it up under any circumstances. Having already prepared a room for her at Molliston, Lydia now offered to prepare two rooms – 'A little flat of your own, where you can come and go as you please.'

Peggy said, 'Thank you, darling, but that's not the point.'

She didn't say what the point was, but Lydia knew it had something to do with Richard and baby Lionel. For Peggy, the house was stained by their deaths, haunted by their cries, and while Lydia understood all that, she wasn't in a position to do anything about it. She never crossed the inner hall without hearing Richard's scream as he'd fallen to his death. The scream was muted now, disguised by time and by the laughter of other beloved children, but she still *heard* it and felt the horror of it, twisting like a wire through her heart.

She couldn't blame Peggy for not wishing to return to such memories, such feelings. But it was such a different *kind* of house now. When Peggy had first moved out it had been empty and echoing, comfortless and sad. Now, although Lydia had never *quite* got around to turning it into a palace, it was a proper family home, full of life, full of people, voices, music and laughter. It wasn't always a happy home (what home always is?) but there was usually someone with a smile to spare, always someone to talk to. Peggy couldn't possibly be lonely at Molliston. Even Gran, on her regular weekly visits, was always cheerful at Molliston. But Gran adored the children, and Peggy . . . it was hard to know what she thought of the children. She could play with them, talk to them, even (on rare occasions) listen to them, but adore them? No.

'Is it the children?' Lydia asked tentatively now. 'Do you think they'd – er – intrude on your privacy?'

'No.' Peggy shrugged with annoyance. 'I just want to be on my own! Is that too much to ask?'

'You'll have to speak to her,' Lydia told Leo. 'If you can only persuade her to come to us for a few weeks, just until we're sure she can manage on her own again . . .'

'That might take a few years,' he said dryly.

'I know that! Can't you be a bit more helpful, damn you?'

Leo blinked. Then sighed, 'I'm sorry, darling,' and reached his arm across the back of the sofa to fondle her ear. It was a trick he'd discovered years ago, when they'd first married. Her ears, like the scruff of a cat's neck, had a paralysing effect on the rest of her body. When he touched her there she went all warm and woozy inside and didn't greatly care about anything except that he should go on doing it. It had brought many a pointless argument to an end, soothed a thousand little sorrows.

'Look,' he whispered now. 'We've still got a week to sort it out and you're tired, sweetheart, you've had enough. Why don't you give yourself a rest for a few days? Pop up to Town, stay at a really good hotel, spoil yourself a little. We'll manage here.'

The ear-massage notwithstanding, Lydia's heart began to thud with annoyance. Manage? How could they manage? She was the only one in the household who could cook anything more difficult than scrambled eggs! Anyway, whether she returned to it or not, Peggy's cottage had to be thoroughly cleaned, Zula had grown out of her shoes again and would need new ones before her toes curled up, and a man was coming on Thursday to lay a new carpet in 'Peggy's' bedroom. Still, Leo meant well and, that being so, she thanked him and said she'd think about it. It was quite difficult, though. She wanted to hit him.

Leo felt like one of the old Crusaders, struggling through to Jerusalem with nothing to support him but his virtue. And his virtue was no war-horse. It was a sad, bony, sway-backed little nag, whose legs could barely hold it, let alone carry Leo. Every time he clambered up on its back, muttering, 'Carry me through, Virtue, old thing,' it wheezed helplessly, '*How* far to Jerusalem?'

A thousand miles. And, while Angela lived at Manor Farm, the distance couldn't possibly get any shorter. Although he felt exactly as he'd felt in his youth, when he'd 'fallen in love' with this girl or that, Leo was aware that he hadn't fallen in love. He'd fallen in *lust*, which was worse: a terrible, all-consuming obsession he could barely control. He didn't care much for Angela's feelings, her character, her husband, her child; he rarely thought of her as anything more than a fleshy landscape of hills and valleys in which he might run free, exploring every golden forest and dark, musk-scented burrow until . . . Until he was satisfied.

But why did he need such satisfaction? For all Lydia's faults (and, if he was fair, she had few enough), she'd always been a wonderful lover. She enjoyed sex as she enjoyed nothing else. She plunged into it with abandon, like an overheated swimmer into a cool sea, shouting, 'Hey, it's marvellous in!' He had nothing to complain of there. She'd been everything he could have wished, except . . .

Could a man sacrifice everything for a yielding handful of flesh? No, no, he couldn't! He wouldn't! But how the hell could he stop himself when every nerve and fibre of his body, every crazy irrational impulse of his mind, prodded him closer to the abyss?

Go up to Town for a few days. Why the devil had he said that? It was like telling his conscience to go away, leave him alone, let him loose to do as he pleased. And yet . . . he didn't *want* to betray her. He didn't want to betray *himself*!

And Angela didn't help. Accustomed to spending months of each year alone, she was extraordinarily competent. She could unblock her own drains, change her own light bulbs, do things with a screwdriver that would make most women reach for their smelling salts. But there were things she couldn't do, and when she needed a strong man – 'Could you spare one, Leo? Just for a minute –' it seemed churlish (not to say self-denigrating), to go off and find one instead of volunteering himself for the task.

She'd moved her bed and got one of its legs jammed between the floorboards. A mere flick of a manly wrist would have shifted it and, had she been Lydia, she'd have left him to it. But Angela helped, bending over to take the weight at her end, squashing her burgeoning hills and valleys into the eiderdown, making him so weak with longing, his manly flick of the wrist had almost ruptured him.

He could think of nothing but Angela, of no one but Angela; and although he *knew* he cared about many other things and several other people, he seemed to have hidden them in the back of his mind's cupboard and slammed the door. Even his own mother was a distraction he could scarcely tolerate, and that wasn't right! He didn't want her to suffer anything that he might, with a little thought, tact and conspicuous concern, divert from its course, yet he couldn't concentrate on her needs when his own were driving him mad. He kept telling himself that Lydia would deal with it, that Lydia could and should deal with it. He was a man; he didn't really understand such matters and would be certain to say or do the wrong thing.

But he knew ... he knew the only wrong he was doing was in doing nothing at all. If it hadn't been for Lydia, his mother might have died, for he'd had no plans to call in on her that day. She mustn't go back to the cottage. She must come home to Molliston. He knew that. He knew too that he'd never forgive himself if any harm came to her later that he could – if he'd tried – have prevented *now*.

He went to the clinic to speak to her. He said, 'Hello, darling. How are you?' heard the first three words of her reply and then ... Nothing. Afterwards, he could recall offering up such glittering conversational gems as, 'Good Lord,' and 'Oh, really?' with an occasional, 'Yes, isn't that interesting?' just to prove he was still there, but he couldn't remember a thing *she'd* said. Had she opened her heart, confessed her sins and bemoaned all her sorrows? Had she asked for a loan or threatened to emigrate? He hadn't a clue.

'What did she say?' Lydia asked when he went home.

He shrugged. 'Nothing, really. I couldn't seem to keep her to the point.'

'That doesn't usually bother you.' She turned away. 'What's wrong? Rust in your tank tracks?'

Lydia had told him once that he had a tendency to drive a tank over his mother, but she'd been joking then and he had a feeling she wasn't joking now.

Wanting urgently to change the subject, he put his arms around her and kissed her neck. 'You look tired, darling. Had a bad day?'

Since David had ceased to scream the clock around, Lydia had learned to measure tiredness on a different scale. 'Tired' wasn't when you had leg-ache, back-ache and a faintly muzzy sensation between the ears. 'Tired' was when you had nothing between the ears but blind rage and every other part of you had collapsed in white-hot embers, like the inside of a bonfire. In short, according to the new measure, Lydia was never tired, so it was slightly annoying for Leo to be always accusing her of being so.

'No, I'm fine,' she said crisply.

'Ah . . . good. I thought you looked tired. Maybe it's your hair.'

'My *hair*?'

'Mm.' He tipped his head and looked at her with a critical, hairdresserly frown. 'I've been wondering if a perm would suit you, give you a bit of . . . bounce.'

'Bounce,' she repeated acidly.

'No, I don't mean *bounce*, exactly. More . . . Well, things are so much better now than they used to be: no rationing, no shortages, plenty of help in the house and grounds . . . Surely you could afford to spoil yourself a little? Buy some really *fashionable* clothes for a change, brighten yourself up. You always look so pale, so worried . . .'

In spite of his wrapping it up in flannel, Lydia knew a complaint when she heard one and it cut her to the heart. She was slicing bread at the time, and made a narrow-eyed appraisal of the knife before cutting the next slice. God, the nerve of the man! She looked *worried*, did she? How worried would *he* look, she wondered, if she weren't around to do all the worrying for him?

She said calmly, 'My hair won't take a perm, and my clothes are suitable for the life I lead. If you'd prefer someone more glamorous, Leo, you'll have to look for her elsewhere.'

He took a few steps backwards and looked at the floor. 'I wasn't criticising, darling. I just thought –'

'No, you didn't think. If you had, you'd have realised that if there's a right time to "brighten myself up", as you so tactfully put it, that time isn't *now*. I've got enough to do, thank you.'

Like most of their minor arguments, this one passed without leaving much trace. It was one of the advantages of having a busy household, with the children's feelings, Nanny's feelings and – to a lesser extent – Floral's feelings to be considered. In their few moments of privacy, husband and wife could snarl and spit as they chose, yet when two minutes later someone else appeared on the scene, they smiled, shook it off and forgot it.

But something reminded Lydia of this particular argument. The next morning, with Leo dressed in his best tweeds for a day at the cattle market, Angela Markham turned up, also in her best, for a day's shopping in Bath. She was there scarcely two minutes (she was catching the bus and had just popped in to drop off a knitting pattern for Lydia), but two minutes was long enough. She looked so *bright* and *bouncy*. She looked so *fashionable*.

So did Leo. His outdoor life had given him a year-round tan (wind-

222

burn mostly) which very nicely set off his sapphire blue eyes and sun-bleached hair. Lydia had almost ceased to notice how he looked, but now she saw that he was an extremely attractive man: tall, elegant, well-dressed. Not a bit like the man she'd married, with his ill-cut demob suit and ill-covered bones . . . She *had* noticed the changes as they'd happened: the swelling of his shoulders, the gilding of his hair, the way his sick, war-time pallor had given way to the proverbial 'ruddy good health'. She'd even noticed how well his tweed jacket had fitted him when he'd first had it made. But she'd never quite noticed how all these changes had come together. She'd never quite noticed that he was . . . beautiful.

But Angela had. She went quite pink when she saw him and said, 'Heavens, Leo, you look jolly smart!'

'So do you.'

He'd have said it, for courtesy's sake, if she'd been dressed in a sack and a dustbin lid. But she wasn't dressed in a sack and a dustbin lid. Her suit was a navy bouclé with a pencil skirt and a long, flaring jacket, her hat a cute little pancake contrivance with a floppy bow at the back. And the high-heels! She'd be crippled before the day was out, but crippled in such *style* . . .

Angela departed to run for her bus. Leo kissed the children, pretended to kiss Floral (who shrieked and ran away) and then dropped an off-hand peck on Lydia's cheek and said, 'See you later,' as he might have said to Mrs Lodge or the barmaid at the Rose and Crown: smiling, but not quite looking at her; with her, but already ten miles down the road.

She could have wept. Instead, as she usually did when her peace of mind was threatened, she strolled down the garden to Richard's Half-acre, taking a short-cut through the alley behind the greenhouse, where Mr Sparrow kept his compost bins. This was the only part of the grounds from which one could command a clear view of the road, and it happened that, just as she arrived there, Leo drove by in the cattle truck. She automatically lifted her hand to wave to him, but dropped it again, partly because he wasn't looking in her direction and partly because Angela Markham was sitting with him in the cab. Both of them were laughing.

Lydia wouldn't have been human if she hadn't asked herself, *What's going on?* and in the same breath supplied the worst possible answer. She knew it was much *more* likely that Angela had missed her bus and flagged Leo down to take her to the main Bath road, where the buses ran more frequently, but . . . Well, only a fool would fail to wonder. How had she got into the cab, for one thing? That skirt of hers had been as tight as a hobble: she'd have had to hitch it up to her stocking-tops just to reach the running board, let alone the passenger seat!

Richard's Half-acre, for once, did not have its usual soothing effect on Lydia's nerves. She went on wondering, thinking of Angela's 'bounce' and her own lack of it, thinking of Leo, who, at forty-two, had come very suddenly (it seemed) into his prime. And he was so like his mother . . . He didn't want to be; he tried very hard to be like his father – responsible and saving, courteous and thoughtful – but at heart he was *just* like his mother. Offer him a little fun and nothing else mattered. And Angela *was* fun. Young, pretty, smart, carefree . . . Her mother always available to take care of the baby, her husband never available to curtail her independence . . .

It was a year, at least, since Lydia had offered Leo any fun. The latter stages of pregnancy, the long months of David's mysterious agony and, now, all the problems with Peggy . . . There had been no time and, if she was frank, no inclination to make the necessary effort. The children, the house, the garden, they were all so much more important. And they took so much *energy*. She still fell asleep at the theatre. As for dancing, the very thought made her long to put her feet up on the sofa and her nose into a good book.

She'd never seen any necessity to apologise for being hardworking and responsible. She'd been brought up to see such things as virtues. But there was a saying, wasn't there, that any virtue taken to extremes can become a vice? And another, that all work and no play makes Jill a dull girl.

Since Dinah's birth, five years ago, Lydia had ceased to think of the circumstances of her marriage to Leo; ceased to feel guilty about it or to think she owed him anything – except the things that were the rightful due of any husband. Now she began to wonder about it again. If she hadn't forced the issue, would he have married her? No. Never. While he'd never been crass enough to have stated his preferences where women were concerned, she'd noticed at various social functions they'd been to that his eyes usually followed the chirpy little blonde with a giggly line in small-talk, or even the statuesque blonde with enormous feet who blundered about the dance-floor like a plough horse.

'Phew,' he'd say afterwards, 'she was an armful,' but always in the sort of tone which indicated that he'd rather have his arms full than not. Angela Markham was an armful . . .

Perhaps Lydia *should* go up to Town for a few days. Her hair wouldn't take a perm, but it could take a decent cut. Her complexion was never going to be roses, roses all the way, but surely a facial would help a little? As for fashion . . . She had a good figure and

224

could wear virtually anything. It didn't *always* have to be sensible, did it?

After her usual visit to Peggy, she spent some time at her dressing table, surveying her reflection in the glass and thinking, oddly enough, of Alec Digger. Although she'd long ago rationalised her feelings for him, he still counted, in a peculiar way, as the love of her life. First love, young love, the love two kids have for each other before they 'eat of the tree of knowledge'. Yet her love for him had been only fantasy, an escape into youthful innocence from knowledge she couldn't bear. His for her had been no more than a schoolboy crush, a sort of heroine-worship. But what would he think if he saw her now? What did a young man of twenty-two think of a woman in her thirties, with crows' feet and frown-lines and four growing children? *How the devil could I have loved her?*

Lord, how depressing . . .

But Alec didn't matter now. Leo did. And Leo wasn't a fantasy; he was her husband.

She spent the late afternoon playing with her hair, her make-up, trying on clothes and a limited selection of jewellery so that, when he came home to supper, she was as bright and bouncy as he had any right to expect.

He didn't notice. Lydia said helpfully, 'Do you think this brooch looks right with this dress?' The brooch was one he'd given her when Dinah was born, worn often enough to be unremarkable. The dress – in Leo's favourite shade of cherry red – she'd worn only once before, during her brief period of slenderness between Zula and David.

Leo blinked. He smiled. He said, 'Yes, it looks fine. I've always liked that brooch.'

'I meant the dress,' she prompted dryly.

'Oh. yes. Yes, of course. That's what I meant, too.'

Lydia sighed and gave up. 'I've persuaded your mother to come to us for a few weeks' convalescence.'

'Hmm? Oh . . .! Well done, darling.'

'If you want her to stay any longer, you'll have to do your own persuading.'

He smiled, but it was evident from the glazed look in his eyes that he was thinking of higher things. As high as the cab of the cattle truck, perhaps?

Chapter Nineteen

Leo was thinking about his mother's cottage, half-hoping that if he could persuade her to move out he might also persuade Angela to move in. It would be more convenient for her than Manor Farm: closer to the village shops and the bus stop, smaller garden. (Angela hated gardening.) But none of these was Leo's real reason for wanting her to move. He just wanted to push her out of sight, tuck her away in a spot where he didn't always have to be tripping over her. His crusading horse was on its last legs and needed to stumble only once more to throw him over its head and into her arms.

He'd discovered today – both literally and figuratively – that Angela was travelling on foot. She didn't have a horse to keep her feet out of the dirt. She was running loose.

'I've missed the bus. Saw it disappearing past the church just as I came out of your drive. Could you possibly . . .?'

She hadn't missed it. One of the advantages of the cattle truck was that it gave Leo a clear view over the hedge-tops, and he'd seen the bus – about half a mile distant – trundling *towards* the village, not away. It would have been the simplest thing in the world to correct her, but the simplest things aren't necessarily the easiest, especially when everything you desire is being offered on a plate and the simplest thing is to say, 'No, thanks, I'm not really hungry.' Instead, aware that the bus would appear within minutes to ruin everything, he'd said, 'Yes, of course; hop in.'

Hop in. Impossible for a woman whose adherence to fashion had effectively tied her legs together. He'd gone quite hot and helpless while she'd shimmied her skirt up over her knees, showing off a dark band of stocking-top and a flash of white thigh and, when he'd dragged his eyes from that view to another, a smile which acknowledged, approved and agreed with everything he was thinking.

He was thinking of Lydia's making love in the back seat of an

Austin Seven (another virtual impossibility) and of how much easier it would be in the cab of a cattle truck.

'Gosh, this is fun!' Angela said. 'You get such a wonderful view of everything, don't you?'

'Yes,' he's said dryly, and they'd both laughed as if he'd told the joke of the year.

Laughter. It was the most potent aphrodisiac in the world. The most potent medicine, intoxicant, sedative. You laughed and nothing else mattered – wife, children, mother, home. You laughed and forgot that you were an honourable crusader, riding the weary nag of virtue.

'Don't you mind living alone so much, Angela?'

'No, not really. I've grown used to it. It's wonderful when Gordon first comes home, of course –' (a sidelong glance, an arch little smile) '– and awful when he first goes away. But I adjust very quickly. The thing I miss most is having a motor car. I should learn to drive, I suppose, but I've never been able to understand how you fit it all together.'

'Fit all what together?'

'The pedals, the steering, changing gear and watching where you're going. It all seems too much to do, all at once. How do you know which gears to choose?'

She was watching his hand on the gear-stick as he changed down to approach the crossroads beyond the village. He remembered other girls, in other vehicles before the war, who'd asked the same question and watched his hand in precisely the same way, with a kind of mesmeric fascination which seemed to be making reference to something else: something a nice girl couldn't mention. Leo had had the answer off pat in those days: *There's no choice involved; it's a natural sequence: first to begin, second to proceed, third to gather pace. After that you just lie back and enjoy it.*

But he hadn't said that to Angela. Infidelity was *not* a natural sequence or, if it was, it wasn't one he could follow to its natural conclusion. If the only food you can get belongs to someone else, you must go hungry. But hunger's a hell of a lot easier to bear when you can't see the plate, let alone have it held right under your nose!

He must get his mother to leave the cottage, to stay at Molliston. Then, somehow (a lower rent might do it), he'd get Angela to leave Manor Farm.

'When will Mother be coming home?' he asked Lydia after dinner that night.

'I don't know. Friday, probably.'

He noticed an edge to her voice which meant she was feeling unhappy about something. Something he'd done or failed to do? Or

227

just something worrying her? His eyes widened suddenly as another thought struck him. Someone must have seen him picking Angela up at the bus stop . . .

'Angela missed her bus this morning,' he said, affecting boredom, although the very shape of her name on his tongue excited him beyond bearing. 'I took her to the crossroads.'

'Oh? That was kind of you.' Still that edge. It reminded him of Lydia as he'd first known her, with her contemptuous looks and her lordly tone, the feeling she'd given him that he was dirt under her foot.

'She stood in the road and flagged me down,' he snapped. 'What did you expect me to do? Run her over?'

Lydia blinked. 'I said it was kind of you,' she reminded him coolly.

'I wasn't questioning your words! I was questioning your tone!'

'Oh, my *tone*! Oh, I'm so sorry. Would you prefer me to whisper, or write messages on a blackboard? I could learn semaphor, if you like. Anything, rather than annoy you with my *tone*.'

'Sarcasm is the lowest form of wit,' he murmured coldly.

'And borrowed wit is the lowest form of wisdom. How did she get into the cab without splitting her skirt?'

One of the most infuriating things about Lydia was that her sense of humour always bubbled to the surface when *he* was picking a quarrel. (If she was doing the picking, of course, it was all deadly serious). But the question about Angela's skirt had thrown him further off-course than Lydia had intended. He could see her thighs and stocking-tops so clearly, he felt sure Lydia could see the reflection of them in his eyes, like a sunset in someone else's spectacles. Guilt made him flush up like a beetroot, so that, merely to have an excuse for being red in the face, he felt obliged to lose his temper.

'Oh, for God's sake!' he roared. 'Don't be so utterly puerile!'

He stormed from the room, feeling foolish, confused, frightened and far more angry than his red face had obliged him to be. He was angry with himself, yet told himself he was angry with Lydia. (Superior little madam! *Borrowed wit is the lowest form of wisdom*. How could she think up remarks like that when he could barely remember his own name?)

He hated her, he hated her. She'd trapped him at the beginning and had kept him tied ever since, depressing him with her po-faced devotion to duty, her relentless efficiency, her remorseless good taste. Even her clothes depressed him. He couldn't count the number of times he'd told her he liked her in *bright* colours, yet still she insisted

228

on wearing her bloody dreary tweeds and bloody dreary twinsets. It was true she had to help with the housework, do the cooking, play with the children, walk the dogs and weed the garden. But so what? Did she have to look like a dark cloud while she was doing it? Did she have to deny him *everything* he wanted?

As this thought crossed his mind in one direction, an image of Lydia as he'd just left her crossed it in the other – Lydia wearing a crimson dress and a gold brooch, Lydia with her usual dragged-back hairstyle softened into waves over her forehead. Oh, how typical of her to prove him wrong just when he most needed to be right!

A cool grey twilight was turning to darkness as he strode through the great hall to fetch his coat, half-blinded by rage, but not so blind that he couldn't see the polished glow of the old refectory table, the glitter of scrubbed yellow stone underfoot, the expensive drape of French-made tapestry curtains which, only a few years ago, had replaced the patched-up remains of the pre-war ones.

Lydia had put her soul into this house. She'd saved it from ruin. But what the hell? It was only a *house*! It couldn't think, couldn't feel, couldn't care! If she'd given *him* only half the attention she'd lavished on her house, her garden and her bloody stupid yew-hedges, he might be a happier man!

'Hypocrite, hypocrite,' his conscience whispered. 'Why did you marry her?'

It was hard to believe, now, that he could have been so stupid, so blind. He should have let Molliston go and saved *himself*!

Chantrys had never divorced. In all of their history, they'd never been divorced. But neither had they had a washing machine, a vacuum cleaner, a television set. *They had them now . . .*

Although Leo never lost his temper about anything important, he had a peculiar tendency to lose it over nothing at all, which Lydia thought even worse. Upsetting everyone just because the butter tasted 'off', or because he couldn't find his cuff-links, had always seemed to her a mite self-indulgent. Silly and childish, a failure of his much-vaunted 'sense of humour'. It was this failure, in fact, that usually made her laugh just as the poor man was winding himself up for the big exit scene. As he'd often informed her, *her* sense of humour wasn't greatly in evidence. She did a fair amount of internal chuckling, but it took something ridiculous to make her laugh out loud. The last time she'd really let herself go had been in Bath, when a woman – dressed to the nines and strutting down Milsom Street as if she owned it – had tripped over a loose paving stone. It wouldn't have been funny if she'd fallen on her face, but she hadn't fallen.

She'd just squawked a bit and flapped a bit and then (this was the part that had tickled Lydia) glanced furtively over her shoulder to see how many people were looking.

Leo's little tantrums affected Lydia in the same way, except that with Leo she was actually *predicting* the loose paving-stones, seeing him make an idiot of himself before he actually did it. And, to his credit, he usually stopped himself and laughed with her before it went too far. But he hadn't stopped himself tonight and his last words, before he'd stormed out, had wiped the smile off Lydia's face just as effectively as if he'd slapped her. Why hadn't the idea of Angela's splitting her skirt amused him? Why had it enraged him so? Was Angela's dignity more sacred to him than his own?

Wanting a distraction, she wandered through to the small parlour in search of Floral. She found her – fast asleep and snoring – in front of the television set. Floral had fallen in love with the television the day they'd brought it into the house (two days before the Coronation) and the only time she stopped watching it was when the BBC stopped transmitting programmes. She'd rush in from the garden, hands still covered in dirt, especially to watch the *Flowerpot Men* or the *Wooden Tops*, although she claimed a profound critical disdain for *Andy Pandy*. She also hated broadcasts of orchestral concerts, which was probably why she'd fallen asleep now. It was Elgar, one of Lydia's favourites. But she couldn't stop to listen. Elgar always made her cry.

She went upstairs to check the children: David still in the old nursery, next to Leo and Lydia's room, and the girls in the new one, next-door to Mary. At six months, David had reached the happy bourne called 'sleeping through the night', which he did in a near-perfect foetal position, as though still regretting his entry to the world and hoping to reverse the process. The girls all slept flat on their backs with their arms above their heads, like three little bank robbers to whom the sheriff had said, 'Hands up!' They looked so angelic asleep and unnaturally clean, as if they'd just come back from the laundry, boiled and starched, rather than simply being sloshed around in the bath in the normal manner. Something to do with being blonde, Lydia supposed. Richard – poor Richard – had never looked so clean.

She rarely wept for Richard these days, but now, perhaps because she felt so miserable about Leo, she did weep. Not much. Just enough to make her eyelids pink and her throat ache with the miserable effort of stopping again before she should wake someone. She waited until she was safely out on the landing before blowing her nose, which was unfortunate, because Leo chose that moment to come back from wherever he'd been and catch her at it.

He stopped on the half-landing of the staircase and looked up at her with a kind of martyred patience, as if crying were something she did twice a day, rather than twice a year. Then, with an obvious effort, he smiled. 'Sorry, darling. Put it down to tiredness, will you? It's been a rotten day, one way and another. Shouldn't have taken it out on you, though, should I?'

She smiled and held out her hand to draw him up the stairs. No sense continuing the quarrel. He did took tired and he had apologised. What more could she reasonably ask? There were plenty of *unreasonable* things she could ask, of course, but they wouldn't help.

'Why's it been a rotten day?' she smiled.

'I don't know. My mother, I suppose. Think we can persuade her to stay? I know I sometimes . . . I know I don't spare her much sympathy, but I don't want anything to happen to her, Lydia. She's always been a bit nervy and while I don't quite understand *why* . . .'

'It's Lionel,' she said softly.

'Not after all these years. He'd be forty-six if he'd lived, for heaven's sake.'

'It doesn't matter, Leo. It lasts forever.'

Leo's gaze followed hers to the part of the balustrade – long ago replaced – where Richard had fallen. He nodded. Wearily he took her in his arms and rocked her, back and forth, but it was as if he was taking comfort, not giving it. She could feel his unhappiness soaking through her, like a sweat, and knew herself helpless to change it.

'Whatever's troubling you,' she said, 'it'll pass, Leo. We've been through a lot together, haven't we? And survived.'

He let her go, smiling stiffly. 'That's true,' he said flatly. 'I just sometimes wonder if survival's enough. Shouldn't there be more? We always seem to be lurching from one crisis to another. There's never any *peace*.'

Lydia had hoped for a soothing reconciliation scene in the bedroom, but knew from his tone that there wouldn't be one. It was time to liven him up, give him something to think about that didn't have 'Crisis' stamped all over it.

'Why don't we give your mother a welcome-home dinner party?' she suggested later when he came back from the bathroom. 'Ask the Moretons. They're always fun, aren't they?'

'Hmm.'

'And who else?' She glanced at him from the corner of her eye before continuing lightly, 'Prue and Gerald. Angela, of course, and that new curate chap – what's his name? Thingummy Robertson-Wood.'

'I thought it was Robertson Thingummy-Wood, but perhaps you're right. Can we ask him without asking the Rector?'

'We'll need the Rector, won't we? Young curate for Angela, elderly Rector for Peggy. Ten for dinner.' She pulled a face, thinking of all the work. 'That's more than enough, isn't it?'

'My mother can't stand the Rector, darling. He bores her to death. He bores *everyone* to death.'

'Only when he talks, and he won't get a word in if we put him between Prue and Peggy.'

Leo laughed and began, in a slow, ponderous voice to mimic poor old Mr Day telling his favourite after-dinner story. 'Ah! Now . . . Ah . . . I've an old chum . . . old Ronnie Gilchrist . . . Scotland . . . Used to go up every . . . Ah . . . Before the war, this was, of course . . .'

It was amazing how Leo's mood had lightened in the instant she'd said the word 'party'. Or had it been the word, 'Angela'? She couldn't remember and, after all, what did it matter? He was a man of honour. He loved his home, he loved his children. His love for his wife (although he'd told her many times that he *did* love her) had always been a matter of doubt, but that was Lydia's fault, not his. She hadn't married him for love, although *she'd* loved *him* – in one way or another – since the day Richard was born. Perhaps most of the love she'd felt for him had been founded on gratitude and respect, but not all. By no means all. Sometimes, when he was irritable, or being childishly playful when she had too much on her mind to be bothered, she'd close her eyes and pray for patience, or imagine how peaceful life would be if he weren't there. At those times, she felt no gratitude to him and little respect, yet the 'peace' she imagined was no peace at all. It was desolation.

In the dark, she turned to him and pressed her lips to his throat, murmuring, 'I love you,' and meaning nothing else, wanting nothing more.

He stroked his palm over her face, as casually as he might have stroked a cat. 'Mm,' he said. 'Sorry, darling. Too tired.'

The latter part of April and the first two weeks of May had been wet, cold and windy, but on the day Peggy came home, summer arrived. It was a glorious day of cloudless skies, fresh green leaves, long meadow grasses reflecting silver and blue, like the sea. The farmyard thermometer was registering seventy-two degrees in the shade and Leo, leaning on the gate in his shirt-sleeves, was beginning to think life wasn't so bad, after all.

The last of his lambs were in their 'racehorse' stage of development, crowding into one corner of the field before galloping hell-for-leather to the opposite corner. It was like a school sports day, seemingly as organised and serving a similar function: to strengthen young legs and expand young lungs, to inculcate the special survival rules of the breed (Rule One: Stick together, chaps; follow your leader).

Nature was wonderful; it had everything worked out in a pattern so intricate, so perfectly drawn, there was no knowing the beginning or the end of it. Was the grass for the sheep or the sheep for the grass? Sheep were good for grass. They cropped it so short, its only hope of survival was to grow more expansive roots, so that when you took the sheep off to graze another piece, you had more grass: thicker, stronger, more vigorous than before. Yet all the sheep did was eat. All the grass did was grow. They existed exclusively for themselves and had no notion of the benefit each gave the other.

If only people were the same: able both to take sustenance and give it without knowledge of the good – or the harm – they might do in the process. Just take what they wanted, unknowing, unthinking, leaving all the consequences to Nature. But people were more powerful than sheep and grass. A wrong word or wrong act, even the right word or act misinterpreted by someone else, could bring the world to its knees.

'Leo?' Angela had inserted herself between a bush of forsythia and a holly tree to smile at him over her garden wall. 'Are you busy?'

He was. His gate-leaning minute had been a minute snatched between one task and the next, a matter not so much of resting as of pausing for thought. He had to go home, have a bath, change his clothes. Go to the bank, go to the feed merchant, restock his supplies of sherry and brandy for tonight's party, fetch his mother from the clinic and get back again in time for milking. In fact, this quiet minute was to have been the last he would have between now and midnight.

But he laughed and said, 'Not terribly. Why?'

'My kitchen tap's dripping. I've got a new washer for it, but I can't –' She held up a spanner and glowered at it comically. 'This thing won't cooperate.'

She was wearing slacks: a new fashion in slacks, very tight and short in the legs, with blue and white stripes which followed the curves of her hips, thighs and calf-muscles and gave her pale, bony ankles a strangely erotic quality. He followed those ankles like a small dog dragged along on a short leash, wanting desperately to stop, to pee against a tree, to think it over one more time. But every thought had flown. It was like being in the middle of a thunderstorm that puts all the lights out yet electrifies the air, intensifying every

233

sense, heightening awareness to a preternatural degree while still, somehow, leaving one blind.

He was aware, for example, that Angela's kitchen smelled of fried onions and soiled nappies, and that the three dirty cups on the table were evidence of sloppy habits, not visitors. The tap, which had been new only a few months ago, was crusted with dried soap and verdigris. The dish cloth was a grey, malodorous heap on a slimy draining board. Although he wasn't sure why, he found all this unbearably exciting. Angela was so neat, so clean and shiny – the archetypal 'English rose' – and the contrast between her person and her home spoke to him of mysteries, secrets, flaws in her character he wanted to dig out, like a splinter from his thumb, and suck until the blood ran.

He fixed the tap, talked, listened and laughed; but he wasn't fully conscious of doing any of it. His conscious mind was occupied with other matters: the shape of her lips (full, juicy and slightly bruised, like over-ripe cherries), the rosy flush of her cheeks, the way the tiny cap sleeves of her blouse emphasised the swell of her upper arms, making him want to sink his teeth into them to find the bone.

'I don't think I've ever seen a man so beautiful,' Angela said. She was talking about Peter Robertson-Wood, the new curate, who (but for a more restrained haircut) looked like an artist's impression of the Archangel Gabriel, with that dreamy, slightly doped look about him which announced, *I am good all through*. But it made no difference who she was talking about. Just the way she said it – the way she widened her eyes and licked her lips – made Leo dizzy with longing.

'Hey,' he laughed. 'You're a married woman, remember.'

'Who cares?' Her wicked little chuckle made her breasts shudder. 'I don't suppose he's available, anyway.' She tipped her head coyly to one side and batted her eyelashes, and although Leo knew she was casting doubt on the curate's manhood, she also seemed to be saying, 'I've no doubts about yours.'

The impulse to pull her into his arms began in Leo's toes and rocketed through him like a tornado. It took a split second to reach the tips of his fingers, which sprang open like the lid of a jack-in-the-box, making the spanner fall from his grasp and drop into the sink with an almighty crash.

'Whoops,' he said. 'Still, I think we've cured the drip. I'd better go.' He was already on his way out.

'Thanks, Leo. You're wonderful.'

She was following him out through the sitting room. He could hear the fabric of her slacks rasping in the fork of her thighs.

'Must dash,' he called out, his voice too loud, too rough, too frantic to be natural. 'See you tonight.'

He sat in his Land Rover for a good five minutes before he stopped trembling. *See you tonight*. Dear God, could he bear it?

The first thing Peggy did when she returned to Molliston was to sneak into the dining room and change all the place-names. Lydia had worked out the seating plan with more than usual care, ensuring that Angela was as far from Leo – and the Rector as far from Lydia – as could possibly be contrived. Once she'd finished setting the table, it didn't occur to her to check it again until everyone was sitting down: Angela next to Leo, the Rector next to Lydia and Peggy snugly placed between Eddie Moreton and Peter Robertson-Wood. Too late to make a fuss. Too unkind to send Peggy a filthy look – it was her welcome-home dinner, after all. But, having prepared the house, prepared the meal and dolled herself up to meet the required standard of glamour, Lydia was already worn out, and when the Rector plunked himself down on one side of her and Prue on the other, a black cloud of depression descended on her and she knew, from that point on, that she was about to 'enjoy' one of the worst nights of her life.

At previous dinner parties (although never before her own), Lydia had noticed that a place-setting of less than a yard wide could seem like a hundred miles when you were on the wrong side of it. From the curate on one side and Helen Moreton on the other, the conversation was going great guns, jokes flying, wine flowing, laughter bubbling from one throat or another, everyone having a wonderful time.

Meanwhile, at Lydia's end of the table, the Rector ate, shovelling food into his mouth as if it was his first meal in a fortnight. Prue picked delicately at her food and, when a roar of laughter erupted at the far end of the table, she smiled into Lydia's eyes and said, '*Isn't* this fun? Awfully good of you, Lyd. Just what Mummy needed.'

It was, indeed, just what Peggy had needed. She was having a wonderful time, flirting with the curate when he'd let her (he was flirting with Helen Moreton), flirting with Eddie (who was flirting with Angela), and snapping, 'Don't be ridiculous, Gerald,' every time her poor son-in-law opened his mouth.

'Drip, drip, drip,' Angela said. 'Absolutely maddening. I didn't sleep a wink.'

'Chinese water torture,' Eddie said. 'Just when you think it's stopped –'

'*Drip*!' everyone laughed.

Wine didn't really suit Angela. It made her flush up like a beetroot. Clashed horribly with her powder blue lace.

'But *could* I get that spanner to shift it?'

'Not really a woman's job, though,' Gerald began importantly. 'I remember the first time Prue tried to change a plug –'

'Don't be ridiculous, Gerald,' Peggy said. 'That's entirely different. *No* one with any sense understands electricity.'

'I do!' Gerald said, and everyone laughed.

'*Isn't* this fun,' Prue said again. 'What did you do with the lamb, Lyd? It's absolutely delicious.'

'*Ham*?' the Rector piped up suddenly. 'Is it? Well, I'm blowed. Nicest ham I've ever tasted, Mrs Chantry, and I must say . . . Ah . . . I know a good ham when I . . .'

'But Leo did it just like that. Two minutes. No nonsense. My husband wouldn't change a washer if his life depended on it. He'd have got a man in.'

'Isn't that what you did?' Eddie teased and everyone laughed again. Everyone except Leo, who chose that moment to reach for another bottle of wine. The lines of recent laughter were still on his face, but Lydia knew him well enough to read embarrassment between the lines. He'd fixed Angela's dripping tap, had he? And never mentioned it?

It was all agony after that. Lydia just got more and more furious as the night wore on, more and more weary and sick of it all. What else had he never mentioned? What else didn't she know?

By the time they arrived at the port and cheese, Prue was seriously tiddly and the Rector almost comatose. Prue jogged Lydia's elbow and gazed at her lovingly, cross-eyed and giggling.

'*Ssn-isn*' this fun?' she said.

236

Chapter Twenty

For want of another example more admirable, Lydia had modelled herself on her grandmother in as many ways as her own nature would allow. She was patient, she was clean and hardworking, she was reasonable, she was kind. Just as she'd seen her grandmother as an unassailable edifice – a kind of fortress behind whose walls nothing bad could happen – so she'd seen herself. She was a safe place for her children to dwell in, a safe place for Leo, for Floral, even for Peggy. She was their well of clear water, their granary, their armoury; she was the roof over their heads.

And now she was crumbling. She knew she was crumbling because it had happened before, when Richard had died: a great, internal, foundation-cracking torment whose name was not grief (grief was a mere layer of dust by comparison) but rage. Rage and guilt. Rage, guilt and self-hatred. *And jealousy*!

She wouldn't have believed she was capable of being jealous of someone like Angela: someone so . . . So young. Angela had had no trouble, no experience of life – or death. She thought one could just bowl along without thought for the consequences: no dread of hard winters or food shortages, no idea that the world was full of monsters whose only purpose in life was to destroy her. She'd been nine at the outbreak of war. She'd understood none of its implications, scarcely registered its threat, remembered it now not as a long, dark labour, a struggle to survive from one day to the next, but as something vaguely exciting which had happened on the periphery of her life. She could remember rationing, of course, but she hadn't a clue what it had meant to the women who'd borne the brunt of it and didn't even *know* that when she said, 'No, I don't remember being hungry,' she owed that not to a bountiful Nature, but to her mother's work, forethought and ingenuity, to her hours of getting soaked, scorched or frozen in bread queues and meat queues, hours of backbreaking

237

labour to turn an ounce of this and two ounces of that into a meal to feed a family.

Even Lydia had failed to understand the burden of such drudgery until the war was over and she'd come to Molliston. By that time, however, rationing had become far worse than it had ever been during the war. And that winter . . . That bitter, cruel winter which had marked the first four months of Richard's life . . . That winter had laid scars on Lydia's mind which would never be erased. Even all these years later, she still spent each summer laying in fuel stocks to see her through an Ice Age.

But for the fact that she had to open her purse to pay for them, Angela thought food, clothes and fuel came from the fairies. She just had to wish – and watch them fall into her lap. Was she now wishing for Leo? And was he falling into her lap? Lydia didn't know and, without exposing her feelings to all and sundry, she was unlikely to find out. *Keep your feelings to yourself; they're no one's business but your own.*

Gran's advice had never been easy to take. Now it seemed next to impossible. Lydia was sick to death of restraint, good manners, civilised behaviour. She wanted to kill someone. Anyone. It didn't have to be Angela. All she really needed was an outlet for her rage. Give her a hatchet and someone to chop into bits with it (a complete stranger would do) and she'd feel *much* better.

But the habit of self-restraint was too deeply ingrained to be abandoned. It was like walking through the village fully clothed: one simply couldn't think of doing otherwise. As the warmth of the season – or her temper – increased, she could leave off certain items: her coat, scarf, gloves. Her smile. The ascending notes of her voice. But it was impossible to give the important parts any air. Let them sweat all they liked, let them break out in heat-rash, those parts *must* be covered.

So when Angela called in the day after the party to thank Lydia for 'a simply *super* time', Lydia gave her coffee as usual and chatted as usual and, after a while, even felt much as usual. One had to hand it to Angela: she was *interesting*. She was modern and stimulating. She was 'fun'. Although she did hardly anything that could be described as hard work (her house was a mess; her garden a jungle), she kept her mind fully occupied with the sort of things Lydia had never deemed important: the latest novels, plays and films, the latest craze in music. For Lydia, most of these things came under the umbrella of 'fashion': things you enjoyed if there was time to spare from real life. But for Angela they *were* real life. She asked what Lydia was cooking and peered inquisitively into the pan on the stove. When

Lydia said she was just boiling up dishcloths, Angela's mouth dropped open with amazement.

'Good Lord,' she said. 'I've never boiled a dishcloth in my life.'

'What do you do when they get dirty?'

'Throw them out. Buy another. Heavens, Lydia, life's too short!'

It had never seemed too short to Lydia. Sometimes, it had seemed too long by half, and that couldn't be right, could it?

'But what does it mean to you,' she asked urgently, 'this short life of yours?'

Angela shrugged and grinned. 'Everything,' she said. 'After all, it's the only one I've got, and – this isn't meant as a criticism, Lydia, it's just a point of view – when my grandchildren ask me what I did with my life, I absolutely *don't* want to tell them I spent any of it boiling dishcloths.'

Although Leo and Peggy had said very similar things over the years (and been ignored), Angela's way of expressing the same ideas made such an impact, Lydia spent most of the rest of the morning thinking it over, totting it up. If she carried on like this until she was eighty, she'd have to tell her grandchildren she'd spent three weeks boiling dishcloths and five solid *years* washing dishes! Not to mention all the floorcloths and the floors, the dusters and the dusting. Ten years? Twenty?

Although she took the whole morning to think about it, she made her decision in the time it took to peel one potato (and wonder how many tons of potatoes she could peel in a lifetime). Ten minutes after that, although the ingrained habits of a lifetime told her she *should* regret what she'd just done, she didn't regret it. Something told her it was probably the best thing she'd ever done; she felt quite filled up with it, overbrimming with it, delighted and thrilled . . . Terrified.

She laid the telephone in its cradle and stared at it with wide, disbelieving eyes, hearing the distant voices of her grandchildren gasping in awe, 'You never did, Grandma!'

'I did,' she whispered. 'I jolly well *did*.'

Leo had expected to have some trouble with Lydia after his mother's welcome-home party. He'd drunk rather too much, hoping the wine might make him numb to Angela's cleavage, but it had had the opposite effect, making him think, afterwards, that he'd spent the entire evening staring into that tormenting violet shadow between her breasts. In fact, he'd spent most of the evening staring at Eddie Moreton's tie, getting a crick in his neck with the effort of *not* staring at Angela's breasts.

He'd also spent some time smiling down the length of the table in an effort to catch Lydia's eye, but she was always looking elsewhere, either mopping up wine and gravy from the Rector's immediate vicinity or trying to prise an intelligent conversation out of Prue (who, after thirteen years of marriage to Gerald, was getting less intelligent by the day). He'd wanted to thank her for being so noble about the seating plan. Giving herself the Rector – and himself and Peggy the full range of good humour and conversation – had been an act of generosity which should not go unmarked. The food was marvellous, the table decorations a joy to behold . . .

He'd travelled to her end of the table with the wine a few times, and on each of these trips had bent to murmur the appropriate compliments in her ear. On the first occasion she'd been talking to Prue about young Jennifer's piano lessons and hadn't even looked up. On the second, she'd bent down to pick up her table napkin so that he'd found himself saying, 'Wonderful dinner, darling,' to the Rector instead. So he'd guessed she wasn't happy. And he'd guessed that her unhappiness had something to do with Angela's dripping tap, her over-enthusiastic report of which had embarrassed Leo so much he'd wanted to kick her. He hadn't told Lydia about the tap. He'd by no means forgotten it – every time he thought of it he went weak at the knees – he'd just found himself incapable of saying, 'I fixed Angela's tap,' without giving something away. A tremor in his voice, a flush of heat under his skin . . . Lydia wasn't stupid. She'd have *known* something was up.

Now he wasn't certain what she knew or didn't know. She'd been a bit surly the next morning, but that could be put down to Rector-fatigue, and by lunchtime she'd been her usual self, meeting his eyes in a friendly enough fashion when he'd said (yet again), 'Thanks for last night, darling. Everyone seemed to enjoy it, don't you think?'

'Seemed to, yes. Will you please eat your carrots, Dinah?'

'I *hate* carrots,' Dinah said.

'If you don't eat them now you'll be eating them for supper, so I'd advise you to get it over with now, darling. Everyone's phoned to thank us,' she added. 'Except the Rector, of course.'

Leo laughed. 'Do you suppose he remembers where he was last night?'

'And Angela.'

'Oh?' He took this as a criticism, as if he was personally responsible for Angela's bad manners.

'She called in. We had coffee.'

'Oh!' He laughed with relief. 'Good, good. What did she have to say about it?'

240

'Nothing much. *Super*, I think the word was. We spent most of the time talking about other things.'

Leo gulped. 'What other things?'

'Life. Dishcloths. To boil or not to boil them: that was the question.'

'Huh!' Peggy said. 'No need to ask *you* what the answer was!'

Although she laughed, there was an unpleasant note to her voice which shocked Leo and, it seemed, everyone else, for even Dinah and Charlotte sat up and took notice. Mary Preece, rarely without her bland, professional smile, lost it for a moment and blinked with embarrassment. Floral's mouth popped open and snapped shut again. Lydia just widened her eyes and said quietly, 'Do get a move on, Dinah. We're all waiting for you. Look, even Zula's finished.'

When she went out to fetch the pudding, Leo found to his amazement that he was thinking about dishcloths, a subject which had never crossed his mind before he'd seen that grey, smelly rag on Angela's draining board. He'd never quite realised that you had to boil them to keep them white, but he was glad Lydia *did* boil them. Now that he came to think about it, he was glad she did virtually everything she did. It was only the things she *didn't* do that sometimes depressed him . . .

After their apricot shortcake, which went down a good deal quicker than the carrots had, Dinah, Charlotte and Zula went off with Mary, while Lydia and Floral cleared the table and fetched in the coffee.

In the short time that he was alone with her, Leo reached out to pat Peggy's hand. 'Lovely to have you back with us, Mother.'

'I shan't stay,' she said.

'But you enjoyed your party, didn't you?'

'It was all right. Gerald annoyed me, as usual.'

'And, as usual, you enjoyed being annoyed.'

Peggy pursed her mouth and said nothing more until Lydia came back with the coffee tray. Then, more loudly than seemed necessary, she said, 'But I don't see why I should be expected to eat with that girl. Who is she, anyway?'

Perhaps it was Leo's guilty conscience that made him think of Angela and scowl with irritation to have her spoken of in such a fashion. 'Really, Mother,' he said. 'You were introduced. You know very well who she is.'

'Yes,' she snapped. 'She's a servant. And I do *not* eat with the servants!'

Lydia cottoned on before Leo did. 'Now, now,' she teased gently. 'Those days are gone, Peggy. Mary and the children can eat in the

241

nursery when you can pay for a cook, two maids and three footmen to do all the fetching and carrying. And since that seems unlikely . . .'

Bewildered, Leo turned to Lydia. 'Have you two had this conversation before?'

'We touched on it after breakfast, yes.'

'But – but it's ridiculous! Mother, this is ridiculous!'

'What is?'

'This – this – eating with the servants business! Who do you think you are, for heaven's sake? Marie Antoinette?'

His mother smiled and got up from the table, dropping her napkin quite deliberately into a brimming coffee cup. 'We were introduced,' she mimicked sweetly. 'You know very well who I am, darling.'

When she'd left the room, Lydia and Leo stared at one another warily, each expecting the other to make some sense of what had just happened. Peggy had never been the snobbish type. It wasn't like her even to think such things, let alone say them.

'She took against Mary at first sight,' Lydia murmured. 'I think I'll get the cottage properly spring-cleaned. The sooner she moves back there the better.'

'Oh!' (But he wanted Angela to move to the cottage!) 'Oh, she'll be all right,' he said. 'Probably a bit under the weather from last night. I was a bit too generous with the wine, wasn't I? Give her a chance, darling.'

Lydia smiled. She nodded. She drummed her fingers on the table. Nothing more was said.

Leo tiptoed back to work as if half-expecting a bomb to drop on him from behind, which Lydia thought it might if he decided to take Peggy's side against Mary. Having resisted having a nanny for so long (mainly because of Peggy's *I always had nannies for mine!*), she was not now willing to do without one – and not just *any* one. Mary was perfect. Mary must stay.

Just in case there should be any trouble, she had a tactful 'word' while she was giving David his lunch.

'My mother-in-law seems a little tetchy,' she said. 'Be a dear, will you, Mary, and take no notice?'

'Oh, that's all right, Mrs Chantry,' Mary said in her gentle way. 'Old people can get like that, can't they?'

This reply surprised Lydia, even shocked her a little. To her, Peggy had never seemed old and it was strange to hear Mary describe her as being so. *Gran* was old. Gran had always been old. Old, wise and stately. But Peggy had somehow managed to get 'fixed', in Lydia's perception, as just on the wrong side of young. Middle aged, not old.

242

But she *was* old . . .

'They get like children, don't they?' Mary said. 'A bit shy of people they don't know. She'll soon get used to me. Don't worry.'

Mary had a special way of saying 'Don't worry' – quiet, easy, almost off-hand – which Lydia suspected could make even the Atom Bomb seem harmless. Yet there was something steely about her, too; something immovable, even cold. She'd said she'd trained as a nanny because she loved children, and it was clear – both to Lydia and to the girls – that she did love them. But it wasn't *real* love. It was professional love: well-trained and narrowly focused, detached. She wasn't linked to the children as Lydia was. She didn't need anything from them. They couldn't hurt her, frighten her, wrench her heart. So it was rather silly, now that Lydia came to consider it, to think that Peggy could achieve what the children couldn't. It would be like water off a duck's back for Mary. She'd scarcely notice.

Nevertheless, Lydia kept a stern eye on Peggy during the ensuing week, noticing that although Peggy was often rude *about* Mary (whom she always called 'the girl'), she was never rude *to* her. In fact, just as Mary had suggested, she seemed a little shy of her, lowering her eyes when she came into the room, skirting warily around her as they passed in the hall, smiling a prim, nervous little smile which suited her scarcely better than it would have suited Leo. Peggy was no more shy than she was a snob (she was known in the village as Darling Chantry, because she called *everyone* darling: even the coalman), so it was all rather puzzling to see her so much on her guard with Mary.

Other things were puzzling, too. She wandered around the house a good deal, exploring every corner of it as if looking for something, but not seeming able to remember what it was. One never knew where she might pop up next. Lydia met her on the back stairs, in the garrets, in the gallery, even in the cellar – and although these wanderings were in the nature of aimless strolls, the minute she realised she was observed she'd quicken her pace, animate her eyes and her smile, make herself look purposeful. Guessing she was bored, Lydia tried to entertain her. She took her shopping in Bath, took her out to tea and to the library, drove her over to visit Gran and Prue. But in spite of all her efforts, Peggy didn't settle. She wanted to go back to the cottage. She never let a day pass without saying, 'I shan't stay,' or, 'I've never liked this house,' or 'I think I'll go home tomorrow.'

Between them, Lydia and Floral and Mrs Lodge had cleaned the cottage, washed the curtains and loose-covers, filled the cupboards with enough tinned and dry goods to withstand a month-long seige.

243

Peggy could go home whenever she liked – and she knew it. But she didn't go.

That there was something 'wrong' with her was a suspicion which played tentatively at the back of Lydia's mind, rather as Zula might play with the china on the dressing table, reaching out to touch, withdrawing when Lydia said no. Was there something wrong with Peggy? No. Was there something wrong? *No*! She couldn't handle that kind of china. It was too fragile. If she touched it, something might break that could never be repaired.

The strangest thing was . . . The strangest thing was that the breakage she feared had very little to do with Peggy. She was afraid for herself, afraid of letting her whole life slip by in steam of boiling dishcloths. Lydia had decided to stop that particular treadmill, to make changes, shake *off* a few responsibilities, not accept more! And if there was something wrong with Peggy, Lydia couldn't leave her; she wasn't the type. So there was *nothing* wrong with Peggy. *No*.

But she spent much of the next few days telling Floral to keep an eye on her. 'Keep her occupied, Floral, will you? And if she goes back to the cottage, go with her, settle her in, check on her, will you, Floral? Every day?'

She told Mary not to leave the children alone with Peggy. 'They wear her out, Mary, and she's not really used to children, you know. She forgets how young they are.'

As the time drew nearer, she became more and more scared, more convinced that she lacked the courage to go through with it. Lacked even a reason to go through with it. Leo wasn't having an affair! He was perfectly happy with his wife and his family! She needn't put herself through all this emotional turmoil, this ridiculous effort to . . . To what? To wake *him* up had been her first objective; to make *him* realise she wasn't just a person who boiled dishcloths.

But, if she didn't go through with it, she *would* be!

Leo was bringing the cows home from the meadow just below Molliston, using the old lane he used to walk before Lydia had bought their first car. Gone now, the faithful old Riley. Lydia drove a Morris estate car and Leo had a very nice Jaguar, a Ford pick-up truck and a Land Rover.

It was a trouble-free walk for the cows. No false roads they could take, no gates or gaps in the hedge. It was just a matter of calling them up and following them home, slapping a few rumps at the end of the line to hurry them along at the front.

He and the rear-guard were halfway along the lane when he came upon Angela and John, huddling together with their faces to the hedge. Angela was trembling with fright, John bawling his head off. Leo understood their dilemma (the cows had horns), but he didn't understand what Angela was doing there; how she'd found herself trapped in the middle of a lane which had a clear view from end to end. She must have seen the cows coming. She must have had time to make a run for it!

'No!' Angela wailed. 'I wasn't even looking down the lane! I was showing John the b-b-buttercups!'

She sounded like Zula when she'd fallen down and hurt herself but was determined not to cry. There was something heart-wrenching about it, something valiant and unbearably sweet. Sex didn't even come into it until he was actually kissing her, but then it came into it so fast it almost knocked him off his feet.

Had he not by necessity taken John in his arms as well as Angela (she was still clutching the child to her chest), there was no knowing what else might have happened, but since nature makes no provision for making love through a fourteen-month-old baby – and since that same baby has lashing fists and an ear-splitting yell to ward off the competition – nothing else happened. Leo dropped the entire armful and turned away, gasping for air and for self-control, only vaguely noticing that his cows had disappeared at the far end of the lane.

'I'm sorry,' he said roughly. He almost added, 'I don't know what came over me,' but stopped himself, partly because they'd both know he was lying, and partly because he felt sure he'd read it in a book, somewhere.

'Don't be,' Angela said. 'You couldn't have done anything better in the circumstances. I was scared to death. I know they wouldn't hurt us, but . . . Gosh, they're so big! And those horns! It was a bit of a tight – *squeeze*!'

He didn't look at her again. He smiled in her general direction, murmured, 'All right now?' and walked away on legs which had turned to jelly. Oh, God, she was so beautiful! So brave and so vulnerable, so fragile, so young! Perhaps 'fragile' wasn't quite the word. And 'brave' didn't properly describe someone who was terrified of cows. But hell, *he* knew what he meant! And he couldn't bear it; not any of it! Every time he saw her they seemed to take one more step down the road to damnation, and they could go only so far before they passed the point of no return.

Lydia would divorce him. He'd thought of divorcing Lydia more than once, but not with any real intent; not at least with any *sense*! She'd go back to Priory Farm and take the children with her, and he couldn't bear that any better than he could bear *this*. What was it, after all? It felt so much like love. Yet when he held Zula in his arms

245

or Charlotte on his knee, when he watched Dinah sleeping and bent to kiss her goodnight, when he gazed into David's face and thought in awe, *my son*, he knew what love was. And it *wasn't* this!

Yet in spite of everything, in spite of all his mental struggles to deny it, he knew he *had* fallen in love and was helpless to change it.

He was still feeling a little shaky when he went home to dinner that night. He found his mother talking to Lydia in the kitchen and although he had no idea of what she'd said before he'd come in, she went on briskly, 'So I think I'll go home tomorrow, darling.'

'Don't be ridiculous!' Leo snapped. 'This is your home and you'll damn well stay here!' Then, impelled more by desperation than common sense, he whirled on Lydia and said, 'Clear the place out! It's *my* property and I mean to let it to someone else!'

Although he was aware that he was prone to such bursts of irritation, he'd never taken them very seriously – they were more a way of letting off steam than of laying down the law – but this time he meant what he said and expected both Lydia and his mother to do as he told them. His mother *couldn't* go back to the cottage. The doctor had said so. And she was more frail than she had been, more vague, less responsible. She needed to be looked after. She needed company and conversation, regular meals, regular routines – everything, in short, that Lydia could give her.

He recited all this to himself while he was having his bath, arguing the case for his mother's welfare almost as if someone was listening – Floral, perhaps – and might applaud at the end and say mawkishly, 'Aw, bless 'im. He's only finking what's best for his ma.' But if Floral *was* listening, she wasn't so easily fooled, for as he reached for the towel she gave him a good punch in the stomach and sneered, 'Bloody hypocrite.'

Was he? No . . . He was just frightened and doing his best to get out of an impossible situation: a situation which might destroy everyone involved if he *didn't* get out of it. Keep his mother here, move Angela into the cottage, find some crusty old Admiral to take over the house at Manor Farm . . . He might not fall *out* of love with Angela if he ceased to see her every day, but at least being *in* love would be less of a torment. It would give him time to think things through, give him space to sort out his priorities. Oh, if only he could talk to Lydia about it! She'd sort it out in a few minutes, he knew; but he couldn't talk to her. She'd read his face, read the truth between the lines. She'd leave him.

He went downstairs smiling. He kissed his wife. He kissed his mother. He said, 'Sorry about that,' and mumbled something about being worried and wanting to do what was best for everyone. Lydia sucked her cheek and said nothing. His mother appeared to have forgotten all about it. Not only that; she was unusually civil to Mary Preece, who was on her way out to the 'pictures' and had turned up for dinner wearing a pink frock instead of her usual blue uniform and starched white pinafore. They talked about Cary Grant and Gregory Peck, both of whom Mary wanted to marry, although she conceded that one might need to look like Doris Day to get the chance. Mary did not look like Doris Day. She was short and dumpy (not fat, but somehow the same width all over) with small, pinkish-blue eyes set too close to a beak of a nose. Pretty hair and sweetness of expression were her only claims to beauty, yet Peggy said briskly, 'Nonsense, my dear. You're a lovely-looking girl. And you can tell this Gregory Grant fellow I said so.'

Everyone laughed, of course, but Leo felt a little disturbed by the whole thing. Was there something *wrong* with his mother?

Chapter Twenty-One

Leo was in that murky territory between wakefulness and sleep, not certain whether he was thinking about Angela or actually dreaming about her. Lydia's bedside light was still on and she was padding about between bedroom and nursery, clinking the things on her dressing table, opening and closing drawers in that dreadfully slow, hushed 'mustn't wake the baby' manner that seems even noisier than if she'd done it normally.

'Get a move on,' he murmured. 'I'm worn out.'

'Oh, sorry, darling. I thought you were asleep.'

'I *was*!'

'Sorry.' She jumped into bed with a force which almost lifted him out of it on the other side. She bounced up and down, pulling her pillows about, straightening the blankets. She turned the light off and was still.

Leo unclenched his teeth, sighed blissfully and drifted away again, holding Angela's hand.

'Have you done the clock?' Lydia asked brightly.

'*Yes*!'

Silence. Peace. Leo raised Angela's hand to his lips and kissed her palm. He kissed the silken skin of her forearm, all the way up to the delectable crease on the inside of her elbow.

'Oh, by the way,' Lydia said. 'I've decided to take your advice, Leo. I'm going up to Town tomorrow.'

'*What*?' Angela's arm was torn from his grasp – as were the parts he'd been saving up for later – and he sat up, his heart thudding, his lungs emptying, his eyes staring into the darkness in a daze of disbelief.

'*Thought* you'd be surprised,' Lydia chuckled. 'I arranged it weeks ago, to tell the truth, but what with your mother and one thing and another, I wasn't sure I'd be able to manage it. Still, everything's ixed now. Mrs Lodge will do the cooking, Mary will look after the children and Floral will keep an eye on your mother. Oh, and I'm aking Charlotte with me. The taxi's fetching us at nine.'

After a relatively successful struggle to get his breath back, Leo ow lost it again. Mrs Lodge, Mary, Floral, Charlotte, Bill Carne vho drove the village taxi and, no doubt, Peggy, all knew that Lydia vas going to London tomorrow and he *didn't*?

'How –?' he gasped. 'How – how *dare* you arrange all this without consulting me? What the devil do you think you're up to?'

'Without consulting you?' Lydia asked sweetly. 'But it was all our idea, Leo. Remember? Something about brightening myself up, vasn't it? Giving myself a bit of bounce?'

'Sweetly' wasn't Lydia's most pleasant tone of voice; it had a accharine taste which made him feel sick as well as furious. He witched on the light, covering his eyes to hide them from the glare. You're going tomorrow?' he asked softly. Then, much less softly, So why the hell didn't you mention it until *now*?'

Lydia smiled. 'I've been so busy, it quite slipped my mind. But I'm ure you understand how *that* can happen, darling. So many things lip yours, don't they?'

She turned over. Turned away from him, nuzzling into her pillow vith all the smug satisfaction of a farmyard cat after a successful atting expedition. Leo's first impulse was to turn her a little further nd beat hell out her sweet *derrière*. His second was to run away: run way to Angela and beg her to save him. His third was to weep. But ie did nothing at all. He was too angry, too bewildered, too rightened, too shocked.

Lydia knew something! But *what* did she know? How *much* did he know? And, when all was said and done, how much did he care? After all, the woman who'd just turned her back on him was the same voman he'd disliked so much at first sight. He'd liked her more since hen – even, from time to time, believed that he loved her – but naybe he'd just been kidding himself. He sure as hell didn't love her ıow!

Although she'd had to tell Floral and Mary, Lydia had told no one ·lse – not even Charlotte – that she was going to London. In more han one way, she hadn't even told herself she was going, or at least, vhen she *had* told herself, she hadn't believed a word of it. Something would happen to stop her. Fate would step in somehow. She wasn't the sort to just get up and go; she wasn't the adventurous ype! And the truth was . . . the awful truth was that she didn't want o go. She wanted to stay safely at home, just as she always had, keeping a close eye on things, keeping everything ticking over. Tick-tock, tick-tock, like the clock in the hall which Leo never looked a except to wind it up every Friday. Their marriage had got like that Worse than that. Not only did Leo never look at her now, he never wound her up, either.

It wasn't his fault. She'd let herself merge with the woodwork and the only way to make herself visible again was to disappear so suddenly that he was forced to ask himself, 'Hey, what's missing?' Most of the things he'd miss, of course, would be the very things a few well-trained servants could supply, but that wasn't his fault either. Lydia had *made* herself a servant – cook, housekeeper laundry-maid, nanny and gardener – and expended so much time thought and energy on being the best servant ever, she'd had nothing left to spare for being a wife. She'd become safe, easy, predictable Nipping off to London on a few hours' notice *wasn't* predictable.

It wasn't safe, either! What if he didn't miss her at all? What if, the minute she turned her back, he breathed a sigh of relief and went off to find his fun elsewhere? It wasn't far away. Just down the lane a Manor Farm. But if that was what he wanted, he could take it whether Lydia was there or not. This was her last chance, her only chance. Risky, but that was what 'chance' meant, after all. *Risky.*

It felt very risky, too, while she was saying goodbye to everyone explaining things to Dinah (who, as could have been predicted didn't give two hoots), meeting Leo's eyes over the breakfast table and saying briskly, 'I'll telephone this evening, darling.'

Everyone was there. He couldn't say a thing about it without causing a dreadful row and she knew he would never do that.

'Where did you say you'd be staying?'

She hadn't said. Now, as if they'd been discussing it for months. 'Barrett's, darling. You know. Where we stayed when we went up to Doug's wedding. Handy for Harrods.'

'You're planning to push the boat out, then?'

'As you said, it's about time I spoiled myself.'

He chuckled uncomfortably. 'Why can't I keep my big mouth shut?'

He managed not to ask how long she'd be away until she and Charlotte were getting into the taxi. 'I don't really know,' she said brightly. 'Depends how long it takes. A few days, more or less. I'll ring you.'

He didn't kiss her. She hadn't wanted to kiss him, but when he made no move to do it, she felt a red-hot, spiky thing, like a three-pronged toasting-fork, piercing her heart.

Yet the pain wore off rather sooner than Lydia had expected; in act, as soon as the train pulled out, and Charlotte, who'd been as solemn as a judge until then, went wild with excitement.

'We're moving! Mummy, Mummy, we're moving!'

Lydia had done a fair amount of train-travel during the war (mostly sitting in the corridor, with crowds of sweaty servicemen) but she'd never felt like this before. She felt like a butterfly breaking free from the shackles of its chrysalis: a little too soft and wet behind the wings to do any flying just yet, but *free* – and, more surprisingly – rather beautiful. She could see her reflection in the window, blurred by dirt and overlaid by the passing scenery, but well . . . Not too bad at all. She'd put on her best summer suit and her most dashing hat (a head-hugging boat-shape of misty blue feathers) and taken the time to twist her dark, silky hair into a cunning little chignon at the nape of her neck. But it wasn't her outfit that impressed her; it was her bone-structure: the clean line of her jaw, the youthful shaft of her throat, the darkness of her eyes, the rather dainty shape of her nose. She must have seen all these things ten thousand times before, but the train window gave them a new, strangely romantic aspect, making her think – for the first time since she'd met her – that Angela Markham wasn't so special after all. A bit over-done, in fact. A mite vulgar.

'Have I been to London before, Mummy?'

'No, I don't think you have, darling. Dinah came with us to Uncle Doug's wedding, but you weren't born then, of course.'

'Mmm,' Charlotte said. 'Ah, yes, I vaguely *remember* . . . You went to see the King, didn't you?'

'Well, we went to see Buckingham Palace, yes.'

'Where the King lives.'

'Well, he *did* live there. The Queen lives there now.'

'Where does the King live?'

'Um . . .' (Charlotte had not yet grasped the nettle of death and dying and Lydia didn't really want her to grasp it; it would worry her so.) 'He moved,' Lydia said.

'Do you know where? Shall we go to see him? I really *should* go to see him, you know, or Dinah will say she's better than me.'

Charlotte said more on that journey than she'd said in her whole life before. It was a revelation to Lydia, a joy and a sadness, for it made her realise how deeply in Dinah's shadow Charlotte was. Heredity was a funny thing. Dinah was Leo's child in every particular: bright, confident and bossy, full of the joys of spring. And poor little Charlotte was her mother's child, always worrying, wondering, patiently waiting for her chrysalis to split open and set her free.

251

'We're going to see things Dinah's never seen,' Lydia promised 'Special things, just for you. The Changing of the Guard, the Zoo *Harrods Food Hall* . . .'

'Gosh,' Charlotte said. 'Isn't this *spiffing*, Mummy!'

Yes, Lydia thought dryly. It was.

Leo spent most of that day in a state of suppressed rage, employing every moment (when he wasn't taking calmly to someone else) to pick an argument with Lydia. He called her all the names under the sun, reduced her to dust more times than he could count. She wept apologised, grovelled. She begged for mercy. Then, when he'd finished slaughtering her and muttered a few cold words of forgiveness, she popped up again, smug as ever, to say again 'Slipped my mind. So many things slip yours, don't they?'

What things? What things? He hadn't *done* anything yet! Hell, a woman couldn't just up and leave a man who hadn't *done* anything yet!

He was aware that 'yet' was the operative word; that but for the act he was as guilty as hell, that his body was set irrevocably on course to commit gross infidelity and that his virtue (such as it was) had almost given up the struggle. And Lydia, God damn her, had made it easy for him! She'd gone away! She hadn't even kissed him goodbye!

Oh, what the hell? She'd just gone away for a few days! But Leo had no doubt that she'd *meant* it as a punitive measure, otherwise why hadn't she told him until the last minute? The sheer impudence of it – *It was your idea, darling, remember?* – made him burn!

It wasn't fair. He'd tried his damnedest to fight Angela off! And he hadn't succumbed – yet! He *hadn't*!

Behind all this rage he detected something worse than rage, worse even than guilt; a thin thread of grief that burrowed its way through his heart like a parasitic worm. He'd turned forty-three last month the thirteenth anniversary of his liberation from prison camp. That day, his thirtieth birthday, had been a joy from start to finish: a dark, trembling joy, marked by so many other emotions he'd scarcely known one from another. Relief enough to melt his bones, hope enough to sear his heart, energy enough to re-build the entire war-torn world, single-handed.

It hadn't lasted. That dark, trembling joy had turned to dread before he'd even reached England, let alone Molliston. And after that, he'd fallen into a pit of depression so deep he'd thought he'd never crawl free of it. He would never have crawled free without Lydia. She'd dug him out. True, she'd given him a few nasty whacks with her spade while she was digging – he still had the scars to prove it – but he couldn't really imagine what life would have been like without her. He'd have lost Molliston . . . He'd have lost everything that was worth having. When a man needs money more than he needs love, can he complain because he has no love?

But as the Book said, man cannot live by bread alone. He needs love too, and she *hadn't* loved him. She'd never loved him. She'd always kept at one remove, loving someone else or something else, putting everything first *except* her own husband. Yet she owed him so much! Without him, her life would have been a desert. Without him, she'd have lived in desolation, rejected by her beloved grandmother and shunned by a society that spoke 'unmarried mother' and 'whore' in the same breath. Yet here she was, Mrs Leo Chantry, the lady of the Manor! Oh, she'd fallen on her feet, all right! He owed her nothing!

It was hard to eat dinner that night without noticing that certain things were missing (the mustard, the table napkins); but even when he complained and Floral supplied these vagrant items, there was still something missing. Not Lydia in the flesh so much as Lydia in spirit, although he couldn't have defined that spirit had his life depended on it. Something to do with safety? He didn't know. He didn't want to know. Dear God, safety was the last thing he needed!

He asked Mary how her day had gone, how the children were. She said Dinah had realised only at bedtime that Lydia wasn't coming home tonight and had cried herself to sleep. Zula had been a little tetchy all day, and David was teething. Lydia had told her to move him into the main nursery, in case he had a restless night.

'Where on earth is she?' Peggy asked brightly. 'It's not like Lydia to miss dinner, is it?'

'She's gone to London!' Leo snapped irritably. 'You know that, Mother! She said goodbye to you three times, for heaven's sake!'

'Cor,' Floral muttered. 'What's Doris Lodge done to this gravy? It's all lumps.'

'When will she be back?' Peggy asked.

He hadn't a clue. And perhaps that was the worst of it. Yes, that was the worst of it, and that was what she'd had in mind all along, the devious little cat. She might be back tomorrow. She might be back next week. And *he* hadn't a clue!

He smiled. He said, 'She'll be ringing tonight, Mother. You can ask her then when she'll be back.' He stood up and threw his unused napkin down on the table. 'Tell her I'm out.'

He thought of going to Angela, not because he wanted her at that moment, but because he wanted to hurt Lydia. Instead he went to the pub. He wasn't the pub-going type, especially in his own village, where the old men, trained in their childhood to salute anything called Chantry, fell silent when he walked in and, to his greetings, mumbled only, 'Evenin' zir,' into their cider. A brave one might occasionally add, 'Nice now, zir,' or 'Cawld, ennit?' but that was generally it unless one of the farmers was in.

Still, the landlord could be incredibly interesting about the weather. He always knew if it was raining (good for the gardens) or not raining (good time for haymaking) and he could reminisce about the Great Flood (if it was raining) or the Great Drought (if it wasn't) from the days when his grandad was a small boy. And he tried his best to draw the others into the conversation.

'Ah, them wuz the days, wa'n 'em, Ted?'

'Ah.'

'Remember that, Alf?'

'Ah.'

So Leo didn't stay very long. Back at Molliston, he killed another half-hour walking around the garden, wondering if it was worth getting the tennis court re-laid, wondering if the weather (damn the weather!) would hold until he'd got his silage in. Wondering how Lydia had felt when she'd telephoned and found him not at home.

Floral and his mother were watching television when he went indoors. Floral offered him some cocoa. He declined, waited a while for someone to say, 'Lydia rang,' and, when no one did, went to bed. He popped into the nursery to check on the children and almost wept to find Charlotte not there. He adored them all, but he loved Charlotte best. And she loved him! She depended on him, leaned on him, turned to *him* to comfort her when she was sad. How could Lydia have taken her to London? She'd be worried sick! He could see her now, her brow all furrowed up, her bottom lip pouting . . . *Are you quite sure Daddy can manage without me, Mummy?*

Had she phoned, or hadn't she? He almost went downstairs again to ask Floral, but his pride wouldn't let him. He didn't care. He didn't care.

But his bed seemed so empty without Lydia in it . . .

Lydia had meant to call Leo just before he sat down to dinner, but there wasn't time. She was busy settling Charlotte into her strange, luxurious divan, telling her a story, murmuring happy things about their afternoon of shopping, sightseeing and (Big Treat) feeding the ducks in the park. She couldn't ring while Leo was actually eating dinner and, after that, she was getting dressed for her own dinner, going down, all of a tremble, and ordering a dry sherry, all by herself, at the bar. She knew she looked good – not just because of her new emerald green gown, nor because she'd managed to re-do the complicated chignon at the nape of her neck, nor because she'd made a near-perfect job of her make-up for once – but because she looked happy, excited, invigorated. Out on the town!

The hotel manager, who remembered her (or at least said he did) from the last time she'd come here with Leo, took her into dinner, pulled out her chair, laid her napkin in her lap and advised her about the menu and the wine list. He was wonderful. But then he left her, all by herself at a table for two and, after that, it wasn't such fun. Except for tea and a bun in the middle of a rushed shopping trip to Bath, Lydia had never in her life eaten alone. Not before witnesses. And all the other diners seemed to be looking at her, wondering who she was and why she was alone.

She imagined trying to tell them. Honestly. No holds barred. My husband thinks me a bore, she announced silently. And he's right, in a way. I don't make time for the more interesting things in life and, when I do, I'm usually too tired to enjoy them. Take this soup, for instance. It's not nearly as good as mine, of course, but do you have any idea how long it takes to make? And have you ever tried getting linen as clean, white, starched and glossy as this tablecloth is? As for cleaning the silver ... It takes hours, my dear. Hours! Is it any wonder I've slept through most of Shakespeare, *School for Scandal*, *Giselle*, *Fidelio*, two pantomimes and *Gone with the Wind*? Is it any wonder that when Leo wants to go dancing, my feet are killing me?

She abandoned her soup, which was tepid as well as tasteless, and picked at a small portion of turbot, served in a slimy pink sauce.

The thing is, she went on sternly, that Molliston isn't the same as Barrett's Hotel. It wouldn't actually *matter*, at Molliston, if the soup came out of a tin occasionally, if the silver went brown, if the linen was limp. I've only just realised it, but it's true, isn't it? For example, I wouldn't give a damn about a limp tablecloth if only you'd *talk* to me, instead of just *looking*!

I used to be able to talk, you know. You name it – politics, architecture, poetry – I could talk about it. But now my head's stuffed with socks and nappies, Brasso and Persil, and if Leo's bored with all that ... Well, you can hardly blame him can you? *I'm* bored with it, for heaven's sake? Life *should* offer more.

It offered a slice of rare beef wrapped in pastry, which was really very nice, but somehow tasted of ashes. Food was no good at all if you had no one to share it.

Afraid she might break down and cry if she attempted the pudding, but equally afraid to walk out of the dining room under the gaze of so many covert watchers, Lydia dug deep for a consoling piece of her grandmother's wisdom: *Seem to be winning*.

'No,' she told the snootily hovering waiter. 'I'll just have coffee, I think. In the lounge.' Then she stood up and strolled from the room, smiling regally at everyone she passed. There was an enormous, gilt-framed mirror just inside the door which reflected every inch of her – from the top of her darkly shining head to the toes of her 'solid gold' (as Charlotte had described them) evening shoes. The tiara aside, she looked every inch a queen; a terminally boring housewife not at all. Leo was a fool.

Yes, Leo was a fool, the type of man who wanted to have his cake and eat it. He'd wanted children, he'd wanted Molliston, but he hadn't wanted all the work, care and worry such blessings bring with them. Lydia had shouldered the whole damn lot of it for him, had volunteered to bear the load just because she *owed* him. Well, she didn't owe him her soul. She didn't owe him her self-respect. She was his wife, not his bloody butler!

Leo was reading when the telephone rang. It was ten past ten. Another ten minutes and she'd have woken him. He wanted to snarl, *Where the hell have you been*? but opted for a bored, 'Oh, hello,' to indicate that he couldn't give a damn where she'd been and cared even less when she'd be coming home. But he did ask how Charlotte was.

'You wouldn't *believe* Charlotte,' she chuckled huskily. 'She's having a wonderful time. She's talked non-stop, ever since the train started moving. I've never seen her so full of beans! It seems she needs to get away from Dinah occasionally, just to have a chance to be herself without being told she's too young to understand, or to make her own decisions about things. And she absolutely adores London! So do I. It's filthy, of course, and the *noise*! But oh, Leo, I'm going to do this more often. It's like ... Well, I feel ... Well, anyway, darling, you were absolutely right. I really *needed* this, and it was wonderful of you to suggest it. Thanks. *Many* thanks. You won't believe what we've fitted in today! We went to Harrods first. I bought a frock and some shoes and some perfume and made an appointment to get my hair done on Wednesday. Then we saw the Changing of the Guard – Charlotte almost fainted with excitement – and bought some bread to feed the ducks. Everything all right there?'

'Fine,' Leo said. 'Dinah –' He was going to tell her that Dinah had cried herself to sleep, but Lydia rushed on breathlessly.

'We're going to have to do something about Dinah, darling. She's absolutely *dominating* Charlotte, and that can't be good for either of them. They're so different – like you and me, I suppose – and need

256

some time away from each other from time to time. We do live too much in other's pockets, don't we? One of the perils of living in the country, I suppose. Not enough contrast. Too small a world. How's David?'

'Teething,' Leo said through gritted teeth. 'Mary's –'

'Mary's marvellous, isn't she? Lord, I wish I'd found her years ago! I would have, too, if I'd taken your advice sooner. Sheer stubbornness, of course. I decided when we got married that I was going to be the perfect wife, but all I've really done is be a perfect donkey. Well, that will change. The housekeeping can go hang from now on and about time, too. How's your mother, by the way?'

'She seems all right. A bit strange.'

'Oh, well, it was ever thus. We can't expect her to change now, can we?'

'That wasn't quite what I –'

'Did Mrs Lodge manage dinner all right? She was a little nervous about it, but I told her –'

'The gravy was lumpy.'

'Oh, well. The food's not absolutely brilliant here, either, and when you think they've got some of the best chefs – Good Lord, is that the time? I must ring off, you'll be wanting some sleep. I'll ring again on Wednesday. Love to everyone, darling.'

'Yes, but when –?'

'And thanks again, Leo. Goodnight, sweet dreams.'

She blew him a kiss and rang off so abruptly it was like being hit over the head with a hammer. Leo stared into the mouthpiece, half-wondering if that had been his wife at the other end or some other woman mimicking her voice. The voice had been perfect – low and husky, with the occasional mouse-like squeak – and all set off by a crisply formal diction which didn't seem to match any of the rest of it.

He realised he'd been holding his breath only when his ears began to whine for lack of oxygen. Then he fell back against his pillows, blinking with bewilderment. Yes, the voice had been Lydia's, but what about the rest of her? Bright and bouncy didn't describe it. She'd gone off like a rocket! And *he* hadn't said anything; she hadn't let him get a word in edgewise!

Hmph! And Charlotte was loving it, was she? Faithless little madam. Not even a word about her poor old daddy . . .

He hadn't said anything. She hadn't let him. She hadn't wanted to know about Dinah's tears, David's teeth, the lumps in the gravy. She'd shaken it all off, ceased to care. And she was thanking *him* for letting her do it!

He turned off the light, gave his pillows their regular punishment and curled on his side to sleep. For the past few weeks, the edges of his dreams had been filled with two women: Lydia at his back, Angela in his arms. Now, in the absence of Lydia, he tried to conjure Angela into her usual place, but the magic wouldn't work. His arms remained empty. And, in spite of the warmth of the night, there was a strangely chill draught at his back.

He woke up in the early hours, hearing Lydia telling him that she'd set out to be the perfect wife. Yes, she had ... But no one was perfect. Succeed in one thing, fail in another: that was the inevitable consequence of being human. But where – really – had she failed? As a lover? As a mother? As a cook, a housekeeper, or in any of the roles that could be asked of the perfect wife? No ... All she'd really 'failed' to do was to be blonde, plump and jolly, and that was *his* failure, not hers. No, not hers.

Blonde, plump and jolly; dear God, what a noble set of values ... To hell with courage and fidelity, hard work and forethought, patience and generosity, grace and good manners. Just give Leo a plump, jolly blonde and he'd be happy.

Would he? Would he hell! He was just like his mother: wanting the best of all worlds and the worst of none.

He hated himself.

258

Chapter Twenty-Two

Charlotte didn't like the Zoo. Lydia had reserved a whole morning for it, but they were in and out within the hour, both of them scowling and close to tears. Lydia was stricken because the best treat of Charlotte's London adventure had come to nought. Charlotte was stricken for reasons of her own, few of which she was old enough to articulate, although Lydia guessed it might have something to do with the smell. The stench of the big cats, the reek of elephant dung, the cloying odours of raw meat and fish – all took up residence in the nose and throat so that it seemed they'd still be catching whiffs of it six months later.

They ended up in the park, feeding the ducks again. Charlotte didn't say much, but Lydia watched as the scowl gradually left her daughter's face and, when all their supplies of stale bread had gone, she finally said (to a duck), 'There, all gone. Now you can fly away if you want to.'

So she'd articulated it very nicely, in the end. Lydia wasn't surprised that she hadn't wanted to discuss it. The idea of freedom was a complex problem for an adult, let alone for a child who'd only just turned four. It had given Lydia some disquiet to see huge lions and tigers, in the wild capable of roaming hundreds of miles, confined to cages so small they could barely turn around. And the polar bear pit, painted to *look* like a hollow in the great Arctic waste, had been just a hole, a filthy, stinking, inescapable hole in which any living thing (bigger than a frog) might go mad with despair.

She thought of Leo, penned up and helpless in a German prison camp for the best part of four years. He'd never talked about it and the nearest Lydia had come to understanding how it felt was when he'd said, 'We didn't know *if* it would end, let alone how. For all we knew, we were there forever.'

The polar bears were there forever . . .

Yet the world was full of cages. Even the ducks, assured of their daily bread by millions of people like Charlotte, were trapped by that assurance, that security. Why should they fly away?

'I think I'd like to go home now,' Charlotte said. 'Daddy will be missing me. D'you think you'd like to go home now, Mummy?'

Lydia rather thought she would. Not because she thought Leo would be missing her, but because she was missing him, missing everyone, missing the peace of mind (regardless of a million worries) which went with being at home. She was like these dratted ducks. Why fly away when there was food aplenty in the park?

'We can't go just yet, Charlotte. Wouldn't it be dreadful if we went home without buying presents for everyone? You'll have to choose something for Dinah and Zula –'

Charlotte cheered up. 'And Daddy, and David, and Floral, and Grandma. *And* Gran and Grandpa!'

'And Mrs Lodge. We mustn't forget Mrs Lodge, must we?'

They spent the rest of the day shopping. Like her mother, Charlotte was a wonderful shopper. She had an 'eye' for the right thing and wasted very little time dithering about it. But, in one way at least, she was even better than her mother, for at the end of the day Lydia was more than three hundred pounds poorer, while Charlotte (clever thing) still had all six of the pennies she'd started out with.

She didn't mention going home again, but Lydia knew she hadn't changed her mind about it. The next few days were going to feel like a lifetime . . .

Leo's night of self-hatred gave his poor, crusading horse the equivalent of a week's soft living in a well-appointed stable. They both felt a little better afterwards, not, Leo realised, because self-hatred is a comfortable condition, but because it shines a ray of light on the engine of one's mind, helps one to see how it works. When he came to take an illuminated view of his own mind, he understood that he wasn't so much like his mother as he was like the rest of humanity, Lydia included. He had standards of 'rightness' which he couldn't bear to compromise. A roof (without leaks) over his head, decent food on the table, a warm bed to lie in, worthwhile occupations for his body and his brain, and a spot of good companionship to smooth off the remaining rough edges. So far so good. One or two saints and nutcases aside, there wasn't a man alive who'd ask less. But there were few men who, given all these things, would not ask for more. It was called greed: the curse of humanity from which all other ills arise.

In perhaps a thousand different ways, Lydia had given Leo his heart's desire and yet, save for the existence of his children, he'd taken every one of those things as his natural *right* and afterwards felt she'd given him nothing. It all arose from the circumstances of their marriage, the feeling he'd always had that she'd cheated him and that she could go on paying the price of it for the rest of their lives together. No matter that he'd cheated *her*. She'd never known about it; it didn't count. And, anyway, he'd been riding the nag of virtue even then. He'd fought her off – and her money – right up until the last moment, only succumbing in the end when she'd given him no choice. But there'd always been a choice. He needn't have married her. He'd married her for her money and for *nothing* else. No virtue involved.

Since then, although they'd never been truly happy (and often downright miserable) they'd lived in peace, in plenty and comfort; and how could a man, who called himself a decent man, ask for more? He couldn't. He wouldn't. He'd made choices and decisions. He'd made vows. Now he made another, and it was a curiously painless one: to ask Angela to leave Manor Farm. He wouldn't even offer her the cottage instead. She'd have to go.

Yet Tuesday passed without his doing anything about it and Wednesday would have passed the same had she not called to him over the wall: 'Just a moment, Leo? Please? I know you're busy, but it'll only take a moment.'

He expected another strong-arm job and instead was confronted with a half-finished oil-painting: a view of Molliston, which Angela had been using her imagination to view, since at this time of year the house was entirely obscured by trees.

'What d'you think?' she asked excitedly.

He thought it terrible. Having been brought up in a house full of paintings – good, bad and indifferent (only the bad and the indifferent had survived beyond his father's death) – he knew a bad painting when he saw one. Yet Angela was clearly enraptured by it, wanting more than anything for him to say, *It's good.* And what harm would it do? He'd said the same about the children's paintings without suffering a moral crisis. But Angela wasn't a child. Not child enough to have dragged him here just to give praise where praise wasn't due.

'Er . . . It needs some work,' he began cautiously.

She caught her breath, and although Leo was looking at the painting, he saw her chin go up and felt, rather than saw, the pain of rejection in her eyes. He couldn't bear it.

'Just a few details,' he went on desperately. 'Otherwise it's quite . . . Quite extraordinary. You've – er – really captured it, haven't you?'

261

'Oh, Leo, thank you!' She'd thrown herself into his arms before he could catch his breath, and by then it was too late. He wanted her! He wanted her! He seemed to see all his virtuous thoughts of the past few days flying away, like so many little beetles – and after that everything went dark. Warm and dark, like a jungle or a tropical sea, where sensation is everything and thinking too terrifying even to contemplate.

She had nothing on under her husband's shirt. It was missing a few buttons and was loose enough to allow his hands to slide beneath it, to feel the satin softness of her skin, the ecstatic swell of her breasts. Her breath was like a storm in his ears, the pulse of his blood a primitive drumbeat, forcing him to dance. He was barely conscious of anything else. He knew only that she wanted him as much as he wanted her, and that from now on he was unstoppable. Her mouth was like an oyster in his mouth. Her scent – of musk and oil-paints and turpentine – an hypnotic drug to melt his bones.

'Oh, Leo, Leo,' she sobbed. 'I've been so *lonely*!' And he tore open the last of the buttons and took her breast in his mouth.

That was when Mary Preece knocked on the door – and opened it.

Angela screamed and ran into the kitchen. Leo let out a groan of horror. He thought it the worst moment of his life. He was soon to discover that it wasn't.

Let loose to go where it pleased (which it rarely was), Lydia's hair reached halfway down her back. But that was all it did. It didn't curl; it didn't wave; it didn't 'bounce'. Just hung there like a handful of wet seaweed, foretelling the weather. She told the hairdresser all this. She told him it wouldn't take a perm. She also told him that if he cut it short and wispy, as was the latest fashion, she'd sue him first and dismember him later.

'I live in the country,' she informed him sternly. 'We wait five years for the latest fashion. Any sooner than that and the hens stop laying.'

He laughed. He said she had beautiful hair and that the only thing wrong with it was its weight. She had a long neck, he said, which meant that if he cut her hair to her shoulders it would still be long enough to 'put up', but not heavy enough to 'just hang there'. And she needed a fringe, he said, to soften the line of her brow. Lydia took this to mean that it would disguise the worry lines on her forehead, which didn't seem such a bad idea, although she couldn't imagine the effect and was afraid she would hate it – or, worse, that Leo would hate it.

She almost said, 'No, just trim the ends,' but before she could speak the hairdresser pushed his hands up through the seaweedy mass so that it sat in a softly billowing curve on her shoulders. 'There, like that,' he said. 'It'll move, it'll *bounce* . . .'

'Do it,' she said.

As was the way with hairdressers, this one interrogated her while he worked, asking her about her home and family; telling her she couldn't possibly have four children (she was too young); drooling with envy when she described Molliston, saying she didn't know how lucky she was to live in so much peace, with so much beauty.

'Yes,' she said wistfully. 'The grass is always greener on the far side of the fence, isn't it? You're lucky to live in London, you know, with so much going on all around you. Theatres, museums, art galleries . . .'

'But no time to enjoy any of them.'

Lydia laughed. 'That's how it is in the country, too.'

'Better views, though. Fresher air. New-laid eggs. Is your husband a gentleman-farmer?'

'He's a gentleman,' Lydia smiled. 'And a farmer. But not a gentleman-farmer. That is, he gets just as wet and dirty as everyone else, but he bathes more often.'

'And –' the man darted a glance at Charlotte, who was having her hair cut too, by someone else '– he's blond, blue-eyed and about six foot tall. Am I right?'

'Six foot two. How do you know?'

'Your daughter's blonde. And you're tall. I can't imagine you with a dwarf. Are you happily married?'

No one had ever asked Lydia such a question and, in any other circumstances, it would have seemed the height of bad manners, but it didn't seem in the least wrong now. Almost a relief, in fact. It was so unlikely that she'd see this man again. She could tell him anything at all and it wouldn't matter.

'I don't know,' she said. 'You're making me wonder – is there such a thing as happiness? A state of happiness, I mean: something you achieve when you marry the right person, for example, and then retain for the rest of your life? Sounds ridiculous put like that, doesn't it? It *is* ridiculous.' She frowned at the mirrored reflection of a profoundly surprised hairdresser.

'But that's the only reason people get married,' he said. 'Isn't it?'

Lydia laughed wryly, remembering the reason she'd got married. 'No, not the only reason, but it's the only reason most people have for living at all, so I suppose it's much the same.'

'And you say it's *impossible*?'

'No, I said it's ridiculous. Ridiculous to expect happiness of one other person, or to imagine that one is capable – on one's own – of making *him* happy. It's so much more complicated than that.'

The hairdresser's eyes brightened, making his thoughts as transparent as water. 'You mean . . .?'

Lydia laughed again. 'Oh, no. What I'm saying is, if you want to be happy, you have to make happiness, not take it. Make it for yourself, I mean, not ask someone else to make it for you. Have you ever noticed that when you're with happy people you feel happy? They aren't necessarily trying to *make* you happy. You just catch it, like measles.'

The hairdresser was quiet for a moment. Then he grinned. 'Yes,' he said. 'I'm beginning to feel that way about you. *Are* you happy?'

Lydia smiled. 'Yes,' she said. 'I do believe I am. And I like the fringe, by the way. You're a genius.'

He laughed. He actually blushed. He said, 'There, you see! You've made me *very* happy!'

'I'm sorry!' Mary Preece gasped. 'I had to find you, Mr Chantry! David's gone! Someone's taken him!'

Leo had turned his back on her, partly to hide his embarrassment and partly to keep himself from killing her. Now he whirled on his heel and stared at her, appalled. '*What*? What d'you mean?'

She'd put him in his pram in the great hall. She was going to the shops and to fetch Dinah from school and had strapped David in before realising she'd left her purse upstairs. Zula was with her and, rather than drag the child upstairs again, she'd left her with Floral in the kitchen. When she'd come back again, having collected both her purse and Zula, David had gone.

'In the pram?'

'No! They took him out!'

'*They*?'

'I don't *know*! Whoever took him!'

She'd looked everywhere: all over the house. She'd asked everyone: Floral, Mrs Lodge, Peggy, the gardeners. But David had disappeared.

The shock of being found *in flagrante delicto* left little room, at first, for Leo to panic about his son. It was a mistake. Mary had only thought she'd strapped him in – he'd probably crawled off somewhere on his own . . . He was already starting up the Land Rover to go home before he remembered that David couldn't crawl: he'd only just reached the stage of sitting up on his own, let alone crawling. Leo began to tremble. Although the drive home took less than three minutes, he could scarcely see where he was going for the throb of blood in his eyes. And nothing Mary said gave him any hope. Although it had been a hasty search, she'd searched every room in the house, asked everyone she could possibly ask.

But the house was a maze with all its interconnecting rooms and several staircases. Even while Mary searched, whoever had taken David could have been ahead of her or behind. His mother was always wandering about the place; she'd nip up the front stairs one minute and be found emerging from the cellar the next. There was no need ever to retrace one's steps at Molliston. One could walk around in circles until hell froze over.

'Right,' he said as they ran indoors. 'Get everyone in the small parlour, Mary, and keep them there. I'll search the house again, and I don't want anyone else wandering about while I do it.'

Panic didn't really overtake him until he saw the empty pram and, in his mind's eye, saw David sitting there, bouncing up and down, chewing his fists, crooning and gurgling, reciting his elocution lessons: Boo-boo, da-da, mum-um, whee! He'd reached that stage: the most charming, most fascinating stage in a baby's life, when he ceases to be just a series of bodily functions and begins to be a person. In spite of all his experience of babies, Leo had never ceased to be awed by them and, in some ways, David had been more intriguing than all the rest just because his early months of life had been such a nightmare. Every time he laughed, smiled, or only burbled to himself while counting his own toes, it seemed a kind of miracle . . .

Leo's internal organs seemed to be collapsing with terror as he raced through the ground-floor rooms, looking for his son under tables, in cupboards, even up the chimneys. He looked under the stairs of the inner hall and felt a shadow engulf him as he cornered at the foot of the stairs. A shadow which darkened as he tore up the stairs. A shadow so black, so dark and solid, it was as if, when he came to the place on the landing where Richard had fallen, he'd run into a stone wall. Shock hit him like a blow to the chest. He stopped in his tracks, doubling up with the pain of it.

They'd lost David! David had gone! And he couldn't bear it, he couldn't bear it. Oh, Lydia, Lydia . . . she'd go crazy with grief! She wouldn't care about anything else, but oh, God, oh, *God*, she'd never forgive him *this*!

He realised he was sobbing only when he stopped sobbing, hearing – behind him somewhere – the sound of someone else sobbing; or, rather, wailing, the way babies do when they're bored with their own company and want some attention. Afterwards, when he was calm again, Leo wondered about the strange, illogical workings of the human mind, the curiously independent way it has of accepting the unacceptable, of believing the impossible. For when he heard that cry, he didn't at first think it was David (David had been kidnapped, taken away) he thought it was Richard, come back to haunt him.

But it was David. He was lying in the middle of Leo's own bed, still dressed in his outdoor clothes, perfectly safe, completely unharmed. He even stopped wailing the minute Leo threw open the door. He just widened his eyes and said, 'Ga-ga-ga!' while Leo turned up his face to heaven and thanked God for salvation.

It was hard not to crush the child in his arms. Hard not to frighten him with tears of relief. Hard even to speak. But he said, 'There you are, you little blighter. What do you think you're up to, hmm? Frightening the life out of everyone, wandering about the house on your own?'

Wandering about the house . . . Had his mother done this?

Although he picked the child up and cuddled him, he was still shaking too much to trust himself to carry him downstairs and instead shouted over the banister, 'All right, Mary! I've found him!'

She and Floral took the stairs almost as fast as he had, but it gave him enough time to get a grip on his thoughts, to calm himself a little.

'Here,' he said. 'He was here. Exactly where he is now. Did you look in here, Mary?'

'Yes! Yes, I –'

'An' I did,' Floral muttered. She was frowning with bewilderment, but Leo saw that her thoughts were following the same course as his own. His mother. But why on earth would she do such a thing? She'd never shown the slightest interest in David – never shown any interest in any of the children until they were toddling about, tripping her up, forcing her to take notice. Why should she take him out of his pram, for heaven's sake? It didn't make sense!

Mary ran off to collect Dinah from school and, while she was gone, Leo asked Floral what exactly had happened; how long it had all taken.

'I were in in the kitchen, 'elpin' Doris Lodge with the veg,' she said. 'An' Nanny come in wiv Zula and asked I to keep an eye while she ran up for her purse.'

'Where was my mother?'

'I dunno.' Floral scowled and bit her lip, but said nothing more, for which – at that moment – Leo was grateful.

'And Mary went upstairs straight away, did she?'

'Yes. No . . . I asked 'er, since she wuz goin' to the shop, to fetch

266

me a few things, but I don't s'pose that took more'n a minute. An' she were a few minutes gone to get her money, so what's that? Four minutes? Long enough.'

'Long enough for what?'

'For someone to unbuckle the babby's harness and take him up the back stairs. Even Doris Lodge'd be nimble enough for that. Not that it *were* Doris, 'cos she were wiv I.'

'So what happened when Mary came back and found David gone?'

'We all run around like a lot o' geese on Christmas Eve, o'course! Nanny thought she'd gone crazy. She kep' sayin' –'

'Never mind what she said. What did she do?'

Like Leo, it seemed, she'd searched under the tables and up the chimneys, in too much of a panic to be logical at first. But then she and Floral had both searched the entire house: Mary using the main staircase and Floral the back stairs that led from the cellar all the way up to the garrets. But there were other staircases – a half-flight leading from the dining room to the second floor, and another half-flight leading from the library to the gallery. It would be impossible for just two people to search the place without giving a third a chance to hide somewhere.

'Did either of you see my mother during all this?' he asked reluctantly, for it seemed all wrong to think she could do such a thing. If she *could* do such a thing, he'd then have to ask why, and he didn't want to know the answer to that. He'd been suspecting for some time that there was something strange about her, something badly wrong, something worse than depression . . .

'Yes,' Floral said sadly. 'She was in the hall when I went up the back stairs. She asked what was goin' on . . . An' I told her us'd lost the babby . . . No, no I never. I said we'd lost *David*, someone took him, I said. An' she said . . .'

'What?'

'She said, "Who's David?"' Floral averted her eyes, evidently feeling as uncomfortable as Leo did. 'One of her jokes, I s'pose,' she added without conviction.

'Yes,' he said, but as soon as he'd said it, realised that he wanted it to be a joke. He didn't want to face the fact that his mother might be crazy. He didn't want to know that her craziness, if such it was, might threaten the safety of his children. But how could he keep his children safe unless he acknowledged their danger? If ever there was a right time to hide from the truth, this wasn't it.

'No,' he said. 'It wasn't a joke, Floral.'

He was surprised by her reaction to this. She'd been looking away

267

from him, frowning. Now she turned to look at him again, her face soft with compassion. 'No,' she said gently. 'No, it weren't no joke.'

He could have wept. He walked to the window and stared out, seeing nothing. 'I wish Lydia was here,' he murmured. 'She'd sort it out, wouldn't she?'

'No,' Floral said. 'She cassn't sort it out, my love. All she can do is keep it hid from thee and there ain't much sense in that, is there?'

'What d'you mean?'

'I mean she's *your* ma, my love, not Lydial's. It ain't her place to sort it out. She don't know much about her, for one thing.'

'Neither do I.'

But even this wasn't as true as it seemed. He'd known his mother all his life, after all, and must know more about her than Lydia knew. Yet he'd never talked to her much and, during her years at the cottage, he'd scarcely talked to her at all. He'd 'popped in' three or four times a week and seen her when she'd come to Molliston, but really it had just been a matter of checking that she was still alive. How are you? Everything all right? Need anything? She'd never given him the wrong answers and, had she done so, what would he have done about it? Told Lydia to sort it out?

'Do you think my mother . . .?' he began hesitantly. 'Do you think she's . . .?'

Floral said nothing.

'Is she ill? I mean – Hell, you know what I *mean*, Floral!'

'Yes. But I don't know the answer, my love. She's never bin the same as the rest of us, and the rest of us ain't so sane we can boast about it. What's it mean, anyway? *Sane*?'

Leo stroked his mouth with a trembling hand. Yes, what did it mean? Understanding oneself? Knowing right from wrong? Controlling oneself? Making the right choice between one set of actions and another? He caught a glimpse of himself, with Angela in his arms, and knew he wasn't sane enough to make any boasts.

Since that terrible moment on the landing when he'd lost Richard and David – and Lydia – in a single, unbearable, stroke of agony, Leo *had* been sane. But before that? Before that, he'd been driven – like an animal – through a mud-wallow of confusion and tangled emotions, still *knowing* right from wrong, but unable to choose between them. It was almost as if his mind had been a railway junction, himself a train, *having* to move the way the points had been set, regardless of the fact that everyone on board (husband, father, son, morally upright citizen) had wanted to go in another direction entirely. There'd been something horrible about it. He'd felt so helpless, *knowing* that he was going to ruin, *knowing* that he'd be taking everyone with him, yet being totally unable to change the points!

If that was how his mother felt – if she, too, was being driven down such a road – what could save her?

Mary came in with Dinah, through the kitchen door, just as Peggy wandered in from the hall. He said, 'Ah, Mother –' just as Dinah wrapped her arms around his legs and cried, 'Daddy, guess what *I* did, today!' It was another example of the railway line. He wanted to speak to his mother, but found himself speaking to Dinah instead. For a moment, though, while he lifted Dinah into his arms, he kept his eyes on his mother. She'd been smiling as she came into the kitchen. Now, as she saw Mary on the far side of the room, her expression changed to one of cold hostility: her mouth pinching, her eyes narrowing defensively before she turned and hurried out again without acknowledging anyone else.

She'd taken against Mary virtually on sight and for no apparent reason. Mary was a fairly typical nanny – stolid, well-mannered, efficient – and there was nothing about her that anyone could reasonably dislike. But Peggy had never been the type one could call reasonable and, given that she did dislike Mary, might she have taken David just to frighten her? Or even to cast doubt on her abilities and get her sacked?

Later, having searched the house for his mother and at last found her in the drawing room (where he'd already looked), he said gently, 'I realise it was just some kind of joke, Mother, but I'd be grateful if you didn't touch the baby again. If any harm came to him, you'd never forgive yourself, would you?'

She took a ball of wool from the table beside her chair and began feverishly to rewind it. 'Forgive myself?' she demanded sharply. 'I've nothing to forgive myself for. I wasn't there!'

'You weren't – where?'

She put her knuckles to her mouth. 'I was ill,' she said. 'I was in bed!' She glared at him, her eyes burning with a strange, hectic light. 'It was the girl,' she said. 'The girl did it!'

The curious thing was that if she hadn't first said she'd been in bed, which she evidently hadn't been, he might have begun to believe her. For a moment, in fact, he did begin to wonder about Mary, but that moment passed, leaving him as helpless as before and wishing with all his heart that Lydia would come home. Without her, everything seemed to be falling apart, and when she discovered what had happened to David . . . Oh, God! She *mustn't* find out, not at least until he felt a little more certain about his mother!

He ran upstairs to find Mary, who was in the middle of bathtime:

rubbing Zula dry while Dinah, still in the bath, played 'slippery-fish' with the soap. He lifted her out and dried her off, chatting and teasing in a general way before saying, 'I shouldn't tell Mrs Chantry about what happened this afternoon, Mary. There was no harm done, of course, but it would worry her. She'd think it was her fault for going away.'

He knew Mary couldn't have misunderstood him, but when she turned to him and asked coolly, 'Don't tell her what?' he remembered Angela, and turned scarlet with shame. He hid his confusion in the damp mass of Dinah's hair.

'Don't tell her anything,' he said quietly. 'It won't happen again.'

Chapter Twenty-Three

After a few days of easy living, being waited on hand and foot, dressing up for dinner and being treated like royalty, Lydia thought she might get used to it. No one could say she was resting – trailing around London was actually harder work than scrubbing floors – but it was lovely to be able to *choose* one's route to exhaustion rather than having it imposed by the dishes in the sink. It was better than resting. It was heaven.

So when she telephoned Leo on Wednesday night (managing to catch him before dinner this time) she still wasn't quite ready to go home. Friday or Saturday she said. Charlotte was seeing Madame Tussaud's on Thursday to compensate for the disaster of the Zoo, and Lydia still wanted to buy out Harrods Food Hall. Rationing lurked like a half-forgotten nightmare at the back of her mind and she felt sure an unlimited quantity of smoked salmon would cure it.

'Couldn't you be more definite, darling?' Leo asked. 'Make it Friday, perhaps?'

He sounded a good deal sweeter than he had on Monday. Mrs Lodge's lumpy gravy was making him think, evidently, but where Leo's thinking was concerned, more was better than less – Lydia didn't want to be missed just for her gravy.

'Oh, I don't know,' she said. 'There's so much I still want to do. Better say Saturday, I think.'

His disappointment, which he made no attempt to hide, gave Lydia a warm glow, deep inside, but by Friday morning, when she finally 'bought out' Harrods Food Hall, that glow was stone dead. She was tired and, even given that she'd never seen so many people all at once, strangely lonely. Charlotte was lonely, too. She wasn't the sort to make a fuss, but since she'd first decided that Leo would be missing her, she'd mentioned him every few hours and was now concerning herself with the rest of the family, too. For a child so apparently lacking in confidence, she had a curious way of thinking that she was the centre of everyone else's world and that no one could survive without her. Who would play with Dinah? Who would understand Zula's two-year-old gobbledegook? Who would help Floral weed between the lettuces or welcome Daddy home? No one could do these things as Charlotte did.

Lydia found this amount of self-importance a little irritating, and they were on their way back to the hotel before she realised that she was exactly the same. Could life at Molliston go on without her? Could the family survive on an unrelieved diet of lumpy gravy? The answer, of course, was yes, and as soon as she realised it she understood too that she (and Charlotte) had been asking the wrong question. The question wasn't, 'Can they exist without us?' It was, 'Can *we* exist without *them*?'

She lay back in the cab, closing her eyes on a smile. 'How would you like to go home now?' she murmured.

'Now?' Charlotte's eyes widened. '*Can* we, Mummy?'

'I don't see why not. Would you like that?'

After the first flush of excitement at leaving home, Charlotte had become quieter and quieter. Now she burst into life again and chattered away nineteen to the dozen. She had so many things to tell everyone, and could hardly wait to give them all their presents!

Oddly enough, the very *best* thing she had to tell them was that she'd been to the Zoo . . .

Except for essential work at the farm, Leo spent much of his time at home since David's 'disappearance'. This was only partly because he was afraid that something else – perhaps something worse – might happen in his absence. It was also because he wanted to steer well clear of Angela. He never wanted to see her again. His fright with David and subsequent anxiety about his mother's state of mind had killed his lusts stone dead. Or perhaps what had killed them had been Mary's arrival on the scene. The shame he'd felt then he still felt, worse with every hour that passed: a seething sickness in his stomach, a dark cloud on his mind. Mary seemed to have forgotten all about it – she was as pleasant to him as she'd always been – but he knew she hadn't forgotten and it was almost as bad to see her, now, as it would have been to see Angela. It was as if he'd tainted them both with his own poison, made them both as ugly as he felt himself to be.

He was afraid, too, that one or both of the women might tell Lydia what had happened, ruining all of their lives for what amounted to an insignificant moment of madness. Insignificant because he'd never really believed that anything more than lust was involved. If any of it had had any significance it was only insofar as it had made him doubt his feelings for Lydia and – now – revealed the truth of his feelings in no uncertain terms. He loved her. He loved her for a thousand different reasons, none of which could be isolated one from another, yet all of which rested on a single foundation: respect.

The more he thought about it, the stranger it seemed to him that he'd respected her utterly from first sight of her to last. On both occasions he'd been angry with her and on both occasions she'd got the better of him. She *was* better than him. From the moment she'd confessed that Richard wasn't his child, she'd rarely put a foot wrong, never done anything dishonest or unkind, never given him anything but her best. She wasn't the kind of woman any man could call exciting – there were so few surprises with Lydia; one always knew what to expect – but there was an enormous beauty in such expectations: a beauty he hadn't begun to appreciate until . . . Until she'd gone away.

Now that *had* been a surprise. And her refusal to explain any of it or give a definite date for her return (he'd buttoned her down to Saturday now, but was by no means certain she'd stay buttoned) was rather more 'exciting' than he could bear. Why had she gone? And why go without warning like that? What did it mean? It was uncharacteristic enough to be frightening. The whole thing – Angela and Mary, David, Peggy and Lydia – had scared him enough to make him think he could expect nothing any more. Nothing good, anyway.

But he was proved wrong, for Friday's post brought him something else he hadn't expected: a letter addressed to 'Mr and Mrs Chantry', postmarked from Bath. It was from Angela.

Dear Leo and Lydia,
Sorry to run out on you like this, but – as I'm sure you will have guessed by now – country living doesn't really suit me. You've been wonderfully kind, but without living absolutely in your pockets, I haven't been able to fight off the loneliness . . .

She'd left. She'd packed up and gone. Leo closed his eyes and sent up a wordless prayer of gratitude. There wasn't even a hint in the letter of her true reasons for going, and he thanked God for that, too, understanding it. Angela had wanted him almost as much as he'd wanted her and, in the end, had given herself, not been taken. She probably thought it had all been her fault and . . . Well, perhaps it had been! She'd certainly made her charms very obvious. And had he pursued her or been pursued? She'd waylaid him for a lift, waylaid him for her odd jobs and 'art' criticism. She might even have staged that little entrapment with the cows in the lane . . .

As the day went on, this line of thought came to be as much of a relief as the letter itself had. His conscience was almost clear; a few smuts remained, but nothing too terrible. He'd been led astray! But as he drove home that evening, thinking (with sinking heart) of having to face Mary over the dinner table, he saw a clear image of himself as Mary had seen him, stooping slavishly to Angela's breast. And that was *no one's* fault but his own . . .

At Molliston, he sat in the Land Rover for long, thoughtful minutes, depressed beyond bearing. This was *exactly* what he'd done with Lydia at the start of their marriage and, in a way, ever since. The blame could be sliced straight down the middle – her fault, his fault – and thus, in a way, no one's fault: they'd cancelled each other out. Yes, it was exactly the same, for his run-in with Angela had almost certainly been *half* her fault. But that wasn't good enough for him. He wanted all the right on *his* side. He wanted someone *else* to take the blame. Ha! He was just like his mother! *It was the girl! The girl did it!*

God, he didn't want to be like that!

He slammed the car door and wandered towards the house, hearing the children laughing in the kitchen without registering that they should, by this time, be in bed. And then, as he passed the kitchen window, there was a wild shriek, and Charlotte flew out to meet him, calling, 'Daddy!'

He couldn't believe it. As he hoisted his daughter into his arms, he found himself almost crying with relief. He'd known he'd missed Charlotte, but he hadn't known how much. He'd known that he'd feared she might never return, but he hadn't realised he'd taken his fear so seriously. He'd known that he'd loved his wife. But when he went inside and found her laughing up at him from a table cluttered with teacups, gifts and wrapping paper, he knew only then that he loved her completely and never wanted to let her out of his sight again.

'Lydia!'

'Hello, darling. Did we surprise you?' She kissed him and he was enveloped in a perfume he didn't know. She stepped back and shook out her hair, letting it swing around her shoulders like a silken veil.

'Like it?'

It was beautiful. She was beautiful. 'Oh, I've missed you,' he whispered.

'We missed you too.'

He believed it of Charlotte, who wouldn't let him go, but he wasn't so sure about Lydia. She looked so different: happy and relaxed and about ten years younger than when she'd gone away – only five days

274

ago. Only five days! It felt like a lifetime.

The children were too excited to go to bed and by the time Leo found himself alone with his wife, it was almost time for them to go to bed, too. He felt strangely shy of this bright-eyed, smartly dressed woman, with her glowing skin, her shining hair, her *fringe*! He couldn't have believed it would make such a difference. She was like someone else: someone he didn't quite know.

'You look – marvellous,' he said hesitantly.

'I feel marvellous.' She grinned. 'It's done me a power of good and I'm going to do it again. *And* again.' She frowned comically. 'And that's not all I'm going to do.'

'Oh . . .?' He wasn't sure he liked the sound of this, whatever it was.

'I've done it all wrong,' she said brightly, 'Life, I mean. I thought it was meant to be difficult. I thought people who had fun at the expense of duty weren't quite decent.'

Leo blushed and looked at his hands.

'But I was wrong,' Lydia said. 'Because duty never ends, Leo. If you show it too much respect, it just gets bigger, more demanding. It never lets you go. So, like virtually everything else in life, it has to be kept in its proper place. Leo, I've had a lovely time in London. It was wonderful not to be chained to the stove and the kitchen sink. It was wonderful to be waited on. It was also wonderful to get away from everyone, to think about people instead of just reacting to them. I've thought about things – especially about you and me – that had never crossed my mind before. I've always thought you a bit irresponsible, for example, but you're not. Not at all. You keep things in proportion. You understand the true value of things.'

Leo continued to look at his hands. He didn't dare look at Lydia. 'What sort of things?' he murmured guiltily.

'Well, everything. That's the whole point, darling. You know when things are serious enough to be taken seriously, but you also know when to laugh at them, ignore them, let them go.' She narrowed her eyes. 'I'm going to *learn* that, Leo. I'm going to learn to *enjoy* life, for a change.'

He laughed at last. Not because she made it sound much fun, but because she made it sound so serious! *Learn* to enjoy life? Was that possible?

'Oh . . .' Lydia reached to stroke his knee, sliding an elegant, freshly manicured hand very slowly along his thigh. 'It's not the enjoyment I have to learn. It's the making time for it, conserving energy for it.' She slid sideways to rest her head on his shoulder. 'I'm full of energy *now*, for instance.'

275

'Are you?' He bit back a smile.

'Mmm . . .'

'Right,' he said ponderously. 'So . . . Let's – um – enjoy ourselves, shall we? What would you like to do? Play tiddlywinks?'

Lydia hit him.

Of all the things Lydia had expected of her welcome home, 'ecstasy' hadn't been one of them. 'Warmth' was as far up the scale as she'd dared to venture, with perhaps a token 'Yippee!' from Dinah before the idea of presents distracted her from the person who had given them (and with difficulty hauled them home). But ecstasy was what she got. The minute the taxi drew up on the gravel, the dogs jumped into the back seat, uttering strangled yaps of joy, Dinah leapt into her lap crying 'Mummy, Mummy, oh, Mummy!' Floral (almost as bad as the dogs) tore out of the house, laughingly hugged the taxi driver and burst into tears – and Zula wet her pants. Even Mary Preece lost her professional calm for long enough to say, 'Oh, Mrs Chantry, we *have* missed you!' before detaching her gently from the general embrace (which, what with Floral's tears, the dogs' slobber and Zula's accident had become rather damp) and organising everyone into some semblance of order.

Peggy showed up just as the taxi crackled off down the drive. Lydia's first impression of her was that she'd aged ten years in less than a week, but her welcome, too, was more than just warm. 'Darling! How lovely to see you! You look so well, so pretty!' She spoiled it by adding, 'How long can you stay?' which Lydia didn't forget, even though the general mood of rejoicing continued, carrying her into the house on such a cloud of happiness she should have forgotten everything. Charlotte, too, was hugged, kissed and admired, but Lydia knew that the best of the welcome was for her alone, that they'd all missed her, that they all cared for her as she'd never suspected they could. A mother naturally expects her children to love her, but the others, too? No . . . The best she'd expected of them was tolerance, respect perhaps, even affection. But not love. It warmed her heart. It made her laugh.

With a little help from everyone else, even David welcomed her home. They thrust him into her arms, told her how good he'd been, showed her his new tooth and said he was getting as fat as butter, as if they'd expected him to waste away in her absence and were frantic to prove he hadn't. She couldn't blame them. She'd spent so much time before she'd gone away 'covering all eventualities', they must imagine she'd spent her entire stay in London worrying about them. Now she came to think of it, it was amazing to think how *little* she'd worried, but maybe that was her reward for covering all eventualities. That, and this. Being missed.

Afterwards, when Leo came home, she realised that she'd been expecting him to give her the same boisterous, noisy greeting, but he looked almost stricken, and when he held her, kissed her, whispered only, 'Oh, I've missed you,' she hardly knew what to do with herself. She understood him well enough to know that when he felt most he said least and hoped with all her heart that he knew her as well, for had she given vent to her own feelings at that moment, she'd have gone all to pieces and wept.

That her little rebellion had worked was a feeling which stayed with her for several days afterwards – in fact, until Leo began his haymaking. Until then, he was at home a good deal, always checking where his mother was, or playing with the children, more Lydia's idea of a family man than he'd ever been. More of a 'baby' man, too (he tended, like his mother, to prefer them when they could walk), for he spent much of his time with David, carrying him about in peculiarly masculine fashion, on his arm, rather than straddling his hip. David was getting to be quite a lump – an active lump at that – and it was rather touching to see how easily Leo managed him.

'I don't remember you being so interested in the girls when they were babies,' she said. 'Is it just because he's a boy?'

'Mmm? No, I don't think so. I just . . .'

'What?'

'Well. They change so much at this age, don't they? I don't want to miss anything. Time seems to pass so quickly . . . I keep thinking I'll come home one day and find he's gone . . . Off to university, or something.'

She laughed. 'I don't think he's likely to do that until he can walk, darling.'

'That's exactly what I mean. It's only five minutes since we were saying the same thing about Dinah, and she's already at school. She'll be getting married next!'

He let out a little sigh. It *was* just a little sigh, and yet somehow it pricked the bubble of Lydia's happiness, making her suspect that nothing much had changed after all. He was still depressed, still worrying about something beyond the reach of her imagination. It couldn't be Angela. She'd been wrong about Angela, who'd moved out of the farmhouse, claiming loneliness, so she couldn't have been enjoying much of Leo's company. Lydia felt bad about that. Glad, too, for even if her suspicions had been wide of the mark, she'd probably have gone on having them while Angela stayed.

'What's the matter?' she asked softly.

'Nothing. Nothing at all. Why?' (Had his cheeks turned pink, or was that Lydia's imagination, too?)

'You sighed,' she reminded him. 'Something to do with Dinah's wedding, I think.'

He grinned. 'Well, think of the expense! And there'll be Charlotte's and Zula's weddings to think about too, you know. And five minutes after that we'll be grandparents . . .'

Lydia tipped her head to one side. 'Ah,' she said. 'Worrying about your age? There's no need, you know. You look younger now than you did when I first met you.'

'Hmph. That won't last. Look at my mother. She stayed thirty-five for the best part of thirty years and then . . .'

'She *is* over seventy, Leo! For heaven's sake, darling.'

'And she's getting weirder by the day.'

'Nonsense.' It wasn't nonsense, but Lydia wasn't equal to facing the truth of it. Peggy would get better. She *would*.

Although Leo couldn't claim to be spending very much of his time worrying about his mother, it was a worry he wanted to be rid of. He didn't realise that he was trying to shift the burden to Lydia's shoulders until, with a shrug, she tipped it back where it belonged, saying nothing about it, but somehow saying everything he least wanted to know. *She's your mother, not mine.*

It was so unlike her. Giving Lydia something to worry about was like giving a dog a bone: she'd gnaw at it for days, bury it, dig it up again and abandon it, eventually, only when the problem was solved. She didn't know what the problem was, in this case, of course. He hadn't told her about David's little vanishing act and probably never would, because . . . Because if Lydia even suspected that Peggy was a danger to the children, she'd have her committed to a mental asylum before anyone else could blink. The thought turned Leo's stomach, but how, in all conscience, could he prevent it? He couldn't. The children's safety must come first.

But surely his mother wasn't a real danger to them? She was getting old and vague, that was all. She wasn't really loopy. Yet every time she said something too obviously 'vague', every time he found her wandering about the house on her own, a faint chill ran up his spine, something he couldn't control and could barely understand. It was something to do with his being her son, flesh of her flesh. It was something to do with her being his mother.

He tried to think of her as his mother, rather than as the elderly stranger she'd become since Richard's death. Richard's death . . . That was the key. He saw it now, as he hadn't at the time (he'd been too concerned about Lydia to spare much thought for anyone else), as too heavy a weight, tipping his mother's life out of balance. And why not, after all? She was more vulnerable than Lydia had ever been, simply because, for as long as he'd known her, she'd *never* been perfectly balanced. She had so few resources: a narrow education, a narrower social circle, no earthly need to strive for anything more important than the latest fashion.

She'd never known a day's trouble until Lionel had died. And after that? After that (perhaps before that; how the hell was he to know?) she'd spent her whole life running from trouble, pretending it wasn't there. He remembered his father asking her about various domestic matters that had blown up in his face: 'Well, really, darling, surely you *knew* about this?' And the answer was always no, even when the truth was yes. She'd been the same when Leo had come back from Germany: she hadn't had a clue why the house was in such a mess, why there was no money, why virtually everything of value had disappeared. The idea was, he supposed, that if she claimed ignorance she could also claim innocence, and although it had never quite worked that way (especially with his father), Leo had in fact spent the first few years of his return to Molliston thinking Floral was to blame for most of it. He was pretty sure now that he wouldn't have had a home at all if it hadn't been for Floral, but that was by the by.

The point was (at least he thought the point was) that Peggy had survived all her life by denying knowledge of everything she didn't *want* to know. But she hadn't been able to deny her knowledge of Richard's death. She'd heard him scream, heard the thud of his poor little body on the cold stone floor . . . It had very nearly broken Leo's mind, and he . . . yes, weak as he was, he'd been stronger than Peggy had ever been.

With Angela gone, his urgent need to keep his mother at Molliston had passed and now he began to wonder if she'd be better if she went back to the cottage. She'd moved out because of Richard and perhaps it was the memory of him that was so disturbing her now. He could pay someone to cook and clean for her; he might even find some woman to live with her (pity Floral wouldn't; she'd be perfect), and he could make his checks on her, as before, but try this time to make them more thorough. He was aware that he'd be serving his own ends in letting her go, but as long as she wanted it too, did it matter? Surely the best solutions were those which served everyone's best interests?

The next time he found his mother alone he said, 'Are you still thinking of moving back to the cottage, Mother?'

She looked up at him, frowning. 'What cottage?' she said.

279

Chapter Twenty-Four

Most of the furniture at Peggy's cottage had come originally from Molliston, so when Leo moved it back again, Lydia rearranged it, as best she could, in one of the rooms adjoining Peggy's bedroom. Peggy took no interest in it at first, which – after all the work it had involved – was a little dispiriting, but about a week later, Lydia found Peggy sitting there, gazing dreamily from the window, and said encouragingly. 'It's a nice room, isn't it, Peggy? Home from home.'

'Yes,' she said. 'I've always liked this place. So much nicer than Molliston.'

These strange little lapses never failed to make Lydia's spine crawl, but on this occasion, more in desperation than hope, she decided to play along. She sat nearby and asked gently, 'Were you never happy at Molliston, Peggy?'

'No. But there was nowhere else to go. It's hard . . . to live all your life without love.'

Lydia smiled encouragingly. 'You loved your children, surely?'

Peggy turned her head, looked at Lydia for a moment and then closed her eyes. She said nothing, but it was all strangely eloquent – and strangely conclusive. The look had said, 'What do you know?' The closed eyes had said, 'Nothing. You know nothing.'

Lydia had too much sense to pursue it, but the exchange stayed with her for days afterwards, depressing her more than anything else could have done. For if she knew nothing, what could she do to help? Eventually she spoke to Floral about it and asked if she knew what it meant. 'Leo's father,' she said. 'Didn't *he* love her?'

Floral sighed. 'Oh, it's hard to say, my love. I didn't hardly know him. Not really. Not till he were bard, and then I s'pose it were too late. He were in a lot of pain. It drove him . . . He weren't in his right mind, half the time. He were a nice man, but . . .'

'But?'

'Sad. I never knowed a man so sad. He said things towards the end . . .'

'Go on.'

'Well, I couldn't make head nor tail of it, my love, and anyway, when a man's ragin', he do say things he don't mean, so . . .' She scratched her head. 'Feelin's is complicated, see, Lydia. Thee can hate someone and love 'em too, cassn't 'ee? One person can't never know the ins and outs of another. It ain't my place to say whether he loved her or he never.'

Floral's diplomacy had foxed Lydia many times before, but she'd rarely felt so disappointed at being foxed. Floral was right, of course; black and white didn't exist in the human heart, only shades of grey. But it didn't help.

She was on her way out when Floral added sharply, 'An' there's another thing, Lydia!'

'What?'

'You can love some people till you'm blue in the face, but if they don't love 'emselves, you'm wastin' your time.'

'Love *themselves*?'

Floral chuckled. 'Ah, sounds all wrong, I know, but you think about it and see if it ain't right.'

Lydia did think about it, but not to any purpose. She'd been brought up to think self-love entirely wrong – arrogant, thoughtless, thoroughly un-Christian – and whenever Floral's injunction, *You think about it*, came to mind, that was precisely what she thought: that it was wrong.

About two weeks after Leo had cleared the cottage of Peggy's things, his land agent sent a couple of men to slap on some paint and wallpaper. Not much caring for the term 'slap', Lydia called in to check that the job was being done properly and afterwards went along to the churchyard to put some flowers on Richard's grave. She didn't stay long but during the time she spent there she was vaguely aware of a tall man strolling up and down beyond the boundary wall. Waiting for the bus, probably. She noticed, as she walked back to the gate, that he had a dark, neatly trimmed beard and moustache which had 'Royal Navy' written all over it, although he wasn't in uniform. She wondered if he might be a prospective tenant for the cottage and, catching his eye as she closed the gate behind her, tipped her head to one side, smiling as though to say, 'If you're lost, I can help you.' He smiled too. He, too, tipped his head to one side and gazed at her, almost lovingly, from a pair of beautiful, sea-green eyes.

Lovingly . . . sea-green . . . *Royal Navy*! Lydia turned pink. 'Alec?' she whispered.

He grinned.

'Alec! Oh, I can't –! Oh, Lord, how –? Alec, I scarcely recognised you!' She was blushing all over, torn in half by an urgent need to hug him – and another, just as urgent, to turn on her heel and run away.

'I recognised you,' he said softly. 'You haven't changed a bit, Mrs Chantry.'

'I –' She burst out laughing. 'I haven't grown a beard, anyway!'

'Like it?' He stroked it, preening himself in the teasing way she'd loved about him when he was a boy. Not that he was much more than a boy now – twenty-three, twenty-four? – although he looked so different, so *much* like a man.

They talked as old friends do, recounting the tale of their lives since last they'd met, and although she heard everything he had to say, Lydia didn't listen very hard. She concentrated on looking at him, remembering him, sorting her feelings into some kind of order. She still loved him. She would love him all her life; but it was a love that would endure like a fly set in amber, perfect in its every aspect, yet incapable of growth or of change. In her heart, he would always exist somewhere between fifteen and seventeen. He would never have a beard. He would always be an innocent village boy, not this experienced, well-travelled man of the world.

'South America?' she gasped.

'And South Africa, and the Med.'

She laughed. 'And a girl in every port?'

'Oh, yes,' he said. 'But only one I love.' The pang she felt then, prompted not so much by his words as by the tenderness in his voice, wasn't jealousy, for Alec the *man* held no attractions for her. It was more a pang of loss. Not the loss of *his* youth so much as the loss of her own. She was almost thirty-five and the tale of her life was very dull compared with his and likely to get duller. Boiling dishcloths . . .

Had the rules of courtesy allowed, she would have left him then and crawled back home to contemplate her stupidity in thinking a few days in London could change anything. But good manners made her gasp a pretence at delight, made her ask, '*Who?* Oh, Alec, where? Is she here?'

He didn't reply at first. He only nodded and at last said gently, 'Standing right in front of me.'

Set in amber, Lydia thought. He couldn't see her new fringe, or the crows' feet around her eyes. He couldn't see the little changes time and care had wrought upon her. They might meet again when she was eighty and, in each other's eyes, still be unchanged.

They shook hands when they parted. Lydia had never kissed him and had no wish to start now. But she looked at his hands and knew that, somehow, they'd put her back together again, taught her, yet again, who she was and what she was meant for.

Leo was just getting out of the Land Rover when Lydia came home. She looked – different. Hopping and skipping like a child, her eyes full of laughter. She leaned against him, tipped her face up to his and wickedly batted her eyelashes.

'What?' he demanded nervously.

'What what?'

He laughed. 'Why are you flirting with me?'

'Why shouldn't I? I love you. I want . . . to lure you into my clutches, lead you astray, sweep you off your size nines and make –' (she pronounced this with a deep-throated growl) '– make a man of you.'

'Good God.' He clutched his throat and affected to go weak at the knees. 'Haven't you left it a bit late?'

'It's never too late. We're young and free, we're strong and beautiful. What more could we want?' She waltzed away from him, danced a tango with a yard broom and waltzed back again, smiling. 'You don't believe me, do you?'

'Umm . . . What's brought this on?'

'You, worrying about your age. Me, worrying about everything.' She wrapped her arm around his neck and followed through with a kiss. 'We could die tomorrow, you know.'

Still bemused, Leo gave her a stern, old-fashioned look. 'You're trying to cheer me up, aren't you?'

She smiled and sighed. 'I love you, Leo,' she said. 'And even if you don't love me, I'm the only wife you've got, so let's . . . live a little, shall we? Before it's too late. The worries can wait, for once, can't they?'

I love you, Leo. She'd said it before. Not as often as he would have liked, but often enough to make it an unremarkable sequence of words, having as much meaning as the weather forecast: a lot or a little, depending on one's need. He hadn't, really, needed it now. He'd been thinking of other things. And yet . . . He'd been needing her to say *I love you*, just like this, for as long as he'd known her: not as a dutiful response to something *he'd* said or done, but because she meant it, felt it, wanted more than anything else to convince him that it was true.

'What's happened?' he asked gently. 'Why now?'

'I met Alec,' she said. 'I'd been to see Richard . . .'

It seemed she'd been worrying about getting old, too – hardly surprising, with Peggy setting them such a miserable example of

283

how it might be – yet she said young Digger had noticed no difference in her and, more to the point, that she'd seen no difference in him.

'He *was* different,' she said. 'He had a *beard*, Leo! But somehow ... somehow he was still the same as when I'd seen him last: seventeen. And I know *I* must look different, but *he* couldn't see it either. It made me think, Leo. It made me think that no matter what happens to us, we're still the same: the same as we always were, because ... because what we are is inside us, not out. And we'll be young for as long as we want to be, as long as we're young *inside*. Alec is still seventeen inside. And so are we.'

He smiled, wanting to say, 'If you wait long enough, it will happen,' but also wondering if perhaps he'd left it too late. True, he *had* been seventeen until ... Until he'd met Angela and realised that he wasn't seventeen: he was forty-two. The shock of that realisation had probably prompted him into everything else that happened – but he saw it now as a last, desperate fling before sinking into the muddy swamp of decrepitude. *Decrepitude*? At forty-two? God, that was just as ridiculous as thinking he was seventeen!

He laughed. He pulled Lydia into his arms and inhaled the scent of her hair. 'No,' he said softly. 'We're not seventeen. We're ...'

'Oh, Leo!' Lydia chuckled. 'Don't let me down now!'

'I wasn't going to,' he said. 'But we have to be realistic, darling. I hadn't met you when you were seventeen, so you'll have to be twenty-two. Take it or leave it. That's my last offer.'

'But you didn't *like* me when I was twenty-two!'

'Didn't I?' He nipped the tip of her ear between his teeth and had the satisfaction of feeling a little shudder ripple through her before he added in a whisper, 'Can't think why. Must have been crazy, mustn't I?'

The children interrupted them at that point (they usually did just as things were getting interesting) but Leo felt that it had marked a major change in their lives: a change more positive and purposeful than anything that had happened to them before. They'd tumbled into their marriage and afterwards had been bowled along by it, never stopping to take a closer look at each other or to ask what any of their feelings really meant. Now, at last, they *had* stopped. And looked. And found that there was nothing much wrong. That, give or take one or two problems, they were really quite happy with it all.

Happy? Well, yes. And why not? They had a beautiful home and four beautiful children. They had health and if not wealth then comfort enough to see them to the end of their days. The world contained many millions of people who managed some kind of

284

happiness without any of those things, so if Leo and Lydia weren't happy, they damn well didn't *deserve* to be.

For the past few weeks, Leo had spent much of his time at home watching his mother, trying to talk to her, trying to discover what was happening to her, even knowing that it was futile and that there was nothing he could do to help. Now, accepting that futility, almost shrugging it off, he watched Lydia instead. She'd said, after her London jaunt, that she was going to let the housework go hang and learn to enjoy herself, but the house was still spotless and, until now, her attempts to enjoy life had been as forced as they'd sounded; but suddenly it seemed she *was* enjoying life. There was something softer about her, something easier in her movements, in the readiness of her smile, in the timbre of her voice. It was as if, ever since they'd met, she'd been encased in a tight, whale-bone corset (probably a cast-off from her grandmother) which she'd only now thrown aside. She could breathe, she could move, she could laugh.

It was evident in everything she did, even in the way she talked to the children and, more especially, in the way she listened to them. She'd never been less than gentle with them and – within her limitations – warm and loving, but she'd always put the practicalities of their upbringing first. Good, nourishing meals, served on time. Clean beds, clean clothes, hair brushed, shoes polished, everyone in bed as the clock struck six. Now, without relinquishing her hold on any of it, she loosened her grip, and although it made no difference to anyone that lunch was ten minutes late, the difference to the children was remarkable. They, too, threw off the inherited whale-bone corset and breathed more deeply, laughed more readily, enjoyed life as they never had before.

So did Leo. Merely in hope, he told Lydia that there was a dinner dance at the Pump Rooms next Saturday. Would she – by any chance – like him to get tickets? She had all those new frocks in the wardrobe; pity not to give them an airing.

Lydia didn't even look up from her perusal of the newspaper. 'No,' she said frostily.

'Oh . . .' He shrugged.

'Well, what do you expect? I can't do every damn thing.' She lowered the newspaper just enough to peep wickedly at him over the top of it. 'And I've already got tickets, you beast. I wanted it to be a surprise.'

So they went dancing and had the time of their lives. They went to the theatre and Lydia stayed awake all through. They went to the pictures and sat in the romantic two-and-nines, munching toffees in the dark. Leo thought Lydia would draw the line at *necking* in the dark, as most of their neighbours were doing, so he didn't attempt it; but he felt as if, in virtually every other respect, they had a great deal in common with the courting couples all around. They'd changed. They'd *both* changed and were getting to know one another again. No, not again. Getting to know one another for the first time, because, until now, they'd each been disguising themselves with various griefs, guilts and regrets, each viewing the other through shaded eyes.

Even in quite trivial ways Leo had *seen* Lydia all wrong. His idea that she could wear only red, for example, wasn't remotely true so why had he thought so? Because it had lent her a warmth and vitality she'd lacked until now? Partly; but also because the true fire of her nature had been too hot for him to handle, too hot even to acknowledge. Since her initial fall from grace when she'd cheated him about Richard, she'd burned a moral flame he'd been incapable of meeting, simply because he'd cheated *her* and never confessed it. (He *must* confess it. *Soon.* Before it could do them further harm.) And for years after Richard's death she'd burned with such rage and grief it had been like a wall of flame between them.

That fire was still burning. It would never go out. But it no longer divided them. Like the fire in the parlour, it gave more comfort than sorrow; they could draw up to it together and talk, warming their toes, 'Remember that awful winter, the year Richard was born?'

'Remember that terrible drive to the nursing home? God, I thought we'd never get there!'

He'd loved her that night. He couldn't pretend to have loved her ever since, but there'd been moments. The day she'd bought the Riley from the Rector's nephew, the night he'd found her by the river, in the very act of 'setting him free'. She'd written him few enough letters, but he'd kept them all, including that suicide note.

I love you and honour you, but without Richard it all means nothing and the best I can do to repay you for all your goodness – both to me and to him – is to set you free. Don't grieve for me, Leo. I'm not worth a single tear.

Yet he'd wept all through the nightmare hour of searching for her and had never forgotten that an hour had been too long. *He* hadn't saved her. She had. Even in the depths of utter despair, she 'hadn't had the heart' to refuse an old woman a kindness and that kindness had given him time to find her. Had that been what she'd been doing all along? Giving him time to find her?

He'd found her now.

Eddie and Helen Moreton, who'd married before the war, threw a party to celebrate their twentieth wedding anniversary in the week before David's first birthday. They'd sent out the invitations two months ahead of time and Lydia had spent most of that time looking forward to it. But with only four days to go, first Dinah and then Zula went down with heavy colds. Charlotte was next. Then David. The girls suffered bravely enough, despite looking and sounding like death warmed up, but David cried. It wasn't as bad as when he'd cried before – he was older now and could, for a few minutes at a time, be distracted from his ills – but it brought back some bad memories and bad feelings. Lydia had tried hard to forget the night she'd lost her reason and almost killed him, but it wasn't something a mother could forget entirely and, when he cried now, she again felt it necessary to make it up to him, to spend every minute with him, to say, 'Cry all you like, sweetheart. I shan't mind at all.'

Had the occasion not been so special for the Moretons, Lydia would have told Leo they couldn't go and spared it scarcely a thought; but she held back, hoping that David would be better the next day and the next. In fact, on the day of the party, he was almost back to normal; a bit wheezy and grizzly, but certainly well enough to clear Lydia's conscience about leaving him with Mary for the evening. After all, it was only a cold.

She wore the simplest (and most expensive) of her London evening gowns: a black lace affair with a wide chiffon skirt and half a dozen stiff net petticoats to give it 'bounce'. Save for a shawl-like twist of chiffon and a large crop of goose-bumps, her shoulders were bare and she didn't really need Leo's off-hand comment, 'It's frosty tonight – you'll freeze,' to make her wish she'd chosen something more substantial.

'At least wear something warm in the car,' he added irritably. 'Or we'll have you going down with pneumonia.'

'Yes, yes.' (The trouble with buying clothes in summer is that you don't even *think* of winter, and the only suitable wrap Lydia had bought was made of taffeta.) She searched through her wardrobe for something warmer. Tweed and camel-hair . . . A motheaten beaver-lamb . . .

'I'll have to wear this,' she said. 'No one'll notice.'

She slipped the coat from the hanger, threw it on the bed and returned the hanger to its rail.

'No, no,' Leo said from somewhere behind her. 'That's no good. Try this.'

A slither of warm satin touched her shoulders; a whisper of fur touched her neck. Leo turned her around to face the glass over the

287

dressing table and she found herself draped in a fabulous evening coat of black figured velvet. Fur collar, fur cuffs . . .

'Oh! Oh, Leo! Oh, oh, oh, *glory*!'

He turned away to fasten his collar studs. 'You don't like it, then?'

She was too busy sliding her arms into the sleeves to bother with a reply. It fitted perfectly. And it was *black*!

'Oh, Leo . . . It's the most beautiful . . . Why not red?'

'Nah. You and yer red. Black d'go wiv everyfing. Red don't even go wiv *red*, if 'tis the wrong red.'

Lydia laughed. 'Floral chose it!'

'She helped. She refused to pay half, though, so don't overdo the thanks in that quarter, will you?'

'How about this quarter?' She slid her arms around his waist and touched his lips with the tip of her tongue.

'Overdo it,' he murmured happily. 'Wear me out with it.'

She tried, but only succeeded in wearing out her lipstick and, when that had been repaired, it was time to go. They paraded their finery for Mary and the girls (still awake, in spite of their colds), and then for Floral, but Peggy had gone off on one of her wandering expeditions and, since they were already running late, they went off in the end without even wishing her goodnight.

They both felt uncomfortable about it. Peggy had been invited to the party, too, but she'd claimed at the time that she didn't know any people named Moreton and although she'd frequently mentioned Eddie and Helen since, Leo had thought it best not to remind her about the party. There'd be so many people there, so much going on, she couldn't be depended upon not to say or do something strange.

'It might have been just the thing to snap her out of it,' Lydia said guiltily.

'Mmm. But what if it had had the opposite effect?'

'Mmm . . .'

A few minutes later, Leo said, 'David seemed all right, tonight, didn't he?'

'Fine. Still a bit snuffly, but he'll probably sleep through.'

She hoped he would, at least. With the girls so poorly and Mary suffering broken nights, they'd moved him back into the old nursery so that Lydia could see to him when he woke at three in the morning. Mary would keep checking him through the evening and Lydia would be home again around midnight, so . . . nothing to worry about.

'Good,' Leo said firmly. 'So let's *not* worry.' Which seemed a bit odd, because Lydia hadn't been worrying. She'd very nearly given up worrying since her meeting with Alec. He'd changed things around, somehow, slotted them into their proper place. He hadn't *just* said, 'Beauty is in the eye of the beholder'; he'd said a thousand other things beside, which – when Lydia recalled Floral's words of a few minutes earlier – had suddenly made perfect sense.

She'd learned from Alec that one person is in fact many people – the sum of several parts – some of which were good, some not so good and some downright awful. She had no doubt that parts of Alec's nature were downright awful. They had to be. He was human. But, for Lydia, at least, they didn't matter, just as for him the awful parts of *her* nature didn't matter. One *could* be loved just for one's virtues. She loved Leo for his virtues, and although his many flaws and minor vices made her grind her teeth (even, sometimes, hate him), when she added up the sum of his many parts the answer was always the same: 'He's a good man and I love him.'

Surely the same would be true if Leo added up the sum of *her* many parts? Yet, until she'd met Alec, in spite of all her efforts to be a good wife, a loving mother, an affectionate daughter-in-law and a not *too* depressing companion for all of them, she'd spent most of her time concentrating on her failures and flaws, giving herself marks for effort but never for achievement. She hadn't *loved* herself. She hadn't allowed herself an inch of the leeway she gave everyone else. And that was all it took, really. A little leeway. There were things she'd done and failed to do that she would never, ever forgive herself for: black marks scored indelibly on the pages of her conscience; but the same was true of them all (Gran, too, probably) and *none* of them was unworthy of love.

And it was strange; as soon as Lydia admitted that she was worthy of love, everyone else seemed to love her more! Even the Moretons seemed fonder of her than they'd been before, welcoming her with open arms, carrying her away to introduce her to everyone, seeming, in virtually everything they said, to make her the centre of attention. She'd never enjoyed a party so much. (When she thought of it later, she realised she'd never enjoyed a party *before*!) And it wasn't really the Moretons who made it so wonderful. *She* made it wonderful just by relaxing and letting it all happen. She ate, she drank, she danced with every man who asked her. She played ridiculous party games without sparing a thought for her dignity. She laughed until the tears ran – and although she *did* spare a thought for the mascara that was running too, a few minutes in the ladies' room soon put that right.

Having thought they'd be home at midnight, it was in fact one in the morning before they began the drive home. Lydia *did* think, as they waved their last goodbyes, *What if David's been crying all night? What if Mary's exhausted and hating me for leaving her?* But

289

what did it matter? Mary could sleep late tomorrow. She could take the day off.

'Oh, Leo, 'she said. 'I don't know when I've ever enjoyed myself so much.'

'Did I ever tell you what an incredibly sexy voice you have?'

She laughed. 'Sexy? No, I don't think you ever did. Frosty, arrogant, aloof . . .'

'Oh, come on, darling. We all make mistakes. It's taken me a little while to get used to it, that's all.'

'Well, yes. It's only twelve years. Imagine being married for twenty years, like Eddie and Helen.'

'Sounds wonderful, doesn't it?'

She laughed again. 'Why do I get the idea you want something?'

But she wanted it, too. There'd been times when *making* love (in the manner of making a cake) had been necessary, because if they hadn't made it there wouldn't have been any. But this was different. This was sheer greed – like the walnuts one ate after the Christmas feast – unnecessary perhaps, yet at the same time completely indispensable.

They kissed as they let themselves into the house, kissed in the great hall while Leo locked the door. They tiptoed through the house, checking fireguards and power-points, whispering and giggling like children. And then, when they were halfway up the stairs, David started crying.

'Oh, dear,' Leo murmured.

'Ssh,' Lydia said. 'He might go off . . .'

Leo draped himself over the newel post at the top of the stairs, his white silk scarf and black tie contrasting wonderfully with the dull gold of his hair, the frosty flush of his cheeks. Lydia reached out a finger to touch his lips. 'Brush your teeth,' she whispered. 'I'll see to him.'

David wasn't crying much. He was still half-asleep and might, if they ignored him, forget why he was crying and settle again. But as Leo disappeared into the bathroom, the cry became a wail and Mary emerged from her own room, still tying the sash of her dressing gown.

'It's all right, Mary. We're home. Go back to sleep. I was hoping he might go off . . .'

Mary smiled and shook her head. 'Doesn't sound like it. He probably wants a drink.'

'Has he been scratchy all night?'

'No. He woke up at about nine, but he went off again as soon as I'd changed him. Did you have a nice time?'

290

'Lovely. Tell you all about it in the morning.' Mary went back to bed. Lydia tiptoed through her own bedroom to offer her son the relief he craved, when he suddenly fell silent. She stopped, blinked, thought about it for a moment and then thought of Leo and smiled.

She was hanging up her new evening coat when an echo of David's cries replayed themselves in her mind. He'd grizzled, he'd wailed, he'd bawled. And then stopped, as a radio might stop when you switched it off. Wasn't that a bit strange?

Her heart thudding, she warily opened the connecting door. Save for the light that shone through from Leo's bedside lamp, the nursery was dark, but there was quite enough light to see what was happening. Peggy, ghostly in a white nightgown, was leaning over the cot, pressing a pillow to David's face.

Chapter Twenty-Five

Leo swallowed a couple of aspirins before he brushed his teeth. He'd had a headache most of the evening, not bad enough to absorb his attention; just enough to take the edge off his enjoyment of the party and make him wish, for a moment at a time, that he could go home to bed. But it had been marvellous to see Lydia enjoying herself so much. He'd noticed quite early that she was the most beautiful woman in the room, and noticed, too, that every other man there was in full agreement with him. As she'd several times said of him, she seemed to have grown into her beauty over the years rather than growing out of it. She had more colour, more vivacity, more energy than she'd had when he'd first met her. He'd noticed all this with enormous pride, but it had taken someone else – a cousin of Eddie's whom Leo had never met until tonight – to remark her voice. 'Oh, my God, what a delicious voice!' Yes . . . Warm and seductive, deep and throaty, the occasional squeaky high notes like chinks in the armour through which one could catch glimpses of the vulnerable woman she was inside . . . *Delicious*. And all his!

He thought, too, about David, who (typical of children) had woken up at the wrong moment and pinched all the 'walnuts'. Leo's headache was, he knew, a symptom of tiredness, not likely to clear up until he'd had a good night's sleep. Which wouldn't be tonight. He had to be up at six and it was already going on for two in the morning . . .

And then, for some reason, he thought of his brother. Or, rather, of his name. 'Lionel' and 'Leo' represented the lion which had been carved over Molliston's front door and on either side of the fireplace in the great hall. It had also been a part of the Litton coat-of-arms and, by coincidence, Lionel had been the name of the first Chantry to live at Molliston. Leo had often wondered about him, suspecting that he'd pulled some wool over a few eyes, perhaps cheated his way into possession of the estate; a bit of an opportunist, perhaps? He sighed, thinking of himself. Molliston would be a row of prefabs by now if *he* hadn't been 'a bit of an opportunist'! It ran in the family, evidently . . .

Leo's habit of timing the brushing of his teeth (never less than five minutes) had begun in prison camp, where there'd been a chronic dearth of tooth-powder and an over-abundance of bald toothbrushes. He'd reached the final minute (his lower molars and one remaining wisdom tooth) when he heard a roar very like the roar of a lion. It came from the direction of the bedroom, a deep, ferocious bellow, which made him whirl on his heel and stare, incredulous and terrified, at the bathroom door. It took him a few seconds to realise that the roar had issued from Lydia. Then he ran, his mouth still foaming with Colgate.

His mother was lying on the little divan bed in the nursery, wearing a white flannelette nightgown and an expression of abject terror. Lydia, with David screaming in her arms, was standing beside the bed, leaning over it, still in her evening gown, her face transformed with a rage which stopped Leo in his tracks, scared the life out of him, just as it had evidently scared Peggy. But she wasn't quite as scared as Leo was. *He* couldn't speak.

'No!' she wailed fretfully. 'I didn't do it! I was ill! I wasn't there! It was the girl did it! The girl did it!'

A great shudder of horror ripped along Leo's spine, making his hair stand on end. She'd said that before! The day David had disappeared!

'Oh, no!' Lydia snarled. '*You* did it! *You* did it, you wicked, evil old woman! And I'll see you dead . . .!'

'*Lydia*!' Leo gasped, but it was as if he wasn't there, as if a wall had come between them, as if he was watching it all on a cinema screen and was helpless to change any part of it.

'I'll see you hanged!' Lydia cried. 'I'll see you rot! And even that's too good for you, you miserable old witch!'

David screamed. Peggy, whose attitude on the bed indicated she'd been thrown there by the full weight of Lydia's arm, now curled herself into a ball and began to sob, 'It was the girl! The girl did it!'

'*No*! It was *you*! I *saw* you!'

Peggy stopped crying. She stared up at Lydia and Leo saw something in her eyes change. He didn't, at the time, know what it was, but afterwards, when he thought it over, he knew precisely what it was. His mother had been mad and suddenly was sane. But she'd been mad for a long, long time. Longer than he'd guessed.

'Yes,' she said dully. 'I did it.'

Lydia swallowed and took a deep, calming breath. From the moment Peggy had said, *The girl did it*, she'd known she was dealing with something beyond her understanding, beyond her reach, a madness which far exceeded the harmless confusions of old age. But she was too angry to control herself, too maddened on her own account: mad enough, almost, not to know what she was doing. She'd known only after the event that she'd hit Peggy halfway across the room, and that if she hadn't fallen on the bed . . . Two murders in one night?

But they were all still alive. David was almost too much alive, screaming and bucking in her arms, terrified by what had happened. Yet she couldn't comfort him. She was too angry and frightened to do anything but hold him, keep him safe from this monster of a woman, this evil, evil old woman who'd dared to harm him!

Yet as soon as Peggy admitted her guilt, Lydia's rage died and was replaced by pity. Pity enough to break her heart – for suddenly she knew. She knew what Peggy had done.

'Oh, my God,' she whispered.

Peggy began to shiver. Lydia turned to Leo and said, 'Fetch some blankets, will you? And my dressing gown. And you'll have to wake Mary. This might take all night.'

'*What* will?' He was almost in tears. 'What's going on?'

'Hush,' she said gently. 'Fetch the blankets, there's a dear.'

He went and, as soon as he was reasonably out of earshot, Lydia gripped Peggy's shoulder and said quietly, 'You killed Lionel, didn't you, Peggy? You killed your baby.'

'I was ill,' she whispered. 'I didn't know what I was doing.'

Lydia knew that, too, for she'd almost done the same thing and known nothing about it until she'd glimpsed her own reflection in the mirror. She saw her own reflection now – in Peggy, who had had no mirror to save her.

The blankets came. Mary took David away to change and feed and comfort him. Lydia wrapped Peggy up and then sat beside her and rocked her gently in her arms, murmuring, 'There, there. It's all right now. You were ill, you say?'

'We all were. It was one of those awful 'flu epidemics . . .'

Almost everyone at Molliston had been ill and when the nanny took to her bed, Leo's father had told Peggy to take baby Lionel, with the young nursemaid, Ellen, to her mother's home in Clifton. Ellen was fourteen years old, a scrawny little thing whose work – in an ideal world – was not to care for the baby but to clean up after him, keep the nursery well-scrubbed and run errands for her superiors in the rigid nursery hierarchy.

'I scarcely knew her,' Peggy said. 'We'd taken her on from the orphanage in Bath. She was . . . Well, I suppose she was like most girls of that type in those days. I suppose she could read and write, but she hadn't been trained to do anything beyond taking orders. She knew nothing about babies. Neither did I.'

Peggy turned agonised eyes to Lydia's face. 'Don't say it. Don't tell me I should have known. You don't know how it was, Lydia. I didn't *have* to know, you see. It wasn't my place to know. All I needed to do . . .' She turned away, hopelessly resting her head on the pillow. 'All I had to do was give birth to him and leave all the rest to those who did know. I had no idea that it could be otherwise until you brought Richard home. It all came so naturally to you!'

'No,' Lydia said. 'I didn't know what I was doing, either. I was groping in the dark, following my instincts. I'd have given my eye-teeth for someone who knew better. If we hadn't been snowed in, I'd have run home to Gran. I would never have coped alone if I hadn't had to.'

'*I* had to,' Peggy said. 'But I didn't! I didn't know where to begin. I was *scared*, Lydia!'

Leo hadn't heard most of this. He'd been busy, taking David's cot into Mary's room, making cocoa for everyone, bringing a portable electric fire to warm the room. Now he came to sit beside his mother on the far side of the bed. He held her hand and gently patted it, but otherwise seemed at a total loss for anything else to do. Lydia threw him a little smile, but she didn't dare lose the momentum of her talk with Peggy who, she sensed, was precariously balanced on the very edge of reason and might easily fall on the wrong side of it if Lydia let her go.

'But you know why you were scared, don't you, Peggy?' she said urgently. 'I know, because I was scared, too. I was scared that some harm might come to Richard . . .' Her voice broke at the memory of her son falling to his death, and at another memory, of her grandmother saying something about lacemaking – the meaning of it all.

'I was scared because I loved him,' she went on gently. 'And without that love why should we be scared? Without that love, what does it matter whether our children live or die?' She stroked Peggy's hair. 'You loved your baby,' she said. 'You loved him, Peggy. I *know* you did.'

Peggy's eyes were closed and she didn't open them. But her head moved almost imperceptibly across the pillow in a nod of assent.

Leo and Lydia exchanged glances, hers desperate, his bewildered. Lydia bit her lip and went on quietly. 'What happened then? You went to your mother . . .?'

'She was ill.' Peggy's voice was soft, lifeless, almost as husky as Lydia's. 'It was different in those days. We talk about influenza now as if it was nothing, but in those days . . . I suppose we didn't have the resistance. People weren't as healthy as they are now. The poor were badly fed and overworked. The rich . . . this was before the Great War, of course . . . there weren't the drugs, the sanitation. After the war there was an epidemic that killed more people than had died in the trenches. They didn't die of influenza, they died of . . . pneumonia. Ellen – the girl – died of pneumonia. In . . .' Her mouth twisted down, as if with nausea.

'In –?' Lydia prompted quietly.

'In prison.'

A spurt of tears escaped Lydia's eyes. *The girl did it!* Oh, God, what a nightmare . . .

'Your mother was ill,' she said. 'Take it from there, Peggy. You went to Clifton –?'

'They were all ill. It was worse . . . We should have stayed here! We should never have gone! I didn't know what to do!'

She began to sob, tearing her hand from Leo's grasp to cover her face. She'd wept, very briefly, earlier on, but this was different: a terrible, racking agony of tears which convulsed her entire body. Leo was appalled. His mouth dropped open and Lydia saw it close again to utter the word, *Don't*! But he didn't say it. Lydia's hand flashed out – like a policeman's to stop the traffic – and Leo subsided, blinking with shock.

Happy and smiling, Lydia thought grimly, *I'll give the bastards happy and smiling!* 'Cry,' she said. 'Cry all you like, Peggy. It's the only thing that can heal you now.'

She gathered the thin, shaking shoulders into her arms, almost lifting Peggy off the bed to rock her back and forth in her arms. But she was crying, too. Crying for wasted lives: Peggy's, baby Lionel's, poor little Ellen's, Richard's . . .

Leo went to the window and stared out into the darkness.

As that long night passed and the story of his dead brother came slowly to light, Leo found things returning to his soul that he'd never quite realised had gone astray. His mother's love for him, his own for her . . . As a child he'd adored her. As a youth despised her. As a man . . .? As a man he'd kept her firmly at a distance, as one might keep a dumb animal, knowing that its differences were a barrier that could never be crossed. One made sure that one's animals were well fed and in health. One didn't try to understand them.

But now he understood. His mother had loved her first-born and murdered him. How, then, could she dare to love another child? Like Lydia, after Richard's death, she hadn't even wanted another child, but such choices hadn't been possible in those days. The only route to a childless marriage had been through a celibate marriage, and what healthy, red-blooded man would consent to that? And Leo's father had never known the truth of it. He'd thought 'the girl' had killed his son.

The girl – Ellen – had fallen ill the day after they'd arrived at his grandmother's house in Clifton, Peggy the day after that. Lionel was only a few months old, still needing to be fed and changed every few hours and screaming when his needs were not met. But with a raging fever, rigors, weakness and pain, his mother had scarcely been able to lift him, let alone fetch milk from the kitchen, three floors below. The room stank of filthy nappies, overbrimming chamber pots, sweat and vomit. A nightmare.

'Was Ellen with you all this time?' Leo asked.

'No . . . She was in the next room, but it might have been ten miles away. She was in a worse state than I was. She couldn't even . . . She was delirious, talking to herself, raving. It seems impossible now. There were seven or eight people in that house, yet no one was well enough to help anyone else! After the war – in the 'flu epidemic after the war – there was a whole street of people, in Wales, I think, one of the mining towns – who died without anyone to help them. Unless you get complications, the worst of it only lasts a few days, but if you all go down together . . .'

It was February and bitterly cold, with no one to fetch coal or light the fires. Lionel was probably freezing, as well as starving and filthy, and the chances were that he'd caught the infection too. He'd screamed and screamed. He'd screamed for two days. And then died.

Remembering how, in the pink of good health, he'd walked the floor with David, wanting to kill him after only a few hours, Leo wondered how his mother had lasted two days in such conditions. How could he blame her? God knew she'd blamed herself enough all these years . . .

It was four in the morning before the last of the tale was told. 'I just couldn't stand it any more, Lydia. I told you . . . I said, "I was ill; I didn't know what I was doing," but that's not true. I did know but it was . . . It was as if I'd forgotten what death means. I just wanted him to *sleep*! And when I was better, when I could feed him and care for him . . .'

'You'd wake him again.'

'Yes! I didn't know . . . I didn't realise . . . Oh, I know it sounds impossible, but when you're so ill and – and desperate . . . I didn't *understand* that he would never wake again, until . . . Until it was too late. And then . . .' There was a long, terrible silence. 'And then I knew they'd hang me.'

'So you blamed Ellen?' Lydia whispered.

'Yes. He'd been screaming for hours. Hour after hour after . . . And then he stopped and she – I don't know how, she was still very ill – she came in from the next room and found him. I remember . . . I watched her . . . feeling her way around the walls, her nightdress drenched in sweat, her teeth chattering . . . She was just a little girl, Lydia! An ignorant, inexperienced child! She didn't stand a chance.'

The irony of it was that barely an hour after Lionel's death, one of the servants had arrived to bring relief. He'd been ill, too, and had only just managed to drag himself from his bed, but he was strong enough to fetch and carry. To clean up and light the fire. He was quite well enough to call a policeman.

'They took her away just as she was,' Peggy whispered. 'Soaked, shivering, terrified out of her wits. She didn't know what was happening to her, poor child. She died a week later.'

Sickened, both by horror and pity, Leo asked softly, 'But how have you *lived*, Mother? How the devil have you *lived* with it all these years?'

'I haven't. That is, I didn't, until . . . Richard. Until then I really believed she *had* killed him. I'd convinced myself of it, I suppose. At the time . . . It was all so confusing! I knew what was happening, but it was as if it was all a dream. A nightmare. And sometimes, when you wake from a nightmare, you aren't really sure which parts your dreamed and which were true. It was impossible to believe I'd killed my own baby! I *didn't* believe it!'

'But when Richard died?' Lydia asked. 'You knew?'

Peggy shook her head. 'No. It was before that. His death . . .' Again she shook her head. 'His death underlined it, made me realise I couldn't go on. I just wanted to die after that. I couldn't bear . . .'

She swallowed and levelled her gaze at the door. 'But it was Richard's birth, not his death, that brought it all home to me.' She laughed shortly and turned to meet Lydia's gaze. 'I couldn't believe what you'd done, Lydia! Fobbing off another man's child on poor Leo! I wouldn't have thought you capable of it! But, having done it, there was no going back. You'd married him and, since Richard was your spitting image, you were completely in the clear!'

Almost proudly – or was it just defensively – Peggy put her chin in the air and continued, 'I would never have told him, Lydia. I knew – God knows I knew – how to keep a secret and I knew – or thought I knew – why such a secret should be kept. What was the point of telling Leo? What was the point of hurting him, of making him your enemy, of exposing yourself – and Richard – to his hatred? You could have got away with it! He need never have known a thing!'

'But –' Lydia began.

'Oh, I know the answer *now*,' Peggy said. 'I knew it then, as soon as I realised you'd told him the truth.' She rested her head on the pillow and closed her eyes with sigh. 'The truth is so clean, isn't it?' she murmured wistfully. 'So clean. Oh, God, I envied you!'

She sighed, closed her eyes and drifted into sleep, leaving her son to reflect on the perfect cleanliness of truth. His mother had been up to her eyes in filth for almost fifty of her seventy years and although Leo couldn't say the same of himself, he still felt a little grimy. He should have told Lydia at the beginning. Truth for truth, shame for shame. Well, he'd tell her now. Right now.

He turned to stare at his reflection in the window, thinking it through, planning the precise order of his words to cause her as little hurt as possible. I love you. I trust and respect you. I worship the ground you tread. But there's something on my conscience, Lydia . . .

No, it would be better to do it the other way around.

'There's something on my conscience, Lydia,' he murmured.

She said nothing and he went on quietly. 'What my mother just said, about the truth being clean . . . it's true, you know, and the truth is . . . the truth is that I love you, Lydia. I married you . . .'

Damn it! Why couldn't he say it?

'I married you with regrets, as I'm sure you realise, yet only one of those regrets has survived until now.'

He turned to face her, his eyes blazing with sudden courage, a sudden knowledge that he *could* say it, *would* say it.

'I regret never having told you –'

Lydia was sitting exactly where she'd sat most of the night, in the nursing chair beside the bed. But her head had lolled backwards, her mouth sagged, her eyes sunk back into her head in a sleep of utter exhaustion.

Leo smiled. He whispered, 'I married you for your money.'

It took the best part of a week for Molliston to go back to normal and even then it wasn't quite the same as before. The night of Peggy's confession had changed all of them. Even the atmosphere was different, as if they'd each been carrying a part of Peggy's burden and hadn't realised the weight of it until it had gone.

Yet 'gone' wasn't quite the word for it. It had been worked into their lives somehow, like a lacemaker's thread. But the pain, eye-strain and frustration of the roses was over, and at last they were making the butterflies. This thought didn't actually cross Lydia's mind until a week had gone by. She was in the drawing room, folding up the Sunday newspapers, which Leo had left, as usual, in a heap on the floor.

He'd just gone out to Manor Farm; the house was quiet, the room striped with wintry sunlight. A marvellous sensation of peace overcame Lydia and she remembered the first time she'd entered this room; how peaceful and happy it had seemed then. It looked very different now. No hole in the ceiling for Leo to worry about . . .

With a good deal of help from Floral, she'd covered the furniture with green tenting canvas from the Government Surplus shop, which had faded over the years to a pale bluey-green, reminiscent of iris leaves. Since rationing (God rot it) had come to an end, she'd added cushions of gold and rose pink, so that in spite of the upholstery's humble origins at a shilling a yard, it all looked as if it was *meant* to be, a perfect foil for the old rugs, a perfect contrast for the ancient stone fireplace and golden panelling.

'What you smirkin' at?' Floral limped in, having trouble with an arthritic knee, yet still managing to look as if she was dancing around a Maypole.

'Our handiwork,' Lydia said. 'Money well-spent, that canvas. Two pounds ten the lot and there's still no sign of wear.' She laughed. 'Unlike us. How's the knee?'

'Killin' I. Cor, them stairs . . . I just bin up to see Peggy.'

'Ah. How is she?'

'Still cryin', bless her. There's a lot still to do, poor thing, but at least she'm gettin' it out of her system. I – er – I asked her. About David.'

It was the one question Lydia hadn't asked; had been afraid to ask. It had seemed too cruel at the time, but since then . . . *Why did you try to kill David*? It was a question they had to ask, or never again sleep easy in their beds until he was fifteen and big enough to fight back. Not that Lydia really feared a repetition. Peggy was sad now, but she wasn't mad. She cried a lot, but as Floral said, she had a lifetime's tears to catch up on.

'She don't recollect it, my love. She got no notion what she were doin' that night. The first thing she do recall is when you told her she were wicked and . . . when you told her she'd get hung.'

Lydia closed her eyes, knowing she should feel ashamed, but instead feeling grateful. That explosion of rage – not the first, but certainly the worst she'd ever allowed herself – had cleared out the cobwebs from more than one mind. Peggy was all the better for it.

So was Lydia. She'd meant to punish Peggy and, in the process, had punished herself. She'd forgiven Peggy. *And* forgiven herself.

'But you were talkin' about David,' Floral went on softly, 'and she were talkin' about her own babby.'

Lydia perched on the arm of the sofa. 'Does that mean we're safe?'

'Oh yes. All that's over and done wiv. But she do want to go away, my love. She don't want to stop here no longer . . . And, if you can afford it, I fink you should let her go. One o' they small hotels by the sea. She'd have all she needed, see, Lydial, and she don't want much . . .'

She'd lowered herself into one of the easy chairs and was massaging her knees, looking at her hands as if, merely by concentrating, she might make the ache go away. Lydia had no idea she was weeping until a tear plopped into the lap of her skirt.

'Floral!' She fell to her knees at Floral's feet and took her hand. 'What's the matter, darling?'

'No!' Floral snatched her hand away. 'Don't go soppy on me, now, my love. I dussn't deserve it. I got a confession to make too. I knowed! I knowed what she done, and I should have told 'ee! I should have told Leo, when she –' She paused, embarrassed. 'Well, anyway,' she added lamely. 'I should have told someone.'

'You knew? About Peggy?'

'Well, to tell the honest trufe, I never *knew*, azzackly. I only guessed from things Leo's dad told I when he was dying. And I'm not sure even *he* knew for certain. Suspected, you might say. Guessed. Put two and two together. But he were good at sums and I ain't. If I'd told you and it *weren't* the trufe . . .' She looked up and performed one of her dreadful, drain-like sniffs. 'Remember what I told you about lovin' yerself? I was thinking about Peggy. No one could love a woman who hated herself so much. But I loves meself *too* bloody much, Lydial! I always looks out for meself, keeps meself safe. But I *should* have said summat! David could've died, and if he had . . . It would have been all my fault!'

'Nonsense,' Lydia said briskly. 'You did exactly the right thing, Floral. You always do. It wouldn't have helped, you see. It would have worried me out of my wits.'

'But at least then she wouldn't –'

'She wouldn't have had a chance to hurt him. But without that chance, Floral, she'd have ended up in the loony bin.' She frowned, thinking about it. 'And so might I,' she added dryly. 'A small hotel by the sea will be much nicer, won't it?'

Yes, Leo thought when he learned of his mother's plans, a small hotel would be much nicer than the loony bin, but that didn't mean he liked the idea. She wasn't well. Her terrible confession had restored her to reason, but it had also weakened her, both physically and emotionally. She looked very frail now and cried a good deal, although not only about her dead baby and the guilt she felt about Ellen. (Mary Preece was Ellen's double, apparently, so that explained that!) She seemed to be crying for everything: a loveless childhood, a loveless marriage, her failures as a mother to Leo and Prue.

Those failures, that seemingly careless detachment from her offspring which had hurt Leo so much, were still – if more obviously and less deeply – hurting him now, for her wish to go away seemed to him to be yet another rejection. For the first time in his life he'd found the heart of her, the meaning of her. For the first time in his life he had a chance to get to know her. And *she* wanted to go away!

These feelings – with a few dozen others – were too complicated to explain and he ended up blustering about it, telling Lydia only his surface concerns, not the depths. 'I don't want her to go! She's too old! She's not well! She needs *us* to look after her, not –'

'But what does "looking after her" mean, Leo? It means answering her needs and her needs are simple enough. Food, cleanliness, warmth. And time.'

'Time?'

'She's over seventy. Her time's running out and for the first time in forty-odd years she has a chance to be herself, a chance to live for herself, a chance to find out who she really is.'

'That's my whole point! *I* want to know who she is!'

'But it isn't really your business, darling. Peggy will be meeting her Maker soon – perhaps very soon. She has to make peace with Him – and with herself – before she goes.'

'But I thought she'd done that when she told us about it!'

'No. She'd spent her life until then believing she had nothing on her conscience, believing "the girl did it". In a way, she did the opposite of what you and I did with Richard. We blamed ourselves for a terrible accident; we called ourselves murderers when in fact . . . Well, maybe we *could* have had the banisters fixed, but if we had, there were still a hundred other ways he might have died. We couldn't do everything, Leo. If he'd fallen out of a tree or under a bus, should we have chopped down the tree or had the bus route changed? It's taken me years to realise this, years to *forgive* myself, and even now . . .' She shrugged. 'It'll never really end. But if I really *had* killed him . . . If *you* had killed him, Leo, how long would it have taken you to come to terms with it?'

Leo nodded, understanding. That his mother wanted to leave

wasn't so much a rejection of him as an acceptance of herself; and the two were connected. He could see that now.

Lydia took his hand and gently squeezed it. 'She needs time, darling. She needs privacy and peace. Let her go.'

'Yes . . .'

'And thank God you haven't any such burdens on your own conscience,' she added briskly. 'Want some cocoa?'

Leo laughed. It had taken him years to get the measure of Lydia's sense of humour. It was a see-saw contrivance, a thing which recognised the underside of darkness and despair, stupidity and selfishness (usually his!) and then came whooshing up to the surface with a grin, a dry little tease or, as on this occasion, a ridiculous touch of bathos, which had the same effect on one's funny-bone as a pantomime custard pie. Life would always be a serious matter for Lydia, but never so serious she forgot the cocoa!

He followed her into the kitchen and hindered her by wrapping his arms around her waist, nibbling her ear. 'I do have a few things on my conscience,' he whispered.

'Mmm. You'll have cocoa all over your shirt if you don't behave.'

'I had a little fling with Angela.'

'Mm. I know.'

'You *do*?'

'Well, I guessed anyway.'

'It didn't come to anything. It was only lust.'

'Mmm. You have a lot of trouble with that, don't you?' She smiled up at him, promising imminent relief from the trouble.

'And also –'

'Oh!' she teased. 'There's an *also*, is there?'

He squeezed his eyes shut, clenched his teeth. 'I married you for your money,' he muttered frantically.

There was a brief – but deadly – silence. Leo opened one eye. Lydia was looking at him as she sometimes looked at Dinah when she'd told one of her awful jokes – dark eyes dancing over a nose wrinkled with disgust, wanting to laugh almost as much as she wanted not to.

Leo scowled and stepped backwards. 'You *knew*?'

Lydia laughed at last. ''Course I knew, you twit! It was obvious! Not so obvious that it became clear all at once, but well . . . Add up the clues! Even for a perfect gentleman, you were much too ready to save my honour – and not so eager to tell me you were broke until *after* the wedding. But you knew about Uncle Avery *before* the wedding. I'd have been as green as a leaf not to have added it all up, wouldn't I?'

'Well,' Leo breathed. 'Damn me.' After a few moments of stunned silence he added helplessly, 'Didn't you mind?'

The laughter died in Lydia's eyes. 'No,' she said softly. 'Never. I had the best of the bargain, after all. Your name, your home, your children. If I'd had ten times fifty thousand, I still couldn't have paid enough.'

'Oh, Lydia . . .'

'And let's not forget your kindness, your gentleness . . .'

Overwhelmed, he closed his eyes. 'My blindness,' he added softly. 'My stupidity and ingratitude, my selfishness.'

'Salt in the spuds,' Lydia said. 'Tasteless without.'

'I love you so much,' Leo whispered.

Postscript

September. A fine, blue day with a clear light and shadows so sharp they seemed to have been drawn in with ink. Lydia stood beside Richard's grave, gazing at the little sheaf of kaffir lilies she'd just placed there. She looked across at Leo and smiled.

'He'd be twenty-four now. Hard to believe, isn't it?'

Looking back, Leo found it all rather hard to believe: that a marriage that had begun so badly and been marked by so many griefs, could have endured to see its silver anniversary. Twenty-five years. Yet it had passed so quickly, it seemed only last week he'd married her and thought he'd caught an incurable disease!

Well, it was that, all right. And it wasn't entirely painless, either; she had some absolutely *filthy* habits, not least of them a tendency to say something totally unimportant just as he was listening to the cricket score.

At close of play, Australia were – 'What the dickens has Zula been doing with my sewing basket?' – *for no wicket.*

But he loved her. Not romantically, not passionately, often noticing her existence scarcely more than he noticed his own. But that was because it was a part of his own, not something separate, alien, detached. If he lost her now it would be like being cut in half. He couldn't live without her now. She was everything.

Lydia knelt to arrange some flowers on Peggy's grave. She'd died, very quietly, in the hospital at Torquay, only a year after she'd left Molliston. They'd both been with her; and it seemed that a year had been enough, for she'd looked very peaceful at the end. Floral had died only two years back and was still greatly missed, talked about and exclaimed over. She'd never told them her age. They'd guessed, towards the end of her life, at 'somewhere around eighty', but it turned out she'd been ninety-three. Lydia still couldn't believe it. She kept recalling their wood-hunting expedition before Richard was born, which meant Floral had been climbing trees when she was seventy!

Lydia put pink roses on Floral's grave. Then she joined Leo on the path and slipped her hand through his arm. She looked tired. They were having a party tonight and she'd been cooking for days, polishing silver, starching tablecloths – the usual stuff. A few hours in bed after lunch would do them both the world of good.

'I think I'll lie down for a few hours,' Lydia said. 'Coming?'

'Wouldn't miss it for the world. It was my idea, after all.'

'It was not!'

'It was. I just didn't get a chance to say it. Typical: I do all the work, you get all the credit.'

They walked up Molliston's driveway, arm in arm, listening to the 'peaceful' sounds of their kids playing tennis.

'Ooh, you little swine!' (Zula.) 'That was out!'

'Liar!' (The son and heir.) 'It was an ace!'

'Oh, come on, you two! It's only a game!' (Dinah, keeping them in order.) 'Was it out or was it in, Grandpa? *You're* supposed to be the umpire!'

'Let!'

'Oh, Lord . . .' Lydia moaned comically. 'Now there'll be trouble.'

Lydia's father had sold Priory Farm for building land when old Mrs Westley had died. They'd thought he'd fade away without his farm to keep him busy and his mother to keep him in order, but the opposite had happened and, at seventy-two, he was like a spring chicken: busy and active, enjoying his grandchildren, playing whist with the village ladies and generally having the time of his life. Another example of things happening you didn't know were happening until they stopped happening! Old Mrs Westley had been *sitting* on him all these years!

At the top of the drive, Leo paused to look at the view which, in the lucid clarity of the day, stretched for miles all around with scarcely a grain-field in sight. The sheep were back where they belonged. All was right with the world.

Lydia couldn't see the view (she still wouldn't wear her glasses) and was crouching to pull a tuft of grass from between two clumps of plate-like pink flowers. As Leo looked down, two butterflies flew from under her hand and fluttered away, to join a half dozen others on a buddleia bush nearby. They were lovely things, coloured like jewels or fragments torn from a Persian rug.

Strange to think they'd once been caterpillars . . .

Coming in Autumn 1997 – Anna Barrie's new novel

THE LINDEN TREE

When her elderly, eccentric employers die, Kate Brookes faces an uncertain future. For the last five years she has taken refuge from her troubled past by helping the Fitzwarrens to make a showpiece of the gardens at Whitsun Gate, a large – and largely decomposed – old house in Somerset. But the reading of the will produces a bombshell: Whitsun Gate has been left jointly to Kate and the Fitzwarrens' nephew Smithy, on condition they run the house and public gardens as their predecessors had for three years.

Kate should be giddy with relief. So why does the thought of sharing a home with the cynical, abrasive ex-soldier fill her with dread? Kate has good reason to be wary of men but in her agitation she is slow to notice that Smithy, recovering from a near-fatal road accident and a failed marriage, is equally disenchanted with women. Perhaps these two damaged people could heal one another – if they don't kill each other first . . .

The Linden Tree is a warm, perceptive and funny novel from the author of *The Butterfly*.

(Available in hardback)

HER FATHER'S HOUSE
Emma Sinclair

Trevellan . . . Her father's ancient Cornish home is the only constant in Jennie Veryan's young life, and Mark Curnow is her only love – though it seems she must lose them both. A proud and old family, the Veryans break up her romance with the land agent's son, for Jennie is the heiress to the estate.

Or so it seems. In 1950 an incredible rumour draws Jennie to Singapore, scene of her father's disappearance in the maelstrom of the Japanese occupation. And in her quest to discover the truth of her father's fate she uncovers a secret so shameful it threatens exile from Trevellan for ever.

With its richly evoked backgrounds, sweeping narrative and enduring romance *Her Father's House* is the long awaited successor to *The Seventh Wave*.

0 7499 3005 5   £5.99

SECOND MARRIAGE
Georgina Mackie

Wealthy Australian Lawrence Seligman is a flawed character, at least in his own estimation. Guilt over the death of his friend Anthony Kenworthy drives him into the arms of Anthea, a Somerset farmer and Anthony's sister. With the passing of years not even his adored daughters can prevent the marriage from crumbling. Beth, a nurse who becomes Lawrence's second wife, is as different from Anthea as two women can be – but before long Lawrence's nature jeopardises this marriage as well.

Only when Lawrence is killed in a shocking accident do the two wives meet for the first time, with predictably stormy results. But as Anthea and Beth discover and accept the kind of man their husband really was, they begin to realise that maybe they didn't know him all that well . . . Only Anthea's mother Amy suspects that Lawrence's influence has not died with him – suspects that perhaps he is with them still . . .

0 7499 3007 1   £6.99

The very best of Piatkus fiction is now available in paperback as well as hardcover. Piatkus paperbacks, where *every* book is special.

The prices shown above were correct at the time of going to press. However Piatkus Books reserve the right to show new retail prices on covers which may differ from those previously advertised in the text or elsewhere.

Piatkus Books will be available from your bookshop or newsagent, or can be ordered from the following address:
Piatkus Paperbacks, P.O. Box 11, Falmouth, TR10 9EN.
Alternatively you can fax your order to this address on 01326 374888 or e-mail us at books@barni.avel.co.uk

Payments can be made as follows: Sterling cheque, Eurocheque, postal order, (payable to Piatkus Books) or by credit cards, Visa/Mastercard. Do not send cash or currency. UK and B.F.P.O. customers allow £1.00 postage and packing for the first book, 50p for the second and 30p for each additional book ordered to a maximum charge of £3.00 (7 books plus).

Overseas customers, including Eire, allow £2.00 for postage and packing for the first book, plus £1.00 for the second and 50p for each subsequent title ordered.

NAME (Block Letters) _____
ADDRESS _____
_____
I enclose my remittance for £_____
I wish to pay by Visa/Mastercard Card.

Number ☐☐☐☐☐☐☐☐☐☐☐☐☐☐☐☐
Card Expiry Date_____